Dear Reader,

Christmas is a season f[...]
also a time to pause an[...]
we have already receive[...]
ourselves to preserving those things that are
precious to us.

One tradition we have established at Silhouette
Books is *Silhouette Christmas Stories.* In our
sixth volume, you will find stories written by
Phyllis Halldorson, Peggy Webb, Naomi Horton
and Heather Graham Pozzessere, all familiar and
favorite names to Silhouette readers. Every author
tells a unique story—as you will see, Christmas
means something different to each writer and to
the characters she has created. What do an
amnesia victim, singing rabbits, single parents and
a hospital vigil all have in common? They are all
elements in this year's Christmas collection. I
hope you enjoy each story.

For the authors and editors at Silhouette, these
stories offer an opportunity to celebrate the
season with our readers. It gives us a chance to
thank you for your support over the past year and
to wish you the very best this holiday season and
in the year to come.

Best wishes,

Isabel Swift
Editorial Manager

SILHOUETTE

Christmas Stories

1991

PHYLLIS HALLDORSON
PEGGY WEBB
NAOMI HORTON
HEATHER GRAHAM POZZESSERE

Silhouette Books®

Published by Silhouette Books New York

America's Publisher of Contemporary Romance

SILHOUETTE BOOKS
300 E. 42nd St., New York, N.Y. 10017

Silhouette Christmas Stories 1991
Copyright © 1991 by Silhouette Books

All rights reserved, including the right to reproduce
this book or portions thereof in any form whatsoever.
For information address Silhouette Books,
300 E. 42nd St., New York, N.Y. 10017

ISBN: 0-373-48234-5

First Silhouette Books printing November 1991

All the characters in this book are fictitious. Any
resemblance to actual persons, living or dead, is
purely coincidental.

The publisher acknowledges the copyright holders
of the individual works as follows:

A Memorable Noel
Copyright © 1991 by Phyllis Halldorson

I Heard the Rabbits Singing
Copyright © 1991 by Peggy Webb

Dreaming of Angels
Copyright © 1991 by Susan Horton

The Christmas Bride
Copyright © 1991 by Heather Graham Pozzessere

SILHOUETTE and colophon are registered trademarks
of the publisher.

America's Publisher of Contemporary Romance

Printed in the U.S.A.

CONTENTS

A MEMORABLE NOEL

Phyllis Halldorson

A recipe from Phyllis Halldorson:

STRAWBERRY SALAD MOLD

2 6-oz packages strawberry-flavored Jell-O
2 cups boiling water
2 16-oz packages frozen sliced strawberries in juice
1 20-oz can crushed pineapple in juice
1 16-oz container sour cream at room temperature

Dissolve the Jell-O in boiling water. Add frozen strawberries, including juice. Be careful not to splash the liquid. To help fruit thaw, cut through the blocks. Add pineapple and juice. Work quickly, before mixture begins to set.

Pour half of mixture into a 13″ × 2″ flat container. Spread sour cream over top. Add remainder of gelatin mixture as third layer. Refrigerate until gelatin sets.

This double-size recipe serves a crowd. I guarantee you'll have none left over. It's bright red, the color of Christmas, and delicious.

Chapter One

It had been one of those hectic nights when all the street crime seemed to be centered in Police Corporal Gregor Remington's district. Now, an hour after he should have been off duty, Greg still had reports to write up before he could head down the peninsula to his duplex in Brisbane, one of the small bedroom communities between San Francisco and the airport.

He opened the door on the passenger side of the black and white car marked S.F.P.D. and looked at his partner sitting behind the wheel as he slid inside. All the backup cars, the ambulances and the vans full of punks had cleared out, leaving the area of the Japanese Tea Gardens littered with broken bottles, shattered window glass and miscellaneous clutter, some of it smeared with blood, but thank God this time there'd been no shooting.

Not that knifings were much better, but at least no one had been killed in this latest scuffle between rival juvenile gangs. For the time being it was quiet again in the dimly lit terrain of Golden Gate Park. Greg wondered if he'd ever get used to the carnage these kids inflicted on one another. Especially now, at Christmastime, when the gayly decorated streets, homes and churches should have inspired the peace and goodwill that the carols extolled.

"I don't know about you," he said to the rookie sitting next to him, "but as of now I'm off duty. Get on the radio and tell the dispatcher we'll take one last sweep of the park and then we're on our way in. If there's any other calls in this area someone else can take them."

Officer Dylan Griffith nodded and started the engine. He was young, twenty-three, and just out of the academy. He'd only been riding with Greg for two nights, and this had been his first gang confrontation. He looked a little shaken, but he'd behaved like a pro. Nice kid, Greg thought; Dylan had the makings of a good cop if he didn't let the violence get to him.

Greg leaned back in his seat and sighed wearily while his gaze darted back and forth ahead of them in surveillance. The object at the side of the road registered in his mind before he was aware of seeing it, and he sat up. "Wait. Stop," he barked as a startled Dylan brought the car to a screeching halt. "Back up, there's something lying on the ground back there."

He reached for his gun and his flashlight, and was out of the car as it rolled to a reverse halt. The park lighting was dim, but the beam from his powerful flashlight revealed a person crouched on the grass, apparently dazed.

"You there," he said, his tone harsh. "Stand up, but keep your hands where I can see them."

The head turned slowly toward him, and he saw that it was a young woman. Her dark brown eyes were blank, and there was a nasty-looking swollen bruise on the right side of her forehead. She put up her arm to shield her eyes from the blinding light but didn't move or say anything.

By this time Dylan was also covering her with a gun, and Greg put his weapon back in its holster and approached her. He directed the light away from her face, then hunkered down beside her and put out his hand to help her stand. She lowered her arm but shrank back and the blank look in her big eyes was replaced with fear.

"It's all right," he said more gently. "I'm a policeman. I won't hurt you, I just want to help. Can you tell me what happened?"

He watched her haunted gaze roam over him from his medium brown hair to his equally medium brown eyes, down his straight nose to his thick mustache, and at last to the blue uniform that identified him instantly to most people as a cop.

She must have decided she could trust him because she pushed herself up to a sitting position and put her hand to her head. "My... my head hurts."

She didn't look like a street person. She was very young, and except for her forehead, which was caked with blood and either gravel or pieces of cement, she was clean. Her dark brown hair was rich and springy as it tumbled around her shoulders, and she wore gray tailored slacks with a bright pink pullover sweater. An outfit that came from a fashion shop, not out of a salvage bin.

"I'm sure it does," he assured her. "You have a nasty bump there. Did someone hit you? Were you robbed?"

The blank look returned to her expression. "I don't know. All I remember is waking up on the ground with a splitting headache." She looked around at the darkness. "I was too dizzy to stand so I crawled over here, but I collapsed and couldn't go any farther. Where am I? How did I get here?"

"You're in San Francisco's Golden Gate Park. Can you show me where you were when you came to?"

"Over there," she said, and pointed northwest, then wrapped her arms around herself and brought her knees up to huddle into a ball. "Oh, I'm so cold."

Greg swore under his breath as he stood and walked back to the car, turning up the collar of his nylon jacket as he went. What was the matter with him? Of course she was cold. It was the middle of a December night and the cool, damp breeze was blowing in off the Pacific ocean. The poor kid had been lying on the ground for God knows how long without a coat or jacket.

He returned with a heavy woolen blanket and knelt behind her as he wrapped it around her shivering shoulders. "Oh, that feels good," she exclaimed, and he let his hands linger on her upper arms to share his own body heat with her.

She was shivering violently, and Greg was afraid she might be going into shock. He looked up at Dylan. "Call the dispatcher, tell them what we have here and ask them to send an ambulance," he said tersely.

He continued to crouch down behind her, sharing his heat and protecting her from the chilling breeze until Dylan called to him. "They can't get an ambulance here for at least thirty minutes."

Greg muttered an oath. "We can't leave her sitting here on the wet grass that long, she'll go into shock. Tell them we're taking her to the hospital."

His face brushed against her thick silky hair as he turned his head to speak to her. "Do you think you can stand up and walk over to the car? It's warm in there."

"I'll try," she answered, and he lifted her to her feet, all the while tightening the blanket around her so she couldn't get her arms free. It was a simple precaution to prevent her from going for his gun. It wouldn't be the first time a woman had cuddled up to a police officer to get his weapon, and Greg had no intention of letting it happen to him.

She leaned heavily against him as they walked to the car, and when he tried to help her into the back seat, she stumbled and fell. The jolt must have triggered a building hysteria in her because she laughed and then began to cry.

Great gulping sobs rocked her, and he picked her up and put her in the car, then climbed in, took her in his arms and held her as her shivering shook them both.

Dylan turned on the siren and they raced through the city streets, crowded even at one-thirty in the morning. Greg was uncomfortably aware of the distraught young woman he cradled against him. It was strictly against regulations, but, damn it, what else could he do? She was chilled clear through and hysterical. He told himself she was little more than a child, but even through the blanket he could feel the soft, fully developed breasts, hips and thighs that pressed so intimately against him.

The problem was that his hormones couldn't tell the difference between business and pleasure and were reacting with alarming forcefulness.

As they drove up to the hospital and stopped, Greg instructed Dylan to go back to the park and search the area where they'd found her for clues as to what had happened. He opened the door and got out of the car, then reached back in and lifted his frightened charge out and carried her into the emergency area where he sat her in a wheelchair. The waiting room was packed as he wheeled her, still sobbing uncontrollably, to the registration desk where his uniform got him the usual immediate attention.

"What's wrong with her, Officer?" the registrar asked.

"Hysteria and a head injury that I know of," he answered crisply. "I think she's been mugged. She was coming to in the park when we found her, and she's cold. Possible shock."

The woman nodded in agreement. "What's her name?"

He shrugged. "I don't know. She's pretty groggy and I haven't been able to get much out of her."

He leaned down and put his hand on the girl's shoulder. "Miss, what's your name?"

She just cried harder.

"Okay," the registrar said. "Not much chance of getting any information until she calms down. I'll put you into a room as soon as I have an opening." She motioned outward. "As you can see, the Christmas season has caught up with us."

Greg looked over the sea of damaged humanity that filled the room, many sitting, others standing, and some lying on gurneys awaiting medical attention. He was profoundly aware of the increase in assaults and other criminal injuries at Christmastime as well as all the other holidays throughout the year. There was something about celebrations that brought out the worst in certain types of people.

It was twenty minutes before an examining room was available, and during that time Greg had managed to soothe the distraught girl enough that she stopped crying but continued to cling to his hand like a lifeline.

Greg knew a good many of the people on swing shift at the hospital since he frequently accompanied prisoners and/or victims here, and the nurse who came for them was one he'd dated.

"Well, well, if it isn't my favorite cop," she said with a teasing grin. "What have you got for us this time, Greg?"

"Hi, Helene," he said, and motioned toward the girl in the wheelchair beside him. "Looks like a mugging, but she's been too scared and disoriented to give us any information."

Helene leaned over to examine the head wound. "Damn creeps," she muttered, "they could at least pick on someone old enough and big enough to defend herself."

She straightened and gripped the handles of the chair. "You can come, too," she said over her shoulder as she started pushing the chair across the room, "but you'll have to wait in the hall while I examine her to see if she has other injuries."

Fifteen minutes later Helene came out to tell Greg that she'd examined the girl and found no other wounds, but also hadn't been able to get any information from her. "I'll bring a doctor here as soon as one is available," she assured him as she sped down the hall to yet another patient.

The young woman was lying on the examination table, wearing a white hospital gown and covered with a heavy quilted warming blanket. She looked up at Greg with obvious relief and murmured, "I'm glad you didn't leave."

He smiled down at her. "I'm afraid you're stuck with me for a while. Do you feel up to answering some questions?"

"I'll try," she said, "but everything's so fuzzy."

He took a notepad and pen out of his shirt pocket and pulled up a stool beside the table to sit on. "Just do the best you can," he said gently. "First, I need to know your name."

She blinked and frowned. "My name is..." She paused, then started again. "My name is..." A longer pause this time, and then she grimaced with frustration. "I don't know," she said on a sob. "It's so close, but it just won't come." Her lips began to tremble. "I can't even remember my own name!"

Greg patted her shoulder. "You will, don't worry. Head injuries sometimes cause a temporary amnesia. Can you tell me your address?"

She compressed her lips, then shook her head. "No. I have no idea who I am or where I came from." Again her eyes filled with tears. "I don't even know what happened to me. What am I going to do if I *never* remember?"

He could see the terror building in her, and moved quickly to deflect it by taking her hand and holding it between both of his. "Try not to be upset," he told her. "You probably have a slight concussion, and it's not at all unusual to have trouble remembering for a while after that happens."

He smiled down at her. "We'll forget about your real name for now and give you an alias. The hospital needs a tag to identify you by, so what do you like? I'm sure we can find something more original than Jane Doe."

She wrinkled her nose in distaste. "What's your name?"

Good. He was finally getting her to show an interest in something.

"My name's Gregor Remington, but my friends call me Greg."

"That's a nice one, but it can't be feminized."

"No, we want something soft and pretty for you. Let's see...how about something Christmassy? Carol? or... No, I've got it. Noel. You look like a Noel."

For the first time she smiled, and it made her seem even younger. "Noel," she echoed. "Yes, I like that. Noel Doe."

Greg frowned. "No. Doe is too ordinary. We want something special."

He thought for a moment and then it came to him. "I've got it. I knew a guy in college who's last name was Santa. He took a lot of ribbing at Christmastime, but it fits just right with Noel. Noel Santa. How do you like it?"

She squeezed his hand. "I think it's beautiful." She hesitated shyly before she added, "Greg."

The way she said it sent a ripple of pleasure through him. "You're very welcome...Noel."

Chapter Two

She lay on the hospital gurney in yet another waiting room and wondered if this nightmare was ever going to end. She'd been poked and probed and x-rayed, and was now waiting for the film to be developed and read.

They'd cleaned and treated the wound just above her temple, then applied a large square bandage before finally giving her something for the pain. Now it had receded to just a dull ache in her head, but that was the least of her worries.

The real terror was her inability to remember. Who was she? Where did she come from? Where was she going? Was there anyone in the world who cared about her?

It was like being born again, only fully grown, but with no past and no sense of future. The only knowledge she had was of what had happened since she came to on the damp ground. The only personal contact was with the policeman who had found her and brought her here.

Greg Remington. He was a nice man, warm and compassionate, but eventually even he had abandoned her. Or was it she who had been separated from him? Yes, that was it. The nurse and orderly had lifted her onto the gurney and wheeled her away from him to another part of the hospital, but that was a long time ago and she hadn't seen him since.

Fear knotted her stomach. What was going to happen to her? Greg had given her a name, and everybody now called her Noel, but where was the real *her?* The woman she'd been until she became just a shell with a made-up "tag", as he'd called it?

Did she have parents? Friends? Maybe even a husband and children? Dear God, how could she function when she had no history?

Her troubled thoughts were interrupted by a familiar voice, and Greg appeared on one side of the gurney with the doctor on the other. In her desperation for assurance she reached out to Greg, and he took her hand and held it.

"It's good news," he said. "There's no sign of fracture or concussion. You're going to be fine once the trauma wears off."

She looked from Greg to the doctor, and he nodded in agreement. "We'll give you a few pills to take until the headache goes away," he said. "It's nothing serious. I know the loss of memory is scary, but you should have yours back in a few hours. Be sure to see your own doctor in a day or two for a checkup."

"But I don't know who my doctor is...." she said, but he'd already turned and was walking away.

"Hey, Doc, hold on," Greg called, and the doctor turned around. "Aren't you going to keep her here?"

The doctor shook his head as he walked back. "There's no need. She's not seriously injured."

"But she has amnesia. Where's she supposed to go?" Greg sounded outraged.

"I'm afraid that's your problem. If we had the space I'd admit her just so we could check on her but it's not medically necessary, and this hospital is filled to capacity. We're still staffing the E.R. but cases that need further care are being sent to other hospitals, and most of them are either full or understaffed, too. You have a dispensary at the jail. Why don't you take her down there?"

That suggestion sent new waves of terror through Noel. "No!" she cried, and rolled to a sitting position with her legs over the edge of the gurney. "Please, don't put me in jail with all those criminals!"

Greg grabbed her and restrained her from standing. "No one's going to put you in jail," he assured her as he glared at the doctor.

The doctor shrugged helplessly. "Sorry, but I can't justify giving her a room that a critically ill or injured person needs, just because she says she can't remember. Sorry, Officer, but those are the facts of life."

Noel gasped, but before she could protest his implication, Greg did it for her. "What do you mean *says* she doesn't remember?" His tone was hard. "Do you think she's lying?"

The doctor sighed. "I don't know, but a lot of the people brought in here do. Especially if it's cold out and they don't have anywhere to go. San Francisco is overflowing with the homeless, and a hospital is a nice, warm place to spend a night or two. Why don't you take her to one of the shelters?"

Greg slumped dejectedly and wrapped his arms protectively around her. "They're all full, too."

They both watched as the doctor shook his head sympathetically and hurried away.

Noel's head swam, and she was trembling with fear and frustration. "Greg, I swear I'm not lying to you. I don't remember a thing. What am I going to do? Where can I go? I don't have any money."

He hugged her close. "Don't panic. I'll see that you're taken care of. My partner's back with the car. He didn't find a thing at the scene except small bloodstains on a cement bench. That's probably where you hit your head. Have you any idea why you fell?"

She shook her head carefully. "I've been trying to remember ever since you brought me here, but I just can't."

"Is there any chance that you had a purse with you?"

"I must have," she said absently. "I always carry one."

Greg looked at her warily. "How do you know that?"

Her eyes widened. He was right, how did she? "I can't explain it, but I'm sure that I always carry a purse. Most women do, you know."

"That's true," Greg said, "but if you had one, Dylan couldn't find it. How about a coat? There's always a cold breeze blowing off the ocean in San Francisco at night during the winter months, but you weren't wearing a coat. Why?"

Her mind drew a blank and she could only shrug. "I'm sorry. If I wore a coat tonight I have no recollection of it."

He sighed. "Well, if you did it's gone now." He picked up the blanket he'd wrapped around her earlier, which was folded neatly at the bottom of the gurney. "If you feel well enough to leave I'll bundle you up in this again and take you down to the station. There may be an empty bed at the dispensary where you can spend the rest of the night."

The thought of spending a night in a jail, even though it was the dispensary, did nothing to soothe her panic. Would Greg just walk away and leave her to the mercy of whoever was on duty? What if, after he left, the next shift mistook her for a real prisoner and locked her up?

She clamped her lips together and turned her face away as she slid off the gurney and onto her feet so he wouldn't see how frightened she was. He'd gone out of his way to be nice to her, and she was determined not to be any more of a burden than she already was.

At the car Greg again helped her climb into the back seat, then got in beside her. When his arm lingered for a moment around her shoulders she snuggled against him, seeking not only his body heat but also the closeness and safety of his arms around her.

Without a word he lowered his arm to her waist and held her while the other officer drove.

It took Noel only a moment to realize that it wasn't firm flesh and muscle she was leaning against but a hard, stiff material, like metal. Greg was wearing something under his uniform that felt like armor!

It was then that she also realized there was something bulky at his waist. His gun, of course, but there seemed to be other hardware, too. She hadn't been aware of all of this when he'd held her on the way to the hospital, but she'd been too hysterical to notice anything then.

She wanted to ask him about it, but was afraid that if she spoke he'd put her away from him. Instead she closed her eyes and relaxed.

At the jail they learned that the few beds in the dispensary were filled, and the nurse was frantically trying to find room in a hospital for an asthma patient. "Sorry, ma'am," the officer on duty said, "but we've got a critical situation in the city right now. Too many patients and not enough hospital rooms. We're having to treat some of our prisoners in their cells when they should be treated in the dispensary. I'm afraid amnesia doesn't count as a medical emergency, and I'm not sure there would be anything we could do about it if it did. We're just praying that none of the prisoners has a heart attack or a hot appendix until this crisis is over."

"But you can't just put me out on the street!" Noel cried, her tone strident with fear. "I don't have any money. I don't know my way around." She clutched the blanket she was wrapped in. "I don't even have a coat."

"No one's going to put you out on the street," Greg assured her as he put his arm around her shoulders and led her to a chair. "Sit here while I see what arrangements can be made."

She sank into the chair but looked at him anxiously. "You won't go away, will you?"

He put his hand on her shoulder. "I'm not going to abandon you, honey. I'm just going to see to it that you're taken care of. I'll be right over there at the desk where you can see me. Okay?"

"Okay," she answered, and watched him walk across the room to talk to the other officer.

She felt like such a crybaby. No wonder he'd called her "honey," as if she were a little girl who had to be soothed. Surely she wasn't like this all the time. She hated being so dependent on the whims of others. It was not only degrading but absolutely horrifying. Without a memory of who and what she was, she was helpless, unable to take care of herself.

Was that why she felt so strongly drawn to this police officer? It couldn't be anything personal; they'd only just met. Her life probably depended on him. For that matter he *was* her life. Without him she'd be completely alone without anyone else in the world.

A wave of panic that was always just beneath the surface waiting to take over shook her, and she huddled deeper into the warm blanket. Was it possible that she'd died from that blow on the head and gone to hell?

Apparently it was, because when Greg came back, he still looked troubled. She stiffened to keep from cringing, but when he spoke, his tone was reassuring. "Dylan is writing up the report, so I'm off duty. I'm going to get my car and bring it around to pick you up. I won't be gone but a few minutes."

"But..." she began, but he was already sprinting toward the door.

True to his word he returned in about five minutes and quickly shepherded her outside and into the passenger seat of a fairly new dark blue sports car. As soon as they pulled away from the curb, she asked the obvious question. "Where are you taking me?"

"I'm taking you to my mother," he said as he kept his attention on the converging traffic.

"Your mother?"

"Yeah. You'll like her. She's a nurse. Works at a medical clinic in Brisbane."

She was trying to absorb what he'd said. "You mean you're taking me to another doctor?"

He turned to look at her then and smiled. "No, Noel, I'm taking you home. I own a duplex in Brisbane, a suburb down the peninsula. My mother and sister, Bevin, live in one side and I live in the other."

She blinked, still a little muddled. "You live with your mother and sister?"

He shook his head. "Not with them, next door to them. The two sides are attached but separate units. If I ever find an apartment I can afford in the city I'll move and rent my side out, but it's almost impossible to find anything in my price range in San Francisco that isn't a dump. I'm in line for promotion to sergeant, and when that happens I can upgrade my search to better neighborhoods."

It was warm in the car with the heater on, and Noel snuggled back against the padded seat. She was exhausted and must have dozed off because the next thing she knew, Greg was shaking her shoulder gently. "Noel, wake up. We're home."

There was a streetlight nearby, and when she opened her eyes she looked directly into his, not more than a few inches above her. They were large and deep set, brown with flecks of gold and topped with thick brown lashes. There was compassion in them, and tenderness. The type of eyes a woman could drown in.

He raised his hand and stroked a lock of hair off her forehead. His hands were rough, but his touch was gentle. "Come on, sleepyhead," he murmured. "I called from the station and Mom's expecting you. She'll put you right to bed, and then you can sleep as long as you want."

If Noel's arms hadn't been trapped in the blanket that was wrapped around her she wouldn't have been able to resist the powerful urge to caress his craggy face, smooth the thick brown mustache and trace the hint of a widow's peak at his hairline.

"I hate being such a bother to her," she said.

He continued to stroke her hair, being careful not to touch the swollen area. "It's no bother," he assured her. "Bevin, my younger sister, is a flight attendant. She's gone most of the time, and just uses Mom's place as home base. You can sleep in her room until we find out who you are. Mom will be glad for the company."

It sounded like heaven. "You're a very nice man, Gregor Remington." Her voice quavered with emotion.

For a moment they just gazed at one another. She was sure her heart was in her eyes for him to read, but he was the one who broke the spell by pulling away and getting out of the car. He came around to her side and opened the door. She turned, and he put his hands at her waist and lifted her out.

The porch light was on over the door to the left, and Noel could see that the duplex had a bluish-gray siding trimmed with white. The two units were separated by a garage in the middle, then attached at the center of the second story.

The front door was opened as they stepped up on the cement stoop, and a woman wearing a turquoise velour robe stood behind the screen. She opened it and smiled at them. "I've been watching for you," she said. "Come in, quickly, it's cold out there."

Noel decided the lady must be in her mid-fifties if she was Greg's mother, but she looked younger. Her round, pretty face had a slight double chin that made her look cherubic, her blue eyes were bright and sparkling, and there was no sign of gray in her dark hair.

"Sorry I had to wake you, Mom," Greg said as they walked across the tiny entryway to the living room, "but I didn't know where else to go."

He turned to Noel. "Noel, this is my mother, Abigail Remington."

Instead of putting out her hand, the woman put her arms around Noel and hugged her. "Call me Abby," she said. "You're welcome to stay here until other arrangements can be made, and right now you look completely done in. I'll turn down your bed and find you one of my daughter's sleep shirts while you say good-night to Greg."

She released Noel and headed for the stairway at the right side of the room.

Noel slid the blanket off her shoulders and handed it to Greg. "How can I ever thank you?" she said. "I...I don't know what I'd have done if it hadn't been for you."

"It's just part of my job." He looked embarrassed by her effusiveness.

"I don't believe that for a minute," she said. "I'm sure that not all policemen bring home the strays they find."

"No," he said softly. "They don't. Mom has to go to work in a few hours, but I'll be right next door. If you need me just bang on the wall and holler. Otherwise, I'll come over at noon and take you to lunch."

He reached out and carefully caressed the swollen area around her bandage. "Sleep tight, Noel, and don't be afraid. The doctor says your memory will come back soon, but until it does, I won't let anything bad happen to you."

Chapter Three

Noel was awakened by the melodic clamor of mockingbirds outside the window. Without opening her eyes, she smiled and burrowed deeper into the soft bed.

When she moved, a dull pain slashed through the right side of her head, and she instinctively put her hand to it. Her palm landed on a thick piece of gauze that had to be a bandage, and her eyes flew open.

This wasn't her room! She bounced to a sitting position, then fell back as a wave of dizziness joined with the pain to momentarily incapacitate her. With a groan she closed her eyes again and clutched at her hand to try to stop the whirling.

Then it came back to her. Not the memory she'd lost, but the recollection of the events of last night. She'd been injured in a park, and a wonderfully compassionate policeman named Greg had found her and brought her home to his mother. He'd held her when she'd needed to be held, and he'd christened her Noel.

She'd been sleeping in his sister's bedroom, and he was probably asleep on the other side of the duplex.

After a while the pain and dizziness receded and she put her hands down and opened her eyes. Last night the doctor had assured her that her memory loss was temporary, that it would return within a few hours, but obviously it hadn't.

The clawing fear returned, and she tried moving backward through time in her mind. It was all clear until she got to Golden Gate Park, the darkness, the pounding pain in her head and the bone-chilling cold. Then everything stopped, as if she had run into a black void. She had no memory of anything that had happened to her before that.

She shuddered and dug the heels of her hands into her eyes. But it wasn't her eyes that were at fault, it was her mind, and that was a devastating thought.

Would she ever be whole again?

After a few minutes she took her hands from her eyes and looked around her. She'd been too tired and disoriented to pay much attention to the room she went to bed in last night. In the bright sunlight of morning she could see that it was small but pretty with white ruffled curtains at the wide window and robin's egg blue paint on the walls.

The furniture was constructed of light wood, and there was a large mirror over the dresser. A 19-inch television set was perched on top of a narrow chest of drawers, and framed travel posters from various parts of the world hung on the walls.

Noel sat up, carefully this time, and put her feet on the bedside rug that protected them from the coolness of the hardwood floor. She glanced at her wrist, but there was no watch there. Where was it? She knew she always wore one, the same way that she knew she always carried a purse.

A glance at the top of the bed revealed a bookcase headboard and a clock radio. It was ten minutes after eleven. Hadn't Greg said something about having lunch with her at noon?

Noel stood, and a mild rush of dizziness returned, but she clutched the headboard and took a deep breath and it disappeared. She was wearing a yellow cotton knit sleep shirt, and there was a white terrycloth robe laid out across the end of the bed. She picked it up and went looking for the bathroom.

Half an hour later, after a brisk, invigorating shower and a session with the comb, brush and curling iron she'd found in a drawer, she wrapped the robe around her and returned to the bedroom in search of her clothes. They were nowhere in sight, and she vaguely remembered Greg's mother gathering them up and taking them with her once she'd seen Noel safely snuggled in bed.

She must have taken them downstairs. They'd been damp, grass-stained and rumpled, so she'd probably put them in a dirty clothes hamper in the laundry room.

Noel was halfway down the stairs when the doorbell rang. She remembered Greg telling her that his mother left for work early so Noel knew she was alone in the house. She hoped he was the visitor. She could trust him, but no way was she going to open the door for a stranger.

As she hurried down the steps, the bell rang again and she looked through the peephole, then breathed a sigh of relief. It was Greg, all right, but he looked different in brown slacks and a sport coat. No less handsome, but not nearly so stern.

He smiled as she opened the door. "Good morning," he said as his gaze roamed over her. "I hope I didn't wake you."

The sparkling approval in his eyes sent a thrill through her. "No, I just got out of the shower and was looking for my clothes," she said as he stepped inside and closed the door.

He chuckled. "If I know Mom she probably took them with her to drop off at the cleaners. My sister has plenty of things. Help yourself to whatever you need. You two are about the same size. She's a little taller, but not much."

His smile disappeared. "How are you feeling this morning, Noel? Do you remember anything?"

She shook her head. "No, I'm sorry but I don't. I don't even know what day or date it is. Last night someone said something about the Christmas season?"

"That's right. Today is Monday, December 16, and the Christmas rush is in full swing." He searched her face. "You look better this morning. Did you sleep well?"

"Like a log, and I feel much better. The headache is still there, but I imagine one of the pills they gave me when I left the hospital will take care of that."

He looked relieved. "That's good. It seems the doctor was right about the head injury not being serious. Your memory will probably return a little at a time. Now, why don't you go upstairs and get into some of Bevin's clothes so we can go to lunch. Mom's eager to talk to you, so I invited her to meet us at the restaurant at twelve-thirty."

Noel argued about the propriety of wearing his sister's clothes without her permission, but Greg was adamant, and a short while later she rejoined him in the living room, wearing royal blue slacks and a matching heavy-knit pullover sweater. She'd found her own black flats under her bed, and her knee-length stockings had been stuffed inside them.

Again the look of open admiration on Greg's face as she walked down the stairs made her tingle, and she knew she'd better get her memory back quickly. This was a man she could like much too well, much too soon.

She didn't know whether or not she was free to bask in the warmth of his approval. Come to think of it, she didn't know if he was free, either. She'd darn well better find out!

The sun was warm, and the long-sleeved sweater kept her comfortable without a coat as they left the house and got into the car.

"Do you have a wife, Greg?" she asked once he'd driven away from the curb and was cruising down the street of small, well-kept middle-class homes.

"Not anymore," he answered, keeping his eyes on the road. "I got married while I was in the army, but it didn't work out. Too many long separations."

"Oh. I'm sorry," she said, but it wasn't really the truth. Actually, she was relieved.

He shrugged. "Yeah, it was rough, but there were no children so at least we didn't hurt anyone except ourselves. She's married again, and last I heard they were living in Sacramento."

Sacramento. The name jarred her, and a vision of shady streets lined with giant elm trees, Sutter's Fort and the golden dome of the state capitol building flashed through her mind. She was familiar with Sacramento.

Greg's voice, still talking, recaptured her attention. "How about you? Is there any chance that you have a husband?"

That thought was disturbing. "I...I don't know. I don't think so. I'm not wearing rings." She held up her left hand for his inspection.

"That doesn't mean much," he told her. "If your purse and coat were stolen, whoever did it would have taken jewelry, too."

She remembered the watch that she was certain should be on her wrist but wasn't and felt a chilling anxiety.

A few minutes later they pulled into the parking lot next to a chain restaurant known for its good food and fast service. "Mom only has an hour for lunch and this place is close to the clinic." He opened his door. "We'll go on in and get a booth."

They did, and shortly afterward were joined by Abigail Remington. She was wearing a tan all-weather coat over her white nurse's uniform. "Hi, you two," she said cheerfully. "I hope I haven't kept you waiting long."

She took off the coat and tossed it to the far side of the bench seat before sliding in across the table from Greg and Noel. "How are you feeling?" she asked Noel. "Have you remembered anything about yourself yet?"

"No, I haven't," Noel said mournfully. "It's so frustrating! I feel like a . . . a nonperson."

Her voice broke, and she swallowed in an effort to gain control again.

Abby put her hand over Noel's where it lay on the table. "Hey, it's all right. Amnesia's not all that unusual. I'll try to make arrangements for you to see the neurologist at the clinic tomorrow. You need to be checked again in any case, and if you still don't remember, he may be able to help you."

Noel's lips trembled. "Thank you, but I can't go to a doctor, I don't have any money to pay him."

Greg started to protest, but Abby silenced him with a look. "There are social services that will give you temporary aid. Greg will put you in touch with them."

She turned to look at her son. "Have any missing person reports fitting her description come in yet?"

He shook his head. "I checked with headquarters as soon as I woke up, but so far nothing. I'm going to take her down there this afternoon and see what we can do about establishing her identity."

An hour later they'd finished their lunch, and Abby had returned to work. Greg and Noel lingered over dessert and coffee, and savored the intimacy of sitting next to each other.

"Your mother is a real treasure," Noel said. "I can't believe there are many people who would take a stranger into their home in the middle of the night."

Greg nodded. "She's a treasure, all right, but she's not in the habit of taking in strangers. I'd never allow it, it's too dangerous. She welcomed you because I asked her to, and I only did that because I knew I'd be in the same building."

Noel's contentment disintegrated. What a fool she'd been to think she might be just a little special to these two nice people. Greg had only enlisted his mother's aid because he was stuck with the hapless victim of a crime and didn't know what else to do with her, but he was letting her know that he didn't trust her.

What upset her even more was that she had no more knowledge than he of whether she was trustworthy or not.

She turned her head away so he couldn't see how much his words had hurt. "Oh . . . yes . . . of course."

Damn, she sounded like a child who'd been scolded and was about to cry.

Taking a deep breath, she laid her napkin on the table. "I really do appreciate your being so kind, both of you, but I can't impose on you any longer." This time her tone was stronger. "If you're finished we'd better get started for the police station. Maybe they can circulate a picture of me or something. Also, I understand that homeless shelters operate on a first come, first served basis so I'll want to check in early."

Greg's attention had been distracted when a teenager suspected of dealing drugs in his precinct walked through the door, and he'd only been half listening to what Noel was saying until the sentence about homeless shelters brought him up sharp.

"What?" he asked harshly as he swung his head around to look at her. "What are you talking about?"

Her face was turned away from him, and he put his hand under her chin and pivoted her head so he could see her expression. She was making an effort to smile, but her eyes were filled with despair. He fought back the overpowering urge to take her in his arms and reassure her.

"Noel, what's this talk of homeless shelters? Don't you like staying with us?" His tone was still too harsh, but she'd shocked him.

Her face registered surprise. "Oh yes, very much, but I don't want to intrude. You don't even know if you can trust me."

He frowned, trying to make sense of what she was saying. "Trust you? Of course, I trust you. Good Lord, you don't think I'd have brought you home to my mother if I'd had any doubts, do you?"

Her lovely eyes widened. "But you said . . ."

So that was it. Something he'd said had upset her.

"What did I say, honey?" This time his tone was soft.

The tip of her tongue appeared and slowly wet her trembling lips, starting an unwelcome stirring in his groin. He'd never known a woman who looked so innocent and so sexy both at the same time.

Even with the bruise on her forehead she was incredibly beautiful. An earthy goddess with wide cheekbones that tapered to a slender rounded chin. The big brown almond-shaped eyes topped with thick dark eyebrows were her best feature followed closely by the full, generous mouth and long sculpted nose that flared gently at the nostrils.

She wore no makeup, and her complexion was smooth, creamy and unblemished, a startling contrast to the rich, luxuriant hair that reminded him of dark chocolate and fell from a side part to bounce buoyantly around her shoulders.

"You . . . you said you wouldn't have taken me to her if you hadn't lived in the same building because you didn't trust me," she said in answer to his question.

Reluctantly he withdrew his hand from beneath her chin before he could give in to the powerful need to explore her upturned face with his mouth and sample those quivering lips.

"That's not what I meant at all," he assured her. "Actually, I was trying to tell you that you were special because I wouldn't ordinarily consider bringing a stranger to Mom for shelter. That's a dangerous thing to do, and I'd never knowingly place her in that type of peril."

This time Noel's smile was genuine. "I'm flattered. Truly I am. Your mom's a wonderful person, and I'd never do anything to hurt or upset her."

She paused a moment before continuing. "Where's your father, Greg?"

A picture of his tall handsome dad flashed into Greg's mind, and he felt the emptiness of loss that was never far away. "Dad was a career army man, a pilot. He was killed three years ago in a training exercise."

Noel's smile faded as her expression changed to compassion. "Oh, I'm so sorry," she said in that breathless way she had of speaking. "That must have been a dreadful time for all of you."

He reached for her hand and held it. "Yes, it was. That's when I bought the duplex. I didn't want Mom living alone, but I wasn't really eager to move back into the family home, either. This way I can be sure she's safe, but we both have privacy."

Her hand nestled warmly in his, and the stirring in his groin intensified. He was both embarrassed and appalled. It was time to start acting more like a policeman and less like a potential lover. He couldn't afford to become emotionally involved with a woman who might at any minute remember that she had a fiancé or a husband. Maybe even a child!

Abruptly he released her hand and stood. "We'd better be going," he said in answer to her startled look. "My shift starts at four o'clock, and I have to stop by the house and change into my uniform before we go into the city. The usual procedure is to change at the station, but I didn't want to keep you waiting while I got into civvies last night so I wore the uniform home."

She slid out of the booth, and he couldn't resist tucking her hand into the crook of his arm as they left the restaurant. "Maybe by the time we get to the station they'll have an inquiry about you," he said, and was appalled at how painful that idea was to him.

Chapter Four

Noel paced curiously through the ground floor rooms of Greg's duplex while she waited for him to change his clothes.

The floor plan was a mirror image of Abby's on the other side of the connecting wall, living room, dining room, kitchen and bath, with two bedrooms and a second bath upstairs, but this one had a definite masculine decor.

The shining hardwood floors were bare except for occasional Navaho-type throw rugs, whereas Abby had room-size Oriental patterned rugs in her living and dining rooms.

Greg's walls were painted beige and were bare of pictures except for a large wood-framed desert landscape over the fireplace mantel, in contrast to Abby's pastel rose walls with delicate floral watercolors framed under glass and hung in artistic clusters around the rooms.

Even the windows denoted gender. Greg's were covered with straight, no-nonsense white panels over metal blinds, while Abby's were hung with ivory lace curtains and dark rose drapes that pulled to the side when not in use.

It was amazing how different two identical homes could look when decorated by people with opposite tastes.

She was in the small cluttered kitchen when she heard his heavy, bouncy footsteps coming down the uncarpeted stairs, and she hurried to meet him in the living room. He was wearing the dark blue trousers and shirt of the S.F.P.D., and, without the bomber-type matching jacket that he'd had on the night before, she could see the paraphernalia he carried with him.

Around his waistband was a black belt from which hung a gun in a holster, a long flashlight, baton, handcuffs, walkie-talkie and mace. Startled, she voiced the first thought that came to her. "How on earth do you keep your pants up with all that metal hooked to them?"

He hooted with laughter as he clasped his hands on her shoulders. "I'll tell you something, honey," he teased. "It's not keeping them up that's a problem, it's getting them off. All that hardware doubles as a chastity belt to keep the police force celibate while we're on duty. By the time we get all this stuff off, we're out of the mood."

Noel could feel the warm flush that suffused her cheeks. She'd asked for that with her too personal question, but darned if she'd let him get away with it without a comeback.

She choked on a chuckle and opened her eyes wide to simulate innocence. "Really?" she said breathlessly. "Gee, I thought men were always in the mood."

She'd expected him to laugh and maybe try to top her with another smart remark, but instead his hands moved up to frame her face and lift it so that they were looking into each other's eyes. "I'm sure they are when they get close to you, my beautiful little foundling," he murmured, and slowly lowered his head to brush her mouth gently with his own.

His mustache was soft, and she felt a glow that started in her heart and spread in tiny circles of delight. Before she could react, he placed a small kiss at the corner of her mouth, then brushed his lips across hers in the other direction.

She draped her arms around his neck, and her mouth parted as his took possession of it. She gasped and clung as his tongue circled her lips then edged slowly between them.

He tasted like the chocolate cake they'd had for dessert, sweet and dark and creamy. A stirring of hunger, but not for food, began in the pit of her stomach, and her own tongue sought and caressed his.

Dropping his hands to her waist, he pulled her closer, but her right hip connected with his long metal flashlight and broke the spell. With a low groan he raised his head and shifted her so she fit against him, then held her there.

"You see what I mean?" he muttered into her hair as he rubbed his cheek in its softness.

"Mmm," was the only sound she made as she snuggled dreamily against his chest. His shirt smelled of laundry soap and freshly ironed cotton, and again he was wearing something hard and unyielding under it. The same armor-type garment she'd noticed on the way to the hospital last night.

She raised her head and put her hand over his left breast. "What's that thing you're wearing?"

He looked down at her through eyes nearly as quixotic as her own. "That's my bulletproof vest. We're required to wear it." He hugged her and grinned. "Still another deterrent to a quick roll in the hay."

He kissed her again, lightly, then put her away from him. "Just keep your distance from me when I'm not in uniform. If I get you in my arms without the impediment, I don't think I'll be able to let you go." There was no teasing in his tone.

They held hands all the way in to the police station, and Noel noticed that Greg seemed to be having almost as much trouble as she keeping track of their conversation. She was too aware of his big, strong hand cradling her smaller one and at times rubbing the back of it with his thumb.

He was always so gentle with her, but she could feel the leashed power in his touch. What would it be like to make love with him when he lost that awesome control?

The very thought made her shiver with desire.

San Francisco was festive with bright Christmas decorations that reflected the brilliant sunlight and cast a sparkle over the city. The streets were swarming with shoppers, their arms loaded with colorful packages labeled Gumps, I Magnin and Nieman-Marcus, and banks of glorious red poinsettias framed the latest holiday fashions in the store windows.

At the police station they learned that there was still no missing person report that matched Noel's description. "Either you live alone and no one's missed you yet, or you don't come from this immediate area," the short, balding officer told her. "San Francisco is overrun with tourists. If you're one of them there's not much we can do until someone starts a search for you. There's no law against an adult voluntarily disappearing."

His gaze roamed over her. "You are eighteen or older, aren't you?"

She shrugged. "I haven't any idea, but I don't feel like a teenager."

He scrutinized her again. "It's hard to judge a woman's age just by looking at her, but I'd say you were between sixteen and twenty-six. Probably somewhere in the middle, twenty or twenty-one. Can you drive a car?"

Instantly her mind took her through the motions of turning on the motor, shifting in reverse and backing up, then shifting into drive and going forward. "Yes, I'm sure I can."

"Well, we can test that out easy enough," he said, "but first we're going to fingerprint you and take your picture, then we'll have the police psychologist talk to you."

He handed Greg a form he'd been filling in. "She's a lucky lady," he said. "Dr. Sims had a last minute cancellation, otherwise she'd have had to wait a couple of days or more. I've assigned her to you, so stay with her and don't let her get any more lost than she already is."

For the next few hours Noel was put through the standard police procedure for tracking a missing person, only this time she was playing a duel role, both the one doing the seeking, and the one being sought.

It was weird and frightening. How was it possible to lose the essence of one's self? She felt like Dorothy in *The Wizard of Oz* who'd wakened one morning in a new and different world and couldn't find her way back. But Dorothy had remembered Kansas and her Aunt Em. Noel didn't know what she was trying to go back to.

The session with the psychologist was frustrating. After talking to Noel for a few minutes, Dr. Sims spread a map of California on the top of his desk. "Study this thoroughly," he said. "Note each town and think about it. Does the name ring a bell? Does it bring to mind a mental picture, or a feeling of familiarity? Anything? Just sit here in my chair and take your time. I'll leave you alone for about fifteen minutes, so relax and let your mind wander."

Noel tried, but it was hopeless.

"I know a little about several of the cities," she told the psychologist when he returned. "Sacramento is the capital, Carmel is an artist's colony, they make movies and television shows in Los Angeles, and Anaheim is the site of Disneyland. I guess that's not much help, is it?"

"Afraid not," he muttered as he reclaimed his seat behind the desk, and she took the one across from him. "Just about everyone who's ever heard of California would know that."

He reached for a folder and opened it. "Now, I have some pictures here. I'm going to show them to you one at a time, and I want you to tell me what they look like to you...."

She was relieved to find that her knowledge of things not related to herself wasn't impaired. She recognized the Rorschach test, and laughingly teased that all the pictures looked like smeared inkblots to her.

Afterward there was a word association test, and by the end of the hour the doctor was more optimistic than Noel was. "When you're alone, just relax and try to free associate," he said. "Your memory will come back, but you can't force it. The harder you try the more elusive it becomes."

Easy for you to say, Noel thought. *You're not the one dependent on the charity of Greg and Abby for your very survival!*

By the time the doctor was finished with her it was almost six o'clock and dark. Greg was waiting for her, and there was an anxious expression on his face. "How'd it go?" he asked. "Were you able to remember anything?"

She shook her head. "No, not a thing. I doubt if Dr. Sims even got any clues from the tests. When he said 'dog' I answered 'cat,' and when he showed me a picture I said it looked like an inkblot. Sounds depressingly normal to me."

He grinned. "That's good, not bad, so cheer up. You'll feel better once you've eaten. Come on, I'll buy you dinner and then take you home to Mom." They headed for the front door.

She hated having to rely on him for everything, even the food she ate. "Oh, Greg, I can't go on sponging off you..."

He stopped and reached in his shirt pocket. "Oh yeah," he said. "I almost forgot." He brought out a folded piece of paper and handed it to her. "This is for you."

She unfolded it and saw that it was a check drawn on the Victim's Assistance Fund account and made out to Noel Santa. The amount was one hundred dollars!

"Oh my goodness," she gasped. "Where did you get this?"

"One of the forms you signed when we first came in was an emergency request for temporary monetary help. I put it through while I was waiting for you, and when it was approved I signed the receipt. You'll have to cash it at the bank it's drawn on, and I'll have to go along to identify you since you're using an assumed name and have no identification."

Noel felt both relieved and repelled. "In other words, it's welfare," she said, and knew with certainty that she'd never before had to rely on public assistance.

He must have seen her distress because he put his arm around her shoulders as they started walking again. "Not really. You 'earned' it by being a victim, but if it upsets you to accept charity then consider it a loan and pay it back when you have the money. The city would be delighted."

For the next two mornings Noel continued to wake up with a blank where her memories should be, and there'd been no missing person report on her to the San Francisco police department. Neither had they made any headway in their efforts to identify her by circulating her picture and fingerprints. She was becoming desperate.

It was not only frustrating but terrifying not to know anything about herself. Like losing her soul!

She seemed to be well educated, with a good understanding of the things she read and heard. She knew where Turkey and Colombia were without consulting a map, she could recite poetry by the early English and American poets as well as Sylvia Plath, and she knew the plots of plays from Shakespeare, through Ibsen to Alan Ayckbourn, but she couldn't remember her own name.

On the third morning Greg again drove her to the police station. By this time she was almost as familiar a figure around there as Greg, and they were greeted by officers and staff who seemed to accept them as a couple.

Nothing could be further from the truth, at least as far as romance was concerned. That one kiss they'd shared apparently hadn't been as special to him as it had been to her. Since that day he'd been treating her like what she was, a guest of his mother's who needed police assistance. No more touching, or holding, or long soulful glances. And definitely no more kissing.

Her disappointment was keen. She had a great need to reach out to him, to feel the touch of his hand, his arms around her, his strong body pressed against hers, hardware and all, but it was all fantasy on her part.

Even if he'd felt the same way, they both knew that any relationship between them was doomed as long as they didn't know who and what she was. It was fortunate for him that he wasn't as emotionally involved as she.

Noel could tell by looking at the officer in charge when she sat down across the desk from him that there was still no report on her. "Sorry, Noel," he said. "I wish I could tell you we have something encouraging, but we don't."

Her spirits sank along with her hopes. "I don't understand," she said, her tone ragged with disappointment. "I very well might have been fingerprinted. I thought it was easy to trace people these days through their prints.''

The officer shook his head. ''Have you any idea how many fingerprints there are on file in this country? It'll take weeks to check them all. So far we've been concentrating on the ones in the Bay area, but there's something I don't think you understand. This is not a police matter. It's true that you were apparently assaulted, but we've completed our investigation into that. Since you can't tell us if anything is missing we can't even classify it as a robbery. For all we know, you may have stumbled and hit your head when you fell.''

Noel couldn't believe what she was hearing. Surely they weren't just going to abandon her!

She gripped the arms of her chair as she turned to Greg sitting next to her. ''Is that true?'' she asked, and knew from his grim expression that it was.

He reached out and put his hand over hers. ''Yes it is, but—''

''Since you aren't in trouble with the law and no one's reported you missing, there's nothing else we can do,'' the officer interrupted. ''We just don't have the time or the manpower to pursue this. I really am sorry, but...'' He shrugged. ''Keep us informed on where you are in case something turns up.''

Chapter Five

Noel was unaware of what was going on around her as Greg talked for a few minutes with the officer, then tucked her hand in the crook of his arm and led her out of the station.

She was too stunned to think, and too frightened to speak. The police department had washed its hands of her! To the best of their knowledge she wasn't a criminal so they were no longer responsible for her. What was she going to do? Where was she going to stay? The Remingtons had only offered temporary shelter, not adoption.

Greg helped her into his blue Nissan 300ZX, and she automatically buckled her seat belt while he got in on the other side and started the motor. Neither of them spoke as they crested a hill and the Pacific Ocean lay ahead of them, dark and angry and shrouded in fog.

It was then that she realized it wasn't only her own little world that had become shadowed in gray, but the whole city of San Francisco. How had it happened so fast? The sun had been bright and shining as they'd driven up the Bayshore highway earlier, and now the sun was gone and fog permeated the atmosphere, as bleak and joyless as her mood.

Noel felt as though she were trapped in a nightmare. Every time she had a glimmer of hope, something happened to push her further into the quagmire of despair that left her suspended in a purgatory between the past she couldn't remember and a future she couldn't get on with.

Greg continued on to the waterfront and parked facing the ocean on the lonely deserted beach. He shut off the motor and turned in his bucket seat so that he was facing her.

He knew what a devastating blow the officer's abrupt dismissal had been, and he intended to raise hell with the man later for his insensitivity, but now he had to convince her that things weren't as bleak as she seemed to think.

"Noel," he said, "there's no need to be upset about this."

"No need!" she blurted. "How can you say that? The police department has just told me that since I haven't committed a crime they don't care who I am or what happens to me."

He leaned forward and took one of her clenched fists in his hand. "Now hold on, that's not what they said, and even if they had, what difference can it make? Noel, you're all wrought up over nothing. We can—"

"Nothing!" This time it was almost a shout. "How can you say that? I'm all alone in a strange city, I don't know who I am, where I came from, or if I have any skill for making a living, and you say it's *nothing!*"

This time he grabbed her other wrist and turned her toward him. "Now just a damn minute." His voice betrayed his hurt and anger. "What do you mean you're all alone? What about me? What about Mother? Don't we mean anything to you?"

He watched her anger drain away and a look of remorse replace it. She raised her hand, with his still attached at her wrist, and stroked his cheek. Her touch was cool and soft and sent tiny tremors along his nerves.

"Oh Greg, of course you do." Her tone was low and sexy. "You and Abby saved my life. I'd never have survived on the streets alone, and I'm more grateful than I can tell you—"

Grateful! The word brought him back to reality with a sickening thud. Is that all she felt for him?

He released her and pulled away from her caressing fingers. "I don't want your gratitude," he snapped. "I'm trying to tell you that I can do as much for you as the department could. They'll send your fingerprints to the national bureau, but it will take several weeks to hear back. Meanwhile we can go to the newspapers and television for help. They're always looking for human interest stories."

He could see that she hadn't thought of that. "Really? You mean they'd print my picture?"

He shrugged. "Sure. Why not? Along with a plea to anyone who thinks they recognize you to come forward and help reunite you with your family for Christmas. It might be picked up by the media in other areas. If not, we can sent out press releases."

Instead of answering immediately, she was quiet for a moment. "Will the police department pay for this?"

He hesitated. "Well, no, but I can get copies of the picture they took of you. It's good, not like the usual police photos. The photographer obviously couldn't resist getting some artistic shots of his gorgeous model."

He'd intended that last sentence to be light and teasing, but it came out sounding like a jealous accusation.

Fortunately she didn't seem to notice. "But Greg, I've only got seventy-some dollars left of that hundred. I bought makeup and a few personal things..."

She sounded as if she were apologizing to him for having spent some of the money, but before he could protest that it was meant for just that, her big brown eyes filled with tears and she looked away. "I can't keep imposing on you." It was a wail of pure misery. "If my memory doesn't come back and nobody comes forward to identify me, what am I going to do?''

The naked anguish in her tone and expression was more than Greg could bear. All his good intentions to keep their relationship platonic until her memory returned melted in the heat of his terrible need to hold her, comfort and protect her.

With a groan he tilted the steering wheel up and pushed his seat back as far as it would go, then hauled her onto his lap. It was a tight fit, but neither of them noticed as he cradled her in his arms and kissed her trembling lips.

He met with neither resistance nor hesitation as her mouth opened under his and she slid her hands up his chest to meet at the back of his head and hold him. God but she was sweet. She even tasted like nectar as her tongue jabbed and parried and made his own work for the glory of catching and taming it.

Deep in his conscience a warning flashed. *This lady is no novice. This lady is no novice,* but it only registered enough in his feverish mind to tell him that he wasn't seducing a virgin. He ignored the more ominous implication.

Instinctive observation showed him that the windows were fogged over on the inside so it was impossible to see into the car in case others drove by. He ran his hand over her back and under her sweater before finding the firm rise of her breast. The muscles in his stomach clenched, and the stirring in his groin escalated to rigidity.

Damn! He took a deep breath and tried to relax. He never should have started this, but now that he had, he wasn't sure he could stop. He was as susceptible as any man to a pretty woman, but none of them, not even his ex-wife, had ever aroused him so hard so fast and without even trying.

It took all his control not to crush her to him and grind his mouth into hers. The lacy fabric of a bra separated his palm from her bare flesh, and he knew he should remove his hand and put her back in the seat beside him.

He also knew that he wasn't going to, and he pulled the lace aside and released her breast, spilling into his eager palm. His involuntary moan caused her to break the kiss and look at him with passion-clouded eyes, but he caught her mouth again and nibbled hungrily at her soft, delicious lips. She responded with the same wild abandon as he gently rolled her hardened nipple between his thumb and finger.

Their urgency grew as he fought to hang on to his sanity while every fiber of his being screamed with the need to possess her, even though he'd have to do it sitting up in the car on a public beach.

The unsavory picture finally jolted him back to his senses. That may be an exciting lark for lovers long used to the ways of pleasuring each other, but not for a first time. Not with Noel. When and if he made love with her it was going to be in a romantic setting where they could work up to it slowly, not a quickie in a car like a couple of overheated teenagers.

His body throbbed in protest as he raised his head and replaced the lacy bra before removing his hand and pulling her sweater down. She sat up slowly, and he almost cried out with the pain of regret that knifed through him. Her eyes were slumberous and her mouth swollen from his kisses, but her expression was dazed, disoriented.

She'd been as far gone as he had. It took all his determination not to pull her back down and take up where they'd left off, and to hell with the consequences.

She put out her hand and touched his lips. "Greg?"

He stroked a disheveled lock of her fragrant hair back into place. "I'm sorry, sweetheart," he said unsteadily. "I couldn't take any more of that. I'm only human, but this is neither the time nor the place. You deserve to be loved, not ravished."

His words brought Noel back to reality with a thrust of shame and anxiety. How could she have behaved like a common pick-up, not only willing but eager to make love in a public place with a man she hardly knew?

She put her hands to her hot, flushed cheeks as her eyes grew wide with anxiety. "You can't really know what I deserve, can you? Neither of us can. I sure didn't act like a flustered virgin..."

One hand moved to cover her mouth as the full force of what she'd done hit her. "Greg, I knew what we were building up to, and I was as desperate for it as you were." Her voice throbbed with intensity. "That was no genteel lady you were making love to. How do you know I'm not a—"

"No!" Greg almost yelled the denial, compelled to stop her from saying the ugly word. "Don't even think such a thing. As a cop I've dealt with hundreds of ladies of the night, and believe me, you're not one of the sisterhood."

His assurance was even more damning. How could he have known what she was going to say if the same thought hadn't occurred to him? Dear God, was this amnesia her mind's way of escaping a life-style she'd found intolerable?

"How can you be so sure?" she persisted, not at all convinced that he was telling her the truth. "Not all of them walk the streets. How do you know I'm not a high-priced call girl?" Her voice broke on a note of pure anguish.

He caught her by the shoulders and shook her. "Stop that, Noel." This time his tone was low and insistent. "A cop develops a sixth sense about these things. We can spot a hooker no matter where she plies her trade or how fashionably she dresses, and I'm telling you, you're not one of them."

She wasn't sure whether she truly believed him or if she was willing to grasp at any assurance that she was a morally responsible woman, but his words calmed her. She took a deep breath and pulled away from him to slump back in her seat.

She was beginning to relax when he delivered a gut-wrenching blow to her emerging peace of mind.

"I've learned in this job to be a good judge of people," he began, and she caught a note of sadness in his tone. "I'd stake my life on your integrity, sweetheart, and that's why we'd better both be prepared for the probability that you are either happily married or have a deeply committed relationship with a lover."

Chapter Six

Noel spent a long and restless night fighting shadows and hiding from double-headed monsters of the mind that threatened to destroy her with their conflicting conclusions.

If her memory came back, she could go home.

But she was home. Abby's duplex had become home to her in this short-term lifetime, and Abby was the mother she'd so quickly learned to love.

If her memory came back, she'd know her name.

But she had a name, Noel Santa, and it fit her perfectly. She was comfortable with it. She felt, looked and acted like a woman named Noel.

If her memory came back, she'd know her life-style.

That's when the nightmare escalated. What if that life-style was the very thing that the amnesia was protecting her from? What if something had happened to her that she couldn't, or wouldn't face?

But what if it hadn't? What if, as Greg suspected, she had a loving husband or fiancé waiting for her to return?

It was at that point that she woke up gasping for air and drenched in sweat. She didn't want a nameless, faceless husband. She wanted Greg!

It was a totally irresponsible desire. She'd known him for only four days, the same length of time she'd known herself. No sane person would be willing to sacrifice her whole past life in order to belong to a man she'd known a little more than one hundred *hours!*

But that's what she was tempted to do. Abandon the past and get on with the future. Greg called her his foundling. They'd been brought together through no fault of their own, as if they were meant to belong to each other, and now that he was talking about going public with her dilemma to hasten a resolution, she was strangely reluctant.

The implications of Noel's soul-searching weighed heavily on her when she struggled out of her troubled sleep on Friday morning, but she'd come to one decision during the night. She was going to find a job.

The doctors had been so sure that her memory would return within hours, but she hadn't had a twinge of recollection. Obviously this wasn't just a temporary aberration, and she couldn't expect other people to take care of her while she waited for someone from her past to find her. That might take months, or maybe years!

She wasn't even sure she wanted to be found.

An hour later she was dressed in Bevin Remington's brown skirt and color-coordinated blouse. The abrasion on her forehead was healing nicely, and with a film of foundation cream under her makeup it was hardly noticeable. After a quick breakfast she put on a gold blazer and left the house.

The dismal fog of yesterday had disappeared in a blaze of bright sunlight, and Noel felt her spirits rise as she breathed in the fresh damp air off the bay and walked westward. Four blocks away, at a main business thoroughfare, she stopped in front of a fast-food hamburger drive-in.

The We're Hiring sign was still in the window. Greg drove by here every time he took her into the city, and the sign had always been there. She didn't know if she was qualified for this type of position, but she could darn well learn. Her choices were limited since she'd have to walk back and forth to work, and this was close.

Inside she asked for the manager, and the girl behind the counter turned and called, "Hey, Joe. Someone to see you."

The man who responded was young, and he eyed her appreciatively. "Hi, how can I help you?" he said cheerfully.

"I'd like to apply for a job," she told him.

His expression changed to disbelief. "You serious?"

Noel realized she'd made a mistake by not dressing more casually. Bevin's clothes were expensive, more suited to a management position than to flipping burgers behind a counter.

She assured him that she was, and his next question was equally disbelieving. "You have any experience?"

That was even more disconcerting. She didn't know whether or not she'd ever worked at this type of job. "Well, I..." Oh darn, it couldn't be all that difficult. She'd fake it. "Yes, some, and I catch on fast. I can handle it just fine."

He hesitated, obviously not believing her. Finally he nodded. "Okay, I haven't had any other applicants. I'll give you a try. The vacancy's on the four-to-midnight shift, and we pay minimum. Any problems?"

There was one. She hadn't counted on working nights and having to walk home in the dark, but she needed the job. She shook her head. "No, that's all right."

He shrugged and turned. "Just a second and I'll get you an application form. You can sit over there at one of the tables to fill it out. You do have a social security card, don't you?"

Oh darn. She hadn't thought of that. She couldn't work without a social security number, and if she had one she didn't know what it was.

She took a deep breath and lied. "Yes, I do, but I lost it, and I never did memorize my number."

He frowned, and she hurried on. "I've applied for a new card, but it takes a while to get it. Couldn't you—"

"So you want to work without one," he said flatly. "How do I know I'm not being set up?"

She blinked. "Set up for what?"

He scowled impatiently. "Oh, cut the innocent act. Are you an undercover agent?"

Oh my. This was even more complicated than she'd anticipated. It seemed obvious that she wasn't a criminal, she couldn't even think up a convenient lie for not having a social security card. She might as well tell the truth and hope he'd believe it.

"No, I'm not an undercover agent. Actually, I don't know who I am. I was apparently mugged in Golden Gate Park five nights ago..." She told him the whole story, and ended with a plea of desperation. "I need this job. You can check with the police department if you don't believe me."

For a moment he stood there frowning at her, then he muttered, "wait here" and disappeared into the back.

She paced around the big open room nervously until he finally returned, still frowning. "Your story checked out with the cops," he told her, "and I need help fast, so I'll take you on, but we're gonna change the rules a little. I'll pay you in cash under the table and you get no benefits, understand?"

Oh, she understood all right, although she didn't know why she did. He meant she wouldn't be listed on the payroll, but he'd keep the money that should be deducted for social security, taxes, and any other benefits the other employees of the company got.

Unfortunately she had no choice but to accept his terms.

After Noel left the restaurant she took a walking tour of the area, familiarizing herself with the upscale neighborhood and admiring the festive Christmas decorations. Most of the homes had lighted trees in their picture windows even though it was still morning, and many of the lawns or rooftops featured large wooden cutouts of Santa and his reindeer or a Nativity scene.

It seemed more like early spring than mid-winter with the trees and bushes still mostly green, and pink and red camellias already bursting into blossom. The climate didn't match the season, and she found it difficult to get into the spirit of the holiday in this warm, gardenlike city.

Could that mean she normally spent her Christmases in the snow? Or was it just because the tradition of a white Christmas was the universal symbol?

It was nearly noon when Noel arrived back at the duplex to be met by Greg glowering with anger.

"Where in hell have you been?" he bellowed from inside as she opened Abby's front door.

He startled her before she saw him standing at the lace-curtained window. She hadn't expected him to be in Abby's living room, and she'd never heard him use that tone.

"I—I've been out," she stammered.

"That's obvious," he said sarcastically. "How about being a little more specific? Why didn't you tell me you were leaving?"

He was speaking to her as if she were an unruly five-year-old who had climbed over the fence and run away, and she resented it. "I wasn't aware that I needed your permission to go for a walk," she snapped.

"Don't be smart with me." He sounded like a drill sergeant. "You don't need my permission, but I think you do owe me a little consideration. Damn it, you scared the bejesus out of me. When I came over here and found you gone without a trace, I didn't know what might have happened to you. I was afraid you'd gotten your memory back and panicked. Hell, for all I knew you could have wandered off and gotten lost, or hit by a car, or—"

He was frightened for her! Why hadn't she recognized that immediately instead of...

She practically flew across the room and into his arms. He hugged her hard and buried his face in the sensitive curve of her neck, sending shivers of delight through her.

He was wearing blue jeans and a sweatshirt, and she could get as close as she wanted without having to contend with all his weapons. Her body melted against him, and his hand settled on her derriere to position her even more intimately.

"Noel, don't ever do that to me again," he whispered brokenly. "I realize that one of these days I'm going to lose you, but I need to at least know that you're all right. Don't ever just walk away and disappear."

She wrapped her arms around his neck and kissed his throat. "Oh, darling, I'd never do that."

"You might," he insisted. "You can't know for sure how you'll react when you remember who you are and where you came from. Please promise that no matter how you feel when that happens, even if there's another man in your life or you're in some kind of trouble, you'll come to me and tell me about it."

He sounded desperate for her assurance, and a strange mixture of elation and sadness overcame her. He really did care for her. He wouldn't have been so upset when he didn't know where she was if he didn't, but was she destined to bring him pain instead of gladness?

Wouldn't it be kinder of her to move out of his duplex and apply to the uncertain mercy of the state to provide for her until she could support herself?

The thought made her shudder. Leave Greg? Never. At least not until he didn't want her around anymore. Why make them both miserable now instead of snatching what time together they could before their happiness was either completed or torn asunder by the return of her memory?

Everyone had to make choices in this life, and she was choosing Greg, for better or for worse, at least as long as she had no knowledge of any other life.

She stroked her fingers through his hair. "Of course I promise," she murmured. "I'll never leave you without saying goodbye. I'll never leave you at all unless I'm forced to."

His arms tightened around her, and he raised his head as he rocked them back and forth in a stationary dance of contentment. "You understand that we may be heading for more heartbreak than we can handle," he reminded her.

She tipped her face up to look at him. "I know, but I honestly don't think I'm deeply involved with another man. At least not happily so. If I were I wouldn't forget him so completely. I'm absolutely sure that a blow on the head could never make me forget you—"

His mouth claimed hers then, and she no longer cared what had happened in the past. Now was all that mattered.

After a few moments they drew shakily apart, and Greg sucked in a steadying breath. "I originally came over to invite you to have lunch with me," he said. "I make a mean omelet, and on my way home this morning I stopped at a twenty-four-hour doughnut shop and got some of those big blueberry muffins."

"Stop," she pleaded. "You're making my mouth water. How could I possibly refuse?"

An hour later, as they lingered over second cups of coffee in Greg's kitchen, he picked up her hand and kissed her palm. "I've got the next two nights off," he said. "What do you say we drive into the city and ride a cable car to Fisherman's Wharf? It's a real tourist attraction complete with the pungent smells from the fishing boats. We can take a tour of the bay, eat crab with our fingers as we explore the ancient restored square-rigger and shop the two-story mall at Pier 39. Later we'll have dinner at one of the gourmet seafood restaurants—"

"Please, Greg," Noel said as she held up her hand to stop him, "you don't need to sell me. It sounds wonderful, but I can't. I have to work tonight."

He blinked. "What?"

She hated having to refuse him but had no choice. "I said I can't go with you. I have to work tonight."

"Work?" He looked totally confused, and she realized that she hadn't yet had a chance to tell him about her job.

"Oh dear, I'm sorry," she said apologetically. "You startled me so when I came home earlier that I never got around to telling you where I was this morning. I walked down to that hamburger drive-in a few blocks west of here and applied for a job. I start work tonight."

He seemed to be struggling for composure. "What do you mean *tonight?*"

"I'm working the four-to-midnight shift."

His confusion was replaced with anger. "Like hell you are. How do you expect to get home in the middle of the night with no car?"

That had worried her a little, too, but she wasn't going to let him know it. "I'll walk, of course," she said calmly. "It's only four blocks."

His expression turned granitelike, set and hard. "Oh no you won't," he grated. "I won't hear of it. Call and tell the manager you've changed your mind."

Her first inclination was to tell him exactly what he could do with that ultimatum, but she fought back her outrage. He probably figured he had the right to tell her what she could and couldn't do since he'd assumed responsibility for her. Maybe legally, or at least morally, he did, but that kind of treatment was untenable to Noel.

She'd learned one thing about herself. She might be a wife or even a mistress, but she was no man's possession!

"Greg," she said carefully, wanting to make her point but not appear rude. "I understand your concern for me and I realize now that I should have waited and told you what I'd planned to do before I went out and did it, but I only decided last night to find a job and I remembered seeing the help-wanted sign in the window of the hamburger place so I... Well, I was in a hurry to get down there before anybody else applied."

"You needn't have worried," he said angrily. "That sign's been there for weeks. The pay's low and the working conditions are intolerable...."

He paused and eyed her suspiciously. "Wait a minute. How did you get hired? You don't know your social security number, do you? Noel, have you had flashes of memory and not told me?"

"No!" She was horrified that he'd think that of her. "I don't remember anything. I, uh, I told Joe, the manager, that I'd lost my card, but had applied for a new one."

She couldn't tell Greg that Joe knew she would be working illegally and was taking advantage of it. That would really set him off.

"That wasn't very smart," Greg said grimly. "Sooner or later you'd have to produce a number, but it doesn't matter. You're not taking the job. Now go put on some comfortable walking shoes while I change clothes. We can stop at the drive-in on the way to the city and tell the manager you're resigning."

His words hit her like a slap in the face with a cold wet cloth. Where did he get off telling her where, when and even if she could work? He may have saved her life, but that didn't make him God.

Even so, she owed him and didn't want to seem ungrateful. She took a deep breath to steady her voice and stood up. "Greg, my decision to take this job is not negotiable. I need the money. I can't go on sponging off you and Abby any longer."

He opened his mouth to say something, but she hurried on as she gathered steam. "My memory may be impaired but everything else works fine. I'm truly sorry that I can't go out with you tonight, but I promised I'd report for work at three o'clock this afternoon for some training before my shift starts, and that's exactly what I'm going to do."

She walked to the back door and opened it, then turned back to look at him. "One more thing." Her tone was strident. "Don't ever again tell me you won't allow me to do something."

With that, she dashed out the door and slammed it behind her.

Chapter Seven

Noel didn't see Greg again before she left for work that afternoon, but at the close of her shift he arrived at the drive-in to take her home. She wasn't sure whether she was grateful or resentful. It thrilled her that he cared enough about her to worry, but he was still sullen, which meant that he was upset because she refused to heel like an obedient puppy.

The next day they arrived at an uneasy truce. She'd walk to work since it was still light at that time, but she'd wait there for him to pick her up shortly after midnight on his way home once his own shift was over.

On Sunday morning she was awakened by the telephone ringing beside her bed. A glance at the clock indicated that Abby would have already left for the early service at church, so she rolled over, picked it up and murmured a sleepy, "Hello."

She was brought fully awake by a female voice asking, "May I speak to Noel Santa, please?"

She'd never received a phone call before. Not one asking for Noel Santa. Who would be calling her by that name? And how did they get this number?

"This is Noel speaking," she said anxiously.

The woman introduced herself as Victoria Langford, a news reporter from one of the major television stations in San Francisco. "We learned about you from the police files," she said, "and wondered if you'd regained your memory yet."

Noel told her she hadn't, and when Ms. Langford asked for more details, she related the whole story.

"That's fascinating," Victoria said enthusiastically. "We'd like to film an interview with you to be shown on all our newscasts tomorrow. It will be a touching Christmas feature, and although we can't guarantee that you'll be recognized immediately, it has been known to happen. If not, we're a network affiliate and the story could be picked up and carried nationwide. What do you say? Will you do it?"

Noel hesitated. What could she say? This was the exposure she and Greg had hoped for. Why wasn't she shouting for joy instead of feeling threatened?

"I... well, yes... yes, of course I will," she stammered as she tried to instill a little enthusiasm into her tone. "That's very nice of you. Will I have to come into the station?"

"No, that won't be necessary. We'd prefer to film it in your home setting. Will four o'clock this afternoon be all right?"

They talked for a few minutes more about appropriate makeup and clothing before Victoria hung up, and Noel went into a state of panic. Was this the end of a brief interlude? Would someone she knew see the interview and come after her? Would she learn that she had commitments that would make it impossible to continue her close, loving bond with Greg?

Dear God, why had she ever agreed to this?

Without bothering to dress, she slipped into Bevin's fuzzy white robe and slippers and dashed next door. She had to talk to Greg.

She pushed her finger into the doorbell button and left it there. It was only eight o'clock and Greg probably wasn't awake yet.

It wasn't long before his voice rang out loud and clear. "I'm coming, damn it! Take your finger off that buzzer. I was asleep, not dead."

The door opened, and he glared at Noel for a second before his sleep-glazed eyes focused on her. Then his expression changed to alarm, and he reached for the lock on the screen. "Noel! What's the matter? Mother...?"

"No, Greg," she hastened to assure him. "It's nothing like that. Abby's fine, but I just had a phone call—"

He didn't wait for her to finish but opened the screen door and pulled her inside. It was then she noticed that he was wearing only a pair of hastily pulled-on jeans. His chest and feet were bare.

For a moment she forgot everything but the sight of his powerful, brawny chest topped by broad sinewy shoulders and the corded muscles in his arms. She'd known he looked great with his shirt on, but without it he was absolutely stunning!

She didn't know how many men she'd seen before without a shirt, but none of them measured up to this one. She would have remembered that.

"Noel. Honey are you all right? What's the matter?"

His words finally registered, and she forced her attention back to the problem that had brought her charging in on him. "Oh, Greg, I'm sorry. I didn't mean to frighten you."

He led her to the sofa and sat her down, then settled down beside her as she told him about the phone call from the television reporter. "I hope you don't mind them coming out here with all their camera equipment. I couldn't get Abby's permission because she's at church, but she's said several times that she'd help in any way she could."

Greg was sitting hunched over with his elbows on his thighs, staring off into space as he listened. He felt as if someone had just dropped the floor out from under him, but that was stupid. He'd known the time would come when they'd have to aggressively search for her identity. He'd even suggested this same course of action when he was still thinking rationally.

But he'd stopped being rational when he'd almost lost control and made love to her in the car that day on the beach. After that, he'd shied away from any thought of searching for her identity, because if she found it she would no longer be his Noel, and that fact was unbearable.

When he spoke, he managed to sound reasonably detached. "No, it's all right. It's better for you if they do it here."

He'd make it as easy on her as he could. God knows he didn't want her to feel the cold empty anguish that had slammed into his gut and radiated in all directions. Of course she had to find her past. She could never be happy always wondering who she was and what had happened to her during those missing years.

He was going to lose her as he'd always known he would, and there wasn't a damn thing he could do about it.

Running his fingers through his hair, he straightened and glanced at her. She didn't look overjoyed, either. She must have been awakened from a sound sleep, too. Her dark hair was tantalizingly disheveled, and her face was free of makeup, even lipstick. In that furry robe she looked hauntingly appealing and even sexier than usual, excepting that it was apprehension rather than desire that shone in her wide brown eyes.

Well, he wasn't going to add to her tangled emotions by confessing his selfish need to keep her ignorant of her background and therefore dependent on him.

He managed a reasonably bright smile and got to his feet, then reached down to help her up. "If this is going to be a Christmas feature we'd better get a tree and decorate it." He strove to sound cheerful. "They'll probably want to photograph you under it. Mom should be home by the time we get dressed, and I'll take the two of you out to breakfast before we go shopping."

He'd intended to send her on her way without touching her, but when they got to the door and she turned to face him, he had her in his arms without even attempting to resist the overwhelming temptation.

Her soft hands skimming over his bare back sent shivers down his spine, and he groaned with the longing she ignited in him. She rubbed her cheek in the hair on his equally bare chest, and he knew she must feel the pounding of his responding heart.

If he didn't send her away right now, he wouldn't be able to, but he couldn't let her go without reassuring her. He moved his hands to either side of her head and tipped her face up. "Don't look so frightened, love." His voice vibrated with his own fear, but he hoped she wouldn't notice. "It looks like your past might finally catch up with you. Maybe you'll be reunited with your family in time for Christmas."

His breath caught in a silent sob, and he leaned down and kissed her trembling lips before ushering her out the door.

Greg, Noel and Abby found a reasonably symmetrical seven-foot pine tree and set it up in the corner beside the fireplace in Abby's living room. They trimmed it with decorations collected from three generations of her family, including a fragile wax angel that had belonged to her great-great-grandmother.

Just holding it in her hands and listening to the story of its history made Noel feel better. In spite of the travail it might cause both her and Greg to learn of her origins, it was necessary. Everyone should be familiar with their family tree, both the blossoms and the blight. Otherwise, how could one find one's roots?

Abby Remington had personally known members from five generations of her family. Noel didn't even have memories of her own childhood. She needed a legacy to hand down to her children

By four o'clock the Christmas decorations were all in place, and Noel had showered, shampooed her hair and, as instructed by Victoria Langford, applied a somewhat heavier layer of makeup than she usually wore. She dressed in her own gray slacks and pink sweater, the outfit she'd been wearing when she'd been found, in hopes that it would be an added mark of identification in case anyone she knew watched the newscast.

Ms. Langford and a cameraman, whose name Noel didn't catch, arrived and set up the interview to take place in front of the tree as Greg had predicted. The room looked lovely with a fire burning brightly in the fireplace, and an antique Dresden crèche, another of Abby's treasures from the past, displayed on the coffee table.

"Try to forget about the camera and relax," Victoria instructed Noel as she positioned her in an ottoman by the tree while the cameraman was busy filming the room. "I want you to tell me your story in your own words. It doesn't matter if you stammer or panic and can't remember. We can do it over, and the whole thing will be edited before it's shown."

She turned to Greg, who was standing across the room. "Oh, and we'll want to ask you a few questions, too, Officer."

Greg shook his head. "No, ma'am, I don't want to be named or photographed, and I'd appreciate it if you wouldn't mention that she's staying with my mother." He grinned sheepishly. "It's not exactly against the rules, but the department frowns on officers taking a personal interest in the victims they deal with. I mean, it's a matter of objectivity."

He had the endearing expression of the proverbial little boy caught with his hand in the cookie jar, but Victoria wasn't buying it. "But that's part of the appeal of the feature," she protested. "The policeman who finds the frightened girl who's lost her memory, and takes her home to his family when she has nowhere else to go. It's guaranteed to brighten the image of the S.F.P.D., and make heroes of the officers."

Noel intervened. "Ms. Langford, I'm not going to do anything to put Greg's job in jeopardy. If interviewing me is going to do that then we'll just have to forget it."

"Noel, wait," Greg interrupted. "Ms. Langford's probably right. In any case it won't jeopardize my career. About the worst they could do is put a letter of reprimand in my file."

Before Noel could protest, he turned to Victoria. "I withdraw my objection. Just give me a minute to change my shirt and comb my hair."

The taping went smoothly and was over in one take. Victoria projected warmth and compassion as she expertly coaxed the story from Noel and Greg, and the experience was more pleasant than either had anticipated.

"I'll introduce this segment when it's shown," she said as she stood to leave, "and at the end we'll ask that anyone who might have information about you contact the San Francisco Police Department, then we'll put the department's address and phone number on the screen."

Again she turned to look at Greg. "I don't have to tell you that you'll probably be swamped with responses. Everybody wants to get into the act in these cases, but most of them will be mistaken identity."

He chuckled. "You're right about that. I'll keep you informed, and if something does turn up I promise you'll be the first to know."

The interview with Noel was first shown on the noon newscast on Monday, and she and Greg huddled in front of the television set.

Noel had the oddest sensation when her picture flashed on the screen. It was like watching a twin sister. Someone who looked and talked like her but wasn't. When Victoria addressed her as Noel, she had to choke back the urge to correct her, to protest, "that's not her name. Her name is..."

But try as she would, she couldn't breach the impenetrable wall that cut her off from her memory.

Other than that she was pleased with the tape. When they'd filmed it, she'd worn her hair down and bouncing around her shoulders during the segment by the tree, but then Victoria had stopped the camera and put Noel's hair up in a graceful swirl on top of her head. When they resumed taping, Noel was positioned standing in front of the fireplace. After editing, this gave the viewer a better idea of her height and build as well as two different hairstyles.

When it was over Greg turned the set off and sighed. "If anyone who knows you sees that, they're sure to recognize you. You photograph like a dream." He paused. "Could you be a model?"

She shook her head sadly. "I doubt it. Mentioning it doesn't evoke any familiarity, and I'm not thin enough."

His gaze roamed over her from her lush breasts, down to her slender waist, the compact roundness of her hips and thighs, her shapely calves and ankles, then back to her generous mouth. "Don't ever lose an ounce," he said huskily. "I love every inch of you just the way you are."

At the start of Greg's shift that afternoon the police department had already had several calls about the amnesia victim. The interview was repeated on the five, six and eleven p.m. newscasts, and by the time he arrived at the station shortly before midnight to write up his reports and check out, the telephone operators were complaining bitterly.

He pocketed the stack of notes containing names, addresses, phone numbers and comments the caller had made, and took them home with him. He'd agreed to handle this as a volunteer project during his off-hours, but there was nothing he could do until the next morning.

Greg and Noel had planned to get together at ten o'clock the next morning and start contacting the callers, but he was wakened out of a sound sleep at eight-thirty by a friend in the missing persons department. "Sorry to wake you, buddy, but I just took a call from a William Trent with an address in Stockton. He saw that broadcast last night and positively identified your gal as his fiancée, Stephanie Gates. Man, this guy didn't have any doubt at all. He says she's a student at the University of the Pacific over there, and he hasn't seen or heard from her since Saturday, the fourteenth."

Chapter Eight

Greg felt as if he'd been poleaxed, but he managed to get the man's phone number before he hung up and groped his way to the bathroom. He splashed cold water on his face and took deep breaths to fight off the nausea that threatened to overwhelm him.

Stephanie Gates, William Trent's future wife!

No! Not Noel. Dear God, please let it not be Noel!

It was a while before he was able to pull himself together enough to make the call, and even then his hands shook so that he kept pushing the wrong buttons. Eventually, though, he made the connection, and the phone at the other end was answered by a male voice. Greg identified himself and verified that he was talking to William Trent.

"Bill," the other man corrected him. "I thought you'd never get back to me. Is Stephanie all right? What in hell happened? Doesn't she remember anything?"

Greg fought back a surge of jealous anger and asked a question of his own. "Why are you so sure the woman you saw on television is Stephanie Gates?"

"You're kidding, right?" The other man's tone was incredulous. "We've been going together for two years and have been engaged for half that time. We're planning to be married next spring after graduation."

Greg bit his lip to keep from groaning. "Sorry, but I had to be sure. We get a lot of crank calls. You'll have to come to San Francisco and identify her in person."

"I'm on my way," Bill said breathlessly. "I should be there in a couple of hours. Where can I see her?"

"We'll be at the police station." Greg gave him the address and directions for getting there. "Ask for Officer Gregor Remington, and tell them it concerns Noel Santa, that's the name she's known by."

Noel had spent a restless night, not fully awake, but not sleeping soundly, either. Greg had told her when he picked her up at the drive-in that they'd already had inquiries about her, but it wasn't excitement that kept her tossing. It was anxiety.

Was she going to regret going public with this? What if she'd been unhappy in her immediate past? Or worse, what if she'd committed a crime and was running away?

She heard Abby leave for work, and when the telephone rang just moments later, she wasn't surprised that it was Greg calling. "I'm sorry to wake you, honey, but we have a lead that sounds promising. We have to be at the station by eleven, so get dressed and come over here. I'll fix us some breakfast."

Her stomach churned, and before she could catch her breath and comment, he continued. "Don't wear your own clothes. Put on one of Bevin's dresses, and could you comb your hair a different way than the two styles you wore on camera? We're going to put you in a lineup."

She rushed through a shower and dressed in a rayon challis print dress featuring a dark smoky-blue background splashed with small mauve, pink and cream roses. It had a charming old-fashioned little girl look with its full skirt, long sleeves, and frilly lace collar and cuffs.

Greg had asked that she improvise a new hairstyle, so she brushed it back and fastened it at her nape with a wide, white enamel and gold filigree clasp. The total effect was that of an illustration out of a Dickens novel.

Greg was waiting for her when she got there, and he looked positively ashen. A wave of foreboding swept over her, and all her fears returned in a rush. "Greg," she said, "what's the matter? What have you found out?"

He didn't answer but took her arm. "Let's go in the kitchen," he said quietly. "We can eat while we talk."

He seated her at the table that had already been set with orange juice and Danish pastry, then poured the coffee before sitting down across from her. "Noel, does the name William, or Bill, Trent mean anything to you?"

Like a flash of lightning splitting apart the black wall to her memory she saw the figure of a golden-haired man, but it was gone too quickly to be sure it even happened.

"I—I don't think so," she stammered.

He was watching her closely. "You remembered something," he said. "Your expression changed. Tell me about it."

"It...it wasn't really a memory." She told him about the illusion.

For a moment she saw anguish in his brown eyes, but he quickly masked it. "Greg, for God's sake, tell me!" It was a cry of terror. "Is this man the 'lead' you mentioned?"

Greg put out his hand and clasped hers on top of the table. "Bear with me, honey. I don't want to influence you. I have another name. Does Stephanie Gates ring any bells?"

This time there was no flash of lightning or cracks in the wall. The name evoked no memory, but without warning her heartbeat speeded up and began to pound, and a film of perspiration broke out all over her body.

She gasped, and her vision blurred. Then Greg was leaning over her, holding her by the shoulders and forcing her head downward to her knees. "Breathe slower and more deeply," he ordered. "You're hyperventilating. Just relax and think about each breath."

She was already so limp that she felt as if her bones had melted. If she relaxed any further she'd slither onto the floor, but she followed his orders, and slowly her head stopped spinning.

When she could sit up again, Greg put the glass of orange juice to her mouth and told her to sip. After a few minutes she was able to hold the glass by herself, and he hunkered down beside her. "Now," he said, "tell me what happened."

She described her puzzling physical reaction as best she could, then added, "I have no conscious memory of anyone named Stephanie Gates, but obviously my subconscious does."

She looked at him and knew he was as shaken as she was. "Is that who I am? A woman named Stephanie Gates?"

He cleared his throat. "Bill Trent says you are, but we can't be sure until he either offers conclusive proof or your memory returns."

It took all her courage to ask the next question. "And what is Bill Trent to Stephanie Gates?"

Greg winced and looked away. "He says he's the man she's planning to marry in the spring."

Noel felt all the breath go out of her. "Oh dear lord, no!" she whispered, and collapsed against him as his arms tightened around her.

* * *

Later, at the police station, the lineup was an unnerving experience. Noel and several other women of the same general age and description were told to stand on a brightly lit stage. Each one was asked to turn right, left, and then walk a few steps.

It was over quickly, and Noel was taken to a small lounge. A few minutes later Greg arrived, and one look at his face told her all she needed to know. She sank down on the sofa and buried her head in her hands. "Is he absolutely sure?" It was more of a cry than a question.

Greg sat down beside her and, taking her hands in his, turned her toward him, thus exposing her white, ravaged face. "Yes, he is. He picked you out the minute he saw you. I don't think he even looked at the other women, just kept insisting that we take him to you."

A dry sob shook her, and Greg pressed her hands between his. "He's waiting just outside. You'll have to see him, honey, but I'll be right here with you. I won't let him touch you unless you want him to."

"No. Not yet," she said frantically. "Just give me a minute..."

Her voice broke, and she wet her dry lips with her tongue. "Greg, hold me. Oh please, I need your arms around me."

He had her in an embrace before she added the last plea, and she clung to him, breathing in the scent of his shaving lotion, stroking her fingers through his soft, luxuriant hair and planting frantic kisses under his jaw.

"Don't send me away," she pleaded as her heart pounded with fear. "Don't let a strange man..."

She could feel him tremble as his arms tightened around her. "Noel, sweetheart, I'll never send you away. Don't you know how much you mean to me? I'm not even sure I can let you go if you want to." There was agony in his tone. "I'm not going to let anyone take you from me. When this is over, if you go home with Bill Trent it will have to be your decision. I won't stop you if that's what you really want, but I'll never let him take you against your will."

A knock on the door reminded them that others were waiting, and Greg reluctantly released her and walked across the room to admit Bill Trent and the sergeant escorting him.

Noel watched fearfully as the blond man dressed in jeans and a red sweater under a leather jacket started toward her. He was carrying a large manila envelope, and instinctively she cringed. Greg stopped him with a hand on his arm.

"Hold it, Trent," he ordered. "That's far enough."

He turned toward Noel. "Do you know this man?"

"Of course she knows me," Bill snapped. "Tell them, Stephanie. Tell them we're in love and going to be married."

Noel blinked. There was something vaguely familiar about him, but he stirred no tender feelings in her. Instead she felt a mixture of anger and fear, but had no recollection of why.

"No, I—I don't think so," she said anxiously. "At least, I don't remember having known him." She looked at the man. "Do you have any proof that I'm, ah, who you say I am?"

"Of course I do." He held out the envelope and once more started toward her, but Greg stopped him again.

"I'll give that to her," Greg said, and took it from him. "Now, Mr. Trent, if you'll just sit here..." He led Bill to a chair at the opposite end of the couch from Noel, then Greg sat down on the couch beside her and handed her the envelope.

Inside were pictures, and Noel couldn't deny that she and the woman in them, whom he identified as Stephanie Gates, were actually one and the same. One was of her in a graduation cap and gown, others of Bill and her together at various places, and one of them with glowing smiles cutting a cake, which he said was taken at their engagement party.

Noel felt sick.

"Please," she said as she handed the pictures back, "tell me about..." She hesitated. "About Stephanie Gates."

Bill looked at her pityingly. "You mean about yourself. You're twenty-three years old and a fifth-year student at University of the Pacific in Stockton. That's where we met. I'm a senior in the fine arts department."

Noel had a vague impression of old and new buildings grouped on grounds with green grass and stately old shade trees. "What is my major?"

"You're studying for a teaching credential. You were born and raised in Fresno, but your mother and father were killed in an automobile accident during your freshman year at U.O.P. They left enough insurance to cover your school and living expenses, so Stockton has been your home for the past four years."

Her jaws and her hands were clenched, and she made an effort to relax. "Do I have any other relatives?"

He shook his head. "Only a much older sister who left home to attend college in the east when you were two, then married and stayed there. You hardly know each other and have had little contact since your parents died. I'm all you have, babe.''

That thought made Noel shudder until Greg spoke. "Don't count on it, Trent." His tone carried an implied menace.

"But I do count on it," Bill answered with equal menace. "We've been together for two years and have great plans for the future."

Noel stiffened. "Do you mean we've been living together?" Her fingernails dug into her palms, and she could feel the same tension in Greg sitting beside her.

Bill took his time about answering, and she was ready to scream at him when he finally said, "No, I live in a dorm, and you have a small apartment just off campus, but that doesn't mean we aren't lovers." His voice rose to a loud, nagging whine. "For God's sake, Steph, how could you forget?''

Her nerves snapped, and she jumped up. "I don't know," she yelled. "Maybe I don't remember because it never happened."

Now Bill was on his feet. "The hell it didn't," he yelled back. "What are you trying to pull, anyway? Just because you've been acting like an ice maiden the past few months doesn't mean we never—"

"Enough!" Greg's roar split the room as he also lunged to his feet.

Suddenly, in the midst of all the shouting and confusion, the wall in Noel's mind crumbled, and Stephanie was whole again with both her past and her present meshed.

For a moment the impact rocked her. What a mind-blowing experience she'd been having this past week!

Never again would she take her memory, or the events of her past, for granted. She hadn't realized how vitally essential they both were to the very essence of living.

The sergeant had stepped in and quieted both Greg and Bill by the time Stephanie regained her composure, and they were all three looking at her, apparently waiting for her to respond to something that had been said.

Instead she looked straight at Bill, and when she spoke her voice was filled with scorn.

"Well, Bill, you took long enough to come back for me. Perhaps you'd like to explain why you left me alone and unconscious that night in the park."

Chapter Nine

Bill Trent's face registered shock, then alarm as he stumbled backward. "I didn't," he blurted. "I don't know what you're talking about. The last time I saw you was in your apartment a week ago last Saturday. We...we'd quarreled and you said you were going away during the Christmas break to think things over..."

Stephanie looked at the man in front of her and wondered what she'd ever seen in him. His poetic good looks and his undisputed artistic talent were all there was to him. He was shallow, vain and self-centered, but even now she found it difficult to believe that she'd misjudged him so completely. That he'd actually abandoned her...

"That's a lie and you know it," she challenged. "It's true that our relationship had been rocky, but that Sunday we'd come over here to San Francisco to see the Klee exhibit at the De Young museum in Golden Gate Park."

"No!" Bill snapped. "I wasn't with you—"

"Now just a damn minute," Greg interrupted, then turned to Stephanie. "Noel, has your memory returned?"

She smiled at him. "Yes, it has. Don't ask me how or why, but all of a sudden it was there. I remember Bill, and I also remember that I broke our engagement and gave him back his ring. That's when he pushed me and I fell."

Greg muttered an oath and started after Bill with mayhem written plainly across his face. "You hit her, you son of a—"

Bill scuttled away and the sergeant caught Greg and held him. "Take it easy," he barked. "We'll deal with this guy later after we've sorted out what really happened."

Greg jerked away from the officer and glared at Bill, but made no more threatening moves.

Stephanie hurried to his side and put her arm through his. She needed to touch him, to reassure him that Bill Trent was no threat to them, but there was little she could do in front of Bill and the other officer.

"It wasn't like that, Greg," she said quickly. "We hadn't been getting along well for months, and on that Sunday everything seemed to go wrong. We'd been late getting to the museum, and then there was another long wait to get in. Once inside, Bill lingered so long at each painting that I finally went outside and sat on a bench for over an hour waiting for him."

"I'm an artist, damn it," Bill said righteously. "I was studying Klee's technique, his grasp of the abstract."

Stephanie sighed. "I know. I should have been more patient, but then in the evening we went to see *The Nutcracker* ballet and Bill didn't like it. He griped through both intermissions and..." She shrugged. "Well, you can see, we were both spoiling for a shouting match."

She paused to collect her thoughts, then continued. "We were both angry when we came out of the theater, and to make matters worse, I misread the map in the dimness of the streetlights and directed Bill wrong so that we ended up back in Golden Gate Park instead of on the freeway.

"He started making snide, sarcastic remarks, and by that time I was furious. When he parked the car to look at the map himself, I got out to move around and let off steam."

She paused as her mind focused on details. "Incidentally, I was wearing my coat and watch so someone must have come by while I was unconscious and stripped them off me. I left my purse in the car.

"My indecision drifted away in the crisp night air, and I finally acknowledged what I'd known for months," she continued. "I wasn't in love with Bill and couldn't marry him.

"He insisted I get back in the car, and when I didn't, he got out, too. I told him I wasn't going to marry him and took off my ring, but when I tried to give it to him, he wouldn't take it."

Reliving that dreadful scene was painful, and she clutched her arms across her chest. "I tried to force it on him, and in the scuffle he pushed me and I lost my footing and fell."

She shook her head sadly. "Which brings us to where my memory was blanked out until just a few minutes ago."

Bill's face was a pasty gray as he slumped down onto a chair and ran both hands through his thick hair. "Oh Lord, Steph, I thought you were dead. Your head was bleeding and you were so white and still. I couldn't find a pulse and I panicked."

His voice broke on a sob. "I'm sorry. I was afraid if I called the police they'd think I killed you, so I ran. When I found your purse the next morning, I burned all identification and threw the rest in a dumpster. I've been living in hell ever since until I saw you on television last night. God, what a relief."

It had been a long, emotional day before all the loose ends were tied up, and it was dark when Stephanie and Greg finally left the police station together. They'd called Abby shortly after Bill's confession to tell her what had happened, but the heightened tension they'd been under had taken its toll, and in the end they'd quarreled over Stephanie's refusal to press charges against Bill.

"Damn it, Noel, uh, Stephanie," he'd exploded. "If you won't charge him with assault at least let me arrest him for endangering your life. The bastard didn't even attempt to get help for you."

She'd shaken her head. "No, Greg. I don't want this to drag on for months. Just make him promise never to contact me again and let him go."

Now Bill was gone, out of her sight and out of her life, but Greg was still angry. The silence between them was palpable as they drove down the freeway toward Brisbane and home.

Home. But was Greg's home still hers? Until now they hadn't had a moment alone since she'd regained her memory. She hadn't yet told him how relieved she was to be free to give herself to him. Nor had he indicated that he still wanted her now that she wasn't totally dependent on him anymore.

Had he lost interest now that she had a life of her own and was capable of taking care of herself?

Greg kept his eyes on the road as he sped through the heavy Christmas traffic. His emotions were in a state of chaos. Happy that Noel's memory had returned, but terrified that now that she no longer needed him she'd go back to her former life without him.

She'd sent Bill Trent away, but their engagement had been broken before she'd lost her memory. It didn't mean that she was choosing him over Bill, only that she didn't want the other man.

Greg wanted her so bad it was like an ache that wouldn't go away, and it was all he could do not to pull off the road and plead with her not to leave him. To beg her to marry him, but he couldn't do that. It wouldn't be fair to her.

Much as he needed her, she had to come to him out of a similar need or not at all. He didn't want her compassion, or her gratitude. He wanted her love.

When they turned off the freeway at Brisbane, the street they usually took to get home was blocked by a truck that had spilled part of its load, and they had to take a less direct route. As they drove past brightly decorated homes, Stephanie heard bells chiming in the distance, and as they came closer, she realized that they were ringing from the bell tower of the small neighborhood church that Abby attended.

Stephanie sat up and peered ahead of them at the cars streaming into the parking lot and the people entering the brightly lit building. Of course, it was Christmas Eve! In all the hectic activity of the day she'd forgotten.

"Oh Greg, please stop." In her rush to get his attention before he drove past, she sounded more urgent than she'd intended.

He slammed on the brakes and halted in the middle of the street. "What's the matter?" he said anxiously.

She smiled and put her hand on his arm. "I'm sorry, I didn't mean to startle you," she said softly, "but it's Christmas Eve, and I'd like to go to the early service here. Do you mind?"

He claimed her hand and raised it to his lips. "I don't mind," he said huskily.

Inside the small sanctuary they sat among the splendor of stained glass, masses of red poinsettia plants and the soft glow from dozens of white candles, and listened to the glorious Christmas music sung by the choir.

Greg reached over and took her hand in his, and all the tension drained away as the melody of familiar carols drifted around her.

Silent night, holy night. All is calm...

She squeezed Greg's hand, and he looked at her, his eyes filled with tenderness as he squeezed back. Was it just coincidence that she and Greg, who lived nearly one hundred miles apart, both happened to be in Golden Gate Park at the same time on that night of her accident?

Or was there a higher power who directed their destinies? Had they been born to meet and fall in love?

Hark, the herald angels sing...

Did she have a guardian angel who placed her under Greg's protection? A feeling of peace left her open to just such a possibility. Why not? Surely anything was possible at Christmastime.

When the service was over, Greg put his arm around her as they left the church and walked to the car, but once inside he didn't reach for her again as she'd hoped he would. Instead he started the engine and concentrated all his attention on maneuvering the sports car out of the crowded lot.

Her glow of contentment dimmed and was replaced with a chill of uneasiness as he continued on home in silence. What was the matter with him? This wasn't just pique over her refusal to press charges against Bill. It went much deeper than that.

When they reached the duplex, Greg drove into the garage. Abby's car was gone, which meant she'd already left for the Christmas Eve dinner party the doctors at the clinic were hosting for the staff.

Greg got out of the car and turned on the garage light, then helped Stephanie out. "We have to talk," he said, and ushered her into his house through the kitchen door.

Inside he switched on the kitchen light, then continued on to the living room where he lit the antique brass lamp that sat on an oak table beside the couch. Stephanie approached him from behind and put her arms around his waist as she rested her cheek against his back.

"Greg, what's the matter?" she asked anxiously. "I thought you'd be happy that I'd finally regained my memory."

"Happy!" His voice was raw. "I'm sick with dread."

Stephanie gasped, but before she could speak, he'd turned around and had her in his arms and cradled full length against him. "Ever since I brought you home looking like a bedraggled, abandoned child, I've known I'd have to give you up eventually. I thought I was prepared for it. Oh, I expected it to be painful, but nothing like this agony that's tearing me apart...."

His voice broke, and he buried his face in her hair.

Her joy was confined only by the depth of his despair. Her arms tightened around him, and she kissed his throat at the open neck of his shirt. "Darling, I'm not going to leave you unless you send me away. I was afraid you didn't want me anymore."

"I've been going crazy with wanting you." His voice was muffled in her hair. "But there are strings attached."

She blinked, and raised her head to look up at him. "Strings?" Was he going to tell her he just wanted a temporary relationship, not a permanent one?

"Yes, strings," he answered as his gaze met hers. "I won't settle for a superficial sexual encounter before you leave me to go back to college and take up your life where it left off a week ago. I love you, sweetheart, and I want to marry you. I want us to belong to each other legally. I want to spend the rest of my life making love to you, raising our children, enjoying our grandchildren and growing old together.''

Stephanie was so stunned by the beauty of his proposal, the depth of love that vibrated in his tone, that she literally couldn't speak. For a moment all she could do was look at him and hope the love she felt for him was shining from her.

Apparently it wasn't, because she saw uncertainty darken his face and pain dim his eyes. "If . . . if you don't want these same things, I'll understand." His tone had lost all its vibrancy. "It's presumptuous of me to think you might, but I couldn't stand it if we were to make love and then I lost you. It will be bad enough as it is. . . .''

Stephanie finally caught her breath. She put her fingers to his lips and smiled. "Greg, will you please stop talking and take me to bed? Or are you going to make me wait until we can get a marriage license and a minister?"

A look of overwhelming relief lit his face, and he kissed her fingers. "No ma'am, I'm not," he said huskily. "I'm not even sure I can wait until we get upstairs to the bedroom.''

She looked around her. "The floor's a little hard, but the couch will do just fine," she suggested.

The corners of his mouth lifted in a half smile. "Oh no it won't," he said, and swept her off her feet and into his arms. "When you and I come together in passion, it's going to be a consummation of our love, not our lust.''

He carried her up to his room, then stood her on the floor beside the bed and took her mouth with his. It was a sweet, almost innocent kiss in the beginning. His lips were warm and firm, and his thick mustache brushed lightly against her skin in an enticing caress that alerted all her senses.

She reached up and stroked his temples as she opened to his gently probing tongue, and when it slid inside, she felt the reaction in the deepest recesses of her femininity. She wrapped her arms around his neck and snuggled closer. He widened his stance and pressed on her hips to bring her hard against his arousal.

She moved against him, and he drew in his breath and shivered as his fingers located the long zipper on her dress and pulled it down. His hands found her bare flesh and stroked upward to unfasten her bra. They were policeman's hands, big and callused, but their gentle roughness only added to the seductive effect as they cupped her tingling breasts.

She reached under his loose-fitting velour shirt and explored his bare back. His flesh was warm, and his muscles contracted under her palms. Her own muscles tightened as his fingers brushed across her nipples and sent spasms of heat to her already liquid core, eliciting a moan of desire.

He was as eager as she as he slipped the dress and bra straps off her shoulders and let the garments fall to the floor, then pulled his shirt over his head.

They finished removing their clothes and turned down the bed, then stood, nude, facing each other, their only illumination the full moon glowing outside the window. Slowly Greg reached out and put a hand on either side of her waist. "I knew you had a beautiful body," he said raggedly, "but I didn't expect perfection."

His touch and the ardor in his voice accelerated her smoldering heat, and she trembled as her gaze roamed over him. Talk about perfect! She'd seen statues of Greek gods that didn't measure up to his muscular virility.

She put her hands on his shoulders and massaged them gently. "I love you, Greg," she said. "Not just because you rescued me and took care of me when I couldn't care for myself, although that's part of it. I love you because you're kind and thoughtful and unselfish. You were willing to risk a negative report on your record rather than leave me alone and unprotected in a strange and violent city."

He drew her close and nuzzled her throat. "When a wise man is given a treasure, he cherishes and protects it," he said huskily. "You are my treasure, my love, my Christmas miracle. I'll never believe that we were just thrown together by accident. We were meant for each other, my lovely Stephanie Noel, and I think I knew that the first time I held you in my arms just minutes after we found you."

Slowly she moved her hands up to cross her arms around his neck and nibbled his earlobe. "I felt it, too," she whispered. "Even dazed from a blow to the head, I knew that you were special. There was a unique magnetism that drew me to you. Frightened though I was, I knew I was safe when you were with me."

His hands roamed over the rise of her hips. "Are you frightened now? Is this really what you want?"

"Frightened? Oh no." Her arms tightened around him. "I want to belong to you physically and spiritually as well as legally." She sighed. "It sounds as if I were selling myself into bondage, but that's not it at all. I want you to belong to me in all those ways, too."

He kissed her then, and carefully lowered them both onto the bed. Before she closed her eyes, Stephanie caught a glimpse of the myriad stars in the clear sky outside the window. One was bigger and brighter, and twinkled more merrily than all the rest.

The Christmas star? Had it brought her to San Francisco? Maybe, and maybe not, but there was one thing she knew for sure.

She was going to name their first daughter Noel.

* * * * *

Author's Note

We've always opened our Christmas presents on Christmas Eve. It was a tradition started before I was born, and one my husband and I carried on after we were married. Our first Christmas together was spent with our families, but by the second one, we were living halfway across the continent in Baltimore. Although we were happy and content to be together, it was our first Christmas away from our parents, brothers, sisters and friends, and we felt isolated and alone.

By the third year, we were again far away from our families, this time in Sacramento on the West Coast, but there was a marvelous difference. We were starting a family of our own. Our first child, a blue-eyed, golden-haired daughter, was born three weeks later, and we were never alone or lonely again.

There are now twenty-nine of us, counting children, children-in-law and grandchildren, and we all get together at our house on Christmas Eve to exchange gifts, eat a buffet supper, and catch up on what's been happening since the last time we were all together.

It's truly a time for rejoicing and for giving thanks to God for our many blessings.

Merry Christmas.

Phyllis Halldorson

I HEARD THE
RABBITS SINGING

Peggy Webb

A recipe from Peggy Webb:

BANANAS FOSTER

This recipe is from the famous Brennan's in New Orleans. I use it for my Christmas Eve brunch because it is special and very festive.

2 tbsp brown sugar
1 tbsp butter
1 ripe banana, peeled and sliced lengthwise
dash of cinnamon
½ oz banana liqueur
1 oz white rum
1 large scoop vanilla ice cream

Melt brown sugar and butter in flat chafing dish. Add banana and sauté until tender. Sprinkle with cinnamon. Pour banana liqueur and rum over all and flame. Baste with warm liquid until flame burns out. Serve immediately over ice cream.

Makes one serving. Multiply according to the number of guests.

Chapter One

"Johnny, you've got to come home."

John Davis didn't answer immediately, but held his hand over the receiving end of the telephone and looked at the stack of files on his desk. They were all criminal law cases, and they were all waiting for his attention. Then he glanced out the window at his sweeping view of Seattle. The city was strung with colored lights and tinsel trees and bright baubles, in preparation for the big holiday rush. He didn't have time for any of it—neither the sentimentality nor the frantic buying urges that seemed to overtake people during the Christmas season.

"Uncle Roscoe, you know I can't come home. I've already explained that to you...I'm preparing for a very important trial." He tried to be patient; after all, Uncle Roscoe was eighty years old and John's only living kin.

"Piffle. I figure a young feller like you, handsome and smart and getting rich, to boot, can do just about anything he wants to do."

"You know I'd love to see you...."

"No, you wouldn't. If you wanted to see me all that bad you'd've come back to Mississippi a long time ago."

John felt a twinge of guilt, but it was only a small one. He didn't neglect his uncle—far from it. He called twice a week and had his secretary select birthday and Christmas gifts to send him every year at the appropriate times. Besides that, the overseer who lived on Uncle Roscoe's farm checked up on him faithfully, and he had both John's numbers—at the office and at home.

"I'll call you Christmas Day, Uncle Roscoe, and we'll have a long visit. How does that sound?"

"Like some big, slick, city lawyer trying to patronize his foolish old uncle. Anyhow, Christmas Day is liable to be too late."

"Too late for what?"

"For me. I heard the rabbits singing last night, Johnny."

John went very still. Although he'd long ago abandoned the foolish fancies of love and hope and faith that had been a part of his small-town upbringing, he had never forgotten the legend of the rabbits.

Years ago—he'd been eight years old, he remembered—he had come home from school to find his house filled with strangers, grown-ups in officious-looking suits and scary-looking uniforms. He had stood in the doorway watching as they wrapped his mother in a white sheet and carried her out the door.

Uncle Roscoe, his mother's brother, had taken him aside.

"She heard the rabbits singing, son. She called me last night, when the snow was on the ground, and said they were gathered on the front lawn, singing to her."

John had been too scared to ask any questions. He'd huddled between Uncle Roscoe's knees and looked at the empty bed where his mother had slept.

"Rabbits know when someone is going to die, Johnny," his uncle had told him. "When that time comes, they pay a visit to the house of the dying and sing their farewell. It's a gift God gives this lowly creature, a voice to use on one occasion. You won't ever hear a rabbit singing unless somebody is going to die." Uncle Roscoe had hugged him close then, whispering, "It's going to be all right, Johnny. I'll take care of you."

John held on to the telephone, remembering. He had gone to live with Uncle Roscoe. His uncle had taught him to play ball, helped him with his math, wiped his nose when he was sick and sat on the front row when he had received his degree from Vanderbilt School of Law. And now it was his turn.

"I'm coming home, Uncle Roscoe. Don't you worry. I'll take care of everything."

"I knew you would, Johnny. I knew it all along."

"Your move, Uncle Roscoe."

Roscoe advanced his checker across the board, jumping his black over two of Ruth Mobley's red.

"Crown me," he yelled, slapping his knee. "Heh, heh, heh. I'm beating your socks off."

"You always do. But I'm going to get you one of these days. Just you wait and see."

Ruth crowned Roscoe Blake's checker, all the while thinking how much she enjoyed these weekly games with him. He wasn't really her uncle, of course. She had met him six years ago when she'd brought her second-grade class to the Senior Citizens' Center to present a Labor Day program. They had been fast friends and checker-playing buddies ever since.

She glanced down at her watch. "What time did you say your nephew is getting here?"

"It's supposed to be five o'clock, but you never can tell with airplanes."

"Are you sure you don't want me to take you to the airport to meet him? I'll be happy to. Or if you don't feel like going, I'll go by myself."

"You just sit tight and finish the game. He'll rent a car. Besides, I want to surprise him."

"I hope he likes surprises." Ruth made her play on the checkerboard, but her mind wasn't on the game; it was on the nephew. If he were anything like his uncle, he would be delightful. She loved getting to know people, and she could hardly wait to meet John Davis.

The big car turned into the driveway just as the game was drawing to a close. Uncle Roscoe shaded his eyes against the evening sun streaming in through the window.

"I'll bet you a pretty that's him. He always did love fancy cars. That's just like him to rent the biggest one at the airport."

The black Lincoln slid to a stop beside an oak tree, and Ruth watched as a tall, dark-haired man got out. He was extraordinarily handsome.

Suddenly she wished she'd changed clothes. She was still wearing her saddle oxfords and the wool skirt and sweater she'd taught school in. On the other hand, if she had dressed for the occasion he might have gotten the wrong idea—that she was a woman on the prowl, for goodness' sake. Not that she had anything against men. On the contrary. She had always believed there was a Mr. Wonderful waiting somewhere for her—a generous, warmhearted, compassionate man very much like her own father. What she didn't understand was why it was taking him so long to find her.

She leaned forward in her chair as John Davis came up the brick walk toward the front porch. He was probably the finest-looking man she'd ever seen, broad-shouldered and slim-hipped, and he walked with the beautiful, manly grace of an athlete. He wasn't, of course. Uncle Roscoe had said he was one of the best criminal defense attorneys in Seattle. She guessed he worked out.

She reached up to pat her hair into place. It had slipped from the elastic band holding it in a ponytail, and loose tendrils were everywhere. She wished she had taken the time to fix it. But now it was too late; John was already coming up the porch steps.

He'd just have to take what he got—a thirty-year-old schoolteacher, plain as the day was long, unmarried, unspoken for and looking, but not so you would notice.

Ruth watched through the picture window as John Davis stood on the front porch, surveying his surroundings. She supposed he was feeling the same thing she always did when she got to Uncle Roscoe's farm—peace. There was nothing quite like a vast stretch of tree-shaded land to make a body feel that all was right with the world.

"Ruth, why don't you go to the door and let him in?" Uncle Roscoe said.

"Are you sure? I'm a stranger to him."

"So am I. It's been four years since he's been home."

An urge to shake John Davis settled over Ruth. How could he neglect such a lovely old man as Roscoe Blake? Her mouth tightened in a self-righteous line, and then she heard her mother's advice from long ago: *Don't judge, Ruth. You never know until you've walked a mile in another man's shoes.*

By the time she opened the door, Ruth was smiling.

"Hello. You must be John Davis."

She had to give the man credit; he didn't blink an eye at being greeted by a stranger.

"And you are..." He politely left the question hanging.

"Ruth Mobley, your uncle's friend." She opened the door wide. "Won't you come in?"

"Come in here, you old peckerwood," Uncle Roscoe yelled, "and let me get a gander at you." He picked up his glasses from the table beside his chair and slid them onto his nose. Then he turned his head from side to side, studying his nephew from all angles. His watery blue eyes began to twinkle. "Lord, look what they've done to you out there in that big city. Is that gray I see in your hair? A man your age. You ought to be ashamed of yourself. I didn't get a speck of gray till I turned sixty."

John smiled as he strode across the room and leaned down to hug his uncle.

"How are you, Uncle Roscoe?"

"Seventy was better, but eighty is not so bad once you get used to it. What I liked most of all, though, was being your age. Why, when I was thirty-six, I had women hanging all over me like bees on a honey pot."

"I see your condition has not dampened your spirit."

"Naw. I don't have time for the mully grubs." He waved his hand toward the sofa. "Sit over there, Johnny. You, too, Ruth. I want the two of you to get to know each other."

John Davis's smile of pleasure disappeared when he swung around to look at Ruth, and a smooth hard mask dropped into its place. She figured she could have been a delicious seven-layer chocolate cake or a coiled-up rattlesnake and still receive the same steady perusal. He made her vaguely uncomfortable. She had always thought she could hold her own with anybody, even high-powered criminal defense lawyers who drove big black Lincolns. But there was something about this man that gave her the shivers.

"I really should be going," Ruth said, turning away from John's disturbing scrutiny to look at Uncle Roscoe.

"It was kind of you to sit with my uncle until I arrived, Miss Mobley." John Davis was dismissing her.

"Sit with me! Shoot, boy, you act like I'm a pumpkin casserole that's about to rot. Ruth wasn't sitting with me— she was playing checkers. And I was beating her socks off."

Ruth laughed, and John glanced from her to his uncle. Just what in the devil was going on here? he wondered. Uncle Roscoe certainly didn't look like a dying man, and as for Ruth Mobley... He studied her the way he would study the prosecuting attorney in a court of law. It always paid to know your opponent. Furthermore, it wouldn't take him long to figure out her game.

"Now, sit down over there. Both of you," Uncle Roscoe roared. "The two of you are making me dizzy, standing up like your legs won't bend."

Ruth sat on one end of the sofa and John sat on the other. It was the same old sofa Uncle Roscoe had had for thirty years, the red roses faded a dusty pink and the cushions lumpy with age. For a moment John felt a bit nostalgic, as if he were eight years old again. It was an entirely foolish notion. Rural northeast Mississippi had always exerted a strange power over him. He had thought that years of living in Seattle had rid him of any excess emotional baggage left over from his childhood. He'd have to be careful. He had too much to do to let emotions get in the way.

"Well, now. That's better." Uncle Roscoe rose from his chair, his old joints creaking and popping. "I'm going to get us some cookies."

"I'll help you." Ruth stood up.

"Sit still, girl, and visit my nephew. When I get too old to walk to my own kitchen to get homemade cookies, you can throw me in the grave and pitch the dirt in on top of me.''

Ruth and John watched as he made his slow way to the kitchen. When he was out of sight, they were left with each other for company.

John turned his piercing black eyes on her. She really was a good-looking woman—fresh-scrubbed and wholesome. Just the type he mistrusted. "Don't let me keep you, Miss Mobley."

"Mr. Davis..." Ruth folded her hands together before she continued, and bright color flooded her cheeks. "I don't know what kind of society you are accustomed to in Seattle, but here in Tupelo we're accustomed to manners." Her chin went up. "I don't like being shown the door."

"Was I showing you the door?" John's mouth quirked with amusement. The woman had guts, he thought.

"Yes. And it's not even your house."

"As a matter of fact, it's not. It belongs to a very old man. A vulnerable old man, Miss Mobley."

"Don't let Uncle Roscoe hear you say that."

"*Uncle* Roscoe?"

"That's what I call him."

"Why?"

"Why..." Ruth Mobley was obviously flustered. She sucked in her breath, and her eyes got wide. Blue eyes. John hadn't noticed before. "Because I like him, that's why. Mr. Blake sounds far too formal, and we are *very* good friends."

"Just how good is that?"

Her cheeks blazed. "Are you implying..." Her mouth snapped shut as she glared at him.

"What am I to think? A young woman like yourself. Unattached. You are unattached, I assume. Or does your game include a silent partner?"

Ruth jumped off the sofa and held her hands pressed together flat over her stomach to stop their trembling. She had never been so mad in all her life.

"Mr. Davis, you are the most vile man I have ever met. And to think . . . I was looking forward to meeting you."

"I find it hard to believe that your motives are all that pure. I've seen the dark side of human nature, and my uncle is a wealthy man by many standards."

"You are lower than vile, Mr. Davis. You are despicable. And if it wouldn't hurt Uncle Roscoe's feelings I'd march into that kitchen and take my chocolate-chip cookies back home. I don't like to think of you enjoying a single thing I've spent my time making."

He almost smiled again, in spite of himself. "If it will make you feel better, I won't eat a bite of your chocolate-chip cookies."

"Nothing you can possibly say or do will make me feel better. I'm sick all the way to my toes that Uncle Roscoe has a wretched nephew like you." Ruth whirled around and started toward the door. "Please tell Uncle Roscoe I had to go." She turned and shook her finger at him, just as if he were one of her naughty second-graders. "And don't you dare burden him with your nasty suspicions."

"I'll handle my uncle, Miss Mobley. Leave him to me."

"I most certainly will not. He's my *friend,* Mr. Davis. I'll be back. You can count on it."

Ruth Mobley made a nice exit, her head held high and her back held rigid. John went to the window and watched as she climbed into her car and drove off. It was an old car, and not in good condition from the sound of it. He could see how a woman like her would find Uncle Roscoe easy pickings. A lonely old man, dying, with nobody around to protect him.

Well, he was home now, and he'd make it his business to see that Miss Ruth Mobley and anybody else like her didn't take advantage of Roscoe Blake.

"Where's Ruth?" Uncle Roscoe stood in the doorway, holding a platter of chocolate-chip cookies.

"She had to leave. She said to please give you her apologies."

"That's not like her to run off without hugging me goodbye."

John didn't like to see the look of disappointment on his uncle's face, so he offered further explanation, inventing as he went.

"She had some errands to run. Christmas errands, I believe she said. You know how busy everybody gets this time of year."

"Yep. Been thinking about what I want to buy for Christmas myself. This year I thought I might put a nightcap under the tree—to me from Santa Claus. My head gets cold at night."

"I'll get you a nightcap, Uncle Roscoe."

"Shoot. You're not supposed to tell. You know I like secrets." Roscoe set the platter on the table and sank into his chair. "Here. Have a cookie. I know they're good because I've already had six."

They did look good—fat and chewy, with hunks of real chocolate and lots of nuts. John was hungry. He hadn't had anything to eat since Dallas, and that had been airplane food. He looked at the cookies with regret.

"No, thank you, Uncle Roscoe. I'm not hungry."

Chapter Two

Ruth was not even out of Roscoe's driveway before she began to feel guilty. She had let her temper get the best of her. There she was, a *guest,* for heaven's sake. And she had said awful things about John Davis. Her cheeks burned at the things she had called him: vile, despicable, wretched. Oh, her tongue had really run away with her. Of course, he *was* all those things. The very idea. Thinking she had anything less than honorable motives where dear old Roscoe Blake was concerned. Still...she had no right to call his nephew to task.

There was only one thing to do—apologize. She thought of turning her car around right then and going back to say, "I'm sorry," but it was getting late and they would probably be eating dinner by now, and she had school papers to grade, and, besides all that, it was almost Christmas, and she had a million things to do. There were lots of reasons why she was going to wait until tomorrow. Being cowardly wasn't one of them. She was certain of that.

By the time she got back to her little duplex apartment on Church Street, Ruth had figured out exactly what she would do by way of apology. Tomorrow was Saturday, the perfect day for driving back into the country and helping Uncle Roscoe put up a Christmas tree. That's when she'd amend her wicked ways with John Davis.

John was up with the first light on Saturday morning. Bleary-eyed from lack of sleep and still weary from his cross-country flight, he made his way down the hall of the old house to Uncle Roscoe's bedroom. John eased the bedroom door open and stood looking at his uncle. He was flat on his back, his mouth open like a fish, snoring gently. Smiling, John closed the door. His uncle had made it through the night.

The first thing John had to do was set up an appointment with Uncle Roscoe's doctor and find out exactly what the prognosis was. "A little trouble with the old ticker," was the way Uncle Roscoe had described his condition last night. John wanted the facts.

The next thing he had to do was put his uncle's legal affairs in order. Dying was never easy, but organized dying was much better for everybody concerned. John prided himself in being an expert on organization.

He went back into his room and dressed with the intention of making breakfast so he could get started organizing the rest of his uncle's life. But the call of a mourning dove drew him to the window.

In the distance he could see the barn, sitting lopsided on the hill like a tired, dusty, raggedy old man in need of a good bath and a new pair of pants. The dove cooed again, high up in the barn loft, and John was transported back in time. He was twelve years old, and he could feel the hay tickling his stomach and the sun warming his back as he stretched out in the hayloft, shirtless, to watch the doves search for loose grains of corn scattered on the ground below him.

His memories drew him on until he was out the door, racing through the morning sunshine, feeling the dew under his feet and smelling the mingled fragrance of rich black earth and sweet ripe hay. The old barn door squeaked on its rusty hinges as he pulled it back and walked inside. Shafts of sunlight shone through the rafters and streaked the loamy dirt under John's feet. Uncle Roscoe's donkey brayed his greeting from a stall.

"Good morning, Henry," John called. Ordinarily he might have stopped and stroked Henry's ears, for he was fond of the ornery old animal, but this morning he had other things on his mind.

Walking quickly, he made his way to the ladder that went straight up into the loft. The ladder was old and rotting, but his footing was sure. When John reached the square opening to the loft, he poked his head through. A few mice scurried out of sight, and two doves took flight. He squeezed through the opening, a big man who remembered the loft as a thing of grandeur and mystery.

Sweet-smelling hay crunched under his feet as he picked his way carefully across the loft. Viewed from the loft's wide opening, Uncle Roscoe's house looked small and far away. John lay on his stomach and gazed out across the farm. From this height, everything seemed remote and less significant, even the solid hundred-year-old oak trees standing in the front yard.

The hayloft had always been his dreaming place. When he had been a child, he'd pictured heaven as being like this: a high place that looked down at the petty doings of mere mortals. He had imagined his mother with wings, floating somewhere far above him, looking down and smiling. Suddenly he pictured Uncle Roscoe ascending to some high and holy place, accepting a pair of wings, then zooming around the Glory Land, laughing and shouting his pleasure.

The vision lasted only a second, and then John's common sense asserted itself. "Don't be a fool." He spoke aloud so the sound of his own voice would restore his sanity. This place was getting to him.

He was lifting himself up onto his elbows in preparation for leaving the loft when he saw an old car coming up Uncle Roscoe's driveway. Ruth Mobley. He recognized the car immediately. What was she up to now? Hadn't he made his position plain enough yesterday?

He watched as she climbed down from her car and made her way across the yard. She had a jaunty walk, one that showed her slim hips to good advantage, and the morning sun made her hair sparkle. His heart climbed high in his chest, and his mouth got dry. For a few minutes he was twenty-nine-years old, still idealistic and rapidly earning a reputation in the Seattle law community and Suzanne Cramer was walking across the street, the morning sun gilding her blond hair and her soft skin. She had been the most refreshing, most appealing woman John had ever met, and he'd fallen madly in love with her. Too late he'd discovered that her innocence was for show and her softness a facade. She was bait set out for him by the DA's office, a paid informant, sent to learn all she could about his client in the case of the State vs. Matkins.

He made a sound in his throat and looked down at his clenched hands. He was squeezing the life out of a clump of hay. In disgust, he tossed away the hay and took the time he needed to calm himself down. Then he got up and left the loft. A woman like Ruth Mobley, with her sweet smile and innocent talk of friendship... It wouldn't do to leave her alone with Uncle Roscoe.

John made his way across the yard. He found Ruth in the kitchen, an apron wrapped around her tiny waist and her hands dunked into a bowl of dough. She obviously hadn't heard him come in, for she was bent over the dough, humming "White Christmas."

"Do you always come into people's houses uninvited, Miss Mobley?"

She jumped at the sound of his voice, then turned around, her cheeks as rosy as the blouse she wore. One hand flew up to her cheek.

"You startled me." She gave him a brilliant smile. It would have been beautiful if it hadn't been so practiced and calculated. Since Suzanne, he'd seen it more times than he could count on the faces of women whose names he could no longer remember. Clever witches, all of them.

"I didn't hear you come in, John."

So he was John now, was he? She was changing her game tactics.

"You didn't answer my question."

Her color got higher, but her smile never wavered. She gave a determined toss of her head.

"Is this a cross-examination, Counselor?"

He didn't smile. "I never get sidetracked, Miss Mobley. You should know that about me."

"I have a key." Her chin rose just a fraction. "When I want to surprise Uncle Roscoe with something special, I often let myself in. This morning I thought I'd prepare a good home-cooked breakfast."

"The way to a man's pocketbook is through his stomach. Is that it, Miss Mobley?"

Her blue eyes flashed fire; then she carefully wiped her hands on a tea towel and crossed the room to where he stood, leaning on the door frame, hoping to look casual. As she came closer, he saw a fine dusting of flour she'd left on her cheek. Seven years ago he might have leaned down and wiped it off. Now he stood his ground, trying not to be seduced by the enticing smells of biscuit dough and honeysuckle she brought with her. He guessed the honeysuckle must be something she rubbed on her silky skin after a bath. He was sidetracked a moment by that thought; then he pulled himself together.

Ruth Mobley moved in on him, coming so close he could see a dewy line of perspiration on her upper lip. Obviously, cooking was hot work. He didn't know why, but that little line of perspiration disconcerted him.

While he was trying to think of what he should say, Ruth spoke.

"I feel sympathy for you, John."

"Save it for a more appreciative audience."

"Apparently you don't understand friendship."

"Don't try to play me for a fool, Miss Mobley. You're liable to be disappointed."

She opened her mouth to reply, then snapped it shut and took a step back. He could see the struggle she made to control her temper.

"I didn't come here to fuss with you this morning."

She looked at him expectantly, but he wasn't going to make anything easy for her. His expression never changed as he studied her with the piercing dark-eyed look that had earned him the nickname "Hawk" in the courtroom. He had to give her credit; she never quivered, not even once.

"I came to apologize," she said.

"Accepted."

Ruth had expected more from him. On the ten-mile drive from her house, she had actually convinced herself that John's behavior of last night was due to fatigue, that this morning he would be as pleasant and ordinary as the men she was accustomed to. But she had been wrong. If anything, the night's rest had made John Davis colder than ever.

For a moment, she thought of leaving and not coming back until John Davis was off the farm and back in Seattle. But that was a cowardly way out, and, besides, she couldn't desert Uncle Roscoe, not this near Christmas. He needed her and she needed him.

She studied the forbidding man before her, studied him frankly and in a manner her mother would have called rude. He looked younger this morning. Perhaps it was the clothes. Today he wore jeans and a sweater instead of a business suit. And his hair... It was blacker than the wings of starlings, with small streaks of gray at the temples that only added to his appeal. And it was slightly disheveled, like that of a small boy who had just come back from a romp in the woods.

She started to turn her gaze away, and then she saw the hay. A small golden straw was clinging to the shoulder of John's sweater. Funny that she hadn't noticed that before. Ruth smiled. John Davis had been romping in the hay.

She reached out to pluck the hay away. John's eyes darkened, and his hand slammed over hers, pinning it to his chest.

"There's no need to carry your apology that far, Miss Mobley. I'm not susceptible to feminine wiles."

Her cheeks stained a darker pink. Good grief. The man thought she was trying to seduce him, right in Uncle Roscoe's kitchen. As if that weren't humiliation enough, she was feeling jolts of current from his hand. He was still pressing her hand tightly against his broad chest, and the tingling that had started in her fingertips was working its way up her arm.

She guessed the proper thing to do was jerk away, but she was powerless to move.

"I was..." Her voice faltered. She flicked her tongue over her lips and tried again. "You have hay," she whispered.

"Hay?"

John suddenly felt like a fool. Here he was, hanging on to Ruth Mobley's hand as if he had never been touched by a woman, and worse yet, accusing her of malicious intent.

He dropped her hand with such alacrity, she stepped back; then he plucked off the hay and tossed it into the nearby wastebasket.

"I was checking on Uncle Roscoe's donkey." He didn't have any idea why he felt compelled to hide the truth.

"I see." Ruth surveyed his disheveled hair once more, then she burst into a peal of merry laughter. "For a minute there, I thought you were going to admit to enjoying a morning romp in the hay."

The laughter caught John off guard. He almost laughed with her as his defenses slipped. Then he remembered all the devious ways of women. This one, with her look of absolute purity, was worse than most. He'd have to play hardball. Perhaps a little shock treatment would send her scurrying for cover.

"A romp in the hay sounds intriguing...and just the thing I need to clear away jet lag." He held his hand out to her. "Care to join me, Miss Mobley?"

He was almost sorry when her smile faded and the music of her laughter stopped. But the feeling was fleeting. He had never let emotion interfere with his job.

Ruth backed against a straight wooden kitchen chair and watched him with wide blue eyes. If it was an act, she was good. Damned good.

"You're kidding, of course," she said.

"Try me." He took a step closer. It seemed he had found the perfect weapon to chase the gold-digging schoolteacher away—fear. "From time to time I find myself in need of a woman." His eyes were bold as they assessed her. "You will do quite admirably, Miss Mobley."

"You would take me for a romp in the hay... a woman you have never called by first name?" Her chin came up in a gesture of defiance.

"Names aren't important to me. Only pleasure."

She was silent for a while, her eyes luminous, and then she said solemnly, "My name is Ruth."

Once again, he admired her spunk. Apparently he had misjudged Ruth Mobley. She wasn't going to be easy to dissuade. For an instant he was thrown off balance. He wasn't accustomed to making mistakes in judgment. His instincts had failed him only once, and now he found himself face-to-face with this paradox, this soft-looking schoolteacher with the will of a dictator and the dignity of a queen.

"Ruth..." John made his voice low and seductive as he closed in on her. Oh, he knew how, all right. Seduction was a game, just like everything else. "I think a sample is in order before we get to the hayloft." He clamped one hand on her shoulder and lifted her chin with the other. "Don't you?"

To her credit, Ruth didn't flinch. Only the slight tremor of her lips gave her away.

"If you think to chase me away with these tactics, you are mistaken."

"I never make mistakes. Not about my opponents and certainly not about women." John traced her soft cheek with the back of his hand. Touching her was almost his undoing. Ruth Mobley had soft skin and lush lips and she smelled like honeysuckle. It was a near-fatal combination.

John ignored the stirrings of his own emotions and pressed on. He circled one finger slowly around Ruth's lips. When they parted and he felt their warm, moist interior, he almost forgot the game he was playing.

"We're going to be good together, Ruth."

The sharp intake of her breath was his only answer. He had thought she'd be on her way out the door long before now. His heart thudded heavily as he bent over her.

"You're going to be a tasty morsel. I might have you for breakfast and lunch both."

Still, she was silent, standing quietly in his embrace with her warm breath fanning his cheek.

Something inside John snapped. He took her swiftly and without mercy. She made a small sound of surprise, and he felt her body go rigid. For a moment, regret sliced through him, but there was no backing down now. He had to strike fear into the heart of Ruth Mobley.

His kiss was expert and thorough, and totally without feeling. It was a survival tactic he'd learned long ago, after Suzanne. He could feel Ruth's defenses falling, one by one. Her body loosened and sagged against him, her lips softened and flowered open.

His tactics were working. When he finished with her, she wouldn't be able to get to the door fast enough. John continued his manipulation, exulting in the power of winning. And suddenly a strange thing happened: he fell victim to his own game.

Feelings he'd thought long-dead stirred deep in his soul. Tender feelings, gentle feelings. With something akin to wonder, he realized his hands were cradling the back of Ruth's head and his fingers were trapped lovingly in her silky hair. His emotions were as strong as the tides, and just as inexplorable. Nothing short of a miracle would stop them.

Ruth provided the miracle. She cupped his face and gently pushed him away. Her shining eyes rivaled the brightest star in the heavens as she gazed at him.

"That was a lovely acceptance of my apology, John," she said softly, "but I do have breakfast to prepare."

He watched, astonished, as she walked to the kitchen counter and plunged her hands into the biscuit dough.

Chapter Three

Ruth congratulated herself all the way to the counter. How she could stand on her legs was purely a miracle. They were as limp as wheat that had been left out in the rain.

Except for the loud ticking of the clock on the wall, the kitchen was as quiet as an empty church. Why didn't John say something? She kept her back to him, concentrating on the bowl of dough. What was there to say? She had gotten herself into a fine pickle, coming out here thinking she could deal with the likes of John Davis. She was out of her league. Way out of her league.

Why had she come in the first place? Oh, she knew she'd told herself she was coming to apologize, but was that the whole truth? When she had first seen John standing in the kitchen this morning, her heart had saluted like a well-trained Marine. And now, kneading the dough as if her life depended on it, she was having the devil of a time to keep from reaching up and touching her lips.

His kiss had been divine, heavenly. All she wanted to do was settle into a quiet corner somewhere and contemplate the strange and wonderful feelings that had ripped through her when John Davis had held her in his arms. And what did that say about Miss Ruth Mobley, unattached schoolteacher?

It said that she was a fraud, that was what. All this time she had been telling herself that she wanted a quiet, compassionate, wonderful, *gentle* man, just like her father;

and she had let herself get carried away by the first ruthless dictator who had touched her. No wonder she was still
unattached; she had been looking in all the wrong places.
Apparently she should have been looking behind the bar-
ricaded doors of big-city criminal attorneys for the kind of
dark-humored, cynical man who could make her go
mindless with pleasure.

Ruth almost groaned aloud.

"Are you going to squeeze that dough all day, Ruth, or
do you plan to turn it into biscuits eventually?"

She gave a start at the sound of John's voice. She had
been so busy with her own thoughts, she hadn't heard him
approach. And now he was standing behind her, too close
for comfort. He was a big, solid presence that made her go
buttery-soft inside.

"I don't wonder that you're hungry." She smiled over
her shoulder at him, and she thought her cheerful attitude
was a masterpiece of deception. Maybe she had missed her
calling. Maybe she should have been an actress.

"A man who uses as much energy as you do trying to
scare a poor defenseless schoolteacher off is bound to eat
a lot."

"I would hardly call you defenseless."

Did she hear a little uncertainty in his tone? she wondered. Good. Perhaps she could survive John Davis after
all if she could only keep her wits about her.

She laughed. "I'll have these biscuits turned out in a
jiffy. Why don't you set the table—" she turned to give
him a pointed look "—for three."

John was alarmed at how easily she had twisted him to
do her bidding. Suzanne had been like that, too—big-eyed
and innocent and impossible to resist.

He rummaged through the cabinets, looking for dishes.
At least it gave him something to do with his hands—

something besides pulling Ruth back into his arms and tasting her mouth once more. She had been an incredibly sweet-tasting woman, and she had somehow wormed through all his defenses and made her way straight to his heart. He could still hear his own blood roaring in his ears, the blood she had set coursing through him like a wild river.

It couldn't be the woman herself who created this explosive chain reaction. It had to be the land, this place, Uncle Roscoe's farm. Or perhaps his heart and soul weren't as crusted over as he had believed. It was a disturbing revelation.

Holding on to three of Uncle Roscoe's blue china plates, he turned and studied Ruth Mobley. She was not beautiful, not in the head-turning sense of some women he had seen. Her face was quite unremarkable when he studied each feature separately. Her mouth was too wide, her nose was slightly uptilted and her eyes were like any other blue eyes—pretty but not astonishing. And yet, taken as a whole, Ruth Mobley was not a woman you wanted to look away from. There was something warm and comfortable about her, something *felt* but not seen that made a man want to get closer, to reach out and touch, even to covet.

He quickly shut his mind to such nonsense. He didn't believe in miracles anymore. And he certainly didn't believe in the myth of love and the institution of marriage. His own father had deserted John and his mother two days after John was born. As if that didn't tell him enough about love and marriage, there was Uncle Roscoe. That wise old man had never married. He must know something. And then there were all the nasty divorce cases John had seen. His law partner was a divorce specialist. That there were specialists presiding over its demise was in itself a sweeping indictment of marriage.

Ruth Mobley might make his body go up in flames, but she certainly couldn't change his mind or his heart. He took one last look at her, then turned to set the table.

"If I didn't see it with my own eyes, I wouldn't believe it," Uncle Roscoe said.

John and Ruth looked up at him, standing in the doorway, his white hair slicked down over his round head and his face wrinkled with mirth. Neither of them had heard his approach. Grinning, Uncle Roscoe made his way into the kitchen.

"I guess I must be living right. Two of my favorite people in the whole world standing in my kitchen, waiting on me hand and foot." He sat down at the table and took up his fork. "When's breakfast going to be ready? I'm starving."

"Coming right up," Ruth said. Relief flooded through her. Now she had a buffer. She scooped hot biscuits and scrambled eggs onto Uncle Roscoe's plate, then sat down beside him.

John sat across the table from Ruth. He felt as if he were a criminal who had just been granted a reprieve.

"Ruth dropped by for breakfast," he said.

"I can see that, Johnny." Uncle Roscoe winked at Ruth.

John could almost see the wheels turning in his uncle's head, but he couldn't deal with that right now. All he hoped for was enough control to get through breakfast. And then Ruth Mobley would be gone. He'd find some way to see that she didn't come back. Apparently she was as dangerous to him as she was to Uncle Roscoe.

"Biscuits, Johnny?" Ruth was handing him biscuits now, smiling that Madonna smile of hers and calling him Johnny.

He took three, snatching them from the plate like a thief. He gave her a curt "thanks" and retreated into a black and terrible silence. Let her think what she pleased. She had already called him vile and wretched; maybe she was adding barbaric and antisocial to her list. He hoped so. He was going to need all the help he could get to keep her at a distance.

Ruth and Uncle Roscoe carried on a lively conversation, their voices blending like music, swirling around John as he sat at his end of the table, brooding.

"Johnny...Johnny!"

Uncle Roscoe's loud bellow suddenly caught John's attention. He looked up to see both Ruth and his uncle staring at him.

"Did you say something, Uncle Roscoe?"

"I said, 'Ruth's come to help us put up a Christmas tree.' Isn't that nice?"

"That's a kind offer, Ruth, but we can manage without you." John made himself speak politely for the sake of his uncle. What he wanted to do was stalk around the table and grab her by the shoulders and say, "Leave before we both get burned."

"I've been helping Uncle Roscoe with his tree for six years. He'll be disappointed if I don't help this year."

"You're darned tootin'." Uncle Roscoe stood up on his creaky old legs and faced his nephew. "You two go on out to the barn and hitch old Henry up to my cart while I go and get my sweater."

"Uncle Roscoe, I don't think you should..." Uncle Roscoe left the kitchen before John could finish his protest. What was more, he was chuckling.

Ruth stood up and began to clear the dishes from her end of the table. "If you don't want to go, John, I'll understand. You must be exhausted from your long trip."

"What I am, Ruth, is exhausted from dealing with a stubborn man and an equally stubborn woman. Age is Uncle Roscoe's excuse. What's yours?"

Holding on to two china plates, Ruth turned to face him. She was in such a state—due mainly to his behavior—that she wanted to smash the plates on the floor. But if there was one thing her mother had tried to teach her, it was manners. Another thing her mother had tried to teach her was the facts about men, but apparently that lesson hadn't sunk in. Her mother and father had had a wonderful marriage—warm and loving. "Marry a man like your father, Ruth," Sarah Mobley had said when she was in a lecturing mood. "A good man like Wade will never let you down. Remember that."

Even now, as she wanted to throw the plates across the room, Ruth still felt the irresistible pull of John Davis's strange power. Her eyes were drawn to his lips, those lips that could be both cruel and exquisitely tender. She gripped the plates till her knuckles turned white. *God help me deal with this man,* she silently prayed.

"Love is my excuse," she finally said. A expression almost like pain came over John's face. "I love your uncle, Johnny."

John felt his will swaying and bending in the face of Ruth's quiet dignity. Was it possible that she was the innocent she pretended to be? Was it possible that the instincts that served him so well in Seattle didn't apply in Mississippi?

"Most people spend Christmas with their own families," he said, moderating his tone.

"I have no family."

A look of such longing crossed her face that John wanted to take her into his arms and comfort her. The feeling was as foreign to him as buying a coat three sizes too small—and just as uncomfortable.

"I had a family," she continued, "a wonderful family. But Mom was killed in a car accident when I was twenty-three, and Dad sort of wasted away after that. He fell victim to one illness after another, and complications from pneumonia finally killed him."

"I'm sorry."

Ruth studied him. He really meant it. It was probably the first genuine thing he'd said to her since they had met.

"Hey..." Smiling, she threw off her feelings of nostalgia. "Look at the two of us. We're supposed to be hitching Henry to the cart." She reached for his hand. "Come on."

Once more John found himself racing toward the barn with the exuberance of a teenager. But this time, he was holding on to the hand of a woman who was turning his life upside down. Ambivalent feelings coursed through him. He wanted to slam his fist into a brick wall and curse the Fates, and he wanted to take Ruth into his arms once more and bury himself in her sweetness. In his present state of mind, the barn with its hayloft was a dangerous place to be.

Ruth dropped his hand and raced ahead of him to shove open the barn door. Henry brayed a welcome.

When John arrived, he saw Ruth leaning over Henry's stall, crooning to him.

"How are you, you old sweetheart? Have you been missing me?" She rubbed the donkey's ears and patted his muzzle. "Just look at you, all fat and sassy. You're turning into a pig, that's what."

"Henry usually doesn't like strangers." John took the harness off the wall and approached the stall door.

"Oh, I'm no stranger to Henry." Ruth smiled at him, flushed from her run across the yard and as fresh and inviting as a box of bonbons. A shaft of sunlight slanted through the rafters, catching her in a golden spotlight. There was a sound of scurrying above them, and a sprinkle of hay drifted down from the loft.

John's hand tightened on the bridle. His heart and his mind were at war, and he had no idea which would win. He stepped closer to Ruth, drawn toward her as if invisible strings were pulling his soul.

"So...you have both my uncle and his donkey under your spell."

"Are you accusing me of witchcraft, Counselor?"

Her smile was still intact. She knew because she could feel her mouth stretched in all the right places. But her heart was doing such a fandango, she figured he could hear its beat. John looked formidable coming toward her—formidable and determined. Oh, Lord, what was he going to do now? If he kissed her again, she knew she'd make a fool of herself.

She glanced upward, toward the hayloft. She could smell the rich fragrance of the hay; she could almost feel the spongy texture of it under her back. When she looked back at John, his eyes were piercing.

"You need not worry, Ruth. I've long since given up the notion of a romp in the hay with you."

She blushed furiously. He had read her mind.

"I wasn't worried," she whispered, then flicked a nervous tongue over her lips.

John nearly dropped the bridle. *Damn her blue eyes.* Didn't she know how close she was to being ravished? He made himself take the next two steps that put him beside her at the stall door. Her honeysuckle fragrance, made richer and sweeter by the closeness in the barn, invaded his senses. Her body heat reached out to him, warm and enticing.

She's only a woman, he told himself, but at that moment he wasn't sure if that were true. Ruth Mobley had a way of making him believe she was someone special. She had a way of making him believe in a kind and gentle world where such old-fashioned virtues as love and truth and kindness existed.

But he knew better. Damn it all, he had seen the wretchedness man was capable of, the malicious intent, the *evil.* And in his own way, he had experienced it.

He slung the bridle and harness over the stall door and turned to her, his face fierce. "Are you sure that wasn't disappointment you were feeling, Ruth?"

Her whole body jerked, and her hand came up. It wavered in the air between them, and he could almost feel the stinging slap on his face. He waited, hoping it would come. The slap would prove to him that he was right, that Ruth Mobley was just another pretender who had been found out.

When her hand connected with his face, it wasn't in a slap; it was in a caress as gentle as the wings of a Christmas angel.

"Oh, Johnny... how you must be hurting inside."

"Hurting?" He grabbed the stall door with one hand and rammed his other one in his pocket. He had lost control once when she had touched him; it wouldn't happen again.

"Yes. I understand why you are lashing out." Her fingers glided softly over his cheek. "Uncle Roscoe told me the legend of the rabbits... and that he had heard them singing." She moved in and circled her arms around his waist. "I'm sorry, Johnny. So sorry," she said softly. Then she laid her head on his chest.

His heart set up such a thundering he imagined it was echoing through the downy cheek resting on his chest. Oh, she was a practitioner of witchcraft, all right. And he was dangerously close to being under her spell.

Chapter Four

Uncle Roscoe paused just inside the barn door, wheezing for breath. Durn, he couldn't depend on his ticker for a short walk across the yard anymore. He blinked once or twice, getting his old eyes used to the semigloom. When he opened them the second time, he saw John and Ruth pressed together as close as a bookend to a book. Her hair was spread across the front of his sweater like wheat in Kansas, and his hand was hovering in the air, just inches from her head.

Roscoe almost jumped up and down for joy. Not that he was a matchmaker, not by any stretch of the imagination. He had never been much of a believer in marriage. That scoundrel his sister had married had treated her like dirt. And personally he had never found a woman he'd thought worthy of him. But Ruth and John were a different matter. John was the son he'd never had, and Ruth was like a daughter to him. There were no two finer people on earth.

Wouldn't it just be a dandy twist of fate if they fell in love? Now that he had thought of the idea, there might be a thing or two he could do to give love a little boost.

The first thing was to stand still and let nature take its course....

Uncle Roscoe tiptoed into the barn and sat quietly in the shadows on the top of an upturned wooden keg.

John's hand barely brushed the top of Ruth's head. Then he pulled it back as if he'd been electrocuted.

"Don't, Ruth," he said.

"Don't what?" She lifted her head to look at him.

John untangled her arms from around his waist, and stepped out of her reach. "I don't need your false sympathy."

"False? You think I'm false?"

"Either false or a damned good actress." John flung open the stall door and reached for Henry. The old donkey backed against the wall, rolling his eyes and hee-hawing.

Uncle Roscoe's hopes fell. Shoot, even Henry could see that Johnny was making a jackass of himself. He rose from the keg, imagining the majestic figure he cut as he marched across the barn.

"I hope that ol' donkey kicks you in the seat of the pants, Johnny."

John and Ruth whirled around, looking like two guilty children caught with their hands in the cookie jar.

"Shoot, when I was your age I'd a been rolling a pretty woman like Ruth around in the hay, especially since she gave you such a good opportunity." Roscoe stopped when he was even with her and leaned close, squinting into her face. "You would have liked that, wouldn't you, Ruth?"

"Uncle Roscoe!" Ruth said.

"You're off base and out of line both, Uncle Roscoe." John glared at his uncle, then turned his fierce look on Ruth.

She suddenly felt hot all over. She pushed at her hair and turned her back on the stall. She didn't dare let John Davis study her face. Of course, she would have liked rolling in the hay, romantic that she was. Oh, she was beginning not to like this Christmas at all; it was bringing too many surprises. And the most surprising thing was herself. Here she was, thirty years old, and she didn't even know who she was anymore. The only thing she knew was what she wanted: she wanted John Davis. Never mind that he had a chip on his shoulder as big as Nebraska and that he never laughed and didn't even know the meaning of the word *gentleman*. Her father had been a true gentleman, a kind and courtly man who would never have put a woman in the hot spot. Wanting Johnny, wanting to abandon herself in his embrace, she felt almost as if she were defacing her father's tombstone.

"I think I'll wait outside while you two get Henry hitched to the cart," she said, already fleeing toward the barn door.

The December breeze was cool on her hot face as she leaned against the barn, trying to get herself back together again.

"Go home now, Ruth Mobley," she whispered fiercely to herself. "Go home while you still can."

But her stubborn streak prevented her from moving. She had come to help decorate a Christmas tree, and by George, she was going to stay until it was done—no matter how many times John Davis tempted her!

"All set." John's voice, coming from just inside the door, startled her.

"Good. Let's get going." She didn't dare look back at him, not yet anyhow. Maybe the great outdoors would blow some sense back into her brain.

The Christmas tree hunters started across the fields, with Ruth and John plodding solemnly on either side of the cart, being careful not to look at each other, while Uncle Roscoe rode in high style, carrying on a rip-roaring conversation with his donkey.

"How about that pair of lovebirds, Henry? Don't they beat all? Why I knew the minute I saw them in the barn that something was going on between them, and here they are acting like they don't even know each other, let alone *like* each other. Life's too short for that kind of shenanigans.''

''The only person cutting any shenanigans is *you*, Uncle Roscoe.'' Under different circumstances John would have found his uncle's comments funny but there was nothing at all funny about hearing a truth he didn't want to hear.

''John's right,'' Ruth said. ''You should be ashamed of yourself, Uncle Roscoe.''

''Nope. The only one I'm ashamed of is Johnny. Why, when I was his age, I'd have been sparking a sweet thing like you up one side and down the other. Heh, heh, heh.''

John would have thought his uncle was getting senile if he hadn't known better. Uncle Roscoe's mind was as sharp and clear as it had ever been. It was his manners that had deteriorated.

''Boy, I sure am having fun,'' Uncle Roscoe yelled. ''What about you, Henry?''

Henry stopped dead in the middle of the path, turned his head to look at Roscoe, then brayed.

''See there—he agrees with me.'' Uncle Roscoe snapped the reins, and Henry turned back around and plodded on. ''God makes the animals talk at Christmas. They tell the truth, too.''

John decided that it was going to be a very long morning.

Ruth found three perfect trees, each one just right for digging up, balling into burlap and transforming into a Christmas tree. She found them with such alacrity that John guessed she was just as anxious to end the outing as he was.

Uncle Roscoe turned all three trees down. One was too puny, the second was too pale and the third had an attitude, whatever that meant.

John quickly turned his uncle's attention to another group of potential Christmas trees, all perfect. Roscoe nixed those, too.

John supposed his uncle would have played his little game forever if he hadn't called a halt.

"Enough is enough, Uncle Roscoe. Don't think I'm not on to your tricks," John finally said after an hour's search. "I'm digging a tree and taking you back to the house. A man in your condition needs his rest." He jerked the shovel out of the cart and stalked toward a small cedar tree.

The hard physical labor of planting the shovel in the earth and ramming it deep with his foot was almost cathartic. John needed something to vent his rage. He wasn't angry at his uncle, and not even at Ruth. The person he was truly mad at was himself. He felt like a different man when he came back home. Somewhere out in Seattle, the real John Davis was sitting behind his desk in his law office, as cynical as ever and very much in control of his own destiny. But down here in the South, this new John Davis couldn't even control his eighty-year-old uncle, let alone his destiny.

Behind his back, Uncle Roscoe was still chattering to his donkey, plotting John's downfall, no doubt.

By the time he had finished digging the tree and they all got back to the house, John felt almost normal, even jaunty. His hard labor, plus the sun, had warmed him so that he had stripped off his sweater. The brisk breeze felt good whipping through his T-shirt. He covertly studied Ruth. Apparently the outing had helped her, too. She looked fresh and wind-blown and serene... and extraordinarily appealing. Fortunately he was back in control and very much immune.

"I'll set up the tree so that you two can do the decorating while I unhitch Henry." His Uncle Roscoe didn't protest, and Ruth was silent. Feeling victory near at hand, John lifted the tree off the cart and carried it into the house. Uncle Roscoe kept a huge tub, painted red, in the hall closet for his Christmas tree. John got out the tub and arranged the tree in the corner of the den, being careful of the roots, for the tree would be replanted after Christmas. "There. All done." He stood up. "It's ready for the ornaments, Uncle Roscoe."

Uncle Roscoe sank into his rocker and flung his hand over his forehead. "I'm all tuckered out from the tree hunting."

Ruth hurried to his side and knelt at his chair. "Uncle Roscoe, are you all right?"

"I just need a little rest, Ruth. I guess you two will have to carry on without me." He peeked at his nephew from between his fingers. John looked about ready to bite tenpenny nails and Roscoe Blake, to boot. Roscoe bit his lip to keep from giggling.

"Let me help you to bed, Uncle Roscoe." John practically lifted him out of the chair and led him into the bedroom. He helped him onto the bed, then squatted and removed Roscoe's shoes. "Shall I call your doctor?"

"This is not my ticker, Johnny. Just my age. You two go on and fix my tree up for Christmas. Have some fun."

John narrowed his eyes. "Are you putting on an act, Uncle Roscoe? Because, if you are and I ever find out about it, there will be hell to pay."

"Would I put on an act, right here at Christmastime? You know me better than that. I'm being as good as I can be so I'll get a nightcap in my stocking."

John smoothed the sheet over his uncle and patted his hand. "I'm sorry, Uncle Roscoe. It's been a trying day. You get some rest."

He left the room, and Roscoe called after him, "Don't you mess up my tree. Ruth will show you how to decorate it."

Ruth was waiting in the den for John. "How is he?"

"Tired, I think, but otherwise okay."

"That's a relief." She glanced from John to the tree. "I'll get the ornaments."

"You don't have to stay. I can do the tree."

Ruth felt a small thrill. He wasn't exactly on hands and knees begging her to stay, but neither was he showing her the door. All in all, she thought he had improved considerably since early this morning. Maybe there was hope for him, after all. Maybe there was hope for *her.*

"I want to stay." She looked straight into his dark eyes and got lost for a while, sucked into the black depths and drowned in confusion. What she had said to him finally registered on her laboring brain. She hastily sought to make amends.

"What I mean is . . . I've always helped Uncle Roscoe decorate his tree. For the past six years, that is."

"I know how to decorate a tree." John hadn't moved from his spot just inside the den door. He looked as if he had been planted there, like a tree, big and solid and every bit as inviting.

"You do?" Ruth's throat felt parched, her skin felt hot. Maybe she was the one who should be lying in bed. Another image came to her: she was lying in bed, stripped naked, and John was beside her, his jeans molded to his hips and his damp T-shirt stretched across his wonderful chest. Her eyes flew to his chest. It *was* wonderful. And his

T-shirt was slightly damp from all the labor. He was making her mouth water.

"Yes, I do." John started toward her, and for a moment Ruth thought he was going to touch her. But he stopped beside the rocking chair. "Perhaps my actions have made you believe I was spawned by the devil, Ruth, but I was actually conceived the normal way and born into a real family." His face hardened. "At least, it was a normal family for two days."

"What happened?"

John looked beyond Ruth, his eyes distant and his expression blank.

"What is it, Johnny? What's wrong?"

Suddenly he smiled, but it was not a smile of mirth. It was such a dark and lonely twisting of his features that Ruth actually shivered.

"You may do as you please, Ruth. Decorate the tree or go home. Uncle Roscoe is resting. Please don't disturb him when you leave."

He brushed past her without looking at her. The front door slammed behind him.

"Johnny," she called. "Johnny, wait." She rushed to the door, but John was already heading toward the barn with Henry and the donkey cart, his back stiff and unyielding.

Chapter Five

Ruth fought back tears. Never had she felt such defeat.

"What am I going to do?" she whispered. The happy day she had imagined lay shattered at her feet: Uncle Roscoe was in bed, worn-out from the excitement of plotting an impossible romance; Johnny was at the barn, probably planning some awful revenge; and she was left to decorate the tree alone. None of this would ever have happened if she had stayed at home. If she had gotten up this morning and called John Davis on the telephone and said, "I'm sorry I called you names," she would be in her own cozy apartment, wrapping gifts and maybe making a big pan of chocolate fudge.

On the other hand, if she had stayed home she would never have known what it felt like to be cradled in Johnny's arms. How long would he stay at the barn? Would he hurry back so he could be with her? Would he touch her again?

She closed the front door and faced the empty room. "Ruth Mobley," she said to herself in her best schoolteacher voice, "wishing and wanting never changed a thing. Decorate that tree and go home."

She got the box of decorations from the top shelf of the closet and separated the tree lights from the ornaments. After all were strung, she felt better. Activity always did that for her.

John still hadn't come back. How long did it take to unhitch a donkey, anyhow? Well, she wouldn't worry about that. What she would do instead was go into the kitchen and make herself a bracing cup of tea; then she'd come back and finish her job.

In the barn, John unhitched Henry, rubbed him down, then turned him out to run in his enclosed pasture. The job didn't take long—not nearly long enough for Ruth to decorate the tree. Was she still there? Was she standing in front of the tree, looking as bright as the tinsel she held in her arms? There were two ways to find out: go back to the house or climb into the loft. Call it cowardly, but he chose the easy way.

He climbed into the loft and gazed toward the house, looking for her car. It was still there. He sat cross-legged on the hay, waiting. It was close and warm in the barn and he began to feel drowsy. What he should do was just curl up and go to sleep and forget the whole thing—Ruth Mobley and her enticing ways and Uncle Roscoe's shenanigans.

He waited in the hayloft twenty minutes, but still Ruth's car sat in the driveway. Suddenly he sat up and brushed the hay briskly from his jeans. What was he doing? A grown man, hiding in the hayloft? If his law partners could see him now they would either die laughing or send someone with a net to get him.

There was only one thing to do: go back to the house and put an end to this nonsense.

Ruth was bending over the box of ornaments when he walked in the front door. For a moment he was distracted by the view; then he hardened his heart.

"I thought you would be finished by now."

She jerked around, her face flushed. Her hand flew up to her cheek, and she pushed back a stray lock of her silky hair. John suddenly wished he had stayed in the barn.

"I can't find the star," she said.

"I beg your pardon?" He was seeing stars, two of them, in her shining blue eyes.

"I know it was in here somewhere. I'm almost certain I saw it."

John fought off the urge to become involved in her star-finding scheme. How easy it would be to get sucked into all of Ruth's innocent-seeming schemes.

"The tree looks grand." He glanced in that direction to see if he were telling the truth. Actually, he was. Bright lights and garlands of tinsel and shiny ornaments transformed the cedar tree into a thing of wonder and beauty. Ruth seemed to have a knack for turning the ordinary into something special. "It doesn't need a star."

"Every tree needs a star." Ruth turned back to the box. Her hands shook as she rummaged through the leftover ornaments and bits of silvery icicles, pretending to be looking for the elusive star. Actually, she was keeping her hands off John. He had been in the hayloft again; she had seen a small piece of hay clinging to the front of his jeans. Erotic images spun through her mind.

"Ruth." She didn't turn around when he spoke her name; she couldn't. Not yet. "Ruth, look at me."

There was an icy edge of command to his voice. She turned around, slowly and reluctantly.

"The tree is finished," he said.

"Are you showing me the door again?"

"Call it whatever you like."

"Why?"

John was silent, for he didn't intend to tell Ruth Mobley exactly why he didn't want her around anymore.

"I've done everything I could to be friends with you," she said. "I apologized. I made chocolate-chip cookies and breakfast. I gave up my Saturday morning to drive out here and decorate this tree."

"You don't have to give up any more of your time. I will take care of my uncle."

"I gave my time willingly."

"In that case, will a check for five hundred be satisfactory?"

"Five hundred dollars?" Ruth's head spun, and she felt faint. She had never known that rage could be so devastating. "You think you can buy me off for five hundred dollars?"

"You want more?"

"What kind of man are you?" She advanced on him, her hands balled into fists.

"A practical man, a worldly man."

Ruth continued her determined march across the room. She knew that rage was keeping her going, for otherwise she would have turned and fled in terror. John Davis stood before her like some avenging god, big and formidable and deadly. Only the slight movement of his T-shirt across his broad chest told her he was a living, breathing man, not made of stone.

She didn't stop her march until she was almost nose to nose with him. She was no shrimp, herself. She tipped her head back and pinned him to the spot with her blazing eyes.

"How dare you treat me like some opportunist? How dare you try to toss me out of Uncle Roscoe's house? I wish I had back every one of the biscuits I made for you."

"For me?"

"For Uncle Roscoe," she amended quickly. She was rapidly losing her starch. Her hands itched to touch him.

Her heart cried out to hold him. Her mind yearned to probe the depths of him, to discover all the reasons for his moods.

"You can have your tree without its star, John Davis. I'm going home."

"Have a safe trip."

"But don't think I won't be back."

"One would certainly expect not. Do you thrive on rejection?"

"No, I thrive on challenge."

"I would advise against taking me on, Ruth. I never lose."

"Don't be conceited, Johnny. It's not you I plan to take on. It's Henry."

"The donkey?"

"Every year he's the star of my second-grade Christmas pageant. He's ornery as all get-out and a pain in the neck—rather like you, John. But still, I wouldn't dream of doing the pageant without him." Ruth snapped him a smart salute. "Good day, John Davis. Until we meet again."

"Over my dead body," he muttered, once she was out the door and out of earshot.

Out in the yard, her old car growled to life, and she spun out of the driveway, slinging gravel. She was as mad as any woman he'd ever seen. And she had been magnificent.

John sank slowly into Uncle Roscoe's rocking chair. He felt as if vampires had sucked all his blood away; he had no energy left. They had eaten his heart, too. He felt a big aching void where his heart used to be.

Some women got ugly when they were mad. Their noses turned red and their faces blotched. Some even cried. It was just his luck that anger turned Ruth into magnificent blue-blazing steel.

He leaned his head against the back of the chair. He had been ruthless. He didn't like to think of himself as a ruthless man. Nothing less than that would have turned her away, though. Of course, she had said she would be back . . . for the donkey.

He'd fix that. He drew a deep breath. His brain felt oxygen starved. Closing his eyes, he took another. Was that cigar smoke he smelled?

John bolted out of the chair and hurried down the hall to Uncle Roscoe's bedroom. That sneaky old codger was sitting in the middle of his bed, the covers pulled up to his chin, puffing away on a big cigar.

"Uncle Roscoe, you know you're not supposed to smoke."

"Piffle. A man can't do anything he likes anymore." Uncle Roscoe took the cigar from his mouth and offered it to John. "Here you are."

He was giving in too easily. John was immediately suspicious. He walked to the bed and took the cigar.

"What have you been up to?" he asked as he crushed the cigar in an ashtray.

"What makes you think I've been up to something?"

"That guilty look on your face."

"You're not in a court of law, Johnny—you're in my bedroom." Uncle Roscoe closed his eyes and leaned back on his pillows. "Go on, so I can get some rest."

"Uncle Roscoe . . ." John started to leave, and then the instincts that served him so well in a court of law came to his rescue. He bent over and pulled back the bedcovers. Uncle Roscoe was wearing his shoes. And hidden under his left thigh was the star Ruth had been searching for.

John picked up the star. "I see you've been busy, Uncle Roscoe."

"Shoot. I had to do something. She was going to leave before you got back from the barn if I didn't." He chuckled. "I snitched it when she went to the kitchen."

"You were supposed to be resting, Uncle Roscoe, not meddling."

"Meddling's more fun." Uncle Roscoe swung his feet off the bed and faced his nephew. "How come Ruth's not still here? Did you two fight again?"

"I never fight, Uncle Roscoe. I merely state my case."

"Humph."

John knew he should drop the subject, but he felt compelled to defend himself. "We simply had a disagreement."

"What kind of disagreement?"

Before answering, John thought of Ruth Mobley and his futile efforts to handle her. Now that she was gone and he could gain some perspective, the entire situation seemed to him almost funny. Here he was, a man who struck fear in the hearts of his opponents and the only thing he managed to strike in the hearts of Ruth and his uncle was stubborn determination to do exactly as they pleased.

Suddenly he laughed. Although Uncle Roscoe didn't have any idea what John was laughing about, he joined in. The two of them laughed until tears rolled down Roscoe's cheeks. Finally Roscoe wiped his cheeks and climbed out of bed.

"That made me feel so good I'm fixing to get up. If you'd tell me what it was all about, I might feel even better."

"I was laughing about Ruth Mobley. She actually believes she can stand up against me and win."

"Win what?"

"Henry. She wants him in her Christmas pageant."

"And what did you tell her?"

"I'm going to tell her 'no.' A man in your condition doesn't need to be worrying with getting a donkey off to a school pageant."

"Henry's going to be madder than hell. He likes that pageant. Looks forward to it every year."

"Donkeys are not capable of abstract thought, Uncle Roscoe. Henry doesn't even know it's almost Christmas."

"Don't let him hear you say that. He's liable to think up a terrible revenge."

"I can handle Henry." In charge once more, John became brisk. "Now, I'm going into the kitchen to make us some lunch, and then I'm going to check all your legal documents to be sure your estate is shipshape. I don't want you worrying about a thing."

As Roscoe followed John into the kitchen, he thought, hard and fast. Now that he had caught a vision of what the future could hold—Johnny and Ruth cuddled together in Roscoe's house, making babies for him to dandle on his knee—he was determined to do something about it. Those durned rabbits that had been singing would just have to think up a new song. Maybe they hadn't even been singing to him in the first place. Maybe they had meant to sing to a neighbor and got mixed-up and came to the wrong house. Or maybe he had just *thought* he heard rabbits. After all, he was getting old and his hearing wasn't as good as it used to be. It might have been whippoorwills making all that racket.

Whistling, Johnny dug sandwich fixings out of the refrigerator, while Roscoe sat in a kitchen chair, watching and grinning. Johnny was not one to whistle. The cause of his newfound joviality was bound to be Ruth. Roscoe was willing to bet money on it.

Roscoe ate his lunch obediently, all the while shaping his plan. When lunch was over and John suggested they go through his uncle's papers, Roscoe put his plan into action.

"That sounds right depressing to me, Johnny. Let's don't do legal stuff yet. It makes me think I'm going to die sitting right here in this chair."

"I'm sorry, Uncle Roscoe. Of course we don't have to discuss business this afternoon."

Uncle Roscoe beamed. Johnny was not even suspicious.

"What I want you to do, Johnny, is go Christmas shopping for me. My list of people I want to give presents to is all made out."

John agreed to the shopping trip.

After he had changed clothes he left the farm in his rented car.

Uncle Roscoe made his way to the barn. When he came to the pasture fence, he whistled. Henry trotted close and leaned over so Roscoe could scratch his ears.

"The two of us have a lot to talk about, old fella. And I don't want you giving me any sass."

Ruth was in the midst of Christmas shopping when she saw John Davis standing at the cosmetic counter of Reed's Department Store looking helpless. Her first instinct was to hide behind the bubble bath display, then sneak out the door. Seeing him reminded her all too vividly of what had happened in the farmhouse that morning. She still smarted every time she thought of the way he had tried to bribe her to leave sweet, dear old Roscoe Blake.

Her second instinct was, of course, to go on with her shopping. She was no quitter, and besides, she didn't have that many days left to shop before Christmas. She tilted her chin up and kept right on with her shopping, selecting just the right bubble bath scent for each of her fellow teachers. From time to time, her eyes strayed to John Davis. He was bent over the perfume bottles now, removing caps and sniffing and looking more and more like a lost little boy.

What was there about a helpless-looking man that tugged on a woman's heartstrings? And what kind of fool was she, to be exposing her heartstrings to a cynic like John Davis?

She turned her back on him and paid for her purchases. But even with her back turned, she was still aware of his presence. It was almost as if he stood beside her, making the heat rise in her face and turning her legs to butter. Try as she might, she couldn't make her body behave. What was she going to do?

"Merry Christmas, Miss Mobley," the salesclerk said as she handed Ruth's credit card back to her.

"Merry Christmas."

Ruth was halfway to the door before she knew she couldn't go on. She couldn't leave the store while John Davis was there. Call her foolish; call her softhearted; call her romantic. The man who made her feel special in his arms was within calling distance, and she couldn't walk away from him.

She tightened her hold on her shopping bag and walked briskly back to the cosmetic counter. John didn't see her coming; he was still involved in his perfume dilemma. When she was so close she could almost count the silver strands shading his dark hair, she spoke.

"Hello, Johnny."

He turned to her, and only the brief light that sparked in the center of his eyes acknowledged that he knew her. Then his face became expressionless.

"I didn't expect to see you here, Ruth."

"I didn't expect to see you, either."

His scrutiny of her was intense, and he seemed to be trying to make up his mind whether she was telling the truth. *Oh, Johnny,* her heart cried silently, *trust me.*

Suddenly he smiled. John Davis with a genuine smile on his face was a beautiful thing to see. His dark eyes glowed and crinkled at the corners, and his face took on the happy mischievous look of a ten-year-old boy.

"Since we are on neutral ground, I suppose the least we can do is be civil to one another," he said.

"It's the least we can do." Smiling, she stepped closer. When her arm brushed against his side, she knew it was no accident. She *wanted* to be within touching distance of John Davis. She held her breath, waiting for him to pull away, but he made a half turn so that his leg came in contact with hers.

Ruth thanked God for small favors. The Christmas spirit surged through her, and the haunting sounds of piped-in carols surrounded her. Her day was colored rosy.

"Are you buying perfume, Johnny?"

"Yes." He smiled again. "Unfortunately."

"Perhaps I can help. Is it for someone special?"

He studied her for such a long time she felt a flush come into her cheeks. She was drowning in his dark eyes.

"You might say that," he finally said.

"Oh…well…" Ruth felt her spirit draining away. It had never occurred to her that John Davis might be attached, though why she hadn't thought of that was a mystery to her. He was simply gorgeous and very successful, and he probably had women on every street corner of Seattle.

"Well," she said again, forcing some cheer into her voice. "If you'll tell me what she is like, perhaps I can help you."

"Sometimes she's like a summer storm, rumbling and threatening and flashing blue fire. Other times she's like a violet hidden in a wooded glade, lovely and delicate and shy."

His eyes caught and held hers. She could hardly breathe.

"You must love her very much, Johnny," Ruth whispered.

Oh, God, he thought. Was that what had happened to him? Had he fallen in love with this woman? That was impossible. Love was for fools, and he was anything but a fool.

John turned away from Ruth and picked up the nearest perfume bottle. His tone became brisk.

"So...what do you suggest, Ruth?"

"For a woman like that...you definitely want to get a fragrance that reminds you of summer flowers."

Honeysuckle. The answer was so obvious John didn't know how he had missed it. Of course, Ruth wore honeysuckle. Even now, standing in the vast interior of the department store, he was aware of her sweet fragrance. How could he have forgotten? When he had held her in his arms the fragrance had been tangled in her hair and embedded in her silky skin. He ached just thinking about it. And that was no condition to be in.

He stepped away from her, relieving himself of the sweet heat of her arm pressing against his.

"Thank you, Ruth. You've been most kind."

Ruth read his dismissal once more, but she didn't fight it. "I'm glad I could help," she said, already separating herself from John. She gave a little wave over her shoulder, and left him at the cosmetic counter with a cut-glass perfume bottle in his hand. For another woman. He was buying perfume for a woman he described in poetic terms.

Ruth actually clutched her heart as she hurried toward the socks and ties. When she was out of his sight, she parted the neckties and peered through. Goodness, what would her mother say if she were alive? Ruth could imagine.

Don't tell me you're pining over a man who loves another, Ruthie! For goodness' sake, dear. Show some backbone. Show some pride.

Of course, her mother had never met a man like John Davis. Ruth squashed her pride and kept her nose between the neckties, spying on the man she loved. She couldn't bear to miss one moment of seeing him, even if he did belong to another.

"Can I help you, miss?"

Ruth nearly jumped out of her skin. Still clutching the ties, she turned to the salesman who had appeared behind her.

"Would you like one of those ties? They make lovely Christmas gifts."

"Well . . . yes. I'll take this one." She handed the clerk one of the ties gripped in her hand.

Following the clerk to the cash register, she told herself over and over, *it can't be possible.* She couldn't possibly have fallen in love with John Davis on such short notice. Maybe it wasn't love; maybe it was just hormones; maybe it was the season.

The sales clerk handed her the tie. She added it to her shopping bag and took one last look toward the cosmetic counter.

John Davis was gone. Maybe she wouldn't give the tie to him; maybe she'd strangle him to death with it. It would serve him right for loving another.

Chapter Six

Henry started braying at nine o'clock Saturday night. John and Uncle Roscoe were sitting in the den playing checkers when the donkey chorus began.

John looked up from his checkers. "What's the matter with Henry?"

"It's probably going to rain. You know he always hollers like that before a big storm."

"The forecast is for clear skies."

"Shoot. What do weathermen know? Henry can predict circles around them." Grinning slyly, Uncle Roscoe slid his black home. "Crown me," he yelled. "You're not paying attention tonight, Johnny. Ruth can play circles around you."

"That's what you said about my gift wrapping."

"You should have let me call her to do it, like I wanted to. She sure can tie a pretty bow. Of course, she does everything well. She's smart, too. Did I tell you about that teaching award she won?"

"Three times tonight.... You're pushing your luck, Uncle Roscoe." Out in the barn, Henry begged to disagree. He created such an ear-splitting ruckus that John got up and shut the curtains, as if that would help. "What could possibly be the matter with that donkey?"

"I guess he's mad 'cause you said he couldn't be in Ruth's pageant. He likes Ruth."

John didn't dare let Uncle Roscoe know how much he liked her. More than liked her. Against all his better judgment he was dangerously close to being in love with her. But he was not one to take no-win risks, and love and marriage definitely fell into that category. There was no use in getting his uncle's hopes up.

From the barn came the sounds of the donkey's misery. Henry didn't believe in suffering in silence.

Abruptly, John shoved the checkerboard aside and stood up. "I'm going out to the barn to see if I can't calm that donkey down."

"Fat chance," Uncle Roscoe said after John had disappeared. Then he sat in his chair, grinning and chuckling to himself until John returned from the barn fifteen minutes later. He was disheveled and disgruntled.

"That donkey has gone mad." John paced, running his hands through his hair and shaking his head. "He's kicking the side of his stall and rolling his eyes and braying without ever stopping for breath. I've never seen him act like that."

Uncle Roscoe had, but he wasn't telling. "Why don't you calm him down, Johnny?"

"He won't let me near him."

"I'll call Ruth. She can handle him."

"This is my problem and I'll handle it. It's getting late, Uncle Roscoe. You go on to bed, and if Henry keeps this up, I'll call the vet. Maybe Henry has a stomachache."

John was barely out the door when Roscoe reached for the telephone. There was no need for him to get the directory. He knew Ruth's number by heart.

Ruth was alrady dressed for bed when her phone rang. The minute she heard Uncle Roscoe's voice, she panicked.

"Is anything wrong?" she asked.

"Everything will be just dandy when you get here."

"You're not sick, are you?"

"Nope. I'm fit as a fiddle. And I'll feel even better when you get here."

Ruth glanced at her clock. It was after nine-thirty, and while she wouldn't have hesitated to go to Uncle Roscoe under ordinary circumstances, she had no desire to go to his farmhouse late on a Saturday night and face another scene with John Davis.

"Where's John?" she asked.

"He's out in the barn."

"At this hour?"

"Ruth, I need you to get out here right away. Henry's cutting a ruckus and John can't do a thing with him."

"Uncle Roscoe, you know I'll come any time you need me, but I do think John is capable of handling Henry."

"I guess you don't love me anymore."

Ruth laughed. "That's emotional blackmail, Uncle Roscoe. It won't work."

"Well, shoot, if you don't come out here everything I've planned will be spoiled, and I'll feel so bad about it I might get really sick. I might even stop eating."

Ruth hung onto the receiver, undecided. Uncle Roscoe was far too wise to stop eating. On the other hand, she certainly didn't want to take any chances. Surely she could stand another chance encounter with John for the sake of a dear old man like Roscoe Blake.

"I'll be there," she said.

Even as she cradled the receiver and reached for her clothes, she knew that the state of Roscoe's health wasn't the only thing that could entice her out of her night clothes late on a cold December evening. John Davis was the drawing card. She would fall in with any scheme that allowed her to see him again, even if she caught only a glimpse. She had never dreamed that love was like that—

being grateful for one stolen moment of seeing the man you loved, even if you knew he didn't love you back.

It took her twenty minutes to dress and reach the farm. Roscoe was waiting for her in the den.

"What's the matter with Henry, Uncle Roscoe?" she said as she sat in the chair opposite his rocker.

"Onions."

"Onions?"

"You know how he hates them." Ruth nodded, and Uncle Roscoe continued. "Well, I had my overseer tie a bunch of onions to his stall about nine o'clock. Henry hasn't shut up since."

"Uncle Roscoe! Whatever for?" Ruth already knew the answer to that question. Roscoe Blake was matchmaking. And she was ashamed at how eager she was to go along with his scheme, whatever it was. Grasping at straws— that's what she was doing.

"I want me some great-nieces and nephews, and the way you and John have been looking at each other, I figured you might give me some if I got you two together."

"Oh, Uncle Roscoe." Ruth began to laugh. Roscoe joined her, and they had a good chuckle. When she sobered, she scooted her chair closer so he could see how serious she was. "John doesn't love me. In fact, I don't even think he likes me. I believe there is a woman in Seattle..." Her voice trailed off. She shouldn't be discussing John's private life. It was not her place. Even loving him didn't give her that right.

"Do you love him?"

Uncle Roscoe's blunt question took Ruth aback. Knowing how her story would end—that John would eventually go back to Seattle and she would go back to her job, still unattached and brokenhearted—she thought about lying to Uncle Roscoe. Why build up false hopes? But lying was not in her nature.

"Yes, Uncle Roscoe. I love him."

"There is no other woman, Ruth. Let me tell you a story...."

It took Uncle Roscoe ten minutes to tell Ruth about John's father and about Suzanne and about the years of seeing only the bad side of marriage in the divorce courts that had led to John's aversion to women. Roscoe Blake was a wise old man. He understood his nephew well and loved him even better. The insight he gave to Ruth came straight from his heart.

After he had finished his story, Ruth sat very quietly in her chair. Then she leaned over and kissed his cheek. "Why don't you go to bed, Uncle Roscoe?"

"Where are you going, Ruth?"

"To the barn. There are two wild beasts out there I need to tame."

John didn't hear Ruth come into the barn; Henry was making too much racket. He'd been trying to calm the animal for some time now, but the donkey was kicking his stall and braying as if all the demons in hell were after him.

"Easy, boy. Easy, now." In a last-ditch effort John tried to get close enough to wrap his arms around Henry's neck, but the flailing hooves kept him at a distance. "Nothing is going to hurt you, Henry. Easy now." John held out his hand. "Come on ... let me see what's bothering you."

"I know what's bothering him."

John spun around at the sound of Ruth's voice. She was standing in the darkened barn, lit by a shaft of moonlight that filtered through the rafters. Quick joy surged through John at the sight of her. He felt as if his entire body were weightless, and that with very little effort he could float straight up to heaven.

"What are you doing here?" John left the stall and stood just outside the gate.

"Uncle Roscoe called me."

They stood facing each other, as tense as two Roman gladiators about to enter the arena and fight to the death. All the love she felt for John sang through Ruth's spirit until she wanted to cry out her feelings, but caution held her back. And John was filled with such longing that he had to ram his hands into his pockets to keep his hands off her.

Henry's plaintive call of distress brought them out of their trance. Ruth brushed softly past John, leaving a heady trail of honeysuckle fragrance in her wake. For a moment, John was too caught up in her presence to guess her intent. When she put her hand on Henry's gate, he grabbed her shoulders.

"You can't go in there. You'll get hurt."

"I have to get the onions out so Henry will calm down."

"What in the devil are you talking about?"

"Uncle Roscoe had onions put in Henry's stall so he would create a ruckus. Henry can't abide onions."

"Damn. I should have known Uncle Roscoe was behind this. Do you know where they are?"

"In that sack hanging on the other side of Henry's stall." Ruth pointed.

John released her shoulders and unlatched Henry's gate. Ruth had a vision of his being trampled under Henry's flailing hooves. Suddenly it didn't matter that he waxed poetic over another woman and that he would be going back to Seattle and that hers was an unrequited love; she had to let John know how she felt.

"Johnny... wait." He turned slowly back to her, and Ruth cupped her hands on his cheeks. "Do be careful. I couldn't bear it if anything happened to you."

John couldn't trust himself to speak. Never had a woman's touch made him feel so special. Never had a woman's concern brought such a warm glow to his heart. He wanted to stand in Uncle Roscoe's barn forever, feeling Ruth's hands upon his cheeks. He wanted the rest of the world to disappear so that nothing existed except Ruth and this warm, dark barn with the inviting smells of honeysuckle and the endless possibilities of the hayloft. He had fallen in love. Against all his instincts and his years of caution, he had let this guileless woman with the soft skin and the innocent smile burrow deeply into his heart.

Suddenly he was afraid. He had handled the toughest criminal cases in Seattle, but he couldn't handle love.

"Henry won't harm me." John became brusque, pushing Ruth's hands aside and striding back into the stable. "Settle down, Henry. I'm going to remove the onions."

John wasn't sure whether Henry understood what he was saying or whether he merely obeyed the command in his voice. In any event, the donkey ceased his racket and stood still while John unhooked the sack of onions and carried them outside the barn. In the cool of the night, he thought about fleeing toward the house and leaving Ruth to her own devices. It would be a painless, easy escape. It would also be wise. Falling in love was not a part of his life's plan. And now that it had happened, he didn't know what to do about it.

John turned his face up to the stars as if he could read answers in the sky. He saw nothing except a vast expanse of blackness shot through with a few bright winter stars. Behind him, the barn door yawned open, beckoning to him; and he felt the irresistible pull of Ruth's presence. He had never walked away from a challenge. With one last look at the sky, John hurried back inside.

Ruth was standing beside Henry's stall, stroking his ears and speaking softly to him. Her voice was like music. John felt his body tighten as he imagined hearing that velvety musical voice whispering love words to him in the darkness. The vision was so vivid he groaned aloud.

"Johnny?" Ruth turned at the sound. For a moment she stood very still, smiling at him with her face as radiant as an angel's. Then she was running, arms outstretched. He reached for her automatically.

She came straight to his arms, pressing herself against his chest and gazing up at him with shining eyes.

"Oh, Johnny. I think I would have died if Henry had hurt you."

John tightened his hands around her small waist. He wanted to believe what he was hearing, but cynicism dies hard.

"There was no need to concern yourself."

"There was *every* need." She reached for his face, and her hands were soft and warm against his skin as she caressed him. "Don't you know what has happened? Don't you see?" One of her fingers traced his cheekbones. "I love you, Johnny." She slid her fingers downward to trace his lips. "I didn't mean to tell you, especially knowing how you feel about me..."

"You have no idea how I feel about you." His voice was rough with the love he couldn't speak. John had never dreamed that he could believe in love again, but Ruth had won his heart completely. Perhaps his own need was the reason for believing in her declaration. With passion turning his blood to a raging river, and need throbbing in his loins, perhaps he had lost all his perspective.

It was almost impossible not to give in to her, not to lift her into his arms and carry her into the hayloft and bury himself in her sweet warmth. Still . . . she might control his heart and his body with the ease of a master puppeteer, but she could not control his mind.

He studied Ruth's face, and the hope shining there almost blinded him. How easy it would be to join her fantasy and forget the real world.

"I don't expect anything from you, John. You don't have to say words you don't mean, but I have to be honest with you. I love you, Johnny. I didn't plan for it to happen. I didn't even want it to happen, but it did." She leaned so close her warm breath fanned against his cheek. "I love you."

"Prove it," he said, even as guilt smote him.

"Come." She took his hand and led him toward the hayloft.

"Where are we going?" He knew, but he wanted to hear her say the words. He had to be absolutely certain that she knew what she was doing.

"Up there. . . ." She lifted her face toward the loft, and a piece of hay drifted downward and caught in her pink sweater. "Because I love you, Johnny, I want to give you the greatest gift of all—myself."

It's a trap, his mind screamed, and yet his body was in no condition to pay attention. Call it passion, call it curiosity, call it any damned thing except love. John *had* to see how far Ruth's gift would take her. Mutely he followed her up the ladder, reaching upward to span her waist and help her negotiate the broken boards.

Chapter Seven

Ruth knew she was doing the right thing. It wasn't something she had planned in advance; it was merely instinct, and it felt good. She had fallen in love with a man she would never have chosen if common sense ruled, but apparently common sense had no say in matters of the heart. Everything about John was the exact opposite of what she had expected to see in the man she loved; and yet, she sensed unseen qualities in him—goodness and tenderness and a sense of fun, too long bottled-up inside. By giving herself to him unselfishly, she sought not only to prove she loved him, but also to unleash all the fine qualities he'd kept under wraps for so long.

She stepped into the hayloft, into a stream of starlight coming through the wide opening, and waited for John to join her. When he stood beside her, she reached for his hand.

"Come. Let me love you, Johnny."

She pulled him down onto the hay. Together they sank into its fragrant, spongy depths, their bodies pressed together and his lips seeking hers.

Ruth cupped the back of his head and gave herself up to John. All the love she felt for him poured forth in the way she touched him, the way she held him, the way she kissed him.

She made soft humming sounds of pleasure as she snuggled close, fitting herself perfectly to him. "Love me,

Johnny," she whispered when his lips left hers to brush tenderly across her cheek. "Love me."

"Ruth...Ruth..." John couldn't get enough of her. She was delicious beyond belief and tempting almost beyond enduring. And he would stake his career that she was not playing him false. Her sincerity made her all the harder to resist.

He had no intention of taking advantage of an unsophisticated, love-struck woman, no matter how much he wanted her; but he couldn't turn away from her—not yet. His mouth came down on hers once more, and he plunged his tongue into the warm inner recesses of her mouth. She responded with an eagerness that nearly toppled all his barriers.

She pulled his shirt loose and ran her hands over his back. Her touch on his bare back electrified him. He almost took her then, without thinking. His mouth skimmed down her throat and nudged aside the neck of her stretchy sweater. The heady combination of honeysuckle fragrance and satin skin drove him wild.

Groggy and half-mad with passion, he lifted himself onto his elbows so he could look into her face. "Do you know what you're doing, Ruth?"

"Yes."

He stared down at her for a long time, trying to read treachery in her eyes; but all he saw was innocence and a love so open and radiant her face fairly shone.

"Do you know how hard it is for a man to turn away from a woman once he's reached a certain point?"

"Don't turn away." She caressed his face. "Please, Johnny."

"You don't know what you ask."

"I don't mean to ask anything of you. I merely want to give." She brushed her fingertips across his lips. "Make love to me, Johnny."

"You tempt me." The starlight shining on her hair turned it into fairy gold. He buried his face there for a moment, inhaling her fragrance and reveling in the feel of the satiny strands against his cheek. His face was grim and determined when he lifted it. "Do you know what a man like me could do with an innocent woman like you?"

"You're a wonderful man, Johnny. I just don't think you've given yourself a chance to know that."

"Don't try to make me a saint. You'll be terribly disappointed." Suddenly he sat up, taking her with him. "Go home, Ruth." He brushed hay off her skirt and straightened her sweater. Only the small muscle ticking in the side of his jaw showed his turmoil.

"Don't, Johnny," she whispered.

"You can't stay here. There's only so much temptation a man can stand...and I've already reached my limit."

"Why are you turning me away?"

John was still a long while, studying her. Suddenly he caught her shoulders and pulled her fiercely to him so that her nose was almost touching his.

"Don't waste your time with a man like me, Ruth."

"I love you."

"I don't believe in love."

She refused to be daunted. In her world, love conquered all, and she had just begun to fight.

"Love is not an intellectual pursuit." She put one hand on his cheek. "What do you *feel*, Johnny?" He didn't answer. "I care what you think, but right now I want to know what you feel." Still, he was silent. She could feel his turmoil in the heat of his eyes and the tremor that ran through his body. "I *know* you feel something for me. The way you hold me, Johnny... the way you kiss me. Tell me you feel the same warmth, the same joy that I do." Her own face became fierce. "Tell me."

They were both so still it seemed the hayloft had been transported into another realm where only starshine and moonlight and the passions that washed through them were real. Suddenly John put Ruth gently away from him.

"I can't tell you the fairy tales you want to hear, Ruth. I can't promise love and marriage and living happily ever after. I'm a hard-driving, cynical man who makes his living defending men you would shudder to meet." He stood up and turned his back to her. "Go home, Ruth. Find yourself a man who can give you a cozy little house and three children and a big shaggy dog and cookouts on Saturday and church on Sunday. Find yourself someone who will be PTA president and leader of the Boy Scouts. Find yourself a man worthy of you."

She was quiet for so long he almost believed she had left without making a sound. When she finally spoke, her voice was strong and steady.

"I'm not asking for commitment. I want you. Only you, Johnny."

He was ashamed of the joy that coursed through him. Slowly he turned to face her.

"Ruth Mobley, you are the most stubborn woman I've ever met."

She smiled. "Thank you."

John struggled with the need to take her into his arms again and the desire to do what was right and even noble. For many years he had maintained a tight control of his life, keeping everything in perfect order. Ruth had upset that balance, had caught him off guard. He felt as if he had walked into a trial totally unprepared.

"I don't want to hurt you, Ruth. God knows, I've already hurt you enough."

"We've both spoken words in anger, Johnny. I don't think either of us meant them."

"You're too generous with me."

"I love you."

For an instant John wondered what it would be like to abandon all he believed to be true about life and simply declare his love for her. Was it possible that he actually could marry and live happily ever after? Was it possible that he and Ruth could beat the statistics? It was a foolish notion, of course. Besides, a woman like her would never survive Seattle. It was a harsher climate, a harsher society than Tupelo. A gentle, guileless woman like Ruth would wither and die.

He reached for her hand and, squeezing it between both of his, looked deeply into her eyes. "I'm sorry, Ruth . . . sorry this happened."

"Are you sending me away, Johnny?" she whispered.

"I'm . . ." He hesitated, searching for the right words. "No. I won't do that again, Ruth, but I want you to know that there is no hope. And it has nothing to do with you. You truly are the loving, gentle, sincere woman you seem to be, and I'm flattered that you settled your affections on a man like me." He released her hands and rammed his into his pockets. "I'm not the loving kind, Ruth."

Ruth knew that she was defeated—at least, for tonight. There was no more she could do, no more she could say, to win the heart of this implacable man.

"Miracles can happen, Johnny," she said softly. Then she left him standing in the hayloft.

He listened to the sounds of her leaving, all the while stifling the urge to call her back. But what good would it do? He had done the right thing. It was best for all of them not to complicate life with emotional entanglements that would lead to certain heartbreak.

When he heard her old car backfiring in the distance, he turned and looked through the huge loft opening. Ruth was merely a speck, rapidly disappearing down Uncle Roscoe's tree-shaded driveway. It was funny how his heart already ached, and he had made no emotional commitments whatsoever.

Ruth was shivering when she returned to her home. She felt as if every nerve ending in her body were raw and bleeding. John had turned her away, but she didn't have a single regret. If she could go back to the farmhouse, she would declare her love all over again. She believed in truth.

Back inside her house she hugged herself. There had to be a way to win the man she loved. She would bake cookies until she melted and carry him casseroles until she turned into Betty Crocker. She would hug him and hold him and tell him she loved him until he *had* to respond. She would...

Suddenly all the starch left her legs. She was a stubborn woman, and all the pushing in the world wouldn't make John Davis love her. Love took two.

What she was going to do was behave like any normal thirty-year-old woman with a wounded heart and go about her duties and leave John Davis alone and see what happened. Maybe there would be a miracle.

She left her clothes in a tidy pile in the bathroom hamper and climbed into her lonely bed.

The next morning it didn't take Uncle Roscoe long to figure out what had happened. Johnny's expression said it all.

"You turned her down, didn't you, Johnny?" Uncle Roscoe slurped his coffee, then glared at his nephew over the rim of the cup.

John was in no mood for a lecture. "Were you staying up all night against everybody's orders, spying? Or were you just up thinking of another scheme to throw Ruth and me together?"

"Heh, heh, heh." Uncle Roscoe slapped his thigh. "The onions worked pretty good, didn't they?"

John reined in his temper. He'd had a sleepless night, but his own ill mood was no reason to be cross with a sick old man.

"I don't want to disappoint you, but I don't want to give you any false hopes, either. Ruth is a lovely young woman, and I'm sure she'll make some man a wonderful wife. But I'm not that man." He stood up and began to clear breakfast dishes from the table. "I think it will behoove both of us to concentrate on setting your affairs in order and getting ready for Christmas."

"Humph. I'd fancied a Christmas wedding, myself."

"You'll just have to settle for something to keep your head warm, Uncle Roscoe."

"Maybe so, but I don't intend to settle gracefully."

He didn't, either. The rest of the day he thought up ways to irritate John. He smoked in places he knew he would get caught; he refused to engage in any of his favorite board games, neither checkers nor chess; and long after he should have been in bed, he sneaked into the kitchen and made enough racket so John would catch him drinking Old Crow straight from the bottle.

"Uncle Roscoe, what am I going to do with you?" John asked, as he took the bottle from his uncle.

"Don't bury me unhappy. Call Ruth and at least take her out to dinner."

"Uncle Roscoe..."

"You'll never know whether love can work until you give it a try."

John didn't mention that his uncle had never given it a try. Instead, John took his arm and led him from the kitchen. "Come to bed, Uncle Roscoe. You're bound to be worn-out from all the shenanigans you've pulled today."

"Well, I am right tired, now that you mention it." He allowed himself to be led placidly to bed, and when the covers were pulled up under his chin, he said to John, "If you hear those durned rabbits singing, tell them to go away, I'm not ready yet."

John smiled. "I'll do that. Good night, Uncle Roscoe."

On Monday, John made his long-awaited visit to his uncle's doctor.

"I see no cause for immediate alarm over your uncle's health," Dr. Wayne Wright said. "As long as he obeys orders, his chances of living out his full life are very good. Of course, you have to take his age into consideration. At that age, there's always the unexpected."

John thanked the doctor and took his leave. He felt better after hearing what he considered expert medical testimony; still, he couldn't discount the legend of the rabbits. He had seen the legend work, and although he was no longer a child, he still could not discredit that part of his past.

He had intended to complete his Christmas shopping after he left the doctor's office, but the route to the mall took him past the elementary school where Ruth taught. He was certain he hadn't gone there intentionally, but he found himself putting on his brakes and craning his head for a glimpse of her. That was ridiculous, of course. It was two-thirty, and she was obviously still in her classroom.

He turned the rented Lincoln left at the corner, with one last glance in the rearview mirror at the school building. It was just the way he remembered it—old-fashioned and homey, a holdover from the 1950s. John found himself appreciating that—a vintage building still serving the youth of Tupelo, a blending of the past and the present. He realized that was one of the things he missed in Seattle—a sense of the past.

He flicked on the radio and began to hum along to the song on the radio, Elvis Presley singing "Blue Christmas." There was another tradition—Tupelo's most famous native son singing an old favorite holiday song.

John's car turned left at the next block, almost of its own volition. Suddenly he smiled. He wasn't going to the mall after all; he was circling the block, going back to see Ruth. He didn't know exactly what he would say when he got there, but he would think of something. After all, it was the Christmas season. A man could stop by and say "Merry Christmas" to his uncle's dear friend, couldn't he?

Chapter Eight

Ruth was surrounded by chattering seven-year-olds when John walked into her classroom. From the doorway it looked as if she were being mobbed. He stood quietly, watching her. He had always believed that a man could best judge his opponents if he caught them off guard. Not that Ruth was his opponent—not anymore. What she was exactly, he couldn't say. All he knew was that seeing her bending over her students and smiling, he felt as if he had accidentally stumbled into a candy store and been told it was all for him.

When she looked up and saw him, her smile became positively radiant. She held out her hand.

"Johnny!" Twenty curious students turned to gawk and giggle at him. Ruth stood smiling for another heartbeat, and then she became brisk. "Students." She clapped her hands for their attention. "I want you to meet Mr. John Davis, Uncle Roscoe Blake's nephew."

"Are you the man with the donkey?" a small boy asked.

"That's my uncle," John said, coming into the classroom.

"Miz Mobley says his name is Henry." A tiny girl with blond angel hair was the speaker. She brushed her hair out of her eyes and peeked up at John. "Miz Mobley says the donkey won't be pa . . . puh . . ."

"Performing, Clara," Ruth prompted.

"How come?" Clara's lips poked out. "Can you tell me how come, Mr. Davis?"

"Well . . ." John was completely at a loss. Telling Ruth that Henry couldn't be the Christmas donkey had been one thing, but facing a crowd of determined seven-year-olds was another.

Ruth rescued him. "Children, I've explained to you that Mr. Blake isn't well this year. We don't want to cause more worry for him by asking him to bring Henry to our pageant."

The school dismissal bell saved Ruth from further explanation. John stepped out of the way of twenty eager children rushing for the door. After the last student had gone and Ruth had closed the door behind them, he took his lead from the students.

"I came by to tell you I've changed my mind, Ruth." A quick flush of excitement came into her cheeks, and John hastened to make amends. The hayloft scene was vivid in his memory, and he didn't want any repeat performances. He might not escape Ruth's empty classroom as easily as he had escaped the loft. "I'm talking about Henry."

"Henry?"

"I was wrong to deny you and Uncle Roscoe the pleasure of letting Henry be in your pageant."

"I was wrong to insist. Wrong and stubborn. After all, Uncle Roscoe isn't well. . . ." As she spoke, she gravitated toward John as naturally as a moth moves toward flame.

"His doctor says the heart condition isn't life threatening." John took a step toward Ruth, drawn by an invisible tugging on his heartstrings.

"That's wonderful news!"

Ruth lifted one hand, and he could almost feel the caress against his cheek. He longed for her touch, willed her to give it to him. But she let her hand fall, and he silently cursed himself for being a selfish fool. It was time to leave this room, time to leave this temptation.

"Well..." he said, backing away from her. "If you change your mind about Henry, let me know."

"I've decided to change my stubborn ways. Christmas is not the time for demands—it's the time for gifts." She squeezed her hands tightly together. "I won't change my mind, Johnny... about anything."

Ruth had tossed the ball neatly into his court. Two days ago he would have thought her shrewd; now he knew that she was merely sincere. Always, Ruth had come to him. She had not backed down, even in the face of anger and rejection. Boldly she had declared her love for him without any hint that her love might be returned. But having declared that love, she was leaving the next move to him.

While John had always been fearless in a court of law, he was helpless in the realm of love. There was nothing to do except retreat.

"Merry Christmas, Ruth."

"Merry Christmas, John."

Ruth watched him leave the classroom. There were many different kinds of heartbreak, and she decided that in the past two days she had experienced all of them. She walked to her window and pressed her face against the glass. John was getting into his Lincoln. For a moment he turned his head toward the building, and she thought he saw her at the window. But he made no sign. Instead, he climbed into his car and drove away.

She frosted the windowpane with her breath and traced hearts there. "Merry Christmas, my love," she whispered. Then she closed her eyes and prayed for a miracle.

The next two days were the longest of John's life. Ruth didn't come by; she didn't call. It was almost as if she had vanished from the face of the earth.

At the end of the second day, he jumped out of his chair and stalked across the den. Uncle Roscoe's rocker stopped its squeaking.

"Johnny, you're prowling around here like a cat in heat."

"I'm going to get another stick of wood for the fire."

"What you're going to do is go out there in the yard and look up at the moon like some old lovesick bull moose. Don't think I haven't seen you doing it."

"You've been spying."

"It helps to pass the time now that you've run Ruth off."

"Uncle Roscoe . . . that discussion is closed."

"Not by me." Roscoe set his rocker into motion once more. "Now, if I wanted to let a certain young woman know that I'd been a fool, I'd take Henry to school tomorrow about two o'clock for that Christmas pageant of hers. And then I'd hustle backstage and lay a sweet word or two on her, and then I guess I might run off to a motel and start making babies before I got too old to know how to do it." He chuckled. "A word to the wise, Johnny."

John smiled. "Does that mean you're planning another onion trick if I don't take your advice?"

"Maybe even worse. Henry and I are full of dirty tricks."

A loud braying came from the direction of the barn, as if the donkey had been scheming with Uncle Roscoe and knew his cue. John laughed as he opened the front door.

"I'm being blackmailed."

"Worse things could happen, Johnny. You could lose her."

Outside under the stars, John thought about the things his uncle had said. If he let this chance for love slip by him, what would the rest of his days be like? Orderly, busy, productive. That much was a certainty. But what about his nights?

He stayed a long time in the chill of the December evening, contemplating his future.

Ruth stood backstage, holding the prompting book and watching her second-graders present their pageant. The curtains in the school auditorium had been drawn, and the stage lights added an air of mystery to her little tableau.

A cradle of hay awaited the baby Jesus, and a crooked cardboard stable filled with make-believe animals awaited Mary and Joseph. The doves, in gray cotton suits with turkey feathers glued to their hoods, were talking with the cows—cumbersome two-part creatures whose back ends sometimes failed to go in the same direction as their front ends.

"Did you see that big star in the sky?" Little Clara, the dove, announced to Bruce and Wanda, the two-part cow.

"Yes," said Wanda, the front of the cow.

"I wonder what it means?" asked Bruce, the back of the cow.

There was a scurrying at the back of the auditorium that meant Mary and Joseph were right on cue for their march down the center aisle. Ruth was pleased. Her children were doing a beautiful job. All that practice was paying off.

There was hardly a sound from the audience as the elementary school children paid rapt attention to the Christmas story.

"It means that a great…" Clara the wise dove began in a loud voice, and then she faltered.

"Event," Ruth prompted from the wings.

"It means…" Clara started her speech over.

"Look," yelled the back of the cow. "It's Henry."

"It's Henry," Clara screeched.

The audience erupted. Children clapped and screamed. "It's a real donkey! It's a real donkey!"

Ruth dropped her prompting book. With a trembling hand she parted the curtains. There, coming down the center aisle were Joseph and Mary, dressed in chenille bathrobes, and Henry, the donkey, wearing his halter with bells and his best smile. And in a front-row seat sat Uncle Roscoe.

"It means a great event," Clara yelled.

"Hee-haw, hee-haw," Henry chimed in.

Ruth's hand flew to her throat and tears came to her eyes.

"It means I love you."

John spoke from directly behind her. Still clutching her throat, Ruth turned slowly around.

"How did you get here?" she whispered.

"A miracle." He pulled her into his arms. "I love you, Ruth, and I didn't know of any better way to show you than to bring this gift to you."

"You brought Henry just to say you love me?"

"I wanted to ride him down the aisle myself, but Joseph argued that I was too big." Smiling down at her, he sifted her golden hair through his fingers. "Am I too big, Ruth?"

"You're just right."

Her eyes twinkling, she tipped her face up for his kiss. They kissed for a long time, mindless of the doings on-stage. Meanwhile, the back ends of three cows had drifted upstage to get a closer look at Henry, while the front ends practiced butting the cooing doves with their cut-out horns. Joseph had abandoned Mary to tumble in the hay, and a dozen little boys from the audience had come on-stage to join him. Henry contributed to the general confusion by giving his loudest donkey yell.

John lifted his head. "We're about to miss the main event."

"You're my main event, Johnny." She reached for his face once more. "I can't believe you love me. It's a miracle."

"Indeed, it is." He scooped her into his arms and carried her onstage. He set her on her feet next to the manager, and kneeling in front of the cardboard stable and an exuberant audience of five hundred elementary schoolchildren, John took her hand. "Will you marry me, Ruth?"

"Yes, Johnny. Oh, yes." She sank to her knees and embraced him.

Clara, the wise little dove, took charge of the pageant. Going to center stage, she faced the audience and yelled, "Mary took all these things and plundered them in her heart. God rest ye merry gentlemen and to all a good night."

"That child deserves a medal," John told his betrothed as he helped her off the floor.

"I'll give her one as soon as I finish with you." Ruth moved into his arms, and Uncle Roscoe, who knew his cues perfectly, rang down the curtain.

John and Ruth were married on Christmas Day in the farmhouse den in front of Uncle Roscoe's tree. The ceremony was brief and beautiful. Afterward John lifted Ruth to put a new star at the top of Uncle Roscoe's tree. It was an exquisite crystal star that caught the lights and spread them in a rainbow across the room.

"We have a new star to guide us on our new life together, Ruth," John said.

"What I want to know," Uncle Roscoe said, "is when you're going to start making babies."

"We're working on it, Uncle Roscoe."

John winked at him, and led his new wife down the hall to their private honeymoon bower in the far west wing of the old farmhouse.

Roscoe sank into his chair and began to rock. From outside the window came a strange, haunting sound. He left his chair and looked out the window into the soft evening light. A light snow had begun to fall, and a small group of rabbits had gathered on the front lawn. Roscoe opened the window to listen. They were standing on their haunches, singing their special song.

Roscoe Blake smiled. "Shoot. I reckon rabbits just like to sing 'cause it's Christmas."

Epilogue

The sound of footsteps on the stairs awakened John. He rolled over in bed and reached for his wife. Nuzzling his face in her golden hair, he whispered, "Ten years has not dimmed my enthusiasm for you, Mrs. Davis."

"I should hope not, Counselor." She stretched and yawned, then pressed herself closer to him and began to caress his back in the way she knew he loved. "Prove it," she said, smiling.

He did. By the time he had finished proving his love, the sun had crept over the eastern horizon and spread its glow throughout the rambling old farmhouse. From their bedroom in the new upstairs addition that had been added six years earlier, John and Ruth listened to the sounds of their children discovering Christmas.

"Look what Santa brought me." The piping voice belonged to their four-year-old son, David.

"Ohhh, just look at this." Obviously, six-year-old Anne had discovered her doll.

"Aww, that's little-kid stuff. Look at my new bike." Their son Roscoe was feeling the superiority of his nine years.

John and Ruth held hands and lay side by side in their bed, smiling.

"Do you ever miss what you had in Seattle, Johnny? The big criminal cases? The fancy office? The fancy income? Is law practice in Tupelo sometimes too tame for you?"

He leaned on his elbow and grinned down at her. "Let me 'plunder' those questions in my heart for a while."

"Oh, you..." Ruth swatted him with her pillow and climbed out of bed.

"What time is it?" John asked.

"Quarter after five. You know how the children are about getting up early on Christmas. They're afraid they'll miss something." Ruth hurried into the shower, singing.

John stripped off his clothes and joined her. Taking the soap from her hand, he began to scrub her back. "I know someone else who's afraid she'll miss something."

"Who?"

He nuzzled her soapy neck. "My wife."

"Well...who knows what sort of miracles Christmas will bring?"

By the time John and Ruth came down the stairs, the den had grown quiet. Thinking the children might have gone back to bed, they tiptoed. When they reached the doorway, Uncle Roscoe stamped his cane on the floor and yelled at them.

"Hurry up. You're going to miss my story." The three Davis children were gathered at his knee, waiting for his annual rendition of the Legend of the Rabbits.

Ruth and John sat side by side on the sofa, holding hands as the story began.

"Once upon a time, many years ago when the snow was falling on the earth, I heard the rabbits singing."

That was Anne's cue. "Why were they singing, Uncle Roscoe?"

"Well, first of all, they were singing because it was Christmas, and they were happy. God likes for his creatures to celebrate the birth of his Son."

"And what else, Uncle Roscoe?" Young Roscoe knew his cues, too.

"Now, this is the best part of all. They were singing to celebrate the marriage of your mother and your daddy, but most of all, they were glad because they knew that all of you were going to be born."

"Will they sing again, Uncle Roscoe?" Anne climbed onto his knee and cuddled against his chest.

"I don't know, little Annie." Roscoe turned his watery old eyes toward Ruth and John. "Will they?"

"Listen," Ruth said, putting her finger to her lips. "Do you hear that?"

"Yes, yes," her children said.

"By durn, I hear rabbits," Uncle Roscoe added.

From the distance came the sound of music. Whether it was rabbits singing or early morning carolers, Ruth didn't know. She smiled.

"Next summer," she said, "when the grass is green and the flowers are in bloom, another baby will be born in our house."

"Will it be a baby sister?" Anne wanted to know.

"I don't know, sweetheart," Ruth said.

Her husband squeezed her hand. "It will be another miracle."

* * * * *

Author's Note

We have two Christmas traditions at our house: decorating the tree and Christmas Eve brunch. I initiated the first when my children were tots. (They are twenty-two and twenty-five now.) I *stole* the second one when they were teenagers.

First, the tree... I have always loved a real tree, smelling of the outdoors and decorated with a hodgepodge of ornaments that have special meaning. When my children were babies, I bought each of them an ornament every year and held the children up so they could hang the ornaments on the tree. As they got older, we launched into the ornament-making business. One year, we painted precut wooden ornaments. That was the year we ended up with an angel with black wings and a red-and-yellow-striped rabbit. Those two ornaments are still among my favorites.

Our ornaments became more sophisticated as the years went by. One year, we made elaborate eggshell ornaments covered with satin and velvet and trimmed with gold braid. Each shell had a miniature scene inside—tiny gold reindeer standing beneath plastic trees; exquisite angels flying over miniature villages; fat little Santas riding in tiny sleighs.

Both my children are gone from home now—my daughter is living in New Hampshire with her husband, and my son lives on his fish farm here in northeast Mississippi. We no longer have time to get together to make ornaments, but the tradition continues. I'm back to buying one for each of them every year. Our Christmas tree is a grand hodgepodge of ornaments that trigger stories that begin with "Remember when..."

The other tradition at my house, Christmas Eve brunch, I had to literally steal from my mother and my husband's mother. Over the years, our extended families have grown large—my husband's brothers marrying and having children, my sisters marrying and having children, *their* children having children. Still, my husband's mother and mine clung to their Christmas traditions: Christmas Eve dinner at the Webbs', Christmas Day lunch at the Husseys'. When my own children were nearly grown, I realized they would always remember Christmas as going to the grandmothers' houses. (It's a lovely memory, but I wanted them to remember being *home,* as well.)

And so I stole Christmas Eve morning. We gather around the table—my husband, my two children, my son-in-law and I—while my husband reads the Christmas story from Luke 2:1-16. Afterwards, we share our special brunch and have a wonderful time of fellowship.

For me, that is the best part of Christmas—being with family and friends and remembering together that it is a celebration of the birth of Christ. And for all of you, my dear readers, I wish you a most joyous Christmas and a glorious time with your loved ones.

Peggy Webb

DREAMING OF
ANGELS

Naomi Horton

NANAIMO BARS

(pronounced na-NIGH-mo)

According to legend, a local housewife entered her family's favorite recipe for chocolate squares into a magazine contest. Out of civic pride, she called them Nanaimo Bars. When her recipe won, our city became immortalized. Others have tried to claim the recipe as theirs—New York Slice, for instance!—but they are all impostors.

Here is the *real* recipe, right from Nanaimo, British Columbia, Canada. Enjoy!

Base Layer
½ cup butter or margarine
¼ cup sugar
5 tbsp cocoa
1 egg, lightly beaten
¼ tsp vanilla
2 cups graham-wafer crumbs
¾ cup fine- or medium-shredded coconut
½ cup chopped walnuts

In a double boiler, melt together butter or margarine, sugar and cocoa. Add egg and vanilla. Cook, stirring constantly, until mixture thickens. Stir in graham crumbs, coconut and walnuts. Press mixture firmly into a 9″ × 9″ pan. Chill.

Middle Layer
4 tbsp butter or margarine
2 tbsp milk
2 tbsp custard powder or instant vanilla pudding
2 cups confectioner's (icing) sugar

Cream together butter, milk and custard powder. Add confectioner's sugar and blend well. Spread over base layer. Chill.

Top Layer
2 squares semisweet chocolate
1 tbsp butter

Melt together in double boiler. Let cool to room temperature. Spread over middle layer. Chill until top layer hardens. Cut into squares.

Makes 16 to 20 of the best chocolate squares you've ever eaten.

Variations
Add flavoring or food coloring to the custard mixture. Mint is fabulous. So is orange. For a mocha taste, use strong coffee instead of milk. For a different effect, add peanut butter to either the base or middle layers.

Prologue

Blinded by wind-lashed snow, he squinted through the windshield of the pickup and swore in a tired monotone. The muscles of his shoulders ached from the tension of gripping the steering wheel and fighting the wind and ever-deepening drifts that were starting to pile up across the road.

He was crazy even thinking about driving through to Denver tonight. The radio had warned of road closures and blizzard conditions, and no man in his right mind would do what he was doing.

The thought made him smile grimly. Hell, he hadn't been in his right mind for nearly six months now. Not since he'd lost the only damned thing that had ever mattered to him.

He spared a quick glance at the gift-wrapped box on the seat beside him. He'd made his decision last night, and nothing was going to stop him now.

A swirl of snow enveloped the truck, and he eased off the gas, swearing again. Then suddenly, with no warning at all, the flare of brake lights lit up the blowing snow and the rear end of a station wagon materialized in front of him.

He had the flash image of a child's face staring out the back window at him, eyes wide with fright, and then another swirl of snow obliterated it and he was pumping the brakes, praying for traction.

Then he was on ice and spinning out of control, crossing the center line. There was a sudden blinding glare of headlights as a tanker truck came booming through the storm toward him, and Gage closed his eyes, knowing it was too late. That everything was over.

And he found himself wondering just before the impact if someone would find the package and give it to her. He hoped so. God, he hoped so. . . .

Chapter One

The call came a little after eight.

Kathleen was unpacking the tree ornaments when she heard the phone ring. She started to get to her feet, but Beth, who was standing in the kitchen door with a mug of eggnog in one hand and a piece of fruitcake in the other, motioned her to stay where she was, and Kathleen sank back to her knees gratefully.

It would be another well-intentioned friend, no doubt. Calling to see how she was. To ask, in that careful voice she was beginning to hate, if she had anything planned. And, if not, how they'd love to have her over.

It was all part of the season, Beth said. All part of being a friend. Of caring.

Except she wasn't in any mood to celebrate anything right now, least of all another Christmas. She didn't want to have to look at one more politely strained smile, hear one more platitude about how it was "for the better," how she could now "get on with her life."

It hurt, damn it.

But then, giving up on love always did.

She hadn't planned on celebrating Christmas at all. There were too many memories associated with it, ones she didn't want to deal with, and she'd *planned* on going away to somewhere warm and foreign, or maybe just working through the holidays.

Problem was, Beth knew her too well. Anticipating just that, she and Doug had turned up on her doorstep a few hours ago with a fifteen-pound turkey, a tree, boxes of presents and food and two kids so jazzed up on raw energy that her small apartment sizzled with it. And they'd told her—a trifle grimly—that she was going to have a merry Christmas if it killed them all.

In spite of herself, Kathleen had to smile. She handed the glass star she'd just unwrapped to Jimmy, Beth's seven-year-old son. Smiling shyly, he slipped a hook into the loop, then handed it to his father.

"A real assembly-line operation," Doug said, laughing. He reached down to tousle Jimmy's hair, but he was looking at Kathleen, his eyes worried. "How are you doing?"

"Great," she lied, forcing herself to keep smiling, to keep the memories at bay. "Just great. I'm glad you guys came over."

"Liar," he teased. "You wish we'd stayed home and minded our own business. But you know Beth..."

Kathleen's laugh rose with honest humor. "Yes, I know Beth. But I *am* glad you're here. I know it's not much fun for the kids, missing Christmas at their grandparents and having to sleep on the floor and—"

"I *like* sleepin' on the floor," Jimmy said firmly. "It's just like campin' out. 'Sides, Daddy says Santa knows we're here. And we're goin' to Granny's right after, anyway."

Kathleen smiled and gave the boy a hug. Then, to keep herself from bursting into tears, she reached into the cardboard carton beside her and picked up the next ornament.

It was an angel—a crystal one, with spun-glass hair and wings of gold. For a split second, Kathleen just stared down at it, her heart in her mouth. It couldn't be, she found herself thinking dazedly. It couldn't be the same angel. Not the one Gage had given her that second Christmas they'd spent together.

It wasn't, of course. Feeling her heart start to beat again, Kathleen continued to unwrap the small ornament, wishing her fingers would stop trembling and making the tissue paper crackle so. It couldn't be that angel. That one had been broken and discarded long ago, shattered in a fit of anger.

"Careful," she whispered as she handed it to Jimmy. "It's very delicate."

Like dreams, like hearts, crystal broke so easily....

"Kathleen...?"

It was Beth's voice, oddly strained, and Kathleen stood up. Beth was staring at her from the kitchen door, her face pale, one hand on her chest as though to still her heart. And Kathleen felt something cold grip her own.

Doug, who had glanced around at the same time, stepped off the ladder. "What is it, Beth? What's wrong? Is it your dad?"

Beth shook her head, her gaze riveted on Kathleen's. "It's... Gage."

Doug slipped Kathleen a quick, sidelong look, then swore. "She's not interested in talking to him," he growled, striding toward Beth. "I'll get rid of him."

"No." Beth's hand caught her husband's arm as he went to step by her. "It... it wasn't Gage on the phone. It was his father. Gage—" Beth's eyes sought Kathleen's again, holding them, filled with fear. "He's been in a car accident, Kathy. Gage, I mean. A bad one. They... they need your signature. For surgery. And... and for the organ donor forms."

"Organ... donor?" Kathleen heard her own voice, but it sounded thin and faraway. The room seemed to tip slightly and she felt displaced and strangely unreal. "You mean he's dead?'' *Dead?* The word meant nothing. Gage, dead? Easier to believe the moon had fallen from the sky. Nothing could bring Gage down. He was a Ramsey. Decker Ramsey's son. Unassailable. Perfect. Immortal.

"No." Beth sounded calmer. "But he's badly injured. And they don't know..." She let it trail off as though not having the courage to word the rest.

"My God." It was more whispered prayer than exclamation, and Kathleen closed her eyes as the room started to tilt. "Not Gage."

A strong hand caught her by the arm, steadying her. "Sit down, Kathy." Doug's voice was tight. "I'll drive over and take care of it. You don't have to come. I'll explain everything. I'll explain that you're not his—"

"But I am," Kathleen whispered, idly wondering why—now—that suddenly seemed important. "I am his wife, Doug. Still."

"Damn it, Kathy," he said with quiet urgency, "you've been separated from the man for nearly six months. You don't owe him a *thing!* Not even this. Not after the way he's treated you."

"I'm his wife," she repeated quietly. She looked up at Doug, an odd calmness washing through her. "Gage is my husband. And I have to go."

"Kathy...!"

"Doug." Beth's quiet voice held steel. There was a sudden bustle of activity, and in the next instant Beth had shoved Kathleen's heavy jacket into her arms. "Doug will drive you. I'll stay with the kids until Mom can pick them up, then I'll come to the hospital myself."

Numbed, Kathleen pulled on the jacket, fumbling with the zipper, taking her handbag automatically when Beth put it in her hands. Suddenly she was cold, and she shivered violently, her teeth chattering. "I can drive," she whispered. "I can drive."

"Doug, you stay with her until I get there." Beth's voice was crisp with efficiency. "And don't you let any of *them* near her, do you hear me? Not his sister, not any of those brothers of his. And most especially not Decker. They're like piranhas, the lot of them . . . one taste of blood, and they'll eat her alive."

"Don't you worry." Doug sounded grim. "If Decker Ramsey wants a piece of her, he'll have to get through me to get it."

Something was wrong.

He was in a dark, cold place, and he couldn't move. There were voices in the darkness: wordless, meaningless whispers that drifted in and out, and he wondered, suddenly, if he were dying.

There had been an accident, he could remember that. Blinding snow swirling in the truck headlights, a patch of black ice and the unexpected flare of brake lights in front of him, then that sickening sideways wrench as the pickup had slewed out of control and had started to roll . . .

Maybe he was already dead.

He thought about it dispassionately. Found the possibility less frightening than he'd thought it would be. Without her, there had been precious little worth living for anyway.

Then the slip-slide toward the darkness speeded up and he was frightened suddenly, and he cried out for her. Knowing she couldn't hear. That she wouldn't come. But needing her . . . wanting her more than even life itself . . .

Doug didn't say much on the drive to the hospital. And Kathleen, huddled into the folds of her jacket and racked by one shiver after another, was just as glad. They'd grown up together, Doug and Beth and her; they had shared homework and afternoons at the movies and dreams. But neither Doug nor Beth had ever fully understood why Kathleen had done it. Why she—of all people—had married one of the Ramsey boys.

After all, she was Brue Langford's daughter, and the Langfords and Ramseys had been feuding over land, water, women and anything else that came between them for three generations. Besides which, everyone knew that the Ramsey boys were pure trouble. They were every young girl's dream and every father's nightmare, and their reputations as hell-raisers and womanizers weren't entirely without foundation.

She'd never tried to explain. How could you explain, even to a best friend, that you were marrying to fulfill a promise to a dying father? That it was just a sham, a paper marriage. Just...business.

As Doug slowed for a traffic light, Kathleen stared out into the magical night. The city streets looked like something out of a fairy tale, ablaze with Christmas lights and tinsel and brightly colored decorations. It was snowing again, and the flakes whirled and spun through the glitter of lights as traffic crept through the slushy streets, wary of slick intersections and the crowds of last-minute shoppers scurrying everywhere, heads down, collars turned up against the cold, minds on everything but watching where they were going.

It still caught her unawares at times, the hustle and lights of the city. This was ranch country and she was a rancher's daughter, and the city was, by definition, an alien place. Yet this is where she'd come when she'd walked out of Gage Ramsey's house and life six months ago. It had seemed like a haven back then, a place where a woman could lose herself and become someone other than Gage Ramsey's wife.

Just as she'd once been Brue Langford's daughter. Property, almost. Just one more asset among the tally of land and cattle and horses and hired hands.

Growing up on High Mesa ranch, she hadn't seen it like that at the time. She'd grown up more comfortable on a horse than on foot, happier to be out riding than inside on the phone with other girls her age, trading giggle-laced whispers about boys and first kisses and all the mysteries that went with both.

It was only later, when she'd actually started taking an interest in those same boys, that she started to understand some of what being Brue Langford's daughter meant.

"It *means*," her father had told her in no uncertain terms one afternoon when she'd been about fourteen, "that every worthless young buck in the country's going to be after you—except it isn't you they want, it's the land. My land. High Mesa is worth millions, girl, and you're going to marry exactly who I say you're going to marry. Get that straight right now."

It hadn't seemed very important at the time. There had been plenty of ranchers' sons around who one day would be eminently eligible, and odds were she'd find at least one she could fall in love with.

Kathleen gazed out the window at the glittering lights and wondered, not for the first time, what might have happened had her father not gotten too sick to carry out his threat to marry her off to the man of his choice. Had High Mesa not been nearly destroyed by neglect and high interest rates. Had drought not devastated the neighboring ranches, the Ramsey's Tanglefoot spread among them. Had Gage not come by that afternoon with his offer of the perfect "deal"....

So many "ifs," she thought desolately. So many other ways it could have turned out. Although, in the end, there was probably no other way it could have happened. Because falling in love had been the easy part.

She could still remember not only the exact day it had happened, but almost the precise *instant*. It had been that day at Fireweed Creek, three weeks after her sixteenth birthday.

Kathleen smiled, gazing out at the Christmas finery garlanding the streetlights, and remembered....

It was the cow she had heard first, bawling loudly somewhere down by Fireweed Creek. Curious, she turned Red down the hillside and touched him lightly with her heels, urging the big horse through the scattered underbrush.

It didn't take long to discover the problem. The cow and her calf had been part of a group of cattle that had drifted away from the main herd and had come down to the creek to drink. A few hundred sharp hooves had churned the creek bank into one huge mudhole, and there in the middle of it, mired to his belly in the thick, sticky mud, was a week-old calf.

It had driven itself deeper into the imprisoning mud with its struggles and was panting with fright and exertion, eyes rolling, its bawls thin and high with panic. A cow—obviously the mother—was running back and forth along the bank, legs caked with drying mud, her sides heaving like bellows as she called frantically to her mired calf.

Kathleen gazed distastefully at the mud, then sighed and dismounted. If the calf had been older and stronger she could have just roped it and used Red to haul it free, but it was too tiny and stuck too deep to risk injuring it. Perching on the trunk of a fallen tree, she pulled off her riding boots and socks, then rolled the legs of her jeans to her knees and walked gingerly toward the calf.

It was becoming more agitated now, clearly as terrified of her as it was of the mud, and Kathleen started talking softly to it. Behind her, the cow was growing even more frantic, and Kathleen gave her an uneasy look, hoping she wouldn't charge.

"This is really a *dumb* idea," she told the calf conversationally. She was thigh-deep in water and syrupy mud by now, and just as she reached it, the calf gave a desperate heave and managed to get itself half-free. It fell back with a bawl, and a sheet of muddy water hit Kathleen squarely, making her catch her breath and swear in shock, drenched to the skin.

"You miserable little—" Wiping mud from her eyes with her arm, Kathleen gazed malevolently at the calf. Its coat was stiff with mud and it was clearly terrified. She started talking softly to it again as she leaned over it and ran her hand down its foreleg and into the thick mud, cradling it in her other arm.

Grasping the calf's hock firmly, she pulled gently until the slender leg came free with an evil sucking sound, then she shifted her grip and started working its hind leg free, gritting her teeth as the calf started bucking and flailing against her and a sharp little hoof grazed her shin.

"I don't suppose," a quiet, laughing voice said from somewhere behind her, "that you could use a hand, could you?"

The calf chose that instant to give another violent heave and the two of them fell sprawling, the calf giving a bellow of terror and Kathleen a sputter as she inhaled a mouthful of gritty water. Coughing, she released the still-mired calf and struggled to her feet. And turned to see a golden-haired Adonis gazing down at her from the bank with a lazy grin.

Gage Ramsey. All six foot plus of him, sitting astride a long-legged chestnut gelding and looking every inch the heartbreaker he was rumored to be. Even at eighteen, he had the height and solid, broad-shouldered build of a Ramsey. The classic Ramsey features, too, straight and even, with just the right amount of ruggedness, and a thatch of thick, honey gold hair, eyes the color of summer skies, and that rakish, go-to-hell Ramsey grin. If it had been anyone else—had *she* been anyone else—the effect would have been devastating.

As it was, she simply stood there, clenched hands on hips, and glowered at him. "This," she said with precision, "is Langford land. You're trespassing."

It didn't seem to make much impact. He just grinned all the wider, those sky blue eyes holding hers with a defiant boldness that was decidedly unsettling. "I heard the racket all the way up on the ridge and thought I'd better come down to have a look." He let his gaze wander over her with a casual interest that made her stomach give an odd little quiver. "You've sure made a hell of a mess of yourself, girl."

To her intense annoyance, Kathleen felt herself start to blush. She felt awkward and self-conscious, suddenly aware of the picture she must make, dripping mud and dirty water, and with her hair all stringy and her clothes plastered to her. "If you don't like the way I look," she said with some hostility, "go away."

But for some reason Gage wasn't smiling now. He had an odd expression on his face she couldn't quite interpret, and as his eyes captured hers, her stomach gave another of those peculiar little quivers. "I didn't say that," he told her quietly. "I just never noticed...you're not as young as you used to be, are you?"

The inanity of the question must have hit him just then, because he gave a snort of laughter and tipped his Stetson back, settling it more firmly over his wheat-colored hair. "What I meant was—"

"We're losing him! We're losing him!"

"No respiration...no pulse."

"He's in V-fib. Get the cart."

"Start CPR..."

"One-one thousand, two-one thousand, three-one thousand..."

"Okay, get the board under him."

"Get me a laryngoscope and an eight tube."

"Let's defibrillate at 200. Pass me the paddles."

"Hold it—I've got a pulse!"

"Pressure?"

"Yeah...yeah! He's stabilizing. We've got him back."

"He did it himself. This guy's a real fighter."

"That's one thing in his favor, then. About the only thing."

"Let's hope it's enough. Now let's get inside and get this bleeding stopped. He can't do it all by himself...."

He'd been dreaming, he remembered that. Before the darkness had come crashing down around him again with its seeping, sucking cold and those distant whispering voices. Gage tried to ignore them, willing them away. Wanting, instead, to gather the remnants of the scattered dream together... it seemed very important for some reason, as though—as long as he clung to the dream—he'd be safe. He let himself drift in the darkness, away from the

cold and the pain and the fear. Back to Fireweed Creek
where Kathy was waiting...

It was at that moment that the cow, reaching the end of
her bovine patience, decided to charge. She gave a bellow
of anger and started for the Langford girl at a ponderous
gallop, mud and water flying, and Gage reacted instinctively. He wrenched his horse around and rammed his heels
into its flanks, reaching for the coil of rope tied to his saddle even as the horse shot between the enraged cow and the
girl.

His gelding didn't need to be told what to do. It cut the
cow off expertly and turned its charge away from the girl,
churning the water to froth as it wheeled and blocked,
edging the animal back toward the bank.

The cow gave up finally and headed for higher ground
with a snort. Going after it, Gage dropped his rope around
its horns and half led, half dragged it to a nearby tree
where he tied it securely. Then, tossing his hat and boots
aside and rolling up his sleeves, he waded out to give the
girl a hand.

Woman, he corrected himself, admittedly intrigued by
what he was seeing. The last time he'd looked at little
Kathy Langford she'd been nothing but elbows and knees
and adolescent giggles. Strange how she'd grown up right
in front of him and he hadn't even noticed.

Or maybe not that strange. Kathleen Langford had always been strictly off limits for the simple reason that her
father was Brue Langford, so perhaps he simply hadn't
wanted to notice.

But he was noticing now. She was tall, for one thing, and
reed-slender, although the soaking denim shirt and jeans
that were plastered to her revealed an interesting landscape of thoroughly satisfactory curves and feminine

swells. Under the mud and angry scowl was a face guaranteed to make a man look twice, and he found himself wondering if that lush little mouth was even half as kissable as it looked.

It amused him to realize that his frank perusal hadn't gone unnoticed—and that Kathleen was blushing furiously under the smears of mud. She wasn't giving in to it, though. Chin tipped up at a pugnacious angle, she was glaring at him.

That in itself intrigued him even more. Even at eighteen he'd never had any trouble attracting women. If anything, the opposite was more often the rule. Being a Ramsey had its rewards, but it had its drawbacks, too. And being loved—if that was the word—for his name and all it meant was one of them.

He couldn't remember any woman looking at him the way Kathleen Langford was looking at him right now. And it was refreshing to realize that far from swooning willingly into his arms if he made a move, she'd more than likely slap him silly. Or knee him, he decided with a smile. She didn't look like the type to let ladylike inhibitions stop her from making a point.

Deciding this wasn't the time or place to find out, he simply bent down and wrapped his arms around the calf and gave a pull.

Nothing happened for a moment, then the calf gave a bawl of fright and swung its head back, catching Gage squarely on the cheekbone. He swore and nearly let go, blinded by pain and flying mud, and the calf started struggling wildly when it felt his grip loosen. Then Kathleen was there, holding the young animal's head firmly under one arm while trying to pull its front hooves free of the sticky mud, and together they managed to wrench it loose.

The calf started flailing wildly the instant its legs were free, and Kathleen lost her balance in the thick mud and half fell. Then Gage caught his foot on something and went down beside her, the calf still in his arms, and in the next instant the three of them were up to their necks in mud and water.

The calf plunged out of his grip and toward dry land with a frantic bleat. And Gage, spitting mud, stood up and then reached down and pulled Kathleen to her feet.

Mud and black water poured off her, and she just stood there for a moment, blinking through a mask of mud, arms outstretched, looking down at herself in disbelief. Then, slowly, she lifted her head and looked at Gage. And a moment later burst into gales of laughter.

It was one of those moments too rare to pass up. Grinning broadly, he reached out and planted one hand squarely in the middle of her chest and gently pushed. She teetered for an instant, a look of shock flickering across her face, then she got her feet tangled up in the mud and fell sprawling.

The look of outrage on her face was almost too good to be true, and Gage was still chuckling when he reached down to give her a hand. Her slim, muddy fingers grasped his firmly, and in the next instant he found himself being wrenched off his feet. He gave a yelp of surprise before he did a belly flop beside her.

He sat up, blinking muddy water out of his eyes, just as Kathleen started struggling to her feet, and he gave a shout of triumph and made a lunge for her. "Not on your life, sweetheart!"

"No!" She tried to bolt away from him, but the water was too deep, the slippery mud too treacherous, and as he caught her around the waist with both arms, they went down in a tremendous splash.

She was as slippery as an eel, but Gage managed to hang on to her, and suddenly they were both laughing and floundering around, holding on to each other as they tried to get their feet under them. Her wonderfully lithe body kept turning and moving against his, and Gage felt his mouth go dry, his arms and hands filled with delicious soft curves and feminine warmth.

And then she felt it, too. Laughing and panting for breath, she suddenly went still, fingers tangled in his shirt where she'd been clinging to him for balance. When her eyes met his they were wide and a little puzzled.

He could have kissed her right then. And if he had, he somehow doubted she'd have protested. But suddenly there didn't seem to be any hurry. Instead, he just held her close and grinned down at her. "Are you going to send me home like this, mud puppy, or invite me in for a swim?"

She grinned back at him, her teeth small and white against the mud caking her face. "Daddy would have a fit if he knew I let a Ramsey swim in our creek."

"We don't have to tell your daddy."

She gave a delighted laugh, eyes shining with mischief, and in that moment Gage knew he had to have her. One way or another, regardless of who her father was and what his own father would have to say about it, Kathleen Langford was going to be his.

They wound up laughing like a pair of kids and wading hand in hand back up the creek to where it widened into a deep pool at the foot of the low falls. There they scrubbed the mud and grit from each other's hair, breathless with laughter and teasing. Then Gage slipped out of his jeans and shirt, and after a while, shy enough to stay submerged but reckless enough to dare, Kathleen did the same.

They stayed there for nearly an hour, swimming leisurely in the spangled sunlight dancing through the leaves, and when he finally slipped his arms around her and lowered his mouth to hers, they both knew it was what they'd been waiting for.

He kissed her lightly, letting his lips rest against hers and tasting her breath mingled with his, as she shyly, almost hesitantly, responded. Her skin was like wet silk in his hands, and as she moved her legs gently to stay afloat, they tangled with his evocatively. He let his hands move over her lightly, caressing her bare back and shoulders, needing to touch and hold her so badly he was crazed with it, and yet not wanting to hurry her.

There was something wondrously innocent about her, a shyness he knew was unfeigned, an inexperience that had to be genuine. He found himself captivated by the trust in her eyes, in the unfamiliar way she returned his kisses, caressed him, moved against him.

"We're asking for trouble," he murmured against her mouth. Her breasts brushed his chest and he gritted his teeth at the friction of lace on flesh, drew her more firmly against him. Her belly was flat and smooth, and he could feel the jut of her hipbones as she pressed against him.

"I didn't think you Ramsey boys were afraid of a little trouble," she whispered, nibbling his lower lip.

He was playing with fire, he knew that. Much more of this and he'd be making love to her... did she know that? he wondered. Did she have any idea of what she was doing to him, any idea where their increasingly intimate caresses were leading? There were different degrees of innocence, but he was pretty damn sure hers was real. Making love to a woman was one thing; making love to a girl quite another.

Damn it, was he ready for this...?

Her thigh brushed between his, touching him, and he recoiled with an inhaled hiss. He wanted her and yet didn't, ached to make love to her and yet longed to postpone the agony of anticipation, found himself torn between raw physical need and that damned, nagging feeling that he was getting in way over his head.

She was just a kid, damn it! Brue Langford's kid, and a virgin to boot.

"How old are you, anyway?" he growled.

Her teeth settled across his lower lip, withdrew an instant later, and were replaced by the slow caress of a silken tongue. "Old enough." Her lips curved in a smile against his. "Sixteen."

Sixteen. He groaned. She was moving against him again, teasing his already overheated body with hers, and he felt his precarious willpower start to slip. "Kathy...honey, I'm not sure—"

"I am," she whispered. "You're not like the others, Gage. You've always been . . . special."

"Your daddy's going to have a fit if he finds out...."

"My daddy'll never have to find out," she said with a throaty laugh. "I'm not going to tell him. Are you?"

There was no answer but the one she wanted.

He dropped his mouth over hers with a groan, tossing common sense and good judgment aside as he filled his senses with her, his caresses becoming less gentle, more demanding. And she responded just as greedily, her hands and mouth moving with surprising skill.

"Hey, you there! What in the hell do you think you're doing! Get away from my daughter or I'll shoot you on the spot!"

The voice shattered the silence around them like the crack of a rifle shot, and for half an instant Gage actually thought her father had made his threat real.

Kathleen jackknifed out of Gage's arms and he turned to see Brue Langford glowering down at them from the creek bank. He was astride a big gray mare, and she was fighting the bit, tossing her head and snorting as he reined her up tightly.

"Gage Ramsey! I should have known!" Langford lifted his rifle and fired inches over Gage's head, and Kathleen gave a muffled scream of stark terror.

"Daddy! My God, Daddy, stop it! You're going to kill him!"

"Damn right I'm going to kill him," her father bellowed, dismounting and striding across to the bank of the creek.

"Stop it! It was my fault! He was helping me, that's all. A calf was stuck in the mud and Gage helped me get it out."

"I don't see any calf stuck in the mud," Langford shouted, his face red. "All I see is a Ramsey with his hands all over my little girl!"

"We were covered with mud and came up here to get cleaned off!" Obviously torn between fury and shame, Kathleen swam into the shallows and pulled herself out of the water, snatching her drying shirt off a nearby bush.

"What the—! What are you doing swimming around half-naked! By God, Kathleen Langford, I'm going to—"

Her father's face was mottled with rage, and he took two long strides toward her, but in that instant Gage was out of the water and standing between them. "She didn't do anything, Langford," he said quietly. Calmly. "We were wet and muddy and decided to come swimming to wash off, just like she said. I tried to kiss her and she pushed me away—that's all that happened."

"Gage!"

"I'm not interested in your daughter, Langford," Gage said in a hard voice, ignoring her. It was a blatant lie—even as he was saying it, he knew he wanted Kathleen Langford more than he'd wanted anything in his life before.

But he couldn't afford to admit it. Not to Langford. Not to himself. Not even to Kathy. Once the heat of their embraces had cooled, she'd realize how impossible it was, so there was no point in teasing himself—or her—with what they couldn't have.

But what he could do was protect her. "I can have any woman in the county—what would I want with a scrawny, scared little virgin like her?"

"Lay a hand on my daughter again, Ramsey, and I'll kill you, you got that?"

Gage gave a snort and turned away, not looking at Kathleen as he strode across to where he'd hung his jeans and shirt to dry. "Don't worry about it, Langford. She's just a kid. And she doesn't have anything I'd want."

Chapter Two

Doug swore under his breath, braking impatiently for a red light, and Kathleen gave a slight start, looking around a little dizzily. The memories had been so real she could still almost taste Gage's mouth on her own, and she found herself reluctant to let them go. She'd been thinking about that day with Gage down at Fireweed Creek again and she smiled, remembering her anger that afternoon. Anger at herself, at her father. And most of all, anger at Gage Ramsey's betrayal.

She had to smile again. Gage had been every inch the hero that afternoon, but it had taken her years to realize it. At the time, about the last thing she would have called his behavior was heroic.

He'd been true to his word that day. Whether in anger at himself or at her, or out of honest fear of her father, he'd gotten dressed that afternoon and had mounted up and ridden away without even a backward look. And afterward, whenever they'd met unexpectedly, his eyes would hold hers for the briefest moment then turn away, cool and remote, as though he didn't even know who she was. As though they'd never shared those hot, tempestuous few minutes in the pool beneath the falls.

She'd been furious and insulted and thoroughly embarrassed, and she'd stayed that way for weeks. It hadn't been until years later that she'd understood that it had been an act, that he'd dismissed her so brutally simply to protect her from her father.

And she had, eventually, gotten over it. Her pride had been more bruised than anything, and she'd turned the sense of betrayal into anger and had kept it that way, refusing to allow herself the luxury of hurt feelings. Her father got over it after a while, too, and they never mentioned it again. Then her mother died and her father became ill, and over the next few years things had just gotten steadily worse.

They'd nearly lost High Mesa. Her father hadn't been well enough to handle things and had been too stubborn, too prideful, to ask for help. She'd done the best she could, but she'd had to fight her father every step of the way, and what she was able to do had been too little, too late. And it had been sometime during those long three or four years that he'd made her promise that she'd never sell High Mesa.

"Do anything you have to, Kathy," he'd told her with fevered intensity. "*Anything!* But never sell—promise me that. Promise me you'll never sell this land. It's the only thing that's kept this family going...never sell High Mesa!"

She'd promised him, of course. What else could she do? There had been a bad couple of months when she'd thought he wasn't going to make it, but he'd rallied finally and had fought himself back into another run at life, but by then it had been too late. High Mesa was all but bankrupt, the herds gone, the land mortgaged to the hilt, the bankers starting to circle like vultures. There had been no way out. None at all.

And then Gage Ramsey had come one day, knocking at the front door and proposing—not marriage—but a business deal. A merger, he'd called it. A way out.

Letting her mind drift, Kathleen allowed the memories to wash over her again. Remembering...

* * *

"I don't understand what you're talking about." Kathleen started pacing again, angry and upset but refusing, so far, to give in to either emotion.

He'd come walking into her home as though he had some right to be there, suggesting . . . well, she didn't quite know *what* he was suggesting.

"Hell, Kathy," he drawled, his dark blue eyes holding hers with lazy amusement, "I figured it was plain enough. I just asked you to marry me."

There. He'd said it again. *That* word. "It didn't sound much like any marriage proposal I've ever heard," she said testily. "It sounds more like a . . . a—"

"Business proposition?" he offered helpfully. "That's what it is, sweetheart. Business, pure and simple. You wouldn't want it any other way, would you?"

His eyes seemed to hold hers a little too long, filled with things she didn't want to see, and she wheeled away from him and strode to the window, staring out across the rolling hills. "I'll give you one thing, Gage Ramsey," she said in a hoarse voice. "At least you're being honest that it's the land you want, not me."

"It's not your land," he replied affably, "it's your water. The one thing you have that I need."

And that, in a word, was why he'd come. The drought that had racked the country for almost two years now had all but left High Mesa untouched, but bigger spreads like Ramsey's Tanglefoot had run on hard times.

"We've cut the herds by over half," Gage was saying, "but if this water shortage goes on for much longer, we're headed for real trouble. With High Mesa water, we can hang on for as long as we need to."

She watched an eagle glide in ever-widening circles in the cloudless skies over the south pasture. "Why marry me for it, Gage?" she asked wearily. "Why not just buy it?"

There was a long silence, and Kathleen glanced around finally to find him looking at her with an odd predatory look that sent a tiny shiver down her spine.

"Your old man won't sell this land, and I can't afford to wait until he dies," he said with brutal honesty.

His bluntness sent a second shiver after the first. "And you think he'll let me marry you?"

"I think you're old enough to make your own decisions." He held her gaze steadily. "I'm talking a business merger, Kathleen. Nothing more. Tanglefoot and High Mesa are both in trouble—you need money, I need water and time. I don't have the cash I'd need to buy the place outright, even if I could convince your father to sell, but I've got enough to get the creditors off your back and keep them off, and to turn this place around and make it a solid, working ranch again."

"And?" She felt empty and cold for some reason. Had to swallow, hard, to keep her voice steady. It shouldn't have mattered. She'd always dreamed of being with him, had known it was impossible for too many reasons to count. So it shouldn't have mattered that he didn't love her....

"We'll draw up a contract. You'll stay with me, as my wife, until the drought breaks and land prices come up. By then I'll have built the Tanglefoot herd back up and have paid off your father's debts, and both operations will be solid again." She sensed more than heard him walk up behind her, and she stiffened slightly.

"Your father isn't going to live forever," he said quietly. "It'll gut him to see this place sold to its creditors, you know that. By marrying me and throwing in with the Tanglefoot operation, you can keep the ranch until...well, until you're free to sell it. Then either you and I can agree on a fair price and I'll buy you out, or we'll sell to a third party. I'll take what I figure I've put into the place and you can have the rest and...go your own way."

"No strings?" It was madness to even consider it, yet she found herself thinking how easy it would be. She was exhausted from months of worrying, from arguing with glacial-faced bankers, and from feeling, day by day, the end edging ever closer. It would be so simple to turn it all over to Gage and let him take the burden on.

"No strings." His voice was husky and very, very close.

She knew he was going to touch her and swore she wouldn't flinch, yet she did start slightly when his hands settled gently and warmly on her shoulders. Unbidden, the memories flooded over her....

"Remember that afternoon down by Fireweed Creek?" he murmured, his breath tickling the back of her neck. "It wouldn't be that hard, would it? Being married to me...?"

Carefully, half afraid her knees might turn to water and she'd ruin it by falling flat on her face, she stepped away from him and turned to look at him. "I'll do it," she said coolly. "On one condition."

Gage's eyes narrowed slightly. "Name it."

"I sleep in my own bed. And you sleep in yours. Touch me, and I'll walk out—and I'll take High Mesa with me."

He paused for a heartbeat, his eyes burning into hers. "Damn you," he whispered. "You know how to cut where it hurts, don't you?"

"That's the deal. Take it or leave it."

He gave a snort. "Seems to me you're not in the best bargaining position, sweetheart. The wolf's at the door...."

"I'll turn High Mesa over to the bankers this afternoon before I'll prostitute myself to save it," she said steadily, emphasizing the word just slightly and knowing by the tightening around his eyes that the jibe had worked. "I'll marry you and turn High Mesa over to you for as long as it takes to get both of us out of trouble...and as long as my father's alive. But I won't sleep with you." She smiled maliciously. "You Ramseys always boast you can buy anything you want. I don't imagine you'll have much difficulty buying *that,* either. Just not from me."

She thought for half a moment that she'd gone too far. Gage's face took on a dull red flush and his eyes narrowed dangerously. He took a step toward her, then hesitated, a muscle ticking in his cheek. "I've never had to pay for it before," he said with deliberate crudity. "I doubt I'll have to start now. If that's what you want, you've got it."

"Fine." Kathleen swallowed, suddenly finding her victory wasn't half as satisfactory as it should have been. In fact, she had her mouth open to tell him that she'd just been testing him, that she hadn't meant what she'd said about separate beds, but one look into those smoldering blue eyes made her snap it closed again.

"Do we have a deal?" He was staring at her, mouth and chin hard, eyes cold.

The empty feeling within Kathleen gaped suddenly wider, and she shivered, fighting down cold despair. "Yes," she whispered, turning away so he wouldn't see the tears in her eyes. "We have a deal."

Chapter Three

"I'll drop you off at Emergency, then find a place to park." Doug's voice jarred Kathleen from her brooding. He looked at her worriedly. "Better yet, we can go in together."

"Don't be silly." Kathleen unfastened her seat belt. "I'm a big girl, Doug. I can go in by myself."

But she was screaming inside. She didn't want to go in there. Not alone. Didn't want to face—*them*. Didn't want to have to stand there without Doug's solid presence as some overworked, overtired doctor told her...

"I'll be fine," she said firmly, pushing the car door open. "You don't have to stay, Doug. It's silly, making Beth's mother come all the way over just so you can both be—"

"I'm staying," he said grimly, his eyes fierce in the harsh light from the hospital's Emergency entrance. "Back in a minute."

The corridor leading from the big double glass doors to the admitting desk was long and brightly lit, and the heels of her boots sent sharp echoes ringing back from the bare walls. There were a few people standing around: a couple of ambulance attendants, a uniformed policeman talking to two youths, a very pregnant young woman in a wheelchair.

As Kathleen neared the desk, she realized her heart was clattering against her ribs like something wild and the aching thickness in her throat was getting worse.

Fear, she realized dimly. Not of Decker. Not even of the others. But of what she was going to hear. Of what might have happened in the long half hour it had taken to get here. Maybe someone was phoning her apartment right now, she thought numbly. Maybe it was already too late....

There were two people in the main waiting room besides the admitting nurse manning the desk: a young doctor still dressed in surgery greens, his face drawn and gray with exhaustion, and another man. Tall. Wide-shouldered. Dressed in a sheepskin jacket and faded jeans. Unmistakably a Ramsey, even from the back.

Kathleen didn't need to see his face to know which one it was. Decker. The old man himself, as legendary as the name he carried. And twice as feared.

For a split second, she was struck by the sheer power of the man. He radiated it like heat, that arrogant kind of certainty that comes with knowing your name still makes strong men swallow hard when they hear it. He was talking with the young doctor, standing close to him in that way he had, looming tall and solid and threatening. She was amused to see that the doctor was standing his ground.

Bad career move, she told him silently. That kind of defiance has cost many men their jobs.

It was then that Decker saw her. His gaze met hers across the doctor's green-clad shoulder, and he threw his graying head up like a cow pony scenting trouble, those brilliant blue Ramsey eyes narrowing with rage.

But he contained it, as Kathleen knew he would. This wasn't the place for a confrontation with her, not here where there were too many unsympathetic and overly curious ears. Ramsey problems were handled in private, behind closed doors if possible. It wouldn't do to let the common rabble discover that even legends have their weaknesses and vulnerabilities.

"I didn't think you'd come," was all he said. *How dare you come,* was what he meant.

Oddly enough, she felt none of her usual trepidation at facing him. He was old, she found herself thinking with sudden surprise. Old and worn out and...scared. She could see it in his eyes.

Her heart stopped. Numbed, she could only stare up into that rugged, lined face. "Is he—?"

To even answer civilly was a struggle for him. His mouth twisted, but he finally managed to get the one word out. "No."

"And you are...?" The young doctor's voice was clipped.

"Kathleen Ramsey." She swallowed, meeting his gaze steadily. "I'm Gage Ramsey's wife. And I want to know how my husband is."

That easily, she dismissed the old man. Could feel his hatred and anger. The doctor's eyes held hers for a moment, shrewd and thoughtful and with what Kathleen could have sworn was relief.

"I'm Dr. Haynes. And I'd like to speak with you, Mrs. Ramsey. In private."

"You're not going to talk about my son without me bein' there," Decker growled. "This *woman* doesn't have—"

"Excuse us, Mr. Ramsey," Haynes said smoothly, taking Kathleen by the elbow and steering her toward a side corridor. "If you'd like to join the others in the waiting room, I'll talk with you all later. But right now, your son's *wife* and I have things to discuss." He stressed the word just enough to bring a flare of anger into Decker's eyes, but before the old man could say anything, Haynes had piloted Kathleen down the corridor and into a small, comfortably furnished office.

He nodded toward an armchair and went across to a coffeemaker, raising an enquiring eyebrow at Kathleen as he poured himself a cup of lethal-looking coffee. She shook her head, and he added a heaping teaspoon of sugar to the cup, stirred it briefly, then carried it across to the desk and dropped wearily into the other chair.

"It's bad, isn't it?" Kathleen was gratified at how calm her voice was.

He looked at her for a moment, then nodded. "As bad as it gets." He took a sip of the hot coffee, squinting through the steam as though contemplating how to tell her the rest. "It was a head-on collision. Your husband apparently lost control of his truck trying to avoid hitting another car that had spun out on ice. The truck flipped over and slid into oncoming traffic."

Kathleen listened to the words without really hearing them. *He's alive.* She kept saying the words in her mind like an incantation. *He's alive....*

"A tanker truck hit him. It's a miracle it didn't explode, but..." He shrugged. "Your husband's in critical condition. We're not too sure yet of the extent of his injuries—we've spent the last two hours just trying to keep him alive and get him stabilized."

Numb, cold, she simply nodded. "The...uh..." She had to clear her throat. "They said...on the phone...that you need my permission for surgery."

He smiled faintly. "Technically. Actually you're here because I want you here. Because *he* wants you here."

Kathleen blinked in surprise. "Gage?"

"He regained consciousness briefly after they brought him in. Just long enough to call your name." He looked at her for a thoughtful moment. "His father says you're not married anymore."

A jolt of raw anger shot through Kathleen. "Gage and I have been separated for almost six months, but we're still very married. I suspect you've figured out by now that his family and I aren't . . . close."

A flicker of a smile. "I got that idea." Then his face turned grave again. "They've ordered no life support," he said quietly.

"They *what?*" Kathleen sat bolt upright, her voice snapping through the room.

"Ordinarily it wouldn't be up to them, but there's Ramsey money in this hospital. A *lot* of money. And that means that if the old man takes it to the top, he'll get what he wants."

"Over my dead body," Kathleen said in a cold, even voice.

"I was hoping you'd say that. Not many people are willing to stand up to the Ramseys. I didn't know if you would or not."

"I'm not afraid of Decker Ramsey," she lied. "Or the rest of them, either. It's the land they want. The ranch. Decker's health turned bad about six years ago, and he had to turn over control of Tanglefoot to Gage. He's spent every day since then regretting it. He and Gage don't agree on a single thing with respect to running the ranch—or on anything else, for that matter—but it's his brothers that are causing the most trouble."

Kathleen got to her feet and paced, knowing this was none of the doctor's business and yet just as certain he needed to hear it. Needed to know the real reason behind any plan to let Gage die. "They've talked Decker into believing the days of big ranches are over. That Tanglefoot should be sold off to a gang of investors who have plans of turning the whole valley into some sort of resort."

Haynes gave a low whistle. "That land's worth a fortune, drought or no drought."

"Eight figures," Kathleen said dispassionately. It wasn't just Tanglefoot they wanted to sell, but High Mesa, too. Especially High Mesa, and the cold artesian wells under it with their priceless flow of water. And even though she kept telling herself it didn't matter, that she didn't care, the truth was that she did.

"But Gage won't sell," she added quietly. "He's a rancher, not an investor. He doesn't want the money, he wants the land. And nobody's very happy about it." *Except me,* she found herself adding silently.

"I see. So if I manage to pull him through, they lose their millions."

"So will your precious hospital more than likely," Kathleen said with surprising humor. It astounded her to think she could still laugh at anything. "Can I see him?"

He frowned. "I don't recommend it. There was a lot of flying glass, a lot of blood. And he's being prepped for surgery. It's not . . . well, it's not a good idea."

"And his chances?" She had to ask. Had to know the truth.

"Not good," came the quiet reply. "The damage is extensive and we don't even know the half of it yet. It's a miracle he's alive right now, if you want the truth. But then," he added with a smile, "I guess it's the time of year for miracles, isn't it?"

After she left Haynes's office there was a moment—but just a moment—when she very nearly gave up trying to be brave and rational. She wanted to scream and cry and hammer at the walls with her fists. . . .

But she didn't.

She couldn't afford the luxury. They were out there right now, coming in like sharks to the kill. They'd all be here soon, and she had to be ready for them. Had to let them know that she was in control of things, that Gage's life, the ranch, all of it was in *her* hands now.

Not that it would stop them from trying.

It sent a little shiver of anger through her. *Let* them try, damn it, she whispered silently. Just let them try.

"Mrs. Ramsey?"

The quiet voice behind her made Kathleen glance around. A nurse was standing there, holding a battered sheepskin jacket. "This was all the police were able to salvage from your husband's truck, Mrs. Ramsey."

Kathleen took the jacket numbly. Its weight filled her arms, and the familiar leather scent wrapped itself around her like a hug. And in that instant, she realized she'd been kidding herself all along. That some part of her mind had refused to believe that this was happening, that Gage wouldn't come striding down that corridor any minute now, boot heels pounding out impatient echoes, the lights sparking gold off his hair, vital and alive and invincible.

She mumbled something, fighting tears, and the nurse smiled and held out something else. "And this," she said gently. "It has your name on it. I...well, I think he'd want you to have it."

Kathleen looked at the slim box in the woman's hand. There was some mistake, obviously. The gift was wrapped in blue metallic paper and bound with glittering silver ribbon, and the small tag did indeed read "Kathy" in Gage's ebullient scrawl. But it couldn't be for her. There must be some other Kathy. Someone he'd met recently, perhaps. Maybe that's where he'd been going tonight when—

She realized the nurse was looking at her oddly. "Thank you," she whispered hoarsely, taking it with cold fingers.

"There's a private waiting room through that door," the nurse said softly. "It's quiet in there, and perhaps you'd like a few minutes by yourself before the rest of your husband's family gets here."

"Yes," Kathleen whispered, hardly aware of speaking, of moving dreamlike toward the door the nurse had pointed out. Aware of nothing except for the weight of Gage's jacket in her arms.

Holding it tightly against her chest, she sat down numbly. That was the worst part, not being able to do anything. Having to sit there helplessly waiting while strangers tried to keep him alive.

It should be her in there, she thought inanely. He was *her* husband, damn it. She knew him better than probably anyone, and if he was going to hang on and fight, it would be for her.

If for no other reason, she thought with grim amusement, than to force her to honor her marriage contract right to the bitter end.

You're not going to let me get away this easily, are you, Gage? she taunted him silently. *You never let anything go when you had your mind set on keeping it. So fight for me, damn it. Fight.*

She realized that her cheeks were wet with tears she didn't even remember shedding, and she wiped at them with her hand, then started fumbling through her pockets for a tissue. Gage hated it when she cried. Like most men, he found it unsettling and nerve-racking, and said it wasn't fighting fair.

She gave a sob of laughter, thinking about what he'd be saying now if he could see her. *You never gave up on any-thing in your life, either, Kathy—don't tell me you're giv-*

*ing up on me now. You're stronger than that, Kath. And I
need you, babe. I need you!*

Kathleen frowned, still looking for a tissue. Funny how
your mind worked at times like this. She could hear Gage's
voice as clearly as if he were standing beside her, yet she
couldn't imagine him ever asking for help. Arguing with
her and taunting her, yes, but saying he needed her? Not
Gage.

Wishful thinking, she told herself glumly.

Her search for a tissue turned up nothing, and she swore
wearily. Then on a whim she started rummaging through
the pockets of Gage's jacket. The first held nothing but a
couple of galvanized fencing staples, a pencil stub and a
scrap of paper with some calculations scrawled on it—dimensions for a new cattle shed, by the look of it. She
frowned at it for a moment, wondering if he realized he'd
underestimated the roof dimensions and would be short
about a hundred shingles, then gave herself a shake. It
wasn't any of her business anymore. If he hadn't learned
to double-check his arithmetic now she wasn't doing it for
him, well . . . too bad.

She had better luck with the second pocket. Her fingers
encountered a tissue, and she drew it out. It was wrapped
around something, and she gave it a tug to free it—then sat
there and stared at the small glass angel lying in her palm.

Her angel.

Gage had given it to her for Christmas a year after they
were married.

But it couldn't be. She'd smashed that angel herself in a
fit of rage—she'd *seen* the pieces lying on the floor of her
bedroom!

Yet it was that angel. She could see the rough-edged
cracks where he had inexpertly glued the pieces back to-

gether. She ran her finger over the chipped edge of one wing.

Tears welled unexpectedly, and she didn't even bother trying to wipe them away. *Why, Gage?* she asked desolately. *Why... ?*

And, not even wanting to, she found herself remembering....

Chapter Four

It had been the first real Christmas after they'd been married. As usual, the entire family was expected to spend the holidays with Gord and his wife at their sprawling mansion in the foothills. Decker, who lived at the ranch in an uneasy alliance with her and Gage, had left earlier, wanting to stop in town on his way to visit some of his cronies, and she and Gage had spent the morning getting ready.

Storm warnings had been coming in all morning, but Gage had decided not to leave until the last minute, wanting to make certain things were solidly battened down before heading out. But the blizzard had hit just as they'd been about to leave, and they hadn't gotten even as far as the main road before Gage had stopped the truck, shaking his head, and told her it would be suicide to go on.

He smiled a little ruefully as he said it, his eyes holding hers with an odd intensity, as though wondering how she was going to react to the news. "It's not going to be much of a Christmas," he said quietly. "Alone instead of with family..."

Alone with me, his voice said.

Kathleen managed to smile. She'd have preferred to spend Christmas staked out naked in drifting snow than with his family, but she decided not to tell him that. It would only lead to another argument, and she was tired of the arguing.

"It won't be so bad," she said easily. "We can decorate the tree and make eggnog and watch *A Christmas Carol* on TV."

He nodded slowly, still looking at her. "It means not seeing your dad...."

"He'll understand. He and Aunt Maud are having a gang in for Christmas dinner, so it's not as though he's going to be alone. I'll get over when the roads are clear."

She was talking too much. But for absolutely no reason she was suddenly nervous. It was the way he kept looking at her, she thought uneasily. The way the cab of the truck had seemed to shrink until it was filled with nothing but wide male shoulders and long male legs and that masculine scent of clover hay and horse sweat and leather that she always found so erotic.

"And if the power goes off?" He was teasing her now, the corners of his eyes crinkling slightly as he smiled.

She shrugged, trying to ignore the nonchalant way he'd draped his arm along the back of the truck seat so his hand rested as though by accident against the collar of her sheepskin jacket. He would only have to move it a scant inch to touch the bare skin of her neck....

"We...umm...if it goes off we'll sit in front of the fire and play cards or...something."

Damn it, would he stop looking at her like that! There was something in his eyes, the hint of subtle yet very real sexual awareness in the way his gaze kept lingering on her mouth, the curve of her throat, that made her feel flustered. He hadn't looked at her in quite that way in all the time they'd been married. Not since that day at Fireweed Creek when he'd almost made love to her.

And in that moment, she suddenly realized just *how* alone they were. The housekeeper, Martha, had gone to visit her daughter for the holidays, and Gage had let the ranch hands go for the four days as well. So it would be just the two of them in the big old house. Alone together—really alone—for the first time in almost a year.

"The snow's getting worse." She said the first thing that came into her mind just to break his stare. "We should get back before the road drifts in."

"You're right." Gage's eyes held hers for a split second longer, then he smiled and started the engine. "I'd hate like hell to spend our first wedding anniversary in a snowbank."

Wedding anniversary.

The words went through Kathleen like a crystal blade, piercing her to the heart.

Oh, God, how had she forgotten! It was Christmas Eve. A year ago to this very day they'd been married.

She gave Gage a stricken glance, but he was concentrating on getting the pickup turned around in the blowing, swirling snow without sliding into the ditch, seemingly unperturbed.

He never mentioned the fact that they were married, never referred to her as his wife, never made any sign at all that she was anything other than just one more member of the household. Not quite one of the hired hands, but not family, either. Just . . . there.

Oh, he touched her at times, draping a friendly arm around her shoulders when he was in a good mood, putting his hand on her waist in a proprietary and husbandly way when they were in a crowd, letting his fingers rest lightly on her cheek on those rare public times when he kissed her, his lips no more than a fleeting touch on her cheek or forehead. But most of the time she could have sworn that he found the very thought of touching her repugnant, the pains he took to avoid it.

But then, what had she expected? He'd been honest with her right from the beginning, and she'd come into this relationship—she refused to call it a marriage—with her eyes wide open. If she'd really harbored some silly notion that Gage Ramsey was suddenly going to wake up one morning in love with her, she'd been crazy.

Besides, it was only until Tanglefoot and High Mesa were back on their feet. And as long as her father was alive. A daughter could do that much, at least. It was a small enough sacrifice. If Gage didn't smother her with affection, he wasn't abusive, either. In fact, there were times when his gentleness and the almost tender way he looked at her were worse than nothing at all. Because those moments reignited hope. And hope was perhaps the most painful lie of all.

Somewhere, a telephone rang. Its shrill insistence shattered the dreamlike memories cocooning Kathleen and forced her, unwilling, back into the present. Grimly, she kept her eyes closed, refusing to acknowledge the ugly reality of where she was. It seemed very important for some reason not to let go of the daydream ... as though, by clinging desperately to the memories, she was clinging to Gage himself. Keeping him from slipping that last distance from her. . . .

If she let her mind drift, she could be back there, she told herself determinedly. Back in the truck that cold, stormy morning. Back with Gage ...

"How's his BP?"

"All his vitals are good. How are you doing down there?"

"Better than I'd hoped. This guy's real lucky—a couple of centimeters either way and it would have been all over. Straight mayos, please—and more suction."

* * *

The whispering, wordless voices kept nagging at him, pulling him out of the warmth and safety of his dreams, and Gage fought them irritably. He wanted to be back there with her. He'd be safe there. Protected. The dream had been so real he could feel the crisp bite of cold winter air in his lungs, could hear the whisper of blowing snow against the truck, the squeak of it under the tires. They'd been in the pickup, he remembered, and he'd just told her they'd have to spend Christmas—and their anniversary— alone together. If he concentrated hard enough, he could be back there with her. Back in the truck . . . gratefully, he gave himself over to the past, remembering . . .

This was, hands-down, the worst damned idea he'd ever had, Gage thought disconsolately. The truck hit a drift and reared like a horse fighting the bit, nearly wrenching the wheel out of his hands, and he swore and wrestled it under control.

Why the hell had he ever thought that just getting her alone for a few days would change things? She hated his guts. Getting snowed in for a romantic little interlude wasn't going to make a damned bit of difference.

The plan had hit him sometime yesterday afternoon when the weather reports had first started coming in with their threat of a major winter storm. He'd already given Martha and the hands a few days off, so all he'd had to do was get Decker to go on ahead—not an easy job, but he'd done it—then waste time until the snow got bad enough that Kathy wouldn't suspect his motives for turning back.

And it had worked perfectly. Problem was, now that he had her alone he wasn't any too sure what he was going to do with her.

He glanced at her just as she looked at him, and their eyes locked for a heartbeat; Gage felt his gut twist into a knot. He'd felt it before, that little sizzle of sexual tension, an awareness of each other that hadn't happened in a long, long time. And under it, something else. An awareness, like the other, but deeper—not just of what they were, a man and a woman forced into a loveless marriage neither wanted, but of everything they might have been.

It pulled through Gage like wire through butter, leaving him aching with sudden want, and he had to forcibly keep himself from stopping the truck and gathering her into his arms and bringing his mouth down over hers in the kind of deep, gut-twisting, mind-wrenching kiss he dreamed of every single damned time he looked at her.

He wanted to plunder that strawberry-and-cream mouth until he was filled with her, to kiss her until they couldn't stand it anymore. He wanted to touch her, to run his hands along that lithe, sweet body, to feel her satin skin. Wanted to pull her close and feel her moving against him all naked and warm and silken.

But most of all he wanted to love her as a man loves his woman, as a husband loves his wife. To bury himself in the moist welcoming heat of her body and move within her, to feel her, taste her, to drown in every sensation and texture and response until they were both crazed with it. He wanted to hear her whisper his name over and over, her voice caught with desire, and he wanted to hear her cry out for him at the end when he made it perfect for her and wanted to lift his own head and bay at the moon when his own reality exploded.

It had been over a year since he'd made love to a woman. There were nights he woke up in a cold sweat, his body so achingly aroused that even breathing hurt, and he'd lie in the darkness and think of Kathleen just a few long strides away, sleeping on the other side of the wall. He'd long ago lost count of the number of times he'd gotten out of bed and had walked across to the door separating them, had stood there, hand on knob, willing himself to step through, to slip into her bed and take her in his arms and show her what loving was all about.

But he hadn't. It was more fear than willpower, if he had to admit it. Fear of seeing the disgust on her face. Of having her flinch away and scream at him to get out. She hadn't wanted him to touch her, and so far he'd been able to keep his promise. But he didn't know how much longer he was going to be able to go on without a woman's sweet touch. The thought of being in the same house with her for years, of being so close to her he could touch her if he dared, to smell her perfume in the air, to glance up at unexpected moments and see her there, to hear her musical laugh, to be able to do everything a husband could do but love her...

If he'd known how hard it was going to be, he thought savagely, he'd never have done it. But he hadn't considered this part. Hadn't considered what it was going to be like being married to her but not able to touch her and hold her or love her long through the night.

It had backfired, he found himself thinking wearily. He'd married her hoping she'd fall in love with him—wanting to have the cool, remote Kathleen Langford so madly in love with him it hurt—and wound up having the tables turned on him. Had wound up halfway in love with her instead...

Neither of them said anything on the arduous drive through the blowing snow and drifts back to the ranch. And aside from an oddly self-conscious word or two as they walked into the house together, they didn't really say anything then, either. The house seemed eerily silent and empty, and it heightened that uneasy tension between them to an almost unbearable level. Gage stood it for as long as he could, then he muttered something about going out to check on the stock and got out before he said the hell with promises and good sense and took her to bed.

Or tried to, he reminded himself with a grim little smile as he trudged through knee-high drifts and lashing snow to the nearest cattle shed. Odds were pretty good he'd get about as far as the first kiss before all hell cut loose and she broke his jaw or something. Kathleen Langford wasn't the kind of woman a man took liberties with. Even if he was married to her.

But when he came back in an hour or so later, he found himself unable to stay away and went prowling through the big old house looking for her.

She was in the kitchen, surrounded by mixing bowls and baking pans and the smell of hot gingerbread. The counters were covered with bags of flour and canisters of sugar and spice bottles and batter-smeared bowls, but it was Kathleen he stared at. Cool, distant Kathleen, with one of Martha's big aprons wound around her middle and her hair tousled and dusted with flour and her cheeks flushed with heat from the oven. She was leaning over a sheet of angel-shaped cookies, frowning with concentration as she carefully outlined them with pale pink icing.

"I didn't know you could cook." He wandered across to look over her shoulder, watching curiously as she started sprinkling sugar on the wings to make them glitter.

Kathleen straightened to admire her handiwork, and Gage caught a hint of the scented soap she used, forced himself to ignore it as she glanced up at him with a mischievous smile. The heat in her cheeks made her eyes sparkle, and she had a smudge of flour on her cheek. He found himself wondering if he dared kiss her. Decided not to even try it.

"Of course I can cook," she said with a laugh, brushing a tangle of hair back from her forehead with her arm. And then, as her eyes caught his for an unprotected instant, he knew she was thinking the same thing he was: that they'd been married for an entire year, and in all that time she'd never done more than get him a cup of coffee now and again.

It reminded him of all the other things he didn't know about her, which in turn reminded him of a number of other things he'd sworn not to think about tonight, and he broke her gaze by leaning over and picking up one of the angels.

Kathleen pulled the other rack of cookies toward her. "Christmas wouldn't be Christmas without angel cookies," she said. "They were standard fare when I was growing up. I'd help Mom decorate them—at least that's what I thought I was doing. Actually I ate two for every one I iced."

Gage smiled, biting into the cookie. "I missed all that. I was only two when my mother died. I don't even remember her...."

Kathleen glanced up at him, looking as though she were trying to make up her mind about something. Then, suddenly, she grinned and shoved the icing bag into his hands. "I always say it's never too late to have a happy childhood." He must have looked as startled as he felt, because she laughed. "It's easy. Let me show you...." Gently she put her hands around his and showed him how to squeeze the icing through the nozzle with a steady, even pressure, guiding his hands to outline the angel with pink satin.

They both frowned at the result. "Well," Kathleen said charitably, "it takes a little practice."

Gage gave a snort of laughter. "I hate to break it to you, honey, but this is hopeless. My artistic abilities are limited to painting barns and fences."

"Nothing's hopeless," she said firmly.

"Even me?"

"Even you." She slipped him a teasing sidelong glance that made his heart give a thump, then took his hand between hers again. "Okay, try this next one...."

He didn't have the heart to tell her she was wasting her time. Besides, he enjoyed just being close to her. She was tucked between him and the counter and he could feel the warmth coming off her body. Her hair kept tickling his cheek, and he could distinctly feel the rounded contour of her breast against his arm. He had to force himself to concentrate on what she was saying, his mind tending to drift off into all sorts of directions, none of which had to do with Christmas cookies.

And finally he couldn't take any more. One more minute of this and he'd wind up in serious trouble—pulling her around and into his arms, for instance, and crushing her mouth under his. Or dispensing with the niceties of seduction altogether and simply tossing her over his shoulder and taking her into the nearest bedroom and making love to her until they were both too exhausted to move!

"I've got to go," he said hoarsely, pulling away from her. She started to say something, but he turned and walked swiftly away. Away from temptation. Away from everything he wanted, and everything he dared not ask for. He'd told her it was just a business proposition; he wouldn't go back on his word now.

It was much, much later that he came into the living room and found her sitting in front of the fireplace, staring into the flames with an expression of such wistfulness on her face that it made his heart give a sharp little twist.

He stood there for a moment or two, wondering how the hell he'd gotten himself into such a mess. Life was supposed to be easy if you were a Ramsey—ask and it was given, want and it was yours. Money. Power. Women. Except that for the past year, things hadn't been easy at all.

He shook the mood off and walked across to where Kathleen was sitting on the braided rug, arms crossed on her upraised knee, chin resting on her hand. The room was redolent with the scent of pine pitch and ginger cookies and baked ham, yet he swore he could pick out her perfume from halfway across the room.

She glanced up, her eyes bright with firelight, and he had the sudden uneasy feeling that she'd been crying. But she smiled and stretched luxuriously, and he decided he'd been wrong. "Are you hungry?" she asked. "I baked a ham, and there's—"

"Maybe later." He eased himself down onto the rug beside her, having the feeling—as he always did when he was near her like this—that if he moved too abruptly she'd take off like a startled deer. She didn't like being close to him, he'd learned that the hard way. And maybe he couldn't blame her. It couldn't be easy, being married to a man you despised.

He turned the small gift-wrapped box in his fingers, wondering why he felt so awkward. "I...uh...picked this up in town last week," he muttered. "Thought you might like it..."

The surprise on her face made him laugh, and as she took the box from his hand, he felt himself grinning like a kid. "Open it."

"But it isn't Christmas yet."

"That's okay. It isn't a Christmas present."

Her eyes held his for an instant, then she grinned and tucked her legs under her and started unwrapping the box, her eyes sparkling almost as bright as the silver paper. He watched her as she drew the claret velvet box from the wrapping, saw something change slightly in her expression.

Slowly she opened the box. "Oh, Gage," she breathed. "It's...lovely."

"I figure you got cheated when it came to an engagement ring." On a whim, he reached out and cupped her chin in his hand, then leaned forward and kissed her gently on the mouth. "Happy anniversary, kid. We've made it through a whole year."

Her eyes filled with a sudden sadness, then she smiled and nodded, looking down at the ring again. "Yeah," she whispered, her voice oddly thick. "I guess we have." She drew in a deep breath, then looked up again. "It's gorgeous, but I can't accept it, Gage. It wouldn't be right. Not under the—the circumstances." She looked back down at the ring. "I'd be taking it under false pretenses."

"Damn it, Kathy—" He caught himself, biting down across the words. "I want you to have it," he said roughly, taking the box from her grasp and tugging the ring from its cradle. Catching her left hand, he slipped it onto her ring finger. "I know it doesn't mean a damned thing, but I want you to keep it. Sell it after, if you want. But I want you to have it now."

She looked at him, her eyes uncertain and filled with shadows, but after a moment or two she nodded and set the empty box aside, and Gage felt himself relax slightly. "I didn't get you anything," she said very softly, not looking at him. "Somehow I didn't think you'd want to be reminded..."

I'm reminded of it every time I look at you, he wanted to say. Every time I walk into a room where you've been and smell the perfume still hanging in the air. Every time I get into bed alone at night, and think of you there in the other room so near I swear I can hear your heart beating...

"I didn't expect anything," he said gruffly. "I bought the ring because I figure I owe you something, that's all. You shouldn't come out of this deal with nothing. Consider it an investment for your future, if that'll make it more palatable."

She nodded after a moment, her face still tucked down so he couldn't see her expression, and he found himself wondering how it was possible to share your life with someone and yet still feel so horribly alone.

He raked his fingers through his hair in frustration and swore suddenly, the oath pungent enough to make Kathleen look at him in surprise, and in spite of himself, Gage had to laugh. "Sorry," he muttered wryly. "It's just that I bought the ring to make you happy, not ruin your Christmas."

Something warmed Kathleen's eyes and she smiled, putting her hand lightly on his arm. "You haven't ruined my Christmas at all, Gage. In fact, I was thinking how nice it's been without—" She caught herself. "With just the two of us, I mean. We hardly even talk..." Again, she seemed to catch herself, letting her gaze slide away from his and down to the ring glinting on her hand.

The firelight made her hair gleam like black silk, and Gage gazed down at it, wanting to run his fingers through it but not daring to. This closeness and companionship and sharing was too special to jeopardize with a careless touch.

"It hasn't been easy, has it?" he said suddenly. "Being married like this, I mean."

She shrugged a little too casually. "Not as easy as I expected, I guess." Her gaze met his for a moment, then went back to the ring. "It isn't you," she added very softly. "You've been more than fair. But your family has been . . . difficult."

Gage gave a grunt. "My family's damned near impossible, you mean. My old man can't stand the thought of me running Tanglefoot without his help, and my brothers and Carol are still mad as hell because he gave me the land instead of splitting it up among all of us."

"It makes sense, not splitting up the ranch." She looked at him, and Gage could read what she wasn't saying in her eyes. That he was the only one of the six who actually *wanted* the land, who felt anything for it. That Todd would drink his share away, Gord would lose his in a poker game, Joe would sell his to the highest bidder, Brack would use his to underwrite some questionable business deal, and Carol...well, Carol would use hers to attract another rich husband.

He gave a snort, this one of dry laughter. "Except Tanglefoot's worth millions—the land, anyway."

"Only because of the work you've put into it," she said quietly. "When he gave you the land and the others all that money, Tanglefoot was more of a liability than an asset. You built it up—and now they want it."

It was strange, Gage thought, how easy it was just to sit here in the firelight and talk with her. They were man and wife, yet they hardly knew each other. And for the first time since he'd married her, he had a sense of very real regret for all the things he'd missed. Not just holding her and loving her long into the night, but this, too—the talking, the sharing, the teasing sidelong glances and soft laughter.

The fire crackled lazily, filling the comfortable silence that had fallen between them, and he felt a sudden and unexpected stab of pure loneliness, knowing they'd never be this close again. She was near enough to touch if he dared, and he found himself tracing her profile with his eyes, wondering why he'd never noticed the small, perfect curl of her ear before, or the way her hair fell along the curve of her cheek. She stirred slightly and turned her head, and before Gage could look away, her eyes met his.

They were firelight-warm and as soft as an unmade bed, and Gage felt his heart come to a standstill. It was one of those moments in time that has no measure, a heartbeat on one scale and an eternity on another, and for a moment the room and everything in it seemed to recede and there was just the two of them, man and woman.

Husband and wife.

Gage swallowed and let his gaze move slowly over her small, perfect features. Burnished by firelight, her skin was creamy and flawless, her mouth so lush and moist he swore he could taste it, and without even thinking about what he was doing, he lowered his lips to hers.

He expected her to pull away, but she didn't. Expected an explosion of outraged anger... and got, instead, the delicious sensation of her lips parting invitingly under his, the sweetness of her breath and a swirl of perfumed warmth as she leaned almost imperceptibly nearer.

It occurred to him, as he started to slip his arms around her, that he was asking for serious trouble. But he was relieved and pleased when instead of rearing away she melted into a compliant armful of feminine curves and warmth and softness. Her mouth tasted of cinnamon and brandy, and her tongue curled and moved against his hungrily, sending a flash fire of desire flickering through him.

He didn't even attempt to make sense of what happened over the next few minutes. Didn't remember slipping his hands up under her heavy wool sweater, and yet found his hands filled with warm, silken flesh. Didn't remember pulling her down onto the rug, and yet became dimly aware of lying in a delicious tangle of arms and legs while her slender body moved evocatively and intimately against his.

He heard someone groan and realized dimly that it was his own voice, and he felt more than heard Kathleen whimper in response, knew without even knowing how that it was assent, not denial. And then her small hands were under his shirt even though he didn't remember unbuttoning it, and she was caressing his chest, her fingertips moving with tantalizing lightness around his nipples, and he flinched involuntarily as liquid fire spilled through him, his breath catching on another groan.

If he didn't stop soon he never would. This wasn't any innocent little Christmas Eve kiss, but some very serious foreplay...and things were rapidly progressing to the danger line even while he was thinking about it.

"Kathy..." He wrenched his mouth from hers and held her firmly at bay, his heart going like a trip-hammer and every nerve ending in his body screaming for the touch of her. "This is getting pretty hot, pretty fast, sweetheart. I don't know about your willpower, but mine's threatening to give out any second...."

"Do you want to make love to me, Gage?" she whispered.

She asked it with such quiet simplicity, such sincerity, that Gage could only stare down at her, certain he hadn't heard right. She was silent for a long moment, eyes locked with his, and then she eased herself free of his embrace and sat up. And, without a word, she pulled her sweater up and over her head.

Her hair spilled around her shoulders, and Gage's mouth went dry. She was wearing a lacy peach-colored bra, and he could see the hard nubs of her nipples through the fabric. He stopped breathing as her hand went to the front clasp.

"Don't do this to me unless you mean it, Kathy," he said hoarsely. "Please, Kath . . . don't tease me like this."

The clasp parted soundlessly and her breasts were free. "Touch me," she whispered, reaching for his hand. "Make it real, Gage. Make me your wife. . . ."

And then, after a while, there was nothing but the soft rustle of the flames licking at embers on the hearth and the whispery sound of flesh moving slowly on flesh and the occasional indrawn breath or soft, wordless murmur of pleasure.

And afterward, he held her. Not even bothering to ease himself free of her body, he simply rolled onto his side and cradled her against him. As the tiny aftershocks finally spent themselves and he slipped toward sleep, he smiled against her cheek. Knowing that this was the way it was supposed to be.

And, much later, he handed her the second gift-wrapped box.

"No more rings," she said warningly, her voice only half teasing as she started to untie the ribbon.

"No more rings," Gage assured her dryly. "One engagement per lady is my limit."

Her eyes widened as she slipped the top off the box, and Gage felt a jolt of pleasure at her expression as she lifted the small glass angel from the tissue paper. "Gage, she's beautiful!"

"She reminded me of you." He grinned, loving the delight on her face. "I got you a *real* present—it's under the tree—but this caught my eye and I . . . well, I thought you'd get a kick out of it."

"I love it!" She laughed, her eyes alight with pleasure.

He had to laugh at her, musing, as always, at how she never failed to surprise him. Most women, eyes still aglitter with sapphires and diamonds, would have smiled at the five-dollar glass angel and then set it aside, forgotten. But Kathy acted as though it were the angel and not the ring that was the more precious; the angel, not the ring, that she treasured more.

"I hope you weren't in any hurry for supper," he murmured, tightening his arms around her and drawing her down against him. He ran his hands over her slowly, drinking his fill of the simple pleasure of touching her, and saw by her eyes that she was in no hurry at all.

And a long while later, deep in the slippery heat of her, he watched through desire-slitted eyes as she sat astride him, her lithe body moving like flame over and around him, taking and giving with abandon.

She was his, something sang within him. His to hold, his to keep, and whatever this special thing was that they'd discovered, things would never be the same again.

Chapter Five

"Kathy? Kathleen?"

The voice brought her back into the present with an unpleasant jolt, and she looked up to find Doug looking down at her worriedly. "Oh, hi. Sorry... must have fallen asleep..."

Relief swept over his craggy face. "Have you heard anything yet? Have you seen the doctor?"

She nodded wearily. "They took him into surgery hours ago." Her voice sounded strained and alien, as though it belonged to someone else. "It's not good, Doug," she whispered, her eyes filling. "They... ummm..." She bit her lower lip, trying to steady it. "They don't know if..."

"It'll be all right," Doug murmured, wrapping his arms around her in a huge enveloping hug. "This is Gage Ramsey we're talking about here, Kath—do you really think a little thing like a traffic accident is going to stop him?"

She tried to laugh, not succeeding very well, and Doug released her and looked at her seriously. "I mean it, Kathy. Gage is a fighter, you know that. And a Ramsey. Hell, the medical staff here wouldn't *dare* let him die."

That did make her laugh, finally, and she wiped her eyes with the tissue Doug handed her. "You should go home, Doug. You've been here for hours. It's Christmas Eve, and you should be home with your family. I'll be fine."

"Forget it," he told her gently. "I called Beth a few minutes ago, and her mom finally got there to watch the kids. Beth's on her way down with a thermos of soup and some turkey sandwiches and things that her mother put together for us." He glanced around the room. "Can I get you anything? A blanket? Pillow?"

Kathleen shook her head, and Doug nodded and got to his feet. "Well, I need a sugar fix. I saw a candy machine outside—you want something?"

"No, thanks. I'm fine...."

His smile told her that he thought otherwise, but he just nodded, then headed for the door.

Doug was right. Gage *was* a fighter. But even with the best medical wizardry in the world, a man has to *want* to live. The surgeons would do their best, but in the end, it was up to him and him alone.

"Fight, damn you," she whispered at him, driving her thoughts toward him as though she could somehow infuse the will to live into his very being. "Fight it, Gage Ramsey. You never turned away from a fight in your life—don't you *dare* turn away from this one!"

She looked down at the small glass angel lying in her hand, thinking of those four wondrous days with Gage that Christmas. They'd awakened the next morning to find the storm had blown itself out, and they'd played in the deep snow like kids let out of school, laughing and chasing each other and indulging in all the silliness of new lovers everywhere. In the evenings they would sit by the fire and simply talk, curled up in each other's arms, and then they'd go up to bed and make love long into the night.

If they even made it that far, Kathleen reminded herself with a smile. They'd been drunk with each other for those four magical days, making love where and when the mood hit them, as exhilarated by the freedom of having the place to themselves as they were with the special closeness they'd discovered. In front of the fire, on the big overstuffed sofa in the den, on the kitchen floor with two gray cats looking on in astonishment, on a pile of sweet-scented hay in the barn one afternoon—they hadn't been able to keep their hands off each other.

There had even been that morning when they'd made love in a snowbank, overcome by considerably more passion than common sense as they'd struggled with layers of clothing and half strangling on laughter at the sheer madness of it, not even feeling the cold in the heat of their mutual need. It had been very fast and very good, and as she'd lain in Gage's arms afterward, breathless and flushed, she'd known that nothing would ever be the same between them again.

Kathleen's reminiscent smile faded, and she ran her finger along the angel's wing, tracing the hairline crack where it had been mended. The magic hadn't lasted, of course. Decker had turned up a day later, then the ranch hands and Martha and the others had returned, and life at Tanglefoot had fallen back into its routine.

Almost within hours, Gage had changed. He'd become remote and cool again, distracted by the old tensions between him and Decker, and suddenly the tenderness and laughter was gone. He'd come to her room that night, and for a while Kathleen had thought they might be able to recapture and hold everything they'd felt for the past four days, but their attempted lovemaking had been awkward and self-conscious and they'd wound up arguing instead.

She'd shouted at him to get out finally and he'd gone, his face white with fury as he'd stalked toward the door, and the last thing she remembered of that evening was flinging the glass angel after him and hearing it smash against the closing door.

In the morning she'd looked for the pieces of broken glass, thinking she might be able to glue them back together, but they were gone and she'd presumed that Martha had found them and thrown them out.

Except it must have been Gage who'd found them instead. Gage who'd taken them and had glued them clumsily together again, trying to mend what couldn't be mended. Holding on to the broken bits of glass as though they'd really meant something...

There was a movement at the door to the waiting room, and Kathleen glanced up. Decker was standing there, his face lined and gray, and she suddenly realized how old he looked. Old and afraid. And for a split second it wasn't Decker Ramsey standing there at all, but just a father whose son might be dying.

But then his eyes hardened, and Kathleen felt her sympathy vanish. She stood up, still cradling Gage's coat in her arms. "Have they said anything yet?"

"I didn't think you'd still be here," he rasped.

"You mean you hoped I wouldn't be," Kathleen said crisply. When had she and Decker become such enemies? she wondered idly. Right from the start, probably. Decker ruled the Ramsey clan with an iron fist, demanding absolute fealty, but she'd been the wild card in an otherwise compliant deck, standing up to him at every turn. She was too used to her own father's temper tantrums to turn a hair at Decker's rages, and it had been that as much as his belief that she was behind Gage's rebelliousness that made him dislike her.

"The doctor says it has to be you that signs any papers."

"I'm his wife."

Decker gave a snort. "Seems to me you gave up that right when you walked out six months ago, little lady."

There was no point in arguing with him. No point in trying to explain that she'd left Gage not because she didn't love him, but because she loved him too much. "Did the doctor say anything else? He's been in surgery for hours...."

Decker gave his head a grudging shake, looking uncertain for a fleeting instant, almost frail. Then he rallied, pulling his shoulders back and eyeing Kathleen with his old antagonism. "You turned my boy against me," he said in a hoarse rattle. "A woman oughtn't come between a man and his boy."

"You turned Gage against yourself," Kathleen said, feeling suddenly sorry for him. "You turned the ranch over to him, then refused to let him run it. He's a grown man, Decker, not a boy. It's time you started treating him like one."

"He doesn't know anything about running a ranch! Bringing in them computers, talking with Japanese bankers." Disgust ran through the words. "Man don't need a computer to tell him if the sun's shining or the well's running low. And there's never been a banker yet you could trust."

"It's a new world out there today," Kathleen said wearily, not even having the energy to fight. It was a battle Gage had been waging for the past six years, dragging Tanglefoot into the twenty-first century and fighting Decker every inch of the way.

"Hey, Pop, what did the—" Gord Ramsey stopped dead in the doorway, his florid, jowly face darkening at the sight of Kathleen. Like all the Ramsey boys, he was tall and broadshouldered, but too much rich food, liquor and soft living had thickened him, turning muscle to fat, and the once handsome features were puffy and unhealthy-looking. "What are you doing here?" he demanded belligerently. "Thought Gage had got rid of you once and for all."

He strode across to glare down at her, his breath reeking of bourbon. "I know why you're here, honey, but you can forget any plans you might have of selling Tanglefoot when Gage is dead. That ranch is Ramsey land...and you ain't going to get a finger on it." He smiled unpleasantly. "It belongs to us now. High Mesa, too. And you won't get a penny of it. So don't you even try."

"Your brother is my husband," Kathleen reminded him coldly, refusing to let him see how deeply his words cut. *When Gage is dead...* not *if*, but *when...*

Gord's smile widened. "You might still be married to him on paper," he said softly, "but paper burns, honey. Paper burns."

Kathleen wheeled away, her stomach roiling at the stink of greed and liquor on his breath. He gave a snort of laughter, and a moment later she could hear him and Decker talking, then they walked out together and she was alone.

Her fingers were knotted on the leather sleeve of Gage's jacket, and she relaxed her grip, taking a deep breath. He wouldn't die, she told herself numbly. He wouldn't die.

The voices were still there, nagging whispers on the edge of his mind, but he ignored them, willed them to go away. He'd been dreaming of angels, and he fought to recapture the tenuous images floating through the darkness surrounding him. But they eluded him, drifting away.

And he thought suddenly of the small glass angel he'd bought Kathy that Christmas they'd spent at the ranch alone, remembering the delight on her face when she'd unwrapped it. Remembering coming into her room the night they'd argued and finding it lying broken on the floor.

He'd picked the small shattered thing up carefully and had stood by the bed, gazing down at Kathy. She was sleeping fitfully, her breath still catching now and again on a sob, her cheeks wet with tears. He'd reached out to wipe them away before he'd caught himself. He hadn't even known why he'd gone back to her that night, except at the time it had seemed very important to talk with her. To apologize for the angry words and the impatience and to take her into his arms and recapture the fragile magic they'd woven in those days alone.

But he'd left without waking her, taking the broken angel with him. There hadn't been any point in trying to recapture what wasn't there. Those four days of laughter and sharing and making love hadn't been real at all—they'd just been part of the storm, part of a few stolen days neither would ever refer to again.

It was obvious she was already regretting the impulsiveness that had brought her into his arms in the first place, and he remembered swearing with savage intensity as he'd gone back to his own room, chilled and alone. The truce was over.

The darkness and the pain seemed to well up and over him, threatening to consume him, and he struggled against it, suddenly afraid. Death, always so abstract, seemed suddenly very near and very personal, taunting him with its seductive promise of peace. But he refused to listen, concentrating instead on remembering Kathy's smile, the way her eyes would sparkle in those rare, unguarded moments of laughter, the scent of her skin...

And then there was more darkness, more pain, and he shouted her name into the silence of his mind. Kathy, I need you! Where are you, Kath? Where are you...?

Kathleen came awake with a jolt, Gage's voice still ringing in her ears. She looked around the hospital waiting room stupidly, feeling disoriented and confused, and realized she'd just been dreaming.

She glanced at the big clock over the door, surprised to realize she'd only been asleep for a few minutes. It didn't seem possible that time could move so slowly. Doug had come back and stayed with her for a while, then Beth had arrived with hot soup and coffee and an armful of blankets. She was still there, asleep in a big armchair, and Kathleen decided not to disturb her.

It was easier not having to talk and smile and pretend she was holding up all right. She wasn't holding up worth a damn, and it was sheer exhaustion that was keeping her from flinging herself down and bawling like a baby. That, and the fact she couldn't afford to let the hospital staff think she wasn't up to making any decisions that might have to be made. She was all Gage had, and she wouldn't let him down.

It was like that summer when he decided to break that hammer-headed roan stallion, and had wound up very nearly breaking his neck instead.

It made her smile for some reason, and she pulled Gage's jacket more tightly around her shoulders and closed her eyes, remembering....

She'd been in the kitchen when two of the ranch hands had carried him in, and she'd taken one look at the blood and the glint of shattered bone in his leg and had very nearly fainted on the spot.

But she hadn't. She called the ambulance instead and then made Gage as comfortable as possible, her heart pounding with fear. His face was gray and slick with sweat, but he still managed to give her a reckless grin as he meshed his blood-smeared fingers with hers.

"Don't look so scared, Kathy," he teased, teeth bared in a grimace of pain. "I've been busted up worse than this before. I'll be up and around in no time."

But it had been a lot longer than that. It had taken four hours of surgery just to set the broken bones and sew up the cuts, followed by six days in the hospital, the doctors making certain everything worked normally before releasing him into her care. And then, once home, he was confined to bed until his shattered left leg started to knit.

Confined maybe, Kathleen thought with some annoyance, but hardly tamed. She winced as Gage's impatient bellow rattled down the stairwell, and she exchanged a long-suffering look with Martha, who was putting the finishing touches on a lunch tray for their unwilling—and unhappy—invalid.

"You've been up and down them stairs six dozen times this morning, Miz Ramsey. I'll take this up to Himself if you like—and give him a piece of my mind while I'm at it."

Kathleen had to laugh. "It's going to get worse before it gets better, Martha. He's already tried to get out of bed twice this morning—I finally hid the crutches, so expect a lot more raging before the day's out."

"Damn young fool," Martha muttered, putting a carafe of steaming coffee on the tray. "Hormones, that's what it is. Got too many of 'em at that age, men do—too many hormones, and not near enough brains." She arched an eyebrow. "I got six sons, so I know all about hormones. Fightin' all the time, showin' off, tryin' to prove themselves." She shook her head and pushed the tray across the table toward Kathleen. "Him and Mr. Decker, both. That's why they're at each other like that all the time, each tryin' to be boss. Just hormones."

Kathleen was still grinning as she picked up the tray and headed for the stairs. Some of Gage's irritability might well be an excess of hormones, but most of it was just old-fashioned frustration. He was a physical man, used to being on the go and in the thick of things all day long, and being forced to stay flat on his back and quiet wasn't easy to swallow.

He'd kicked most of the covers off again, and the magazines she'd given him earlier were lying on the floor where he'd flung them angrily. When she stepped into the room he lifted his head like a horse scenting the wind, nostrils flared, and eyed her with hostility. "Sure took your time getting up here, didn't you? I've been calling for fifteen minutes—a man could be *dead* before anyone in this house bothered to check on him."

"You sounded healthy enough," she replied calmly, setting the tray on a table and starting to adjust the sheets. "Sit up so I can plump up these pillows."

"I don't want the pillows plumped, I want my crutches."

Kathleen gave him a sharp look. He was pale and drawn and the hair at his temples was soaked with sweat. "You've been trying to get out of bed again, haven't you! Darn it, Gage, you know the doctor said—"

"I was just trying to get to the damn bathroom," he bellowed in frustration.

"I'll get the bedpan," Kathleen told him matter-of-factly.

Gage gave a bawl of vehement protest, and Kathleen drew in a deep breath. "Fine," she told him with steely calm. "If you don't want *me* to help you, I'll call Martha and—"

"No!" He caught her arm as she started to turn away, his look of alarm very real. "Damn it, Kathy, don't do this to me."

His voice had a touch of pleading in it, and Kathleen paused, realizing how galling it must be for him to have to depend on her and Martha to help him even with this. "All right, all right," she finally said, relenting. "I'll get the wheelchair."

It wasn't easy, but she finally managed to help him out of the bed and into the wheelchair, then she pushed him into the big en suite bathroom and waited outside. There was a series of loud crashes and bangs and enough fiery profanity to singe the wallpaper, but he came out after a few minutes looking considerably happier and even managed a sullen mumble of thanks as she helped him back into bed.

She shook out the pillows and tucked them behind him, then put the lunch tray across his lap. Gage glared down at it. "Soup again? Can't you bring me anything but soup? I'm going to starve to death before this—"

"That's it!" Before she even knew what she was doing, Kathleen had whipped the tray off Gage's lap and had slammed it down on the bedside table. "I've had it with you! I can put up with the occasional bad mood and even an all-out temper tantrum now and again, but I will *not* tolerate this constant complaining and harassment! You're not the only person in this household, you know—there's a whole ranch out there that didn't quit running just because you got hurt. I know you're in a lot of pain and I know you're worried about the ranch, but we're trying to cope as best we can. But from now on you're on your own, mister, because I will *not* be treated like some...some *slave!*" There was a moment of stunned silence, then she turned and stalked toward the door, back rigid.

"Wait—Kath, wait!" There was something in Gage's voice that made her look around suspiciously. He gave her a rueful smile. "Hey, I'm sorry...I know I've been a real pain in the neck. But being cooped up like this is driving me crazy and—'' He shrugged, his grin widening engagingly. "Come on, Kath, don't go. Please? Stay and talk to me.''

"What about?'' Only partly mollified, she took a few grudging steps back toward the bed.

"Whatever you want.'' He held his hand toward her, his smile widening. "Come on, Kath, just sit with me for a little while, please? I get so damn bored up here with nothing but soap operas and the four walls for company. You don't even have to talk if you don't want to. Just keep me company, okay?''

"No more shouting and yelling and ordering me around?''

"Cross my heart,'' he promised, doing just that.

Still eyeing him a bit suspiciously, Kathleen did capitulate long enough to hand him the tray again. "When you're finished, I could give you a sponge bath.''

He glanced up, his expression wary for a half instant. Then he gave her a slow, teasing smile and picked up the soup spoon. "That sounds like it could have possibilities. How about bringing two sponges, and I'll give you one, too.''

It made Kathleen laugh, and she started gathering up the scattered books and magazines as Gage ate his lunch. "You're supposed to be recuperating.''

"What I had in mind would do my recuperative powers a world of good,'' Gage assured her with a chuckle. "It's been a long time since we took a bath together, Kath....''

It had made her blush, Kathleen remembered with a smile. It had been the first time in over six months that he'd made any mention at all of those four wondrous days at Christmas. The first time he'd made any sign he even remembered those long leisurely baths they'd taken together, or the lovemaking that always followed.

"Hey, we may have a problem... this guy's pulse is all over the place...."

"Damn it! Get me a—"

"No. Wait. It's stabilizing...he's stable. Respiration and pressure are okay now. His pulse is still a little erratic...."

"Not surprising, with all the blood he's lost. Are you recommending I continue?"

"Yeah. He's doing okay. Signs are all good. Maybe he was dreaming of his wife... woman like that would make any man's pulse a little erratic."

"Let's stay alert, people. We've still got a lot of work ahead of us..."

Gage hung on to the dream like a drowning man, terrified that if he let go of it he'd go spinning off into that gaping darkness and be lost forever. It was real—as real as the scent of spring coming through the open bedroom window. As real as the look of surprise on Kathy's face when he'd teased her about the bath....

Kathleen looked so flustered and uncomfortable that Gage could have kicked himself. You would think he'd have learned by now not to mention that blasted Christmas weekend! There was a look of sheer panic on her face, as though she was terrified he was going to bring up something she obviously just wanted to forget.

"How are you and Dad getting along?" he asked abruptly, knowing the answer but wanting to keep her even a few minutes longer.

"Okay, I guess."

"Like hell," he contradicted her dryly. "I might have a few ribs stove in, but I'm not deaf. I heard the two of you shouting at each other this morning."

Kathleen put the stack of books down with a bang. "He's impossible! Carl Schumaker wants to buy a couple of Tanglefoot bulls to build up his herd, and Decker has apparently promised him Royal Highland and Comanche Warrior."

"Damn it, those are my two best bulls!"

"I told him that," Kathleen said, the annoyance in her voice matching his. "Just like I told him you're going to send both bulls to every stock show you can book this summer, then use them for breeding. But Decker says you're tying too much cash up in livestock—that it's too big a risk. He wants to sell now and use the money to buy more land."

Gage felt a jolt of familiar anger. "That's what we need—more land! I've got too damned much of it as it is— the taxes alone are killing us, and most of what we have now is too dry to support a rabbit, let alone a healthy grazing herd!" He gestured angrily, forgetting his broken ribs, and the stab of pain made him swear. "Those two bulls can bring in a hundred times their selling price in breeding fees alone over the next couple of years, not to *mention* making the Tanglefoot herd one of the best in the country!"

He swore in frustration, eyeing the closet on the other side of the room. "That damned old man is going to run this place into the ground if I let him," he growled, flinging the covers back and hitching himself toward the edge of the bed. "Get my jeans and a shirt—and those crutches. I'm going to—"

"You're not going anywhere," Kathleen replied emphatically, whipping the sheet and blanket back across his plaster-clad leg so sharply it made Gage blink. "Honestly, you're as pigheaded as he is! You nearly lost your leg, Gage—doesn't that mean anything to you? How much good do you think you're going to be hobbling around Tanglefoot on one leg? I'll take care of Decker."

For some reason, her anger made Gage smile. He grinned at her as she started straightening the pillow behind him, leaning so near he could smell her shampoo. "If I didn't know better, darling, I'd almost think you were worried about me."

"Of course I'm worried about you," she said briskly, not meeting his eyes as she fussed with the pillow. "A one-legged cowboy isn't much use to anyone."

Gage chuckled, and without really thinking about what he was doing he put both hands on her slender waist and tugged her down into his arms. She gave a squeak of surprise and went all stiff and angular, but he hung on to her, wincing as she tried to push herself away. "Careful, darlin'—those ribs you're leaning on don't have much spring left in them anymore."

She stopped fighting him instantly, and the look of concern on her face sent an odd little tingle through him. That, and the way she felt in his arms, soft and feminine and warm. It brought back a flood of memories he'd sworn to forget: memories of how she'd felt in his arms that first time they'd made love, of the sweet scent of her skin, the salty taste of her, the soft intake of breath when he'd finally eased himself down, down into the softness of her....

"Damn it, Kathy, I've missed you." The words were out before he could stop them, but suddenly he didn't care. Didn't care about anything except the lush, warm mouth only inches from his and those wide blue eyes, as soft as suede... And then all the well-intentioned promises he'd made to himself broke with a crash he swore was audible and he was kissing her.

He didn't expect it to last more than a heartbeat, but he didn't care about that, either. Just kissing her—that was the important thing. Having her in his arms and tasting the nectar of her mouth and remembering, even for a flicker of time, what it was like loving her—and having her love him back.

So it caught him a little by surprise when she didn't rear back in anger, and it took him a befuddled moment or two to react to the reality that she was kissing him back. Deliciously. Her mouth moved on his, lips parted in welcome, and when he slipped his tongue between them she shivered very slightly and met its probing caress eagerly.

Then the rest of his good intentions followed the first and he pulled her against him impatiently, ignoring the pain in his broken ribs as he plundered that silken mouth with a groan of relief.

Her tongue flickered against his like flame, consuming him, and then her hands were caressing his face, his hair, and he could feel her heart trip-hammering against his. Desire exploded through him, and then he was wrenching her cotton shirt out of her jeans and fumbling with the buttons until all but one were free, and he simply ripped that one off and pulled the shirt from her shoulders. She shrugged out of it, panting against his mouth, and when he gripped the front clasp of her bra and snapped it roughly, she gave a murmur and pressed herself into his eager hands.

Her breasts were as full and heavy as he remembered, the tips aroused and hard, and she gave a little groan as he caressed them rhymthically with his work-roughened thumbs, her mouth moving hungrily on his. And then, as though suddenly realizing what was going on, she pulled her mouth from his with a gasp.

"Gage, what are we doing . . . ?"

"Making love," he growled, cupping her face in one hand and turning her mouth toward his again.

"B-but we can't!" she protested with a soft laugh. But she made no attempt to pull away, and her hair spilled around his face like sweet-scented water as she nibbled his lower lip. Her hands moved lightly on his bare chest and shoulders, driving him wild. "Gage, this is crazy! Your leg—"

"Won't even be in the way if we're careful," he whispered against her mouth. "Lock the door, Kath. Quick—lock the door."

She giggled and pulled back to look at him, her cheeks flushed, eyes sparkling with mischief. "We can't!"

"We can," he growled. "Now lock the door, then come back over here and let me show you just how good a one-legged cowboy can be when it counts."

He didn't know which one of them was more surprised when she did as he asked, she for doing it or he when she came back to the bed and slipped out of her jeans and panties without even a blush. And in the next moment she was in his arms, naked and satin-warm and so ready for him that even his plaster cast and bandaged ribs provided no more than a momentary awkwardness.

He told her what to do and how to do it in blunt, straightforward English and she came to him willingly, easing her lithe, strong body across his and enveloping him in hot silk. She was so aroused that even that first contact made her groan and buck her hips against him and he gritted his teeth and put his hands on her hips to guide her urgent movements.

It didn't take very long for either of them. To Gage's relief Kathleen didn't even try to hold back, and when she arched against him that last time, biting back a cry of satisfaction, he was there with her only moments later, trying to muffle his own shout of release and pleasure. They lay in a tangle of arms and legs and bedsheets for a long time afterward, even dozing for a while, and when Kathleen finally sat up, scooping her tangled hair back with her hands, she was smiling.

"You weren't in any rush to go, were you?" Gage ran his hands along her shoulders. "The afternoon's young."

"I should," she protested, her cheeks an engaging shade of pink. "I...umm...didn't intend to get so sidetracked."

"I like your bedside manner, lady," Gage murmured lazily. "It's been too long, Kath. There's no reason we couldn't have been like this all along."

She smiled. "It *has* been a little difficult pretending this is only a business arrangement after...well, after Christmas."

"Don't tell me you've been having trouble sleeping, too," he murmured, kissing the corner of her mouth.

"Some." Kathy's blush deepened. "I...umm...have been having dreams. Fairly...explicit dreams."

Gage laughed. "I hope I've been in 'em."

"Oh...yes," she said a little breathlessly. "You have."

"All you had to do was come through that bedroom door and I'd have made them all come true."

"Is that an invitation?"

"Honey," he murmured, "that's an order." He grinned at her and ran a strand of her hair through his fingers. "You know, angel, it's at times like this I have trouble remembering why we're always so mad at each other. Maybe we should try forgetting about the business side of this marriage for a while and start concentrating on the pleasure part.''

Chapter Six

Somewhere, an elevator chimed. Kathleen blinked and looked around, feeling the fear and aching disbelief wash through her again as she realized where she was.

The memories had been so vivid she swore she could taste the sweetness of Gage's mouth in hers, could feel his touch on her skin, and she realized with sudden embarrassment that she was aroused, her body responding to the memories of his lovemaking as vitally as it had to the man himself.

Hot tears spilled, and she pressed her face against the rough sheepskin jacket, hugging it desperately against her as though it were Gage himself, filled with an aching emptiness so vast it threatened to swallow her. It was all her fault, she thought miserably. If she'd kept her promise, he wouldn't be lying in that operating room hovering on the thin edge between life and death. If only she hadn't fallen in love with him!

But she had. She'd been in love with him even before that Christmas they'd come together for the first time, and she'd fallen more in love with him with every passing week. She should have known that it would lead to nothing but trouble—the ease with which she'd tumbled into his bed after his accident should have made *that* clear. It had taken no more than a teasing smile and a kiss and she'd been his, and although the following couple of weeks had been like heaven itself, they'd also been the precursor of the unhappiness that had followed.

They'd spent those two weeks laughing and talking and playing card games and working on jigsaw puzzles and making love like the happily married couple they supposedly were, and for a while Kathleen had actually thought it was going to work out.

She should have known better.

With Gage laid up, Decker had seen his chance to take back control of Tanglefoot—and the dissension between her and the old man had deteriorated into open warfare. She'd tried to protect Gage from the worst of it, and that's where she'd made her biggest mistake. Because when things went from bad to worse, Decker used her as a weapon against Gage and she found herself caught between the two men, a pawn in a power struggle that had been brewing for years. And when it was over and Gage was back on his feet, all the gentleness and laughter and lovemaking was forgotten and the old house was filled with anger and hostility once again.

That's when she knew she had to leave, Kathleen thought grimly, taking a deep breath to fight another spill of tears. She'd simply loved Gage too much to stay. She'd hoped that he might come to love her even a little bit, and when she realized that wouldn't happen, she'd tried to convince herself that it didn't matter. That just being with him was enough.

Except that had been a lie. And she'd decided sometime during that fall that when the time came, she'd walk out the door and put Tanglefoot and Gage Ramsey behind her forever.

But it hadn't been until her father had finally died the following spring, releasing her from the promise that had brought her to Tanglefoot in the first place, that she'd had to face the reality of leaving.

It had seemed as though Gage somehow knew even before she'd told him. In the months following her father's death he'd become withdrawn and silent and moody. He was short-tempered with the ranch hands and uncharacteristically abrupt with Martha, and he hardly spoke or even looked at her, as though just having her underfoot was more aggravation than he could handle.

It shouldn't have mattered, of course. Or, if anything, it should have made leaving easier. But it hadn't. She found herself in tears practically every day over one silly thing or another, and she'd lie awake at night in the loneliness of her room and will him to come to her, to slip into her bed and hold her and ask her to stay. He didn't even have to tell her he loved her . . . just that he wanted her. It would have been enough.

But he hadn't. And finally one day she knew she couldn't live like that anymore, waiting for the love that would never happen, and she told him she was leaving.

Kathleen shivered suddenly and hugged Gage's jacket a little closer. She could hear quiet voices murmuring in the distance, the clatter of a typewriter, a burst of faint laughter. But none of it seemed real. She glanced unwillingly at the big clock on the far wall and drew in a deep, unsteady breath, fighting her fear. Nearly five hours, and still no one had come out to tell her anything. That was good news, wasn't it? Surely if he'd . . . if things had gone badly during surgery, they'd have told her by now, wouldn't they . . . ?

She didn't want to think about it. Everything was going to be all right . . . she had to believe that. Gage was too strong and stubborn and full of life to let go that easily. He'd hang on to life with the same bullheaded tenacity with which he'd tried to hang on to her, standing face to face with death itself with that obstinate Ramsey chin jut-ted out, shoulders squared, blue eyes narrowed and as obdurate as stone.

The image made her smile. No. Gage Ramsey didn't give up *anything* easily. Stroking the lambswool collar of the jacket with absent fingers, she let her head fall back against the cushion and closed her eyes, and remembered. . . .

"No." The word cracked through the room like a gunshot, and Kathleen blinked. Gage's eyes were narrowed and brittle with anger. He faced her with deliberate belligerence, crowding her, forcing her to look up at him. "There's no way you're walking out of this marriage before I'm damned good and ready to let you go, lady," he told her forcefully. "You signed a contract, remember?"

Swallowing, she glared up at him defiantly, trying not to let him see the fear in her eyes. Not of him, but of what he could do. "There is nothing at all faulty with my memory," she said with icy precision, "but I think yours could do with a jump start. The contract was for a limited term. Until Tanglefoot was back on its feet financially, or my father died. Both those terms have been fulfilled. And so is my obligation to you."

"No." Gage shook his head, holding her gaze boldly. "The term was for three years, renewable. We've only been married two and a half. You owe me six months, Kathy."

"I don't owe you a damned thing!" For an instant her anger got the better of her, but she fought with it, bringing herself under control. "Why are you doing this, Gage? You know I married you just to keep Dad from having to sell High Mesa to cover his debts—but it doesn't matter now! If you want High Mesa, you can have it for a fair price and we can go our separate ways."

Something that felt like panic welled through Gage and he struggled with it. He was *not* going to lose her, damn it! Not without a fight. The last two and a half years hadn't been perfect, but there had been a couple of break-throughs when he'd figured they had made real head-way....

"Forget it," he growled, wheeling away from her and stalking back to the big rolltop desk by the fireplace. "You made a deal and I'm holding you to it."

"Gage!"

There was real pain in the cry, and he steeled himself against it, forced himself to sit down and pretend to go through the papers scattered across the desk. It wasn't fair, he knew that. He'd agreed this was strictly a business ar-rangement, no strings attached, but he didn't care. All he knew was that he wasn't ready to give up yet. He wanted Kathleen, wanted her bad, and if he could just keep her there for a while longer he could make her love him, he was sure of it.

If he gave up now and let her go, he told himself grimly, he'd be losing the only woman he'd ever wanted.

He sensed more than heard her come up behind him, soft-footed on the polished hardwood, and braced him-self.

"Gage?" Her voice was gentle. Evocative. "Please, Gage, don't you see that we're only hurting each other with all this pretending? You should be thinking about getting married and—"

"I am married."

"I mean really married," she said with a hint of des-peration in her voice. "You want kids, Gage, you told me that once. And a loving wife...a *real* wife. One who—"

"You are my real wife," he taunted gently. "That mar-riage certificate is as legal as they come, sweetheart."

"Gage, please!" She came to stand beside him, her eyes pleading as they held his. "Why are you doing this to me? You know we don't love each other. You know—"

But you will, he felt like shouting at her. *Damn it, one day you will!* But all he said aloud was, "You're wasting your time, honey. And mine. You're my wife, and you're going to stay my wife until I say otherwise."

"But why me? There are a thousand women out there who'd kill to be married to you, Gage. Why is it so important to—"

"Because you don't want anything from me," he told her point-blank. "Do you know how rare that makes you? You're the only woman I've ever met who didn't give a damn about *who* I am." He smiled grimly. "Maybe I just like the honesty, sweetheart."

"Damn you, Gage Ramsey, I should have known you'd double-cross me! My father always said you couldn't trust a Ramsey any further than you could spit, and he was right!" Eyes snapping with fury, Kathleen spun away from the desk and headed for the door. "If you think you can bully me like you bully everyone else around here, you're crazy. You can keep High Mesa—that's all you wanted in the first place, that damned ranch, so it's yours! I just want my freedom."

Gage swiveled the chair around and leaned back comfortably, planting one booted foot on the edge of the desk. "Try leaving Tanglefoot, honey," he advised her companionably, "and I can guarantee you won't get far."

She stopped. Looked around suspiciously. "And just how do you propose stopping me?"

He shrugged. "You don't have any transportation, for one thing. All the vehicles out there belong to the ranch. That means they belong to me. Take one off the property and I'll have you arrested."

Her eyes widened with indignation. "You wouldn't dare!" But he saw by her eyes that she knew darned well he'd do it. "I'll call a cab."

He smiled lazily. "And what will you pay him with? Witty conversation? The man will want hard cash, sweetheart. And that's one thing you don't have."

"I have money in the bank." Her voice was rough.

"My money. My bank."

He had her. And she knew it. He could tell by the hurt in her eyes that she knew as well as he that she was backed tight into a corner with no way out, and he found himself almost hating how easy it was. "Like I said, Kath. You're mine. And you'll stay mine until *I* decide otherwise."

"I'll find a way," she said in a hoarse whisper, her face riven. "Damn you, Gage Ramsey... I *will* find a way!"

Chapter Seven

And she had, Kathleen mused, rubbing her forehead with her fingers, trying to dislodge the dull ache behind her eyes. It had been her mother's jewelry that had given her the key to freedom. There had been just a few pieces left; the rest had been sold over the years trying to keep the debtors from taking High Mesa right from under her and her father.

They hadn't brought her much, but it had been enough. She'd packed a few things in a bag and had hitchhiked into town, where she'd bought a bus ticket to Denver, and she'd never once looked back. Although she'd wept all the way to Denver, her heart breaking a little more with every mile she put between her and the only man she'd ever loved.

He hadn't come after her.

She'd spent the first week torn between praying he would and praying he wouldn't, but after a while she realized he wasn't going to bother. And tried to convince herself that this was, after all, what she'd wanted.

"Kathy?"

Kathleen looked up wearily to discover Beth standing beside her, her face drawn. "Have they said anything yet?"

Kathleen shook her head, swallowing, and tried to smile.

Beth nodded wearily. "I'm going down to get some coffee. Want a cup?"

"Yeah, all right. Thanks."

Beth smiled and reached down to squeeze her shoulder gently, then she turned and walked toward the door and Kathleen let her eyes stray back to the clock. What could be taking so long! Something must have gone wrong…maybe they just didn't want to break it to her yet. Maybe Gage had died hours ago and—

No. Angrily she got to her feet and started pacing. Gage was not going to die.

The door opened just then and she looked around, her heart in her throat, but it wasn't the doctor she both dreaded and anticipated. Decker gazed at her numbly, his face so drawn and pale that Kathleen felt her heart ache for him.

"Have the doctors said anything to you?" she asked quietly.

He shook his head, looking haunted and lost, and walked across to the sofa so unsteadily that Kathleen wondered for a moment if he was going to make it. He sank into the cushions and rubbed his face with his hands. "It's taking so long," he whispered, his voice ragged. "Why is it taking so long?"

"They said it might be awhile." Kathleen walked across to him and, without really even thinking about what she was doing, put her hand lightly on his shoulder. He flinched, then suddenly he reached up and grasped her hand fiercely, not saying anything. Not even looking at her. "I love him," he said so softly that Kathleen wondered for a moment if she'd only imagined it. "I love my boy."

"I know." She had to swallow, hard, and meshed her fingers with Decker's.

"I'm leaving the ranch," he continued in that ragged whisper. "Buyin' one of the condos in town. A father oughtn't to be trying to tell his son how to run things."

It surprised Kathleen so much she couldn't think of anything to say. And when she finally did reply, it was just to ask where the others were.

"I sent them home." His voice hardened. "Damn useless pups. Gage was the only one who amounted to anything. The only one *worth* anything. And now he's..." The broad shoulders quivered.

"He'll be all right," Kathleen murmured, using the words as she would a prayer. "He'll be all right...."

She didn't even hear the door open a few minutes later, and it was only when a shadow fell across her and she looked up that she realized Dr. Haynes was standing there. He looked gray with exhaustion, shoulders slumped, the green surgical cap soaked with sweat, and as his eyes met hers Kathleen felt the world fall from under her.

"No," she whispered, fighting the scream clawing at her throat. "No..."

"He's alive." He flexed his shoulders and wearily pulled off the cap, rubbing his eyes. "It went well, I think. But we won't know for certain until he regains consciousness. He's in recovery now and his vital signs are all good. But I won't lie to you, Mrs. Ramsey. It was pretty bad, and it could get worse. We had a couple of close calls, but he's got the constitution of a bull—and a strong will to live. He called your name a couple of times when he was coming out of the anesthetic. I think he's hanging on to that somehow."

"Can I see him?"

His eyes slid to Decker. "I'll let one of you in for a few minutes. But just one."

Decker looked at the doctor calmly. "Kathleen should be with her husband," he said quietly. "A wife's place is with her man."

Even braced for it, Kathleen felt a rush of horror as Haynes led her into the small, curtained-off room. Gage lay as still as death, his tanned face sallow against the crisp white pillow and the swath of dressings across his forehead. A battery of monitors flickered and purred on one side, and she stared at the strong, regular tracing of Gage's pulse, cheered slightly by the rhythmic electronic heartbeat that was the only sound.

It took a moment to convince herself that the ruggedly handsome features under the tubing and dressings really belonged to Gage. He was too still, too quiet, and she found herself holding her breath, half expecting those bold blue eyes to flick open and that strong mouth to cant upward in a lazy smile.

She walked around to the side of the bed where someone had placed a chair and sat down, reaching instinctively for the sunbrowned hand lying so still against the sheet. It was surprisingly warm, and she slipped her fingers between his, trying desperately not to cry.

"You can't die, Gage," she managed to whisper, her voice breaking on a sob. "I love you, damn it. I love you!"

He dreamed he heard a woman weeping. He was in a long corridor, and it was dark and very cold, and he was afraid. The whispering voices had gone finally, and with them, the pain. There was nothing now. No sensation, no voices, no anchor to anything that might be called reality.

Nothing but the cold and the loneliness and the fear.

And then he heard her. Kathy. She was calling his name, and he turned awkwardly in his dream and saw her at the end of the corridor, all golden skin and female warmth, her eyes bright with tears. She called his name again and reached toward him, and in that instant the fear vanished.

He should have known he could count on her. Should have known that she'd come after him in this dark, cold place; find him and lead him back into the light.

* * *

He felt like hell.

Gage stared at the ceiling and took a deep, experimental breath, sensing more than actually feeling the pain lurking just on the edge of consciousness. Drugged within an inch of his life, by the feel of it. And a damned good thing, too, by the shape he appeared to be in.

What the *hell* had happened? All he remembered was a swirl of snow, then the flare of brake lights in front of him. Remembered swearing as he tried to swing around the stopped car. The truck had started to roll, he remembered that. Then . . . nothing.

Probably just as well. Whatever had happened, it must have been bad.

He wriggled a couple of fingers and a toe or two, relieved to discover that he didn't seem to be missing anything important and what was still there appeared to be more or less in working order.

He contemplated trying to sit up, then dismissed the idea. Judging by the number of tubes and intravenous bags and clicking bits of machinery involved, he must be busted up pretty bad. And painkillers, he knew from experience, wore off.

He did turn his head, however, and gaze down at the dark-haired woman sitting beside him. She'd rested her arms on the bed and had laid her head on them, and she was asleep now, her cheeks lightly flushed, the thick lashes still damp with tears.

She had been crying. For him.

He felt a tightness pull up inside him, filling his throat, and he carefully moved his hand to cup her head gently. Just seeing her again made his heart soar. He'd missed her so bad these past six months he'd been crazy with it, and he ached to gather her into his arms and tell her what a fool he'd been. To tell her everything he knew now to be true—that he loved her, and always had.

I love you, Gage. I love you.... The words still filled him with their magic, and he felt himself grinning like a six-teen-year-old. That's why she'd left—not because she hated him, but because she'd loved him. Because she couldn't bring herself to stay with a man she thought couldn't love her back.

Kathleen came awake with a little start, disoriented and groggy, wondering how long she'd been asleep. She hadn't intended to, but she'd just put her head down for a few minutes and...

What if something had happened to Gage during those stolen few minutes? Furious with her carelessness, she sat upright and scanned the monitoring equipment, not having a clue what she was looking at but finding all the glowing green lights and rhythmic scans somehow reassuring.

And it was only then that she realized Gage was awake. Not just awake but obviously aware of his surroundings. His deep blue eyes were filled with gentle teasing as they met hers.

"Hey, sweetheart." His voice was no more than a hoarse rasp, but he managed a lopsided smile. "Kind of messed up Christmas, didn't I?"

She gave a gulp of laughter. "Gage! How long... when...?"

"A little while ago." He swallowed painfully. "I was just lying here trying to convince myself that you were really here."

A feeling of relief swept over her like a tidal wave, so strong it left her light-headed. "Damn it, Gage, you s-scared me to death!" Tears spilled and she wiped at them furiously, trying valiantly to steady her chin. "I should call someone and—"

"No. I don't want to see anyone else. I just want to look at you for a while...."

She was blubbering like a complete idiot, but she couldn't help it, and she started laughing through the sobs, wanting to do nothing more than fling herself into his arms. But she settled for rummaging through her pockets for a tissue and blowing her nose instead, still giving a hiccuping little sob now and again. She wanted to tell him she was sorry and to tell him she loved him and that she'd never been so scared in her life, not knowing if he was going to live or die. Wanted to tell him so much.

But all she said was, "It was crazy to be out driving in weather like this! You could have killed yourself and—"

"You're the most beautiful thing I've seen in a long while, Kathy. I've missed you."

"I—I've missed you, too."

"What happened?"

"You lost control of the truck trying to avoid a rear-end collision with a stalled car, and it rolled . . . you wound up in the other lane, right in front of an oncoming tanker." She shivered. "The highway patrol said it was a miracle you weren't killed outright."

He gave a grunt. "How bad am I broke?"

She let a smile brush her mouth, relieved at having at least some of the old Gage back. "Bad enough that it took nearly five hours to put you back together."

He grunted again. "Hope they didn't have too many bits left over when they were finished. I don't trust these hot-shot big-city doctors."

"Dumb question, but how do you feel?"

"Like I got hit by a tanker," he quipped. He let the careless smile fade and squeezed her fingers gently, letting his gaze move slowly, wonderingly, over her face. "It *was* crazy, setting out in this kind of weather, but I had to see you, Kath."

"See me?" She blinked. "You were coming to see me?"

He managed another reckless smile. "Of course. Why the hell else would I be out risking my neck in weather like this?" He gave her fingers another squeeze, then released them and looked at her seriously. "I had a Christmas present for you, angel. I could have sent it, I guess, but I wanted to give it to you in person. Guess it's gone now, though. I'll have to—"

"It's here." Kathleen reached down and retrieved the silver-and-blue box from the floor beside her chair. "The highway patrol found it and brought it in with you. And this..." She held her hand out to show him the glass angel. "You kept it."

He shrugged a little too casually. "She always reminded me of you, sweetheart." He touched the glass wing with a fingertip, smiling faintly. "Funny, I was dreaming of angels awhile ago. This one, anyway. I dreamed I was back there at the ranch with you the Christmas I gave her to you."

Kathleen glanced up at him, her heart giving a little thump, and he smiled again, roughly this time. "Wishful thinking, I guess. I had other dreams, too. About that afternoon at Fireweed Creek—I could have sworn I was back there with you again, it was so real. And that time I broke my leg trying to halter-break that roan and you brought my lunch up one day and got mad, and we wound up making love all afternoon."

Kathleen felt a tingle run down her spine. It was impossible, of course. Just coincidence. And yet... "It's funny, but I was thinking about those same things while you were in surgery. Daydreams, almost. But so vivid...like that afternoon I made the angel cookies and you helped me ice them. I could almost taste the icing.''

"Then later that night, sitting in front of the fire." His eyes caught hers, and she could see he was remembering what had happened afterward, too. "Can people share dreams?'' he asked softly.

"Maybe if they try hard enough," she replied just as softly.

"What time is it?''

"Time?" Frowning, she looked down at her watch. "A little after two, why?''

"It's Christmas. You can open your present.''

She laughed quietly. "Sitting here talking to you is enough of a present. I don't need anything else.''

"Open it.''

She started to protest, then saw by his expression that he wouldn't be put off. If she had any sense at all she'd be calling for the doctor, but she decided a few more minutes wouldn't hurt. She could tell by his eyes that the drugs were starting to kick in again and he was having to fight just to stay awake, and suddenly it seemed very important to do as he wanted. There would be plenty of time later for the doctors.

"I can't imagine why you couldn't just mail it to me,'' she muttered as she pulled off the wrapping paper. "What could possibly be so important that you had to risk your life to—" She stopped dead as she lifted the lid of the box and stared down at the contents.

It took her a moment to fully understand what she was looking at, and even then it made no sense. Frowning, she drew out the diamond-and-emerald ring. The amethyst earrings. The double strand of pearls.

"Mother's jewelry." The jewelry she'd pawned six months ago when she'd walked away from Tanglefoot without a penny to her name, telling Gage she'd rather starve than live under his roof for another minute. "But...how?" She lifted her eyes to look at him and found him watching her, his expression wary.

He smiled roughly. "Not a hell of a lot goes on around here that I don't know about, sweetheart. The owner of the pawn shop called me the day you took them in. I picked them up a couple of days later."

He frowned suddenly and looked down at the box in her hands. "I know how much they meant to you. It didn't seem right, somehow, that you had to sell them just to get away from me."

"Oh, Gage." Tears filled her eyes again and she blinked, swallowing hard, refusing to give in to them.

"I was wrong, Kath," he said quietly. "I grew up thinking that being a Ramsey meant you could have anything you wanted, but I was wrong. You have to *deserve* the things that count. And I didn't deserve you."

"Gage, please..." Her voice was choked.

"There's more." He gestured toward the box. "In that envelope on the bottom."

Blinking her eyes clear, Kathleen tugged the envelope from the box. It had been folded lengthwise to fit, and she fumbled with it, half blinded by tears, but finally got it open. There was a slender sheaf of papers inside, and she drew them out. They'd been torn in half, and she frowned, unfolding them.

"I had no right trying to keep you in a marriage you didn't want," Gage said softly. "I want you, Kath. But not like that."

Kathleen's face felt numb. She gazed down at the papers in her hand uncomprehendingly, wondering what kind of a cruel joke he was playing on her. And then, slowly, realizing it wasn't a joke at all. "Our marriage contract," she whispered.

"I love you, Kathy. Too much to keep you captive in a marriage you don't want." He was silent for a long moment, and Kathleen just stared at the torn documents in her hands.

"But I thought . . ." She lifted her gaze to meet his.

"That it was just business?" Gage smiled ruefully. "Hell, lady, you were never just business. You were Brue Langford's daughter—I knew I didn't have a chance of ever marrying you for real. So I settled for a few years with you and hoped you'd come around sooner or later and learn to love me. Except you didn't. And then I realized I'd fallen in love with you but couldn't admit I'd broken my promise to you."

"And I was scared to tell you for the same reason."

"I've wanted you since that day down at Fireweed Creek," he murmured. "If there'd been any other way, I'd have done it, Kathy. Would you have married me if I'd come right out and asked?"

She looked at him, thinking about it. "No. Not while my father was alive. Your family wouldn't have stood for it, either. As it was, Decker only agreed because it meant getting High Mesa away from my father."

"I love you, Kathleen."

Kathleen smiled sadly, looking at the sundered documents in her hand. "We've wasted so much time."

"Did you hear what I said, Kathy? I said I love you."

She had to smile at the impatience in his voice. He might still have one foot on death's doorstep, he might even be willing to finally put his heart on the line and tell her he loved her, but he was still the old Gage, hating to be kept waiting, even for this.

"I heard you," she teased.

"Well?"

"Well what?"

His eyes smoldered. "You said you loved me a little while ago, damn it! Would it kill you to tell me again?"

Kathleen tried to fight the smile that was threatening to break loose. "I thought you were dying, Gage. Not to mention unconscious. A woman says all sorts of rash things when she thinks a man might be dying."

His gaze darkened dangerously. "Kathy . . ."

She laughed aloud, leaning down to kiss his stubbled, dry cheek. "I love you, Gage Ramsey."

"Enough to marry me?"

She smiled. "We are married, remember?"

But Gage was looking at her seriously. "I mean properly, Kath. No deals, no strings. Just you and me and a church and forever. The way it's supposed to be." He smiled wistfully and reached up to stroke her cheek with the back of his hand. "Tell me you'll marry me, Kathy. Again."

"Yes," Kathleen breathed, and as she lowered her mouth to brush her lips across his, she could have sworn she saw the little glass angel smile. "And I think this time we just might get it right. . . ."

*   *   *   *   *

Author's Note

I've always loved stories set around Christmas. Part of it, I guess, stems from the fact that I'm a hopeless romantic, and part of it is because, for me, Christmas has always been a special time—a time of magic and wonder and generosity, a time when the true spiritual meaning of love is remembered and when anything is possible.

As well, I've always thought that Christmas is a time for renewal, when we're surrounded by old friendships, old traditions and old memories, and we take time from a busy year to reflect about what is truly important in our lives . . . and to remind ourselves that of all the gifts this season brings, love is by far the warmest to give, the richest to receive and the most precious to share.

So what better time than Christmas to find lost love and reaffirm that magic we all carry in our hearts?

I've told Gage and Kathleen's story mainly through memories, because memories have always seemed part of Christmas, too. It's a perfect time to remember things and places and people we've known and perhaps loved. Perfect also to count blessings that we sometimes—in the hustle of everyday living—forget to appreciate.

And so, from my house to yours, I wish you the very merriest of Christmases. And may the coming year be filled with an abundance of joy and love, serenity and contentment, good health and prosperity for all.

Naomi Horton

THE CHRISTMAS BRIDE

Heather Graham Pozzessere

A recipe from Heather Graham Pozzessere:

SISTER SLOAN'S PINEAPPLE-CHEESE CHRISTMAS CASSEROLE

This recipe I got from my sister, who got it from my brother-in-law's sister, Sloan. It was the highlight of the table this year, sweet and tart and different!

2 large cans pineapple chunks
2 cups shredded cheddar cheese
1 cup sugar
6 tbsp flour
1 tube (3 doz.) Ritz crackers, crushed
4 oz butter, melted

Preheat oven to 350° F.

Mix together pineapple and cheese. Set aside. Mix together sugar and flour. Add to the fruit and cheese mixture. Spread mixture in an 8″ × 11″ or a 9″ × 12″ casserole dish. Spread crushed crackers over top. Pour melted butter over all.

Bake for 35 to 40 minutes. Let cool and serve.

Serves 12.

This dish is good hot or cold, so leftovers, if you're so lucky, are a snap.

Chapter One

"And what would you like for Christmas, little girl?" Cary Adams asked. She leaned forward at the table, resting her chin whimsically on her hands as she asked her friend June Harrison the question. Cary's hair, a sleek and shimmering brown, curved around her delicately boned features, and her eyes, a tawny hazel that glittered when she laughed, were as wide and innocent as a child's. Well, it *was* Christmas. Nearly.

"It's not a 'what,' but a 'who,' " June replied with a laugh. "His name doesn't matter. He just has to be tall, dark and handsome. And rich," she added as an afterthought. She grimaced. "It's not that I'm a material girl, but it *is* a material world."

Cary grinned and leaned back. She wagged a finger at June. "Not fair. I can't get you a man for Christmas."

"No? Well, I wasn't expecting one, anyway. But you, Mrs. Adams, deserve one. And he *should* be tall, dark and handsome. And rich."

"What if I prefer a blond?"

June shook her head. "No, I'm sorry. The saying is 'tall, dark and handsome.' Take it or leave it."

Cary laughed and looked around the room.

Despite the fact that it was always held indecently early—at barely a week after Thanksgiving—Cary loved the annual office family Christmas party. She loved the music, the colorful lights, the scent of the holly branches, pine and candles, and today she even loved the snow that was piling up on the sidewalks and streets.

There was another Christmas party held at the *Elegance* office every year, always the night before Christmas Eve. But today's party was Cary's favorite. It was held for the families of the employees. Husbands, wives, children, grandparents and even a few cousins managed to finagle invitations. Every year Jason McCready, the publisher of *Elegance,* rented the ballroom of one of the most prestigious hotels in Boston, and it was pure joy to see toddlers and teens running amok among the handsomely tuxedoed waiters. Champagne, eggnog, beer and wine poured freely for the adults, and Christmas punch—bright red for the season, of course—was in abundance for the underage crowd. There were drawings for huge turkeys and hams, and there was a main prize, too, a microwave oven, a television set, a video recorder or the like. Always the latest, always something that someone would really want. Jason McCready, for all his eccentricities, planned Christmas well for his employees. Everybody went away with something, for there was a draw that he called the seasonal exchange. Each employee drew a name from a hat, someone with whom to exchange a gift. Not that it mattered what McCready called it, for everyone in the office joined in his Christmas party, regardless of their religious beliefs. It was all done with tremendous warmth and goodwill, and though the hall was adorned with a giant Christmas tree and someone was always elected to hand out toys to the children, McCready saw to it that the beautiful and ancient Hanukkah songs were also played, and no one's beliefs were trodden on.

"Hey, kid, you're awful quiet! This is a party, a celebration, remember?"

Cary blinked, then smiled. June, of the magazine's advertising salespersons extraordinaire, was staring at her pointedly. June was her senior by about five years. At first Cary had resented being called "kid" all the time, but she had quickly learned that June used the word with affection. After a rocky start, the two had become best friends.

"I was just thinking," Cary said.

"Horrors!" June murmured in mock protest. She was a striking woman with a headful of wild platinum hair and soft gray eyes. She had the type of figure that might well have once graced the inner pages of a magazine centerfold, but she was as smart as a whip and knew her business backward and forward. June stirred her Irish coffee. "What were you thinking about? Men?"

"No. Actually, yes. One man. I was thinking that McCready throws a fabulous party—especially since he is...McCready," Cary finished a little lamely.

June smiled and shrugged, and Cary knew her friend understood her completely. Jason McCready was a good-looking man—definitely tall, dark and handsome—and he was very young for his position, still a year shy of forty. But it was said that he had been a dynamo in his early twenties—bright, energetic and full of the ideas that could turn a dying biweekly into a respected glamour magazine. *Elegance* had a section on the finest homes in America, an entertainment division, a special section devoted to current politics and one to current affairs. And there was the "American World" column, Cary's own baby, full of insights into people and more personal events. The magazine had a contemporary flair along with the old, traditional values that were intangible and yet all important. And that was Jason McCready's doing.

He was the publisher, and he was also the president of the board. He was an American success story, and years back, long before Cary had come into the business, he had often graced the covers of various other news-oriented magazines. She could remember one photograph in particular, taken when he had been at Rockefeller Plaza with his wife.

Oddly enough, Cary reminisced, it had been a Christmas photograph. And she could remember it so clearly. The huge annual tree had risen behind them, the ice rink had stretched out before them, and New York had been decked out in a fabulous display of colorful lights. Mc-Cready had been in a long black coat that had accented his dark good looks, and his strong, decidedly masculine profile. His wife, Sara, had been in the softest white mink, a complete contrast to him with her feathered white-blond hair and eyes so blue that, even in the picture, their color shone with an almost unreal light. They had been smiling at one another in that picture, the look on Sara's beautiful face one of adoration. And he had gazed at her with a tenderness that was somehow shattering to the observer; one could almost touch it. They had been so stunning, a fairy-tale couple.

The next year, though, Cary knew, Sara McCready had been dead before Christmas.

And Jason McCready had never consented to another interview. Cary had thought to do one for their own magazine. It had been one of the few times she had actually spoken with him.

And he had nearly jumped down her throat.

She could still remember the occasion in his office. She had made an appointment with his secretary, had gone in fully prepared and with a truly intelligent presentation.

She had walked into his sparse office. White-walled, peach-carpeted, two prints on the wall, a massive oak desk, a leather sofa, two chairs.

He had never even asked her to sit.

He had remained behind his desk, his lime green eyes
sharp and cold and so pointedly on her that she'd felt as if
steel blades were stabbing her. He had listened for at least
sixty seconds before the pencil he had held idly between his
fingers suddenly snapped. Then he'd stood, rising to his
full, imposing six-three, and walked around the desk to
stand before her. She had nearly cowered, when his palms
touched her shoulders. Hard. Forcefully. But not violently.

And he had issued one harsh word to her. "No!"

He had stood there staring at her, a strand of his usually impeccable black hair falling over one of his deadly
dark eyebrows. His bronze features had gone tight and
white, and the fullness of his mouth had been compressed
into a grim line. He'd stared at her as if she were an ancient enemy, and she had wanted nothing so much as to
run.

It wasn't courage that had kept her standing there—she
was simply too surprised to move. And at last his hands
dropped from her shoulders and he turned away. "I said
no, Miss Adams—"

"It's Mrs. Adams," she'd interrupted, fighting the tears
that welled in her eyes, wondering why it should matter at
this particular time that she make such a point about her
name.

"*Mrs*. Adams. Excuse me," he said coldly. He walked
around the desk and sat again, with something like an air
of royalty about his designer-suited form. "Could you
leave now, please? I'm busy, and this interview is over."

She stiffened her shoulders, certain that not only had he
refused her, but that he had also fired her. "I can have my
desk cleared out by five," she said flatly. "I shall expect to
see a severance check just as promptly."

Only then did his dark brows arch and a look of fleeting surprise pass over his hard and handsome features. "Why on earth should you clean out your desk, Mrs. Adams?"

She hadn't wanted to falter, but she had. And she knew that crimson flamed in her cheeks. "Mr. McCready, it certainly sounded as if you were annoyed and no longer cared to employ me."

"I *am* annoyed, Mrs. Adams, but I do not fire people simply because they annoy me upon occasion. I find your work excellent. I merely wish that you would vacate my office and refrain from mentioning such an article in the future."

She was still staring at him blankly. She had often wondered if the man read anything that went into the magazine anymore. Apparently he did.

"Is there anything else, Mrs. Adams?"

"No!" she exclaimed. But she didn't move, and she was stunned to hear herself speaking again. "Mr. McCready, this is your own magazine! Why won't—"

He was on his feet again. And, oddly enough, she felt as if she had his attention. Really had his attention, and not just his anger.

"Because I cannot talk about my personal life, and that is that! Do you understand?"

"All right," Cary agreed. He was still staring at her. She felt tremors, hot one minute, cold the next, racing along her spine.

For the briefest moment she saw what might have been a glimmer of anguish in his eyes. And she knew, intuitively, that he was thinking about his wife. He had nothing to say without her in his life anymore.

"I'm sorry—" Cary began.

"Don't be!" he interrupted her.

The words were soft, the emotion behind them vehement. And Cary found herself speaking again despite them. "Mr. McCready, you loved her very much. I can see that. I'm sorry. So very sorry. But you're not the only one who has ever lost someone they love. Perhaps the article is a bad idea. But you should talk to someone. You should..."

Her voice trailed away. He was staring at her with ice-cold fury in his eyes.

"Are you quite finished, Mrs. Adams?"

She nodded. His life was none of her business.

"Perhaps you'd like to get back to work then?" he suggested pleasantly.

She spun. She did not thank him for his time. He hadn't willingly given her any. And she didn't need to thank him for not firing her. Her work was good; that was what mattered. He just wanted her out of his office.

"Mrs. Adams!"

She looked at him.

"I beg your pardon," he said. "I really do beg your pardon." His voice was soft. And, seated behind his desk, his hands folded, his hair so dark and his eyes so startlingly green, he was striking—and more. He was appealing. She gritted her teeth, startled at the temptation to walk to him and slip her arms around him. To offer him some comfort.

It was an illusion. McCready wanted nothing from her. And there were no weak links in his armor. He just wanted her to leave his office.

She obliged him.

And she had never ventured back in.

"He still throws a very nice Christmas party," she commented idly, then cast June a mischievous smile. "Almost as if he still believed in the Christmas spirit. Ho, ho, ho."

"You almost make it sound as if you still believe in it yourself," June said sagely, eyeing her friend across the table.

Cary felt as if her heart slammed against her chest, and it was suddenly difficult to breathe. That hurt. She tried. She tried very hard every Christmas. She had learned to smile and laugh a lot. For her family, if not for herself. She had done very well, or so she had thought.

She had gotten past the shock and the agony and the feelings of utter rage, of helplessness. She had found her own apartment, she had become independent and she had managed to build a new life, filled with her son's school activities, her work and visits to her in-laws and her family. It wasn't in the least fair that June should attack her about her Christmas spirit.

But June wasn't really attacking, nor was she going to persist in that vein. She tossed her wild mane, licked her swizzle stick and used it to point toward the large, intricately decorated cardboard house where Santa was seeing to the little ones. "Jeremy is playing Santa this year, isn't he?" she asked.

Cary nodded. "Padded to the gills, complaining black and blue and having the time of his life. Danny should be just about up to him now. I wonder if he'll recognize Jeremy."

"Let's go see," June suggested.

They rose and threaded their way through the gaily dressed crowd, stopping to call a greeting here or there. Just as they reached the line leading into the house, Cary came to a halt, smiling. It was just about Danny's time to go in to talk to Santa. The little girl in front of him had just been escorted through the bright red curtains. Through a tiny crack in the cardboard, Cary could see Jeremy give

Santa's long-legged and beautiful helper a little pinch where the short-skirted elf outfit left her thigh bare.

"Santa is a lech," she told June with a sigh.

"And Isabelle loves every minute of it, I'm sure," June assured her.

Isabelle, Santa's helper, was the newest college student to take a job in the mail room. And her smile clearly indicated that she was having a good time.

Danny, Cary's eight-year-old son, turned suddenly, sensing that she was there. His freckled face broke into a wide grin at the sight of her, and she felt a sudden, quick pounding of her heart. Danny looked so much like his father. The clear, sky-blue eyes, the blond, almost platinum-streaked hair, the pale spatter of freckles over the bridge of his nose. He was a cute kid, she knew, not just because he was her own. Most kids were cute, she assured herself, but with Danny, it was more. There was something about his eyes...a wisdom in them. Even a compassion. Danny had never grown bitter, even when he had understood what had happened to his father. He had only cried.

He still cried at night, sometimes.

But he had never allowed his father's death to warp his feelings toward others, or even toward life. He had grown older long before his time. Yet it had given him a charm and a sense of responsibility, rare for his age. Talking to Danny was sometimes like talking to a teenager or a young man ready for college.

"Mom! Come on up!" he called to her.

"Go on," June told her. "I'll wait for you by the exit from Santa's hut."

Cary grinned. "All right. I want to get a peek at Danny with Santa if I can, and see if Jeremy holds up."

June nodded. Cary excused herself, as she wended her way through the parents and children to reach Danny. Isabelle offered her a wide friendly smile. "Hi, Mrs. Adams. Is this one yours?" she asked, indicating Danny.

Cary nodded. "He is. Danny, this is Miss Isabelle LaCrosse. She works with us now. Isabelle, my son, Daniel."

Danny solemnly shook hands. "And I thought you were really an elf!" he said with a soft sigh.

Startled, Isabelle stared at Cary, who shrugged, hiding a smile. "He likes elves," she explained lamely.

Isabelle peeked behind the curtain. "I think Santa is ready for you, Daniel. Come on in. Mrs. Adams, if you'd like..."

Cary saw a break in the red curtain where she could discreetly spy on Santa and her son. She offered Isabelle a wide, engaging smile and slipped closer while Danny marched in to sit on Santa's lap.

"Well, ho, ho, ho, it's Mr. Daniel Adams, so it is!" Santa said. Cary watched her son's eyes widen with surprise as Santa addressed him so familiarly.

Jeremy, she decided, was perfect. He was padded wonderfully, and the suit was great. A big snowy beard covered his chin, with a swooping mustache attachment that hid the whole lower half of his face. The red and white Santa hat fell over his forehead, and little gold spectacles sat on the tip of his nose.

"Yes, sir, Santa," Danny said with a certain awe. He had told Cary that he had no intention of sitting on Santa's lap, that he was a big boy. He had meant to stand and talk to Santa man to man.

But he was quickly up on Santa's lap, and he seemed to have no idea at all that he was talking to his mother's cousin.

"I know that you've been just as good as gold this year, Danny. So tell me, what would you like for Christmas?"

Danny hesitated. Cary frowned, watching him. "What would I really like for Christmas?" Danny asked softly.

"Yes, son, of course. What would you really like for Christmas?"

"I believe in Santa, you know," Danny said quickly. "I believe in God and Santa and miracles, especially Christmas miracles. And I know you can help me, Santa—Mr. Claus, I know you can!"

"Danny, I—"

"I'd like a father, Santa. Oh, not a real one! I know you can't bring my dad back. He lives up in heaven, with God, because he was a great dad. God can't give people back once he takes them. And it isn't for me. I'd like someone for my mom. She tries not to show it, but she's so unhappy, and I can see it. I don't think she knows I can see it, but I do."

"Danny—"

"She's a great cook, and a good housekeeper. She makes neat chocolate chip cookies. And she's a writer. She writes all about other people who need help, and sometimes the things she writes get help for them. She's been really good, Santa. Please."

She felt her heart—she could have sworn that she actually felt her heart—swelling. Tears welled behind her eyelids, and she almost choked on them. She swallowed. Hard. A smile slowly curved her lips. I love you, Danny, she thought.

"Look Danny," Santa said, managing to interrupt him at last. "I—I'd like to make you a promise, but I can't. You see, grown-ups have to—well, they have to find people that they like themselves sometimes."

"I know you can help me," Danny said stubbornly.

Santa opened his mouth, then closed it. Danny had a stubborn streak in him. And this Santa knew it very well.

"I'll tell you what, Danny. I'll see what I can do. But that's not an easy Christmas order. It's absolutely the hardest. You may have to give me more than one Christmas to fill that wish, all right?"

"But you'll work on it?"

Santa sighed. "I've *been* working on it," he muttered, then smiled. "Of course I'll work on it. Hard. I promise."

"Thank you," Danny said simply. "I'll help you. I'll wish on the North Star every night."

Santa nodded. "And what about this Christmas?"

"Oh, well, I'd like that computer made especially for kids my age. The one they have at school."

Cary almost muttered an expletive out loud. Danny would never say he wanted anything. And now he was asking for something she could never afford. She knew the computer he was working with at school. It was a wonderful invention, with talk-it-through word processing and talk-it-through graphics for math and art projects.

I'll bet I could even straighten out my income taxes with it, she thought wryly.

But, unlike many other computers, this one had yet to come down in price. The whole outfit cost thousands, and she didn't know if she could manage the payments even if she bought it on time.

Jeremy obviously didn't know the price of the computer. "That's easy!" he assured Danny. "I can definitely work on that one!" He set Danny on his feet and reached into the big red bag by his high black boots. "For the moment, my boy, I've got a remote-control car for you, how's that?"

"Great, Santa!" Danny said. "It's great, honest, just great. And thanks, thanks a lot."

Danny escaped through the curtain, Jeremy started to summon Isabelle to lead in the next child when he happened to look up and notice Cary standing there. He stared at her for a second, then crooked his finger toward her.

"Come here, Cary Adams!" he commanded.

She stepped forward. "Sorry, I was eavesdropping. I couldn't quite—"

She managed to swallow a little squeal as he wound his arms around her and pulled her onto his lap.

"I hear you've been a very good girl," he told her, and winked.

"Would you quit that, you lech, I'm your cousin!" she protested, laughing.

"Second cousin," he reminded her, and sighed.

"Close enough, so behave."

"Well, you heard your son, Mrs. Adams," he told her. "He wants someone for you. And I've tried and tried—"

"Jeremy, you're a dear, and I love you with all my heart, and you know it. And you know, too, that you aren't a bit serious about me—"

"I could be, if you would just get over this relative bit," he said jokingly.

"Jeremy—"

"What about that electrician who was built like a body-builder?" he demanded darkly.

She had to smile. "Sorry. He wore his boxer shorts up to his boobs."

"The lawyer from Concord?"

"He was cross-eyed, I swear it."

"Cary," Jeremy told her sternly, "no one is going to be Richard. That lawyer was not cross-eyed."

She caught her breath and stared into his eyes, seeing his concern and love. She exhaled slowly. "I know no one will be Richard, Jeremy. Honestly, I know that. But he—he would have to live up to Richard, can you understand that?"

He started to nod then maybe he realized that she was very close to tears, so he shook his head vehemently. "Mrs. Adams, your boy has been very good all year. And I think—"

"I think you got me into a lot of trouble!" Cary interrupted him.

"Me?" Jeremy said in mock distress. "I have been an absolute angel!"

"Jeremy, you've never been an angel, but that's not what I'm talking about."

"Oh?" he murmured, wounded.

"You promised him a father!"

"Hey! I gave you a few years."

"Thanks. That was really swell of you."

"I do try to please."

"And then, on top of that, you promised him a gift I can't possibly afford!"

"What?" For a moment, Jeremy was serious, frowning. "I thought computers prices were coming down!"

"They are—but not the setup Danny wants. It costs thousands, Jeremy."

"I'll help—"

"Like hell you will. I don't take charity from the family, Jeremy, and you know it."

"Hey! I have every right to buy my little cousin a Christmas present."

"Sure. And if I ever manage to afford that system, you can buy him a game or some software."

"Stubborn, stubborn, stubborn," Jeremy insisted. Then his eyes brightened. "We might get Christmas bonuses."

"That much?"

"Maybe. After all," he teased, lightness returning to his voice, "you've been a good girl yourself. Too good. Atrociously, boringly good. So I'm going to sprinkle you with Christmas dust. And the next man you see is going to be the man of your dreams. Rich as Midas, sleeker than a Mercedes Benz, tender, gentle and kind. Tall, dark and handsome. Danny's Christmas present—and yours. And the Christmas dust is going to make you run right out and be bad with him. How's that?"

She was laughing. "The next man I see will probably be old Pete from the mail room, he of the ten children and eighteen million grandchildren. But hey, knock yourself out. Sprinkle away with Christmas dust. Maybe I'll at least find a suitable date for the adult Christmas party. What do you think?"

"I think that your time's up," Jeremy said. "If the one adult I get on my lap all day can't ask for one lousy, decadent present, you may as well stand!"

Laughing, she found her feet. "I'm telling you, Santa sure isn't what he used to be," she said with mock horror. She started toward the exit when she stopped short, suddenly aware that someone was blocking the red-curtained exit door.

Someone big. She couldn't see who it was right away, because the flare from the Christmas lights was in her eyes. All she could catch was the form, tall, imposing, totally blocking the exit. Dark. Even forbidding.

For a moment her heart fluttered, and she didn't know why. She felt an acute sense of unease.

How silly, she told herself. She didn't know why she was so startled by the masculine figure in the dark tux.

She took a step forward, then realized who the man was. She should have known him instantly from his height alone.

It was none other than their host himself. Her boss. The illustrious Mr. Jason McCready.

There had been rumors that many a female at *Elegance* had foolishly cast away her heart and pride on his behalf. McCready wasn't interested. He never dated his employees, and when he made his necessary social appearances with women, they were never the same from one occasion to the next. Still, Cary knew that June found him irresistible.

That was undoubtedly because June had never ventured into his office with a story proposal, Cary decided.

She took another step forward, deeply irritated with herself. Then she paused again, because of the way he was staring at her.

Once again it seemed as if those green eyes sliced her like steel blades. The scent of him slowly curled around her; it was subtle, but very masculine and . . . alluring, she had to admit. He was compelling, standing there. So tall, so dark, his shoulders broad, his hips lean. She wondered about his chest. It would be deeply muscled, she was certain. Hairy, or sleek and bare? Hairy, she was sure. Darkly hairy, with a narrow whorl that drew a line from his chest to his . . .

She jerked her head up and stared into his eyes, horrified. He stepped back, lifting the curtain for her.

"Mrs. Adams?"

She gritted her teeth and started forward. She had meant to see him sometime during the day to thank him for the party, but now she couldn't seem to muster up a thank you. In fact, she couldn't seem to speak at all.

"Mrs. Adams!"

She looked up and realized she was very close to him. Close enough to see the texture of his tux, the snow-white pleats of his shirt. The angles and planes of his face, the sensual fullness of his mouth.

"Yes?" she managed.

"I had intended Santa's lap for those children among us who are under, say, fifteen."

How long had he been standing there? How could she explain?

She didn't know if he was seriously angry or if he was teasing her. She still couldn't find a reply. Nor could she seem to tear her eyes from his.

"Mr. McCready, I..."

He smiled, which made him seem more striking, younger. Almost touchable. Her voice died away as he stared at her.

"I do not want your desk cleared out by five, Mrs. Adams," he said softly. "I still find your work exceptional."

"Thank you," she managed. He was still staring at her. She couldn't smile; she couldn't speak. He didn't expect her to. He was just watching her.

She turned away at last and fled down the steps, hurrying toward June. Just as she reached the bottom step, she realized a little girl was waiting on the landing, waiting for Cary to move so she could run up the steps herself.

But the girl waited politely, with a beautiful smile. She must have been about six or seven, and she had light blond hair caught up in pigtails tied with red ribbons. She looked like an angel, delicate, sweet, with a haunting, wistful smile that instantly tugged at Cary's heartstrings.

"Is Santa free now?" she asked Cary.

Cary heard June's laughter, and she blushed. Then she returned the little girl's smile. "Yes, Santa is free, I think.

Of course, there is a line around the other way. I'm not sure—''

"Oh!" the girl cried, stricken. "I have to leave, you see, and my father said it might be okay to slip around this way. But it would be rude to take someone else's place."

"Angela, it really is okay. We'll be quick, and the others will understand," came a deep masculine voice over Cary's shoulder.

She turned in dismay. McCready again. But this sweet, delicate little child couldn't possibly be his daughter....

Yes, she was, Cary realized. She stared from McCready's gaze to the little girl's wide eyes. "Excuse me," she murmured lamely. "Honey, if you have to leave, I know Santa will be thrilled to see you, and no one will mind at all."

Angela McCready smiled again. "Thank you." She started up the stairs, then turned back. "It was nice to meet you, Miss..."

"Mrs. Adams. Cary," Cary told her. And once again that smile crossed the little girl's lips.

"Mrs. Adams!" Angela McCready exclaimed happily. Cary arched a brow, and Angela continued quickly. "You must be Danny's mother."

Cary nodded, still confused.

Angela enlightened her. "We sat together for the magic show. And he taught me how to do a trick. He's really wonderful."

"Yes, well, I rather think so myself," Cary agreed.

"I hope I see him—and you—again," Angela McCready said.

There was such hope on her face that Cary couldn't disappoint her. "I'm sure we'll meet again," she said.

McCready's eyes were on her, sharp, unfathomable. Cary felt herself growing warm. But then he and his daughter disappeared into the cardboard Santa hut, and Cary turned away.

It had all happened in a matter of moments, she realized. Running into McCready, meeting his daughter, sitting on Jeremy's lap...

Jeremy and his Christmas dust! she thought with disgust. So much for Jeremy's prophesies.

"Danny's watching the puppeteer. I told him it would be all right," June said. "Let's go for a glass of that delicious champagne. I don't get to indulge in the really good stuff all that often."

"Champagne sounds wonderful," Cary agreed. She was parched. More parched than she could remember being. Except for the time she had gone into Jason McCready's office with her notebook and great expectations.

They walked to the champagne table, where a polite bartender helped them both. Cary toasted June, then raised her glass and sipped her champagne.

The next man you see, Jeremy had told her. She didn't want a man for Christmas. Sometimes she wondered if she would ever want another man in her life.

And then sometimes...

Sometimes she was lonely and frightened, furious with Richard for leaving her, and sometimes she ached because he had taught her that love could be so very sweet, and then he had been gone, leaving nothing in her life except for the pain and the blackness and the void. She had tried to date, but she had always backed away quickly. Because...

Because no one had ever touched her in the same way. No one had ever made a kiss seem natural. No one had ever seduced her to where she could forget...

"Cary, are you still with me?"

"What? Oh, I'm sorry." She realized she had been ignoring June. They were sipping champagne. It was a party. And she was having a good time. Well, she was almost having a good time.

She started to smile. Jeremy. Santa. Where would she be without him?

Him and his prophesies!

The first man she had seen hadn't been old Pete from the mail room after all.

She suddenly choked on the champagne.

No, it had been someone much worse.

Jason McCready.

Tall, dark and handsome. And rich. Just like June had ordered...

Cary swallowed more champagne.

No, no, no...

So much for Christmas dust and miracles!

Chapter Two

Jason McCready had a headache. One that pounded viciously at the back of his skull as he drove toward his house.

He knew he was disappointing Angela by leaving the party so early, but he'd really wanted to go home.

The party had really been Sara's baby.

Oh, he'd always had a Christmas party. And he'd always tried very hard to do right by his employees. He hadn't been born to money, nor had he inherited the magazine. He had built it. He knew what it was like to work hard. And more, he knew what it was like to dream.

And once he had even known what it was like to hold magic in the palm of his hand. There had been a time when he had had everything.

He'd had Sara.

Sara had loved Christmas. She'd loved winter, the snow and the clean, cold air. She'd loved the bright lights and the decorations, the Santas in the stores and on the street corners, the specials on television. Just sitting with her before a fire had meant more than anything in the world to him. He'd really, truly had everything.

But that had been before the December night when a drunk driver had plowed into Sara's silver sports car with enough speed to kill her instantly. The only miracle had been that she had just dropped Angela off for a Christmas party, and so he was left with his very young daughter when he had been bereft of his wife.

But others had handled Angela for him then. In his grief, he realized now, he had deprived her of two parents instead of one. It had taken months for him to rouse himself enough to care for Angela. And now he was trying very hard to make it up to her.

"Can he, Dad?"

"What? Sorry, darling. I guess I wasn't listening," Jason apologized. The traffic was bad tonight. Fresh snow had made the streets slippery.

"Danny. Danny Adams. Can he come skiiing with us?"

"What?"

"I said—"

"No, no, I'm sorry, I did hear you, I just..."

"He was so nice, Dad. He—he made me laugh. And he understood when I—"

Angela broke off speaking.

"He understood what?" Jason asked her curiously. He braked quickly for a red light. On a street corner, a Salvation Army volunteer was waving a bell that clanged away, chiming out the Christmas season with a cheerful vengeance.

Why did he feel the loss so much more keenly every Christmas? Jason asked himself. It was a time for peace, a time for faith.

"Nothing," Angela murmured evasively. "He's just— he's just great. Couldn't we ask him, please?"

"Honey, his mother is one of my employees. I don't know if I should bother her with this." His mother wasn't just an employee. She was Mrs. Cary Adams, and since he'd been watching her for quite some time now, he could almost guarantee she would tell him no.

Angela didn't seem to see it that way. "His mother was very nice, and I don't think she'd be bothered at all," Angela said stubbornly.

Why shouldn't he ask a friend along for Angela? Guilt plagued him. He hadn't thought how lonely things must become for her now and then. She had the run of the lodge, of course, but it was true. She had no special friends.

Except for now. She was crazy about this Danny.

Jason had to admit that the boy seemed to be a special kid. There was something in his smile. It was nice. It was open, generous. He'd taken a few hard knocks himself, but he'd come through with that great smile. Jason knew about Danny Adams's life because he'd made a point to know something about Cary Adams. He'd done so the day she'd come into his office—and walked out of it with her head held high.

He would never forget that day. Just as he hadn't been able to forget Cary Adams.

She was petite. She had a smooth, soft, melodic voice, but she had a certain essence of steel about her. When he thought about it, he realized that she was a very beautiful woman, with her sweeping dark hair and richly lashed hazel eyes. They burned when she was indignant or angry. He smiled. She wasn't flashy. She was nicely, quietly sophisticated. Something wild or ornate might draw a glance first, but once a person's eyes had fixed on her quiet elegance, they were compelled to stay.

It wasn't her looks that had drawn his interests, for he lived in a world where women were often beautiful and sophisticated. It had been her determination in coming to him, her staying power when he had refused her.

And then it had been the way she had gazed at him with glimmering gold eyes as she had told him bluntly that he wasn't the only one who had ever lost someone. And he had been in a rut, one hell of a rut of self-pity. She hadn't lifted the weight of the world from his shoulders, but her anger had done something, and since that day, life had been a little bit better. He'd made sure it was better. She'd made him see that it was something he had to do himself.

That was why he knew about her. He'd had her personnel file on his desk within five minutes, so he knew that Richard Adams had walked into a burning building because he had heard a child crying, and that he had never walked out again.

"Daddy?"

He sighed. The very beautiful Mrs. Adams might have cast accusations at him, but she had a few failings of her own. He could almost guarantee that she would turn him down. She had the defenses of a porcupine.

"I'll try, Angela."

"Oh, thank you, Daddy!" She threw an arm around him and kissed him.

"Hey! There's traffic out tonight!" he warned her.

"Sorry, Daddy!"

But he caught the look in her eyes. She was smiling. She was radiant.

He'd never seen her so happy or so excited.

Jason tightened his jaw. Somehow he was going to have to get Mrs. Adams to agree to let Danny come with him.

Even a porcupine had to have a chink in its armor somewhere.

It was the very next Monday that Cary found herself summoned to McCready's office.

She had been looking through the photographs for a Valentine's Day special when she sensed someone watching her. Gazing up, she was surprised to find June staring at her with a look that combined excitement and anxiety.

"What is it?"

"McCready's office," June said nervously.

"What?"

"You're wanted. In McCready's office."

Cary's heart lurched. Was she being fired after all? Perhaps he really had been angry to see her sitting on Jeremy's lap.

"Now?" she murmured. Of course now! She rose from her desk and stared at June. Was this how people felt when they walked to the gallows?

No, no, this wasn't that bad! Even if he was firing her, it wasn't anything as terrible as walking to the gallows. She was talented! She would find a new job. . . .

Just a month before Christmas. Danny would never get his computer.

He couldn't be firing her! Not right before Christmas!

But despite his wonderful parties, McCready didn't have any Christmas spirit. His spirit had been buried with his very beautiful wife.

"I'm here for you," June said to her softly.

"I'm fine," Cary muttered. She lifted her chin, squared her shoulders and walked from her office to the elevators. She stepped into an elevator and punched the penthouse-level button. Her fingers were trembling, she twisted them together.

Stepping off the elevator, she saw Billy Jean Clanahan, McCready's attractive and sophisticated secretary. She expected to see pity in Billy Jean's eyes, but there was none. Instead Billy Jean greeted her with a wide grin. "Oh, good, you're here!" She lowered her voice. "He was getting so anxious in there, I thought he was going to head down and accost you in your own office! Go in, go right in!"

Cary had little choice, for Billy Jean was prodding her toward the door.

She was pushed forward, and a door closed behind her. McCready's dark head had been bent over the papers on his desk, but it rose instantly. His unfathomable green eyes were on hers, as he stood and walked around the desk, offering her his hand. "Mrs. Adams! Thank you for coming so quickly."

She wasn't aware that she had offered her hand in return, but his fingers were folding around hers, and she was aware of an electric tension and tremendous strength. And a startling heat.

She drew her fingers away quickly.

"Sit down, Mrs. Adams, please." He pulled out one of the chairs for her, and she sat, very aware of him behind her. He was always impeccable. It was a natural thing with him. And he carried that handsome, subtle scent of aftershave. She suddenly felt a warm flowing sensation cascading all the way down the length of her spine. Her fingers curled around her chair, and she caught her breath. She thought that she would leap up and scream, except that he came in front of her and leaned on the corner of his desk, crossing his arms over his chest.

"I have a favor to ask of you," he told her.

She wasn't being fired. No one fired an employee this way.

She exhaled, then gasped in new air. He was staring at her curiously, and she struggled for an appearance of composure. "A—a favor?"

"Yes. And may I add from the beginning, Mrs. Adams, that your agreement or disagreement will have no bearing whatsoever on your position here."

He was smiling again, she thought. That secret smile of his.

She felt herself flushing, and she sat more primly in the chair, her eyes lowering despite her determination. "I didn't think—"

"Yes, you did think," he said, and she was startled when he laughed. She looked into his eyes, and she was further surprised by the light of humor in them. "You thought that I had decided to fire you because you had been sitting on Santa's lap. Taking time away from the children. For shame, Mrs. Adams."

"Mr. McCready—" She started to stand, utterly humiliated. But his hands were on her shoulders, and his laughter was surprisingly warm and pleasant, even compelling, as he pressed her into her chair. "I understand that you and Jeremy are cousins, right?"

Cary wet her very dry lips. "Yes. But if you—"

"Mrs. Adams," he said as he walked behind his desk, "do you remember the last time you were in this office?"

Of course she remembered it. She would never forget. She was surprised, however, that he had remembered it.

"Yes, Mr. McCready, I do remember," she said with grave dignity.

He was still smiling. "Well, you made a rather personal remark to me. You told me that I wasn't the only one who had lost someone."

Cary felt as if she were strangling. More than anything, she wanted to get out of his office.

"Look—" she began, standing once more. "I'm sorry, I really had no right—"

But again he was before her. "Ah, but you took the right! Mrs. Adams, will you please sit?" She wasn't going to have a chance to rise this time. Casually seated on the edge of the desk before her, he kept his hands on her shoulders. She looked at him, and to her great distress, she felt a heat like the warmth of the sun come sweeping over her. She didn't remember ever being this aware of a man. There was little help for it. His bronzed hands remained on her shoulders. The fabric of his suit was nearly close enough for her to feel the texture. And she could feel that electricity emanating from him, the leashed but still powerful energy.

"Mr. McCready—"

"You saw fit to comment on my personal life, so I think that maybe I have the right to comment on yours. You are sensitive, Mrs. Adams. Very, very touchy. I've never met anyone so defensive, so quick. Will you please relax! Your work is very good, and I admire you very much as a person."

Stunned, she stared into his eyes. "Then..."

"I'd like to borrow your son."

"My son!" she repeated.

"Just for a week. And you have every right to say no, as I explained before. But I'd look after his welfare as if he were my own."

"What are you talking about?" Cary demanded in confusion.

"I'm going on a ski trip next week. Half business, half pleasure. Angela is coming with me. She was entranced with Danny at the Christmas party."

"Oh!" Cary murmured. This had nothing to do with her job. Nothing at all.

And for once McCready was looking at her anxiously. She'd never before seen anything that even remotely resembled anxiety in his eyes.

Something did matter to McCready, even if his wife was gone. Angela mattered.

Dismay filled her. "I really am sorry—"

"It would be a wonderful experience for him. As I said, I'd see to his safety at all times. Mrs. Adams, I'm aware that you do not particularly like me, but Angela has not been so enthused since... well, it's been a very long time. She hasn't been so excited about anything since her mother died. If you feel some bitterness for me, I implore you, think of the children."

Cary shook her head. "No, no! It isn't anything like that at all. It's just that—Danny is diabetic. He is very good with insulin shots himself, but he's still... he's still a little boy. And when he's away, when he becomes involved in playing, he can forget. Really, Mr. McCready, I'd love him to be with Angela, she's a beautiful child. If I could let Danny go, I would."

She was touching him, she realized. While she had been speaking, she had let her hand cover his to emphasize her sincerity.

She jerked her hand away, and her eyes fell from his. "I am sorry."

He moved, first walking around behind her, then behind his desk. He sat and idly tapped a pencil against his blotter. "If that's your real reason, there's no problem at all."

"I beg your pardon?"

"You can come, too."

"Oh, but I can't. Really, I can't."

"Why not?"

"Well, I have work here—"

"You can work in New Hampshire."

"But I may need things that are here—"

"They can be expressed or faxed."

It was so simple for Jason McCready. Everything was always at his fingertips. Well, she wasn't.

"I'm sorry."

"Oh," he murmured. "Well, if you're involved with someone..."

"No, no, it's nothing like that!" she protested. Then she was furious with herself because she had just admitted to this man that there was no one in her life.

She stood up. "Life just isn't like that!" she exclaimed. "You don't live in the real world! No one else can just snap their fingers and have whatever they want!"

He looked at her with a slow, rueful smile curving his lips. "I do live in the real world, Mrs. Adams. I once swore to God that I would trade anything I had if Sara could just breathe, just speak, one more time. It didn't happen. I'm very aware that the world cannot always move my way. There were two reasons I pulled it all back together, Mrs. Adams. This business, for one. Almost a hundred people are dependent on it for their livelihoods. And I held it together for my daughter. I'm not doing anything terrible here. I'm asking you and your son on a week's skiing trip, and you might just forget yourself long enough to allow the both of you to enjoy it!"

Cary didn't know what was disturbing her so much. She leaped to her feet. "I'm sorry!" she snapped again.

And then she spun and hurried out of the office as fast as she could.

June was eagerly awaiting her downstairs, but Cary couldn't talk to June. She rushed past, shaking her head and casting her friend a look that promised she would explain later.

"Were you fired?" June called as Cary hurried by.

"No!" Cary said. She closed the door to her office and leaned against it, looking at her hands. They were shaking.

What was wrong with the idea? Jason McCready had asked her and Danny on a nice trip. She should be grateful and go. Skiing in New Hampshire. It would be beautiful. The snow would be all over the ground. The lodges would all be decked out in their Christmas finery.

She closed her eyes. She knew why she had said no. She didn't want to be somewhere like a beautifully decorated ski lodge. Not with Jason McCready.

Because she found him way too interesting. She had liked him better when he had been entirely cold and distant. She didn't like seeing into any part of his personality.

She was becoming more and more aware...

Of him as a man.

The phone on her desk starting ringing. She walked over and picked it up.

"Cary Adams here."

"Please?"

The voice was low, deep and very rich. And she was startled when she felt a smile curve her lips.

"It's just not possible. I'm sure that it's very crowded this time of year. I'll never be able to get accommodations—"

"Yes, you will."

"It can't be that easy—"

"Yes, it can."

"But—"

"Mrs. Adams," he murmured wearily, "I own the lodge."

"Oh," Cary replied softly.

"Well?"

"I..." She hesitated again. There seemed to be every reason in the world for her to go. Danny would be delighted. And she would please Angela McCready, and Angela seemed like such a sweet little girl. There was no reason at all that she shouldn't go.

Yes, there was. McCready himself.

He hadn't made any illicit overtures toward her, she reminded herself dryly. He hadn't made any overtures at all.

Still, there was something . . .

"Mrs. Adams?"

"All right. All right, we'll come."

"I'll pick you up at your house on Sunday morning. Nine o'clock. Is that all right?"

Her palm was damp, Cary realized. "Yes," she said. Sunday morning.

What had she done?

Sunday morning came, and Cary waited anxiously for nine o'clock to come. How did Jason McCready travel? Would he pick her up with an entourage? In a limo? Maybe a Mercedes. No. A Rolls.

"You all right, Mom?"

She was looking out the apartment window, and she would have been chewing her nails if she hadn't already donned her gloves. Bless Danny. He thought it was the most natural thing in the world that her boss should have invited them on a ski weekend. Oh, the innocence of children!

But then, she had been the only one to see anything at all wrong. June had been ecstatic. "He likes you, kid, he really likes you!" And then, in the middle of Cary's office, she had loudly said "Hmm! He's definitely tall, dark and handsome!"

"And a recluse. And deeply in love with his deceased wife," Cary had remarked flatly.

"Well, look at that, will you? You're deeply in love with your deceased husband, he's deeply in love with his deceased wife. What a couple."

"We're not a couple at all. I'm certain he'll have a date up there for... well, for some function. I'm just going as...as..."

"The nanny?" June had suggested drolly.

"Right. The nanny," Cary had agreed sweetly, making a face.

"Well, we did order tall, dark and handsome for Christmas. And he's rich, too."

"*We* didn't order tall, dark and handsome. *You* did," Cary had reminded her.

"That's right. According to Jeremy, all we needed to find for you is someone who doesn't wear his boxer shorts pulled up over his belt."

"Would you get out of here, please?" Cary had moaned.

"Hmm," June had speculated again. And Cary had thrown her out of her office as nicely as she could.

But now that the time was coming nearer and nearer, Cary was nervous. She might have been invited because of Danny, but Jason McCready had never suggested that she was along to play nanny for the children.

But then, she wasn't one of his real guests, either. So where did that leave her? And why did she care so much?

She leaned her forehead against the windowpane and felt the searing cold come through. Her stomach was in knots, she was so nervous.

Too sensitive. And defensive. She had to relax. Well, she would try.

A Jeep Wagoneer pulled up to the curb as she stared out the window. Her eyes widened when she saw the very tall figure of Jason McCready slide from the driver's seat.

He was in blue jeans and a leather jacket, hatless despite the cold. He looked up and managed to find her face right there in the window. His dark hair was out of order, lifted by the wind, falling over his forehead, and his eyes were very bright. Instinctively, Cary wanted to withdraw. But he had seen her, and he was smiling. Then he waved, and her heart turned another little somersault, because she suddenly realized just how attractive a man he was.

She smiled. So much for the Rolls, the limo or the Lincoln. He'd come in a Jeep.

"He's here!" Danny shrieked delightedly.

"Yes, yes, he's here. Grab your bags, Danny. And don't scream quite so loudly, or we won't last the first day!" she advised him. But Danny wasn't chastised. He cast her a lopsided grin, his eyes alight with pleasure. He scooped up his duffel bag and headed for the apartment door, casting it open just as Jason McCready appeared before it.

"Well, I was about to ask if you were ready or not, but it appears that you are," he told Danny.

"Yes, sir! Thank you, sir! I'm ready. This is great! Just great. Did I say thank you?"

Jason McCready seemed pleasantly amused. "Yes, you did. And I thank you for coming. Angela is very excited. She's in the car. Want to take your things and run on down? I'll get your mom's bag."

Danny ran out, and Cary found herself face-to-face with Jason McCready. She moistened her lips, alarmed that she was so nervous.

It seemed that she stood there forever, feeling those green eyes touch down on hers. And despite the cold of the day, she felt a warmth creeping swiftly through her.

"Is that your only bag?" he asked.

"What? Oh, yes, that's it, thank you," she murmured.

He collected her bag. As he did so, his eyes swept the apartment.

She loved antiques, and they fit well with her building, a three-storied federal brick that had been built in the early eighteen hundreds. The parlor was a compilation of Edwardian and Victorian pieces she had lovingly stripped and stained and polished herself. A braided rug covered the floor before the fireplace, and a deep old leather sofa was covered with an afghan. Little copper pots and other bric-a-brac decorated the buffets and cabinets. Blue and white Dutch patterned draperies hung at the windows. It wasn't contemporary; it probably wasn't in the least what Jason McCready was accustomed to. But it was a warm and very inviting room.

He didn't comment on it, only said, "Ready?"

"Yes."

He smiled. "You're not going off into a den of lions, you know."

She arched a brow and stiffened. Jason McCready's smile deepened. There was no way, of course, that she could know that he was thinking that the spines of his little porcupine were already bristling away.

Cary hurried through the door.

She also didn't realize that, as she brushed by him, he breathed in the clean scent of her hair. Or that the subtle charisma of her perfume trailed sweetly through the air.

She was just too aware herself. Of Jason McCready. Big, so very tall in her antique doorway, his shoulders exceptionally broad and attractive in the leather jacket.

She would certainly have no complaints if she was dating this man, she thought. His underwear was not pulled well over his belt line. His belt line was perfect. All of him was perfect.

That wasn't fair. She knew a lot of attractive men, and she had been teasing about the underwear. It had very little to do with looks. McCready's appeal was all in his eyes, in the little line around them, in the richness of his voice, in his rare smile. . . .

And then she nearly gasped aloud. She wasn't dating Jason McCready. She was accompanying her son on a trip to the man's ski lodge!

With her cheeks flaming, she hurried down the stairs. By the time she reached the streets, she thought she had regained a little of her composure.

The kids were already in back, chatting away. Angela leaped from her seat while Jason packed Cary's bag in the rear of the vehicle. She threw her slender little arms around Cary, so giving, so trusting. "Thank you! Thank you so much for coming. Daddy said you might not let Danny come along, but I knew you would. I'm so glad that you're going to be with us!"

"Thank you," Cary murmured. Jason was coming round to open her door. She stared at him, and he shrugged. She hadn't realized that he knew her well enough to warn his daughter that she might very well refuse.

The passenger door was open, and he was waiting. She slipped into the Jeep, and the door closed behind her.

Jason McCready went around and slid into the driver's seat. A plaid thermal blanket lay on the seat between them. He flashed Cary a quick smile. "It's a long drive. About three hours. Just in case you get cold."

"Thanks," she said.

There was very little traffic, even in Boston. The kids chatted away while Jason expertly steered the large vehicle through the narrow streets, past the Common and toward the turnpike.

"Do you ski?" he asked Cary. She shook her head. He shrugged. "Well, we can solve that in a week."

Her heart skipped a beat. "Really," she murmured. "You don't have to worry about entertaining me. I'm just along for Danny. I'll be all right."

She nearly jumped a mile when his arm stretched out across the seat and his fingers curved around her neck. He flashed her a very quick smile.

"Relax, Mrs. Adams! It *is* a ski lodge. It's where people learn to ski. And you and Danny are both my guests, I'm very much hoping that you'll enjoy yourself."

The most absurd sensation swept through her. Tears stung her eyes, and she suddenly longed with all her heart to move closer against him. To lay her head on his shoulder. To relax . . . to feel his fingers, warm and sure, working away the tension at her nape. . . .

His hand fell away, and she blinked. Hard. Then she managed to smile. "Thank you, Mr. McCready."

"Dad's name is Jason," Angela suddenly volunteered from the back.

"Yes, I know," Cary said.

"Mom's is Cary," Danny offered in turn.

Jason grinned, meeting Danny's eyes in the mirror. "I know, son, but thank you."

"Well, if you both know," Angela said with exasperation, "why do you keep up with this Mr. and Mrs. business?"

Cary, smiling, shifted in her seat to see the wide, expectant eyes of the children. "He's my boss," she told Angela.

"And she's one of my employees," Jason explained.

"That doesn't change your name, does it?" Danny asked innocently.

"No, it doesn't," Jason said. He glanced quickly at Cary. "I can live with Cary, if you can handle Jason."

"I think so. It's simple. Two syllables. I should be able to manage it."

The Jeep sped along the highway. Cary realized that she had actually known Jason McCready for about three years. And now, within a period of fifteen minutes, they were suddenly on a first-name basis.

And she still felt warm. Very, very warm—despite the cold of winter....

Chapter Three

The ski lodge was beautiful.

The place looked like an alpine château, all wood and angles, with beautiful carvings. The reception area in the front boasted a huge stone and wood fireplace that was decorated with Christmas stockings and ran nearly the length of the wall. All around the fireplace were leather sofas and chairs, arranged for small and large gatherings, all offering warmth and intimacy. Hot and cold drinks were served in the area all afternoon, with mulled wines and exotic coffees the specialty for grown-ups, and hot chocolate with whipped cream and chocolate shavings the main offering for the smaller fry.

Jason McCready explained all this to Cary as they stood in the entryway together. He had pointed out the nearly twenty-foot-high Christmas tree in the lobby to Danny when a young blond man came hurrying forward to welcome them. He was anxious to please Jason McCready, Cary decided, but there was also a warmth in his eyes and a pleasure in his voice that could mean only one thing—he liked his boss.

"Mr. McCready, you're here! No bad traffic, I hope. Did the weather slow you down?"

Jason shook his head, drawing off his gloves. "No, Randy, the trip was fine. We got off the highway to take a look at the Basin." He smiled at Cary as he explained. He'd mentioned the Basin when they had stopped for pizza for lunch. It wasn't far from the lodge, just before a little town called Franconia's Notch. It was one of the most exquisite places Cary had ever seen, with falls and rivulets racing over rocks through the snow to reach an otherwise tranquil spot where the water hurtled down with a noise like thunder. A lot of the shallower water was freezing over, but Cary assumed that the place would be beautiful in any season. Thoreau had thought so, too. According to Jason, he had been a frequent visitor to the area, and some of his words were now immortalized at the spot.

The area had been exciting to see. And more so, perhaps, with Jason McCready. Because of the ice, he had kept a steady hand upon her elbow as he had led her along, the children racing ahead. He had watched her in silence as he had shown her the place, and when she had spun with pure wide-eyed pleasure, he had seemed to read her thoughts.

"It's almost like Camelot! In summer, everything is green and lush, and there are wildflowers everywhere. In fall, the colors are simply fantastic. In winter, it's a crystal palace of ice, just as you see. And spring brings the water rushing down at a greater crescendo, sweet and clean, the flowers just budding and the return of the birds . . ." His voice had trailed away, and he'd shrugged. They had stood gazing at each other. He hadn't seemed to need a reply, but she had never seen him so animated, nor had she imagined that he might feel so poetic about any place.

"It's wonderful. Just wonderful," she'd murmured, and then quickly added, "thank you for taking the time to stop for me—and Danny, of course—to see this."

"The pleasure has been all mine, Mrs.—Cary," he'd said softly. Then he had turned and walked away, leaving her to follow on her own.

And she had wondered if he had come there often with his Sara, and if the place had awakened memories.

In the car he had remained quiet. And he had winced when Angela had begged him to play Christmas carols on the tape player. He had caught Cary's glance and tried to smile.

He had played the tape, just as his daughter had asked, but he hadn't joined in any of the songs.

Now, however, he was as polite and easy as could be. He turned, catching Cary's hand and drawing her over to meet the younger man. "Randy, this is one of my top writers, Cary Adams. Cary, Randy Skylar. And this is Cary's son, Danny."

Randy shook her hand and grinned broadly. "Mrs. Adams, it's wonderful to have you." His gaze returned quickly to his employer. "I've readied the suites in the rear, just as you asked. Would you like something sent up?"

"I'm afraid I have a meeting with the sales staff right away," Jason said. "But, Cary, perhaps you and Danny would like something?"

She started to shake her head, but then she thought about the children. "Angela, why don't you come with us to our room for a while? That way we can have Randy send us all some hot chocolate while your dad is busy."

Angela smiled shyly. "I'd like that. May I, Dad?"

"Well, maybe Cary and Danny should have a little time to settle in first—"

"It's fine, really," Cary said, interrupting him. She almost added, We're only here for Angela, but she didn't want Angela to feel that she was a burden, because she wasn't at all. "I'm not tired, and I can throw things in drawers in a matter of minutes."

Jason shrugged. "Fine, then. I'll see you all later for dinner."

He left the three of them with Randy, who escorted them to the room Jason had reserved for her and Danny.

The door to their room was certainly ordinary looking. It was a plain wooden door that opened from the balcony that ran the length of the wall above the Christmas tree. But once that door had opened...

The room was massive, yet cheerful and warm, with its own fireplace against a wall of granite. There was a white leather sofa standing on a raspberry carpet, and beyond a curving pine bar was a full kitchen that appeared to be equipped with all manner of conveniences and utensils. There were two doors leading from the main room. Cary glanced at Randy, then strode across the parlor area to the first door. Opening it, she discovered a bedroom with a huge queen-sized bed covered by a massive quilt. Even here, there was a fireplace. And to one side of the fireplace, set into a small field of white tiles, was a huge Jacuzzi.

Cary left that room behind and hurried on to the next. It was smaller, and it was missing the Jacuzzi, but it was every bit as warm and as nice.

These rooms had been designed as family getaways, she decided. The suite provided a romantic seclusion for adults, while children could be just steps away....

The lodge was his. He had probably designed it, too, Cary thought.

She walked to the main room, and she must have been frowning, because Randy was quick to question her. "Is anything wrong?"

"No, no, of course not. It's just that..." Angela was staring at her anxiously. It's just too nice! she wanted to shout. She hadn't really been invited on this trip—Danny had been the intended guest. And now here she was. In the absolute lap of luxury and feeling very uncomfortable.

"I'm just afraid that I'm taking space from . . . from another guest," she finished lamely.

"Oh, but you're not!" Angela assured her. "There are two of these suites here. My dad and I have the other. See—it's through that door over there. He never rents out these rooms. Never. They're always for guests. Really. I hope you like it."

"I like it very much," Cary told Angela, but her discomfort was growing. She suddenly felt very much like the governess.

"Come, Mrs. Adams," Randy Skylar told her. "You haven't seen the half of it yet!"

He led her through the main room and pushed open French doors that led to a balcony. From there, plate glass stretched above her. Below her, swathed in mist, was an indoor pool. A swirling whirlpool sent water cascading over a rock fall into the pool.

Beyond it, the mountains and the ski slopes were visible through the plate glass. It was breathtaking.

Cary heard laughter and looked through the mist. Some guests had left the slopes to sink into the warmth of the heated pool. Children played on the steps. And a pair of lovers, perhaps the parents, laughed together, the man in the water, the woman stretched out on the tiled rim of the pool beside him.

A knot twisted in Cary's stomach, taking her unaware. Once she had been like that. She could close her eyes and remember when she and Richard and Danny had taken vacations and left their cares behind.

"Hot chocolate has arrived!" Randy announced. Cary turned. A young woman had appeared, pushing a cart holding a silver pitcher of hot chocolate and a plate of Oreo cookies.

"This is living!" Danny announced happily. Then he looked at his mother, remembering that he needed to be very careful with Oreos—their sugar was high, and that was bad for his diabetes. "Can I have some?"

"Yes, of course. A few," she told him, smiling. She made a mental note to test his blood sugar level and give him his insulin as soon as they were alone. They had a small machine to do the testing, and he was accustomed to receiving his insulin three times a day. Even at his age, he knew how to do it himself, and Cary was proud of him for that, but he was still young, and she liked to be there to oversee things.

But right now, she decided, he could have a few Oreos.

Cary smiled at the children. Danny was still watching her. "Why don't you two dig in, and then get into your suits? We'll swim and shower and change, and maybe then your father will be ready to join you again, Angela."

Angela, delicate and pristine even with an Oreo in her hand, gave Cary a beautiful smile. "Oh, he will be. He's always on time, and he never lies."

"Well, how commendable," Cary murmured. She offered the two another smile, thanked the maid and Randy Skylar, then disappeared into the master bedroom. As Danny had said, this was living.

She just couldn't accept this kind of hospitality. It was too much.

She stretched out on the bed and closed her eyes. It would have been so nice if she could have come to such a place with Richard.

In her mind's eye she saw the pool and the snow-covered mountains beyond the glass. She saw a fire burning, and she saw herself, her head resting against the shoulder of a dark-haired man.

She bolted up, setting her hands against her flushed cheeks.

Richard had been blond. As light as Danny. The dark head in her daydreams had belong to another man.

Jason McCready.

She groaned softly and buried her head in her pillow. And she didn't rise until Danny came in to tell her that their luggage had been brought up, so they could change for the pool.

After their swim, Angela went through the connecting door to the suite she shared with her father to change. An hour later she knocked at the connecting door and Cary let her in.

"Has anyone ever told you that you are really beautiful, Miss McCready?" Cary asked her, smiling.

Angela blushed, her cheeks as rosy as her red velvet dress. "Do you really think so?"

"Indeed I do."

"You're very beautiful, too."

"Thank you."

"I told my father that."

"Oh," Cary murmured.

"Yes, she did, but it wasn't at all necessary," came a rich male voice over Angela's shoulder.

Jason was freshly showered and shaved, his hair was still damp, and he was very handsome in a black dinner jacket and red vest. Cary, uncertain of how to dress, had chosen a soft white knit that gently molded her body until it flared slightly into a wider skirt just below the knees. Only the back was low and in the least daring, and she had hoped that her choice would suffice whether she found herself in casual or dressy surroundings.

"I already knew how beautiful you are, Mrs. Adams," Jason assured her.

She felt a flush rising to her cheeks, as red as the color that stained Angela's fair face. But she wasn't young, she told herself. And she wasn't the least bit innocent. She had to acquire a backbone where this man was concerned.

"Thank you. May I return the compliment?"

"You think Dad's beautiful?" Angela inquired, giggling.

"You mean he's not?" Cary said lightly.

"Oh, no!" Angela told her gravely. "He's handsome. Very, very handsome."

Tall, dark and handsome! an inner voice taunted Cary. Ah, but tall, dark and handsome had been June's order for Christmas. Cary had just wanted a man who didn't pull his boxer shorts up to his earlobes.

No. She hadn't wanted a man at all. Jeremy was the one who had wished that upon her. Jeremy and his darned Christmas dust!

"Well, we've got reservations at a place up by one of the other slopes," Jason said. "Not that the restaurant here isn't marvelous—it is. But the week may grow hectic, and you may eat here frequently, so I thought I should get you out while I could. Is that all right?"

"Certainly. It's very thoughtful," Cary told him. "But you really don't have to worry about Danny or me—"

"Tsk, tsk, Mrs. Adams. I realize that I don't *have* to worry. I *choose* to worry. May I?"

There was that smile again. One that was open and honest. The smile that made her feel warm. That made candlelight seem to dance and flicker down the length of her.

Cary nodded, consenting as graciously as she could.

Dinner was wonderful. The owners of the restaurant had managed to combine moose and elk and deer heads on very rustic walls with a certain amount of elegance. Cary had her first beefalo steak, and a delicious salad. Conversation with Jason McCready was proving to be easy and natural, and throughout the meal she was surprised by the range of topics they covered, from the best qualities for grammar school teachers to the situation in the Middle East. And with Angela and Danny there, Cary also found herself laughing through the meal as Danny described the very best way to spit on a ball to give it a fast curve, and Angela sang camp songs that might have repelled a hungry bear. So much for elegance.

When they left the restaurant, it was late. The children were barely in the car before Cary turned and realized they were fast asleep, one slumped on the other.

Jason was silent for a while, and Cary felt her eyes flickering shut. Then Jason suddenly spoke.

"The kids are out?"

"Fast asleep," she assured him.

"I just wanted to say thanks. Thanks very much for coming."

"Thank *you*. The suite is beautiful. Too beautiful. I think I would have been happier with something, er, smaller."

She saw the slow curve of his smile. "Mrs. Adams, you are worth it."

"Well, thank you," Cary murmured. He didn't reply. The motion of the car as it sped through the night mixed with the warmth of its heater, and her eyes kept closing. Then they closed one final time and she couldn't quite get them open.

It startled him when her head fell on his shoulder. Jason almost jumped, but he managed to hold still. The soft, sweet scent of her hair teased his nose, and for a moment he held his breath.

A poignant anguish stole slowly over him, seeming to seep into him like water over porous rock.

It had been so long....

Sara had fallen asleep on him like that.

He'd been out a number of times since her death. And though he was certain that he'd always been courteous, he knew, too, that he'd always been distant, and he'd seldom seen any woman more than once. According to a number of tabloids, he'd become a very eligible bachelor, but in his heart, he knew he would never be that. He couldn't retain his interest in anyone; he couldn't look at beauty with more than a casual eye. He hadn't really dated; he'd had arrangements, and that had been that. Strange, because he had been intimate with some of those women, but...

He'd never come so close that one of them might fall asleep on his shoulder.

And Cary was certainly the only woman he would allow to be there.

He didn't know why. He did know that he hadn't thanked her just for Angela. He had thanked her for himself, as well. It had been years since he had really laughed. Years since he had been anxious for a day to end so that he might see someone—other than Angela—again.

Her hair brushed his chin. Soft and satiny, so warm with its rich brown depths. Like silk, it teased over his flesh. His fingers tightened on the wheel, and he clenched his jaw as he felt sudden, volatile stirrings of desire rise hard within him. His initial anguish had faded away. The present—and this woman—held all his attention. He couldn't remember wanting anyone quite this way. It was ironic.

She was probably the one woman who would not want him.

She made a soft sound in her sleep as she curved against the warmth of his body more comfortably. Her fingers curled over his shoulder. And then her hand slipped and fell to his thigh.

He clamped down on his jaw even harder.

Cary awoke when the car jerked to a halt. Almost instantly, she was sitting upright, wondering how she had been sleeping.

But Jason McCready was already out of the car, and she didn't know whether to apologize or not.

"This is it," he said curtly. "We're here." For once on this trip, he wasn't being terribly polite.

"Yes. I'll, uh, I'll just get Danny."

"I'll get Danny. He's a lot heavier than my daughter. You carry Angela. If you think you can."

"Well, of course I can—"

"I meant that you're so tired yourself. And hell, you're not a lot bigger than either of them."

"I can manage," Cary said irritably.

"Yes, yes, you can manage." Jason quickly had Danny in his arms. She bent down for Angela, and his next words seemed to slap her right in the face. "Have I ever told you that you remind me of a porcupine at times?"

With her young burden in her arms, Cary stiffened and swung around. "What a lovely comparison. Thank you so much, Mr. McCready."

"I didn't say that you looked like a porcupine, Mrs. Adams. You're a very beautiful woman, and you must know that. Even though your husband hasn't been around for a long time to tell you, I'm sure that other men have. Or maybe not. With those porcupine bristles of yours, maybe no one has managed to get close enough."

"Thank you again. You do have my life right down to a tee, Mr. McCready. And with all the women you date! Don't you dare judge me!"

Cary delivered the last statement with her nose in the air, then turned quickly on her heel and headed for the lodge.

He was right behind her. "All the women I date?" he inquired.

"Ah, yes, if it's Tuesday, it must be a redhead," Cary said sweetly as they reached the door to the lodge.

"I didn't know you had been paying so much attention to my dating habits," Jason said.

Cary wasn't able to reply. Randy Skylar was there to open the door for them. "Let me take her," he offered Cary, and without giving her a chance to refuse, he swept Angela into his arms. Cary followed the two men up the stairs to the suites, forcing a smile to answer Randy's polite questions about their dinner.

Jason laid Danny on his bed. Randy had taken Angela into Jason's suite, so Cary and Jason were left alone to stare at one another, the sprawled and comfortable body of Cary's son between them.

"Good night, Mrs. Adams," Jason said softly.

"Good night," Cary murmured. "Thank you for dinner. It was lovely."

His slow, rueful smile curved his lips. "Yes, it actually was." Then he brushed by her and left. And, oddly, Cary could feel the entire length of her side where he had touched her so lightly and so briefly. It was so much warmer than the other side....

Funny, she had been so tired. But even after she had tucked Danny in and changed into a comfortable flannel gown, she couldn't sleep at all.

She pulled the pillow over her head, gritted her teeth and willed sleep to come. But for the longest time it didn't.

She kept feeling the warmth of her side and wondering how closely she had leaned against Jason McCready when sleep had come so easily in his car.

There was a note beneath her door in the morning. It was handwritten, and she recognized Jason's handwriting from the Christmas cards she had received over the last few years. It was a broad, large script, very legible, and somehow like the man, firm and powerful. The message was brief but courteous. He was tied up for the day, but she mustn't feel that she needed to tend only to the children. There were programs for them all morning, movies, lessons on the bunny slopes, whatever. She was welcome to spend her day however she chose, and she shouldn't worry. His staff were wonderful with children.

Cary didn't mind spending her time with the children, but she did have an article she wanted to edit, and with a magazine's deadlines, time could be very precious. She decided to have breakfast with the kids, then work for a while, then go down to the bunny slopes with them.

The day worked out as she had planned it. They breakfasted in her suite; then Angela and Danny traipsed off to see cartoons. Cary started to work in front of the main fireplace in the suite. She wondered if she would be able to concentrate, but to her great pleasure, she found that the comfort of the lodge and the snap and crackle of the fire were definite pluses. She didn't dig her nose out of her manuscript until two o'clock, when she had accomplished everything she had wanted.

Pleased, she dressed in her own best rendition of a ski outfit—clinging knit pants, a warm wool sweater and a windbreaker—and went in search of the children. They were just finishing lunch, and both were pleased that she was going to join them on the bunny slopes.

"I don't ski," Cary told Angela. "That puts me on the bunny slope with you and Danny. Except that I'll bet that you can ski."

Angela could ski. Beautifully. But she spent the afternoon with Cary and Danny and the young ski instructor, laughing delightedly as Cary and Danny struggled with the equipment and a new sense of balance. Cary, overwhelmed at first by the heavy boots, the skis and all the safety tips she was being given, swore she would never be able to manage. But by early evening she was delighted. She was managing the slopes. She was skiing! And she was thrilled with the rush of pleasure and exhilaration that negotiating the small slopes brought her.

She was also cold. She and Danny and Angela headed into the lodge. The children had hot chocolate; she decided on an Irish coffee. It was very good, but since she hadn't bothered with lunch, the hot drink seemed to hit her like lead.

She and the children decided to have dinner in the suite. And by the time they finished with the delicious linguine, the kids seemed willing enough to go to bed. Angela slipped through the door into her own suite. Cary hesitated, told Danny to get ready for bed and followed Angela into Jason McCready's private quarters.

His suite was obviously never rented out. It had the same view of the pool, the same handsome pine walls and deep plush carpeting. There was more of a feeling of home to his rooms. There were beautiful mountain prints on the walls, and a cabinet filled with curious sculptures and knickknacks. A handsome oak secretary was covered with papers, and on a coffee table before the sofa were several issues of *Elegance* and other magazines. On a side table was a picture frame. It contained the perfect family photo. Jason McCready surrounded by the two women he loved, a much younger Angela and Sara, both with their beautiful blue eyes and angelic halos of soft blond hair.

Cary suddenly felt as if she was intruding, and she almost backed away. But Jason McCready had never given her any decrees about not entering his private domain, so she hurried through the living room to tap at one of the bedroom doors. "Angela?"

"Cary? Come in."

Angela was already in her red flannel nightdress, her hair flowing down her back, her eyes wide and bright. Looking at her, Cary felt a peculiar rush of emotion, her heart tearing for Sara McCready. She's so beautiful, Sara! Cary thought. If only you could see her!

"I just came to...to see if you wanted to be tucked in," Cary told her.

Angela's eyes widened. "Yes, please. Thank you very much."

So Cary tucked her in, kissed her on the forehead and promised to see her bright and early the next morning. She went to her suite and tucked Danny in, then changed into her flannel gown. But once again, as exhausted as she should have been, she couldn't sleep. She got out of bed, made herself a cup of tea and wandered to the balcony overlooking the pool and the mountains beyond.

To her surprise, there was activity by the pool. She first recognized Barney Mulray, a salesman from Ohio whom she had met at a convention. Then she realized that the pool was full of *Elegance* salespeople.

And at the far end was Jason McCready.

To Cary's growing dismay, her first thought was that he looked wonderful in a bathing suit. He was bronzed, lean and very well muscled. His chest was covered by a handsome and provocative mat of dark hair. And from the breadth of his shoulders to the clean, lean line of his hips to the powerful thighs below his black bathing suit, he was perfectly formed.

Someone else thought so, too. There was a little young redhead, with a chest that didn't quit, sitting near him. She was talking to him, and Jason was responding. But then Barney called to him across the pool, and Jason was just as quick to respond to Barney. Cary leaned a little over the balcony, trying to hear their words.

"Come on, time for a drink," Barney encouraged.

Jason shook his head. "No, thanks. I'm about to head up to my room. I want to check on Angela."

Other encouragements were called to Jason, who shook his head. The people began to trail out of the pool. All but the redhead. She leaned closer to Jason—with that chest that wouldn't quit.

"Really, Jason. Just one drink. Come on. It's early."

"Trudy, thanks," he said, his voice firm. "But I'm tired. I'd like to be alone now, please."

Not even Trudy would dare to argue with such a tone, it seemed. She rose with a shrug and moved off with the others.

The pool area was suddenly very silent. Only Jason remained at the far end, his eyes closed. Again Cary felt as if she was intruding. Well, she *had* been intruding, eavesdropping. She started to move away, but right then his eyes flew open. Right to her.

"Ah, Mrs. Adams!" he called softly.

"Hello," she called back uncomfortably.

He smiled. Just like the cat who had caught the canary. "Did you have a nice day?"

"Yes, lovely, thank you."

"The kids?"

"They're fine. They're sleeping."

"Angela?"

"She's fine. I . . . I tucked her in."

His eyes widened a bit, she thought, but she didn't know with what emotion—pleasure that she would do so, or annoyance that she would presume to come so close.

"But you're wide-awake, I see," he commented.

"Yes, well, I was going in—"

"Don't. Come down," he commanded suddenly.

Cary hesitated. She should go to bed. She shouldn't go down to him. She felt as if little rivers of water were already dancing down her spine.

This was when memory usually kicked in. When she would remember Richard's smile, his laugh, when she would feel so cold and empty...

But this time she didn't see Richard's face before her. She was caught by the powerful, handsome face of the man in the pool below.

"I just heard you say that you wanted to be alone," Cary murmured.

"Did you?"

Cary flushed. "Yes," she admitted.

"Well, I did want to be alone—then. But I would very much appreciate your company now. Please, come down. The water is wickedly warm."

Much, much more than the water was wickedly warm, Cary was certain.

But suddenly she ached for a taste of that warmth. Just a taste. Jason McCready never offered anything more. And she could never take anything more.

But tonight . . .

Indeed, the wicked warmth seemed to sweep right up and curl around her. She moistened her lips, still hesitating.

"Cary?"

"I'll be right down," she promised.

And to her amazement, she got quickly into her suit and made her way to the pool. To the warmth.

Chapter Four

By the time she reached the pool, Cary was wondering why she had come. Jason McCready was no longer at the end of the pool, and she felt rather foolish standing there, looking around for him.

"In here, Mrs.—Cary."

He'd moved to the Jacuzzi. And he'd watched her arrive. For some reason, that disturbed her.

And there was more to disturb her. There was a tray by his side as he slowly leaned back in the hot swirling water with his eyes on her. There were two glasses of champagne on the tray, and a dish of bite-sized cheeses and shrimp and crackers.

Cary stiffened and tightened the belt on her terry swim robe. But then she heard his husky laughter, and her flesh warmed. "Your quills are bristling, Mrs. Adams."

"Are they?" she said, looking disapprovingly at the champagne. "Was this for my benefit?"

"It was."

"Well, you shouldn't have."

"Why not?"

She waved an arm to indicate nothing—and everything. "Because it's just too...practiced. As if you were going to..."

"Going to what?" He picked up one of the champagne glasses and took a sip.

"If you don't know—"

"If you're assuming that I intend to seduce you, don't you think you're being just a little presumptuous?"

"Oh, my Lord, this whole trip was a mistake. I just knew it—" Cary began, turning, intending to walk quickly away.

But she didn't quite manage it. Jason McCready was out of the Jacuzzi and standing before her, dripping wet, very masculine—and entirely imposing.

"It was a mistake because Danny is having such a miserable time?" he demanded. "Or is it a mistake because you're suddenly afraid of me? Why, I wonder? I'd admired you because you seemed to be the one person who wasn't afraid to say what she was really thinking."

"I'm not afraid of you!" Cary snapped quickly.

"Then?"

"Then . . . why did you invite me down?" she blurted.

He smiled. And there was a gentle humor in his eyes. "I like you. You're my guest here. I've been dealing with business all day, and you've been with our children. I thought it might be nice to talk. And, since it's late and it might also be nice to unwind, I ordered champagne and a snack. I thought you might enjoy it. And you just might, you know, if you let yourself."

She wasn't sure exactly why she felt like such a fool. Maybe she really had been presuming too much. Maybe he didn't find her attractive in the least.

Most probably he was simply stating the truth. And she had been acting like a porcupine.

Her fingers were still knotted over the belt to her robe. Her lashes fell over her eyes. "Is there cocktail sauce for the shrimp?"

"Yes."

"Well, all right, then."

She couldn't quite meet his gaze, so she turned, slipped off the robe and stepped into the Jacuzzi. The steaming heat was wonderful. It seemed to reach into all her muscles and smooth away her tension. Jason McCready stepped in, keeping his distance, sitting across from her. He offered her a glass of champagne. She thanked him, and he leaned back, sipping his own.

"How was your day?" he asked her.

"Great," she said. She told him how the three of them had spent their time. He asked her questions all the while, and it was more the tone of his voice than the warmth of the water that relaxed her. Before she knew it, she was leaning closer and closer. She had consumed half the shrimp, while he had politely preferred the cheese.

And she had allowed him to refill her champagne glass twice.

But when she had finished recounting the day, there was a sudden silence. Jason was leaning back, his head resting on the rim of the Jacuzzi, his eyes half closed.

"Did you...did you design this place?" she asked him.

His eyes opened slightly. They seemed to cast a searing heat as they swept over her. "Yes."

"I thought so. It's so well planned—" She broke off, willing herself not to flush, because he was staring at her so hard. "You designed it for Sara," she heard herself say.

He shrugged. "Yes."

"Then it must bring back painful memories for you."

He shook his head. "My memories aren't painful. And what difference does it make? According to you, I'm a dating machine."

"Well, it's foolish," she told him.

He shrugged again. "It's better than what you do."

"And what do I do?"

"Start off with your quills bristling."

"I don't—"

"Did you know that I'm fairly good friends with your cousin Jeremy? Second cousin, actually, isn't it?"

Cary inhaled and gritted her teeth. Jeremy! What had he been saying about her?

"He says that you've gone out three times in three years. And that each time you acted like an ice princess."

"An ice princess!"

"Yes, an ice princess. And that you never had any intention of enjoying yourself. At least I try."

"I try, too," Cary protested.

He sipped more champagne, watching her. Now he didn't look so much like the cat who had eaten the canary. His eyes were still lazy, half closed, but very green as he stared at her.

"Would you quit that!" she snapped.

"Quit what?"

"Well, I may remind you of a porcupine, but at this moment you very much remind me of a crocodile. So laid back and ready to snap my head off at any moment."

He laughed and leaned toward her. "I'm not going to bite your head off."

He was close to her. Very close. She could see the water beading on his shoulders and chest, and she was very tempted to touch one of those little beads. She was even tempted to move closer, to taste one of those little drops of water, to put the tip of her tongue against his flesh.

"The... the life you're living is very wrong," she told him primly. She couldn't draw her eyes from the water... or from his chest. Think! she warned herself. Remember.

"Is it?"

She heard his whisper, and then she knew that they were even closer. She felt his thumb and forefinger stroking her cheek, lifting her chin. And then she felt his lips on hers.

The rushing warmth of the water seemed to sweep through her like a fever, to touch her mouth, her body, her soul, with the same sweet fever. She had never imagined kissing any man besides Richard.

She couldn't imagine not feeling the touch of this man....

He did not seduce; he did not coerce. He gave so much with the hungry pressure of his lips. They molded to hers; they brought a fantastic warmth, a burst of emotions and sensations to fruition within her.

Maybe she had always known that he would kiss like this. With no hesitation, with a sheer provocative mastery. Maybe she had known that his tongue would move, hauntingly, drawing sensual patterns over her lips, delving between them, seeking the deepest recesses of her mouth, bringing a surge of sweet desire, latent so long, rushing like a cascade of wild water through her.

A sound escaped her, soft, like a moan. A sound of pleasure. Perhaps even a sound of desire. She could never accuse him of seducing her. His first touch had been so light. Even that kiss had provided every opportunity for escape. Perhaps at that point it was she who seduced him. For it was her arms that were the first to curl around his neck. It was she who floated against him as the swirling hot waters of the Jacuzzi lent them aid, seeming to fit their bodies so closely together.

He kissed her again. And again. His fingers traveled down her back, stroking her flesh, her form. She pressed against his muscled body, torn by memory, awakened by it. She was never anything but aware that he was a different man, a very different man, from the one she had married, the one she had loved. But for once her senses were swept away. She wanted this man, and the sensations were so acute and demanding that she didn't want to care about anything else.

She was in his arms, on his lap, yearning for more and more of his touch. His lips rose a fraction of an inch above hers, and he whispered softly, "I think we're both relaxed at last."

"It's the Jacuzzi."

"No, because not all my muscles are at ease," he told her.

Her eyes widened, and she might have been awakened to exactly what she was doing. But he kissed her again as his fingers caressed her cheek, her chin, her collarbone, and his arms tightened around her. The hot whirl of the water was not something outside her anymore, but something that was a part of her.

His lips rose from hers again. "We can't stay here."

"No," she whispered.

"I want this to go on." Again he offered her every escape.

"I know."

"Is it the champagne?"

"It helps, I'm sure," Cary admitted.

She felt him stiffen. He would walk away now, if she chose. But she didn't choose. She moistened her lips and tightened her arms around him. "Please..." she murmured.

He didn't make her say more. They stepped from the Jacuzzi and walked across the pool area to a door that led to a private stairway. It led, she realized, from the pool area straight to his bedroom.

One light was on. It cast a soft, dim glow over the black comforter that covered the large bed, the mountain prints on the wall, the black and brass and glass of the furniture. Cary saw very little of it, for she kept her gaze on Jason McCready, on the green eyes that remained locked with hers. She shivered suddenly, violently, for despite the heat indoors, she had come wet from the Jacuzzi into the air, and now her flesh was chilled. Not for long. For when he had laid her down, he covered her with the warmth of his own form. His kiss seared her with heat again, and his caress became a touch of fire.

Once more, his gaze caught hers, and he offered her a last escape. "Will you stay?"

She wanted to speak, but she couldn't. She nodded, closed her eyes and wound her arms around him, burying her face against him.

"Open your eyes," he commanded her, drawing her away. And she did so, meeting his gaze. "Tell me that you want me. Say my name."

"I want you."

"My name."

"Mr. McCready."

"My first name!" He laughed, and she smiled.

She managed to whisper, "Jason. I want you, Jason."

Then he asked nothing more of her, and the magic began.

He touched her . . . just where she longed to be touched.

And he kissed her . . . just where she longed to be kissed.

Fires rose in the night, the flames sending little licks of sensation to tease and torment and bring sweet pleasure to her. She saw his eyes in the dim magical glow of the night. And she saw his hands, so bronze, so large, so masculine and wonderful, against the pale hue of her own flesh.

And she kissed him. Touched the bare skin of his shoulder with the tip of her tongue, just as she had dreamed of doing.

It had been so long. So achingly long . . .

And what he offered her was good. So beautifully, perfectly good.

For he made love. He took nothing that he didn't give. He demanded; he shared; he held her; he caressed her. He touched her . . . so tenderly. And so passionately.

Almost as if he could love her.

And when the sweet whirl of heat and fever rose from pitch to pitch, when the cascade of need and hunger and wanting came swirling to a peak, it burst upon them both with a volatile climax.

The sensations were so strong, so sweet, that Cary's world went black. And when the light came again, she was still trembling, still drifting. Held in his arms, she shook time and time again with the aftermath of pleasure.

And shock.

It wasn't that she was suddenly horrified by what she had done. She had done it with her eyes wide open.

But she had done it without thinking. And though she still lay in his arms with the soft glow of the night a sweet shield around them, the garish rays of daylight would come streaking down upon her tomorrow, and she would have the future to live with.

She bit her lip, thinking that her suit was lying by the bed. Was there any way to slip into it without feeling awkward? Should she say thank you very much what a wonderful time and try to slip casually to her own room?

Good God, how could she ever go to work again? She had to quit! Unless he fired her. No—it was getting so close to Christmas. She couldn't quit. Danny wanted a computer.

She was thinking about a computer at a time like this?

She started to move, but his hold on her tightened. "I—
I have to go back," she said in near panic. "Danny will be
waking—"

"At one in the morning?" he said. Those eyes of his
were on her again. And he was smiling.

"I have to go back," she said stubbornly.

He kissed her lips. Then he moved away, rising on one
elbow. He watched while she donned her suit, then comfortably slipped into his own. "I'll walk you down for your
robe and back to your room."

"You don't have to."

"I said I'll walk you back."

Cary's suit was still soaked, so cold after the warmth
they had shared! As she hurried for the door to the stairway, she brushed by the bedside table, looking down as she
struck it with her thigh.

And she stared at the picture. The picture of Sara
McCready. Smiling so beautifully.

Oh, God. But Jason didn't seem to notice. He moved
past her, opening the door, then starting down ahead of
her. He found her robe by the pool and set it around her
shoulders, then smiled. "You're shivering."

"I'm cold."

"You could have stayed warmly by my side."

"We both have children."

"We had more time."

"No." She shook her head, backing away from him.

"Cary, if you regret anything—"

"No, I don't regret anything. It was wonderful. You
know that. I mean..." Oh, she wasn't good at this; she
wasn't good at all. She might as well be honest. "It was my
first time since...Richard. And maybe I will be able to
start seeing people again now. Thank you. But I need to be
alone."

"Cary—"

"I have to go!"

"Wait!" he said demandingly.

Why was she feeling such a swift rise of panic and handling things so poorly? "I have to go! And I don't care what my leaving means. Even if you fire me!"

His jaw went very square. "Cary! I'm not firing you!"

The panic left her suddenly. But she still needed to escape. "So I don't have to clean out my desk," she murmured. She wanted to laugh, wanted to cry. She wanted to throw herself against him all over again.

But most of all she wanted to be alone. Alone to deal with the sudden anguish that seized her now. She couldn't let him walk her back. She turned and ran from the pool to the steps that led to the balcony, then back to her own room.

She spent the morning desperately trying to feel and act normally.

She must have done a better job than she had expected, because neither Danny nor Angela seemed to notice anything amiss. Cary didn't know where Jason was; she hadn't gotten a note from him, and he didn't appear at the table when they went down for breakfast.

To Cary's dismay, he did appear at the bunny slopes that afternoon. And although he had a meeting scheduled, he just brought the meeting to the bunny slopes with him. Cary recognized a number of the sales staff. They had looked a little dazed at the locale he'd chosen, but nobody was about to say anything.

Cary thought the whole thing was ridiculous. Especially when she skied down the little slope and, despite her very best efforts and determination, ended up on her hind end in the snow. Jason was there, smooth and sleek and infuriatingly comfortable on his skis, to assist her. "We're going to talk tonight," he told her briefly.

"No! The children—"

"The children are going to the lodge's kids' dinner club. They're going to have hot dogs and play games and pop popcorn to string on the tree. And they're going to sing Christmas carols and make Christmas gifts and have a great time. It is the Christmas Season! Have a little spirit!" he told her. "Be ready at six." By then he had her on her feet and was gliding away.

She couldn't begin to move so quickly. She could hardly move at all.

"Be ready for what?" she demanded.

But Jason McCready either didn't hear her or didn't intend to answer.

Danny left early for the kids' dinner club. That gave Cary time to bathe and dress carefully. She didn't know where she was going, so she chose a black velvet dress that she hoped was both concealing and elegant. She wasn't going to run away tonight. She was just going to explain that they couldn't go any further. Because...

Because she needed her job. And she couldn't bear for things to be awkward.

And because she didn't want to be one of his long string of women.

And that was the real rub, she admitted, seeing her features pale in the mirror as she slipped on her little pearl earrings.

Why? What did it matter? she asked herself. He was good for her. He would open up the world that she had closed away, and then she could go on.

No. She couldn't.

Because she cared about him, she admitted. Because he had fascinated her from the start. Because no one else could draw the things from her that he had drawn so easily. No one else could make her forget Richard.

She hadn't forgotten Richard.

Yes, she had. For those precious moments in Jason's arms, she had forgotten.

She closed her eyes. He had made her say his name. But he had never spoken hers.

There was a knock on the door to the suite. Cary grabbed her coat and hurried out. She didn't want him coming into her room.

His room, really. The whole lodge was his.

She was breathless when she threw the door open and saw him. His eyes were bright. He was still angry, she thought.

And in jeans and a leather jacket, he was far more casually dressed than she was.

"Oh! I'll change," she murmured.

"No, it doesn't matter. It doesn't matter at all. Not where we're going. Come on."

"Where *are* we going?" Cary demanded.

He could move so quickly when he was in a hurry. He had her by her elbow, and he hadn't answered her question. In front of the lodge there were too many people around, all greeting Jason and nodding to her, for her to say anything. But finally they were in the Jeep, and she repeated her question. "Where are we going?"

"There." He pointed to a structure just up the hill. Cary sighed. For a man who wanted to talk, he was extremely untalkative.

And she still had no idea where they were going.

The ride was too short, and yet it was also interminable. As soon as they entered the wooden building on the hill, she realized it was a private château, and that some-one had readied it for their arrival. A fire was burning in the grate, and a delicious aroma was wafting from chafing dishes on the rustic table.

Jason removed his jacket, casting it onto one of the couches. He didn't take her coat, but walked straight to the table, lifting the cover off one of the dishes. "Beef Stroganoff. And, let's see, a very nice white burgundy. Have a seat."

He pulled out her chair. Cary still had her coat on. "Jason, I never agreed to a private—"

"Did you want to discuss our sexual relationship publicly?" he demanded.

"We don't have a relationship!" she insisted.

He smiled. "Fine. Sit down and tell me why."

Exasperated, Cary groaned, doffed her coat and then took the seat he had pulled out for her. He poured the wine, then sat opposite her. His eyes met hers as he lifted his glass to her.

"Well?"

"I just can't see you anymore," she said.

"Why not?"

"You're my boss, for one thing."

"We're nowhere near work."

"But we will be."

"This has nothing to do with work, and you know it."

Cary sipped her wine. "All right. All right—you need another reason? I don't care to be one of the crowd."

"The crowd?" One brow shot up. "Really, it isn't that bad, is it?"

She flushed. "I just don't—"

He leaned across the table. His fingers closed over hers. The warmth was electric. Seductive... frightening.

"I enjoy you. I like you. I admire you."

"You're lost, sunk, in your memories!" Cary told him.

He smiled ruefully. "I am? All right, then, Cary. We have everything in common. You're in love with a ghost, too. But admit it, you're having fun with me. You opened up. You didn't do anything casual or careless last night. You made love with me! And that's a hell of a lot more than you've managed before!"

She jumped up, and his wineglass slammed down. "At least I'm not always trying to run away!" he exploded.

But you're not in love with me, either! Cary thought. And then she paused at the awful realization that maybe, just maybe, she was falling in love with him. It had started when he had picked her up for the week....

No. It had started before that. It had started with the fascination she felt each time she saw him.

And now...

"Give it this week," he said.

"What?"

"You're having fun. Hell, you're even having sex. Give it this week. Then, if you want to stop, we will. We can go back to work and never even nod in the hallways."

She should have said no right then.

He had brought her here, to complete privacy. To complete intimacy. But he would take her home if she wanted. She knew that. She had only to say the word.

But...

She liked the lodge. She liked being with the children. And she liked being with him. She liked his slow smile, his laughter, and she even liked seeing the weariness slip from his eyes.

And she liked his chest. Naked.

The rest of the week...

It was almost Christmas. She owed it to herself.

She sank slowly into her chair. "We'll have dinner," she murmured.

And they did. Just dinner. But then it began to snow, and they stood at the window and watched the snowflakes falling. Then they sat before the fire and started to talk about baseball and all the things that little girls needed, and children in general.

Suddenly they were stretched out on the floor beside the flames.

And Cary knew that she wanted to make love. Again.

The flames in front of them, and between them, began to climb higher and higher.

Outside, the Christmas lights flickered red and green.

And Cary knew that she had given herself a bigger Christmas present than she had known. She had given herself laughter and a little bit of Christmas spirit. . . .

And even a little taste of peace.

Chapter Five

The week passed in a whirl.

And while it was happening, Cary had to admit that it was the best time she could remember having.

For one thing, she became a passable skier. Between Jason and Angela, she had plenty of help. And plenty of laughter each time she or Danny pitched into the snow.

The laughter. Perhaps that was what she would remember the most. Or maybe it was the warmth, the quiet evenings. Or maybe the sheer excitement of feeling alive and aware and sensual again.

He told her to relax, to try to have fun.

And she did. They swam; they skied; they ate. They spent time with the children, and they spent time alone. They took lazy walks, and they played in the privacy of the Jacuzzi in Cary's room. They listened to the endless hum of Christmas carols heralding the season, and they went on sleigh rides with bells jingling.

Danny had the time of his life.

But the week came to an end, and though Jason acted as if nothing needed to change because they went back, Cary knew that it would. The week had been a fantasy. Now they were in the real world. It was an uneasy feeling, and as she lay awake the Sunday night before she had to go to work, she regretted what she had done even as she dreamed about the days gone by.

And then there was Jason.

Courteous, charming. He'd made her laugh so easily. And she'd never imagined a more tender or exciting lover. But now it was time to remember that he moved swiftly, that no matter how easy he had been to be with, he was still in love with Sara, and if he thought that Cary was coming too close, he would move on.

She slept very little that night.

Monday morning passed by without her seeing him. She had lunch with June, determined that she wasn't going to give anything away. Nothing. And despite June's persistence, she stuck to her story that it had been a nice week, that Jason had been charming, that Danny and Angela had enjoyed a great time—and nothing more.

She thought she would see Jason sometime during the day, but she didn't. And she didn't know whether she was anxious, or very, very glad.

A second day passed without her seeing him, and then a third and a fourth. She lay awake at night, tossing and turning. She remembered his every touch, and she clenched her teeth tightly, thinking how ironic it was that she had finally fallen in love again.

With a man who not only couldn't love her, but didn't even want to see her again.

She had warned herself. Again and again, she had warned herself.

By Friday she had stubbornly convinced herself that she was not going to go from living in one kind of hell to living in another. If he asked her to dinner, to a show, to coffee—to anything—ever again, she would refuse.

To make matters worse, June plagued her at lunch every day. And it was the Christmas season. Everywhere she turned, people were singing about tidings of joy.

"Maybe you'll have a date for the pre-Christmas Eve party," June teased her at lunch on Friday.

Cary clenched her teeth. "June, I had a nice time last week. I enjoyed both the McCreadys. That's all."

"And did the McCreadys enjoy you?"

"June, drop it," Cary said warningly.

But it was when she returned to her office after lunch that she found the computer. And, as it happened, June was with her.

"It's that system that Danny wanted so much! The one you thought you couldn't afford!" June exclaimed. "How did it get here? Who would have...oh!" She stared hard at Cary, then she started to laugh. "I guess one McCready did enjoy you. Very much."

"June!" Cary gasped.

"Oh, kid, I'm sorry, I didn't mean anything by that. Except that you must have...well, I mean, you must have had a really good time. And *he* must have had a really good time, too. Oh, I'm not making this sound any better, am I? Gee, I wonder how many other people saw this come in here?"

Damn Jason McCready. He'd forced her into falling for him, then ignored her....

And then managed to turn her into the most delectable piece of office gossip in months.

Cary's cheeks were flaming, and she couldn't think of a single word to say to June. She probably shouldn't accost Jason now, in his office. His secretary would hear her, and the staff would probably be buzzing by the end of the afternoon.

Damn Jeremy and his Christmas dust! Cary thought furiously. The computer was in her office, and it must look like some kind of payment for services above and beyond the call of duty. Well, nuts to timing! She strode out of the office, down the hall and to the elevators. And she didn't wait for Jason's secretary to announce her, she waved and went right through the door.

Jason had been expecting to hear from Cary. He'd been waiting for a call.

This past week had been bedlam—absolute bedlam— and he'd played catch-up from morning until night. He'd driven by her apartment on his way home from work twice, but it had been late, and when he'd been about to go up to see if she was awake, he had been amazed to find his hands trembling, and he'd driven home instead.

Early this morning, he'd thought of the computer. He hoped it was the right one and that she would tell him how much it would mean to Danny. The boy had talked about it often enough on the trip, telling Angela all the wonderful things he had been able to do on it in school.

He wanted to talk to Cary. He wanted to hear her voice again. From the minute he had left her at her door, he had missed her. Missed the gold in her gaze, the curve of her smile. He missed the simple beauty of her face and the lithe, sensual beauty of her form. He missed being near someone who shared his love for children; he missed the way she could laugh at herself when she landed in the snow. He missed her eyes, steady and sure when she told him something she was determined he should hear. And he missed her sighs and her whispers and the wonder in her eyes when they made love. Just remembering made an ache rise hauntingly within him.

He had lain awake all night thinking about it, and he had awakened that morning amazed to feel an aching in his heart. He wanted the week back. He wanted to be with her. For the first time in five years he had been happy. He hoped the computer would make her happy, too.

Apparently it didn't.

He was amazed when she stormed into his office, her eyes gleaming with fury, her beautiful features as tense as iron. There was a pencil between her hands. And even before she began to speak, it snapped.

"What the hell are you doing to me?" she demanded.

Defensively, he was on his feet. He walked around the desk and perched on the edge of it, his arms crossed over his chest. "What on earth are you talking about?"

"The computer!"

"It's for Danny."

"Oh, it's for Danny! But it's also for me. And I can't afford it. And I don't want things from you that I can't afford. It looks like a—a payment!"

"A payment!" Jason roared.

"Everyone must know now that . . . that . . ."

"You're sleeping with me?" Jason suggested. He said it as if it were something evil. But it had meant everything to him. It had meant salvation.

"But I'm not 'sleeping with' you—it's not some ongoing thing!"

"There was no payoff intended, Cary, and I can't believe—"

"Oh!" she ground out with exasperation. "I *am* going to have to quit—"

"Why?"

"Don't you see what you've done? My position is untenable. I just became another of your casual associations, but I have to appear here every day—"

"I wasn't sure that we were involved in any casual associations," he said, his eyes narrowing angrily. "I intended to call you this afternoon—"

"Did you? No! No, it doesn't matter. It can't go on, don't you see? I can't work here and have everyone looking at me as if I were...as if I were one of your women," she finished flatly.

"It was good between us," he said harshly. "Everything was good."

"*Was!* It's over. I will not see you again!"

He was still. Dead still. Absolutely silent and tense. Then he spoke softly. "All right. I'll marry you."

Cary was so startled that she fell silent, gaping. Then she felt tears stinging the back of her eyes. *All right, he'd marry her?* It sounded as if he had come to a compromise on a business proposal. And he couldn't mean it. No matter how...good...it had been between them, he was striking and rich—no, no, how could she forget? He was tall, dark and handsome and rich. Damn June and Jeremy and Christmas dust and the Christmas season! He didn't mean to marry her; it was just something that had come out of his mouth to stall her.

She shook her head. "You can't mean that. It makes no sense. And if—"

"I mean it with every breath in me." He strode toward her, pausing half an inch away. "And it makes perfect sense. You're the one who said we had a lot in common. So we're both really in love with ghosts. I understand you, you understand me. We share something."

Cary shook her head. She didn't understand the pain she was feeling. He did mean it. He would marry her. Just to keep her near. She should have been flattered. Instead she wanted to cry. "I don't need anyone to marry me. You certainly don't have to do anything like that. I can do very well on my own—"

"Yes, yes, I know. But you can do better with me. And I can do a lot for Danny that you can't do."

"I'm a good mother—"

"But you're not a father."

"This is insane."

"Angela loves you. And I do flatter myself that Danny is fond of me."

His hands were on her shoulders, his eyes burning into hers. They were compelling, demanding that she bend to his will.

Excitement began to seize her. She could marry him. He'd offered her something that he hadn't offered any other woman. There was something missing, but what she would have would surely be better than loneliness. She was falling in love with him. And perhaps that would be enough.

"Do it," he insisted.

"I . . ." She jerked free from him suddenly. "I have to go!" she said.

"I'll be home tonight. Get someone to watch Danny. Come see me. I'll want an answer."

She left his office.

She spent the afternoon in misery. Jeremy popped his head in, and it was apparent that he and the entire office had heard about the computer. "Wow! Just imagine what you could get if you went away with him for a month!" Jeremy teased.

Cary felt like hurling her desk at him. "Get yourself and your Christmas dust out of here!" she warned him furiously.

Jeremy couldn't be gotten rid of that easily. He came in and sat on the edge of her desk. Frowning, he looked into her eyes. "Cary, I didn't mean anything."

"Never mind!"

"Cary, I really didn't mean anything. And neither did Jason, I'm certain."

"He's careless! He's accustomed to having everything at his whim, and he's accustomed to money—"

"Cary, he was an orphan. An abandoned boy who grew up on the streets more than off them. He worked his way up to everything he has. He isn't careless."

Cary stared at her desk. She hadn't known anything about his past. He never talked about it. Maybe he had walked the hard and rocky road once, but that had been years ago. Perhaps his career had been admirable. Okay, so he was admirable, and that was how he had managed to slip into her heart. That was why she cared so much.

But it was also true that he thought he could snap his fingers and she would snap to attention.

Well, she wasn't going to.

At nine o'clock that night she was on her way to his house in Cambridge. So much for her best intentions. But as the cab carried her along, she convinced herself again that she would say no. In very certain terms.

The house was beautiful, old and furnished with antiques. She was escorted to an eighteenth-century drawing room where Jason was sipping brandy and evidently waiting for her.

She felt awkward as she walked in. And he had no polite chitchat for her. He simply stared at her, waiting.

"How's Angela?" she asked.

"Fine. Sleeping."

She nodded. "Jason, I can't—"

She didn't see the disappointment in his eyes. His lashes shaded them too quickly. "I really can't do this. I can't do this to you—"

"Do it to me? Cary, I want you!"

"And it seems that you're willing to pay a tremendous price. Jason, I don't—"

"The price doesn't matter, Cary. It's Christmas. You're what I want more than anything in the world."

This year, Cary thought.

"I will do my best to give you anything that you want," he said harshly.

"Jason, it's just that—"

"Cary, you don't want to be one of a number of women. I'll make you my wife. I can give Danny anything in the world. The best schools, anything he wants. A guaranteed future. No worry for you. Cary, it's Christmas! And I can give you and Danny every Christmas gift in the world."

"But there's nothing that I can give you!"

"Damn it, Cary, give us both a break! You'd be giving Angela and me a real home!" he exclaimed.

She felt her fingers curl. It was a business proposition. Pure and simple. But it wasn't such a bad proposition.

"All . . . all right," she told him.

"Done!" A handsome smile slashed his face. In seconds he was across the room. He took her hand, and before she realized what he was doing, he had slipped a diamond on her finger.

It was beautiful. It was large, but it wasn't decadent. It was surrounded by tiny emeralds, and it fit right beside her old gold band.

"Jason, I can't—"

"It's an engagement ring! It seals our promise."

And it fit. It fit her just right, the band snug and warm around her finger. "A ring and a kiss," he told her softly. And she was suddenly in his arms.

The kiss too, was filled with promise. Her anxiety and emotions knotted together, and when his kiss deepened, she found a sweet escape in the growing sensation. It had become so natural to be with him. So natural, so beautiful to feel his touch. To know this wonderful, spiraling desire . . .

She saw his room that night. Saw his large oak ward-robes and dressers, his massive, white-tiled bath, his king-size bed. She lost herself in that bed, in the soft, warm, sinking comfort. She acutely felt his every touch. The sweep of his hand, the pressure of his body, the passion of his being. She rode with him and flew with him, and when it was done, she was once again left shaking with the wonder of their lovemaking.

And once more feeling the growth of tears behind her eyes.

She lay on the soft sheets, feeling his arms around her, and from somewhere she heard the promise of a Christmas carol on the air.

Christmas...

It was for giving, for believing. It was for miracles. It was for faith.

And to have Jason, well...

But there was something missing. And as she listened to the distant beauty of "Silent Night" filling the darkness, she knew what it it was. Love.

He touched her. Touched her shoulder. And his kiss burned into her flesh.

Once more, she thought. She couldn't resist having one last time. And so she moved into his arms, meeting his kiss with warmth, with magic, with a prayer.

Later, while he slept, comfortable, handsome as a boy, his dark hair tousled, she rose and dressed quickly.

"Where are you going?" Lazy green eyes were on her.

"Home. Danny is there."

"I'll take you."

She shook her head. "No, please, it isn't late. I'll be all right."

But she was beginning to know Jason McCready. Even if this had been a casual date, he would still have seen her home. The man she loved had manners.

He took her to her apartment door and paused there. "I smell popcorn," he murmured.

"June and Danny. I'm sure they're making strands for the tree."

He placed a hand on either side of her head. "I love your apartment. Did I ever tell you that?"

She shook her head, wondering if it could be true. His house was so magnificent. "I love your house," she told him.

He smiled. "Good. Maybe you can change it, and I can love it, too." He leaned down and kissed her, and she wanted to pull away, but she couldn't. She clung to him, letting the magic wash over her.

She walked into her apartment, where June and Danny were indeed busy with popcorn strings.

"Hi, Mom!" There was excitement in Danny's eyes. He knew that she had been with Jason.

"Hi, honey." She kissed him on the top of his blond head, her resolve weakening. It would be so good for Danny. Maybe she was thinking like a fool.

No, it would be wrong to marry Jason. She couldn't do it. She had told him that she would, but she couldn't. And she couldn't see him again. Not under any circumstances. Because every time she saw him, she wanted him. For Christmas.

For always.

"Bedtime," she insisted to Danny, and she finally managed to get him tucked it.

June was not so easy. "Well? You're upset. You're going to cry. Oh, that creep! He told you it was over!"

Cary shook her head. "No, he asked me to marry him."

"What!" June gasped. "Oh, how wonderful!" She started to dance around the room with a pillow, but then she paused. "You did tell him yes, right?"

Cary sighed. "Yes, I did. But I'm afraid I'm not going to. I'm—I'm going to resign tomorrow. I'm not going back to the office. I'll finish my present assignment, and you can take in all my paperwork."

"What!" June stared at her as if she had gone insane. She argued with Cary, pleaded with her.

Cary slipped the diamond from her finger and placed it in June's palm. "Take this back, too," she insisted.

"Oh, Cary, you can't possibly dislike him or be angry with him—"

"I don't dislike him and I'm not angry with him," Cary said. She smiled. "Actually, I love him."

Cary knew that June didn't understand, but Cary wasn't going to give her an explanation. She ushered June out and hurried to her bedroom, where she turned on the radio.

Someone was playing "Silent Night" again.

Cary laid her head on her pillow and indulged herself in a cascade of hot tears.

Jason McCready was on top of the world.

Indeed, the world was beautiful. For the first time in years he couldn't wait for Christmas. The pain had been miraculously lifted from his heart, and he loved all the things that had once hurt so badly. They would be married before Christmas, he decided. He'd forgotten to ask Cary to help Angela with a Christmas dress, something special to be worn to church. She wouldn't mind, he was certain.

Sitting at his desk at work, he leaned back and closed his eyes. He laced his fingers behind his head and wondered if Danny needed a new baseball bat, or maybe a glove. Or maybe he had an attachment to his old one. Danny liked collecting baseball cards. He had told Jason that in New Hampshire. There were all kinds of baseball card shows they could go to together.

His secretary buzzed him and announced that June was waiting to see him.

"Send her in," Jason said.

As soon as he saw June he felt a foreboding. He knew immediately, beyond a shadow of a doubt, that something was very wrong.

"Mr. McCready, I . . ." Her voice trailed away.

"June, I have always hoped that all my employees would feel free to come here and say whatever they had to say," he told her patiently.

She went very pale.

"June?"

"Oh, Mr. McCready, I hate being here," she said. "But I . . ."

She stepped forward, and she put his diamond ring on his desk. He stared at it, and then at her.

"Cary is quitting," June said in a rush.

He paled, amazed at the assault of pain that swept over him.

"She couldn't tell me herself?"

June moistened her lips. "I think she was afraid to see you again. Afraid you wouldn't really listen to her. Not that I understand her myself."

Jason stared at the ring, then stood, slipping it into his pocket. He walked to the window.

"She's going to finish up all her work. She just isn't going to come in anymore," June said quietly.

His back was square and straight as he stared at the street. "This isn't like her," he said. "Cary Adams has always had a talent for stating her mind."

She did have that wonderful talent, he realized. Since that day when she'd come here and told him exactly what she thought of him, she'd been changing his life. So subtly, at first. She'd just made him watch her. Watch the sunlight in her hazel eyes. Watch her movement in the hallways. Dear God, he'd come to love her smile.

Christmas bells rang below him. Bright lights in green and red were coming on as the early darkness of winter descended.

A bleakness settled over him. The future was empty without her. Suddenly it hit him like brick as he realized what his despair meant.

He loved her eyes; he loved her hair. He loved her laughter, and he loved her spirit and her mind. He loved the trusting way she looked at him when they lay entwined together. He loved *her,* he realized.

And she wanted none of him.

June realized that he wasn't saying anything. He was just standing there, his shoulders squared in misery as he gazed at the snow. June wanted to touch his shoulders in comfort.

And she wanted to give Cary a good shaking for hurting him so. What was the matter with that woman?

"Cary is usually very determined to handle her own affairs. I suppose she thought it would be easier if she weren't involved this time," June said. Why hadn't Cary gotten Jeremy to come up here? He and McCready were friends, and although June had always liked her employer a lot, she was in a wretched position at the moment. "It's so much harder when you love someone. Though, for the life of me, I can't understand—"

"What!"

June broke off, stunned, frightened by the harshness of his tone. She couldn't remember what she had been saying. "I—er—"

"What did you say?"

"What did I say?" June repeated. "Oh. I don't understand Cary. I don't know why on earth she's doing this. She loves you, and—"

"That. That part. Say that again."

"I said she loves you—"

"How do you know that?"

"Well, she said so, of course—"

Once again June broke off. He was striding across the room to her, and he was moving so swiftly, and with such power, that she almost cried out and leaped away. She didn't get a chance to.

His hands were on her shoulders. She was lifted off the floor, and his lips brushed her cheeks.

The bleakness had fallen from him like a cloak of darkness.

She loved him. And he loved her. And as he broke into a broad grin, he suddenly understood. They'd both been too lost. Lost in the past. Lost in pain that they hadn't managed to let go. And then, like a fool, he'd offered her everything in the world. Everything except what a woman like Cary wanted. Love.

"She *is* going to marry me. Thank you, June, but you don't need to stand here stuttering anymore. She *is* going to marry me."

And then, while June stared openmouthed, he walked past her and out of the office.

By late afternoon Cary had decided that Jason had graciously accepted both the return of his ring and her resignation.

She allowed herself another good cry, then decided she had to try to stop or else she would spend the rest of her days in tears. But it was hard. So hard...

She looked at the phone time and time again, thinking that she should call him. And then her cheeks would flame, and she would be ashamed, because she hadn't gone to see him herself. She should never, never have sent June to face her own particular lion for her.

But she had been afraid to see Jason McCready. Because if he pressed her, she just might want the magic so badly that she would reach for it, even though it was wrong.

Danny came home from school, and she wondered if she should talk with him yet. She had only told him that she was taking a day off from work—she hadn't told him she had quit her job.

After all, it was Christmas.

It wasn't right to be so miserable.

She didn't say anything to Danny, so he spent the night talking about Jason, and about how wonderful it had been at the lodge, and how he hoped that they would get together again soon.

Cary nearly screamed.

At ten she went to bed. She lay staring at her ceiling and willed herself to go to sleep, but sleep wouldn't come.

Tears would. They were just starting to well in her eyes when she heard the first thump against her window. She jerked up, wondering what on earth could be going on. A second thump hit the window, and she jumped up and raced to it, her heart pounding.

Two stories below was a figure standing under a lamppost. And even as she watched him, another snowball came flying at her, thumping against the window.

Her eyes widened in amazement. Jason McCready, hatless and scarfless, was standing on the sidewalk, grinning at her and throwing snowballs.

She threw open the window, shivering against the sudden cold.

"Jason! What are you doing down there?"

To her utter amazement, he began to sing. "I'm dreaming of a white Christmas..."

His voice was good. Very good. Rich. He could croon out the tune with almost the same appeal as Bing Crosby.

The window next to hers suddenly flew open. Mrs. Crowley, from the apartment beside hers, looked out. "What in heaven's name is going on?"

"Jason, hush!" Cary pleaded.

"...may your days be merry and bright..."

Another window burst open. It was old Mr. Calahan from the apartment below hers.

"Hey, not bad!" Mr. Calahan said, chuckling. "How about 'Deck the Halls'?"

"Jason, please, what are you doing?"

"Trying to get your attention."

"Well, you've got mine, young man," Mrs. Crowley informed him. All bundled up in her thick robe, she was a cheerful picture, with her red cheeks and bouncing pink curlers. Jason grinned at her.

"I came to ask Cary to marry me again. I just wanted her to know that I have lots of Christmas spirit. She thinks she knows all about me, but there are a lot of things she hasn't realized."

"Jason!" Cary cried in horror. "I told you I can't marry you—"

"Why not? Specifically."

Mr. Calahan craned his neck. "Yes, why not? Specifically."

"Jason!" Cary cried, mortified.

"That's all right. I already know," Jason told Mr. Calahan and Mrs. Crowley. But his eyes, green, bright and with such a tender expression, remained on Cary. She felt her heart beginning to ache and her limbs to burn.

"I asked her for all the wrong reasons, you see. I said that we'd be good together. That we'd be good parents for each other's children. That we'd keep each other from being lonely. I have a nice business, and I told her that I could take care of her."

"That doesn't sound so bad to me," Mr. Calahan said.

"Go on!" Mrs. Crowley insisted.

Jason smiled. A beautiful, slow, crooked smile that filled his face with wistfulness and longing. "I want to restate my proposal. I want to tell her that I want to marry her for just one reason. For the most important reason in the world. Because she brought light back to my world. She made my every hour worth living. Because I love her with all my heart."

"Oh, Jason!" Cary whispered.

"How romantic!" Mrs. Crowley clapped her hands.

"Well, tell him yes, young woman!" Mr. Calahan commanded. "Tell the poor fellow yes before he expires out there!"

"Yes! Yes!" Cary cried. "Stay there. Stay right there! I'll be right down!"

He could have come up, but she wasn't thinking clearly. And so Cary rushed down the stairs and into the snow, where she threw herself into his arms.

"Oh, Jason! Really? Can it be true?"

He cradled her chin. "Yes, it's true. Cary, I do want to give you things. I want to give you and Danny everything I can. I want to make you happy. I want you to keep working, if that's what you want. And I know that Angela and Danny will be delighted. But, Cary, I do love you with all my heart.''

"Jason! I love you, too."

"Kiss him!" Mrs. Crowley called out.

"Are you still eavesdropping up there?" Mr. Calahan demanded.

"Oh, shut up, you old goat!"

"Hmph! All right, young lady, you go ahead and kiss him. And come inside! That way we can all get some sleep."

Cary decided to oblige. She stood on her tiptoes and kissed him. Long and hard.

Mrs. Crowley sighed. A window closed.

And suddenly little flakes began to fall. Beautiful, intricate little snowflakes. It would probably be a very white Christmas.

Jason's lips parted from hers. Cary caught his hand, and they rushed up the stairs.

Once inside her apartment, she was in his arms again. And when the kiss at last seemed to end, she leaned against him, dazed, amazed, dazzled, and then worried and afraid all in one.

"Jason, this still isn't quite fair. You've given me so much already. What will I ever give you?"

"What I want for Christmas most of all."

"And that is?"

"You," he said. "In a red ribbon. And nothing else. Just you."

She smiled shyly, and he kissed her again. Then he broke away. "Maybe something else, too."

"What?"

"I always imagined a wonderful family, a big family. I grew up alone, and somehow that makes you really love kids. We have a great boy, and a great girl, but maybe we could go for two more somewhere along the line. If you're willing. What do you think?"

"I think kids are just great," Cary whispered.

He already knew that.

"So will you marry me?"

"Yes, Jason, yes. Oh, yes, I'll marry you."

"Wow. Oh, wow! Wow, oh, wow, oh, my!" came a little boy's voice.

Danny was up. And Danny had been unabashedly listening to the whole thing.

"Really?" Danny said.

"You're supposed to be in bed," Cary said.

"Really," Jason told him, grinning.

"When?" Danny demanded. "It has to be by Christmas."

"Danny!"

"By Christmas it is," Jason agreed.

And they *were* married by Christmas. The ceremony was on December twentieth. Danny and Angela were both there, along with Jeremy and June and the entire staff of *Elegance*.

They were holding off on a honeymoon because they didn't want to leave for the holidays. Jason and Angela planned to stay with Cary and Danny at her apartment until New Year's Day; then Cary and Danny would move into Jason's house.

And make it a home, Jason knew.

On Christmas Eve they all went to church. And when they came home, everyone sang carols and set packages around the tree.

But once the kids were tucked in, Jason turned on the Christmas lights and was startled to find a note to him hooked on the tree.

"I have a special gift for you. My room. Five minutes."

Curious, intrigued, Jason waited the five minutes, then rushed to Cary's bedroom.

And there, curled up on an expanse of snowy sheets, was his wife.

His gift, his greatest Christmas gift ever.

His wife.

And she was decked out beautifully in nothing—absolutely nothing—but a big red bow.

He paused just a moment, breathing out a prayer. Thank you, God.

And then he walked forward, laughing, and swept his Christmas gift tenderly into his arms.

Epilogue

It was very late, but Danny slipped out of bed anyway. The house was quiet; everyone was sleeping at last.

He ran to the Christmas tree. He was so startled that he paused, his mouth a large O.

He had expected gifts. But he hadn't really expected so many.

And he certainly hadn't expected to find his brand new computer, all set up, with a big red bow on it, just awaiting his touch.

He closed his eyes and opened them again. The gifts were all still there. Wait till Angela saw...

But Angela already knew about the gifts, he was certain. And she would be excited, and she would be pleased, because she was Angela, and she was just great, even if she was a girl. His sister now. They'd both been very lucky this Christmas. They'd already gotten the things that money just couldn't buy. He had a new father. Jason McCready would never replace his real dad, just like Cary could never replace Angela's real mom. But both were the second best thing. And they both had the very gift in the world to give. Love.

Danny knew that Jason would always be willing to leave work early to throw a baseball. And Angela would have a mom to take her to her Brownie meetings, and Cary would fuss over her hair, tie it up in those pigtails and dress it up with barrettes.

Danny found himself shaking suddenly. This was just the best Christmas in the world.

He took a walk across the room, going to the beautiful little crèche that his mother had set up. He reached over and very carefully fingered the little Christ figure, then walked to the window.

He could just see the North Star. He knew which one it was because Jason had shown it to him. "Hello," he murmured. He cleared his throat. That wasn't how you were supposed to pray. "Dear Lord," he began again softly. "I just wanted to say thank you. I—well, I do believe in the Christmas spirit and miracles, but I know that the Santa I spoke to was my cousin Jeremy. So I know that everything I got—all the miracles—was because of you." He smiled. "A new dad, and a computer!" Maybe you weren't supposed to joke with God. No, God would understand, he decided. But his smile faded anyway. "Thank you so much!" he whispered earnestly. "Once you gave us all your Son. And now you've given me a dad, and Angela a mom. And I have a sister, and she has a brother. And Mom has Jason, and Jason has Mom. It *is* a miracle! Thank you!" He stopped because he didn't have any more words that could express how grateful he was.

The North Star seemed to sparkle suddenly with a dazzling light.

And then it began to fade.

Danny stared at it for a while, then he smiled. The star was fading because it was Christmas. Christmas day.

He let out a wild whoop and went running for Angela's door. "It's Christmas, sleepyhead! Wake up!"

Angela, with her eyes barely open, appeared in her doorway in a fluffy robe. "It's so early!" she breathed. "Can we wake them up?"

"Sure. We're kids. And it's Christmas," Danny told her.

Cary awoke to the children's shrieks of delight, yet she was afraid to open her eyes.

Knowing that the kids would be up early, she and Jason had put on pajamas before they fell asleep. His arms were around her tightly; she was pulled against him so that his chest met her back, and they were curled together like a little pair of mice. She felt him, felt all his warmth, and didn't dare open her eyes. She didn't want him to be a Christmas dream.

But he wasn't. She was his wife. She was in love with him, and miraculously, he was in love with her. No gift could be greater.

"Mom!"

"Dad!"

It was Danny who called her name, and Angela who woke Jason. Yet when the two came flying into the bedroom, it was Angela who landed on her, and Danny who tackled Jason.

"Whoa, hey, what is this!" Jason protested gruffly. But he was laughing.

"It's Christmas!" Danny announced indignantly.

"Wow, you mean we might have missed it?" Cary said, wide-eyed.

"Mom!" Danny moaned. "Will you two please get up!"

"I'll make coffee," Cary volunteered to Jason. Then she smiled and slipped out of bed. She winked at the kids as Jason tried to fall back asleep, and as she left the room, she could hear a burst of laughter as the two attacked Jason, tickling him mercilessly.

And apparently Jason was just as merciless in return.

Coffee and cocoa were ready when they all traipsed out to the living room. Cary seated herself by Jason's side, comfortable in the crook of his arm, as the children opened their gifts. There was paper everywhere. And she was pleased to see that Danny was as impressed with the small things as he was with the wonderful new computer. And Angela, bless her, was thrilled with her gifts, too, even though she'd grown up with everything money could buy.

And Jason McCready, the self-made man, seemed more touched by Danny's home-made Christmas card than by any gift he might have received.

Cary had just stepped over some of the paper to get more coffee when the doorbell rang. She arched a brow to Jason.

"Don't look at me," he told her. "It must be your cousin Jeremy."

And it was. Except that he had run into June in the doorway, so both of them were standing there arguing, with their hands piled high with boxes for the children.

The two were quickly inside, and there was more mayhem as the children kissed them and thanked them for their gifts. Jason poured the coffee while Cary supervised the gift giving. Pandemonium seemed to reign for quite a while; then at last the room grew quieter. "I wanted to know if I could take the kids to the Parade of the Elves. It's not far from here—I'd only need to steal them for a couple of hours," June said.

Jason seemed uneasy. "June, I know it's Christmas, but it might be a little wild out there today. Are you sure you want to take the kids by yourself?"

"Jeremy will come with me," June said.

"I will?" Jeremy began. June kicked him. He stared at her indignantly, then he seemed to realize that June was trying to give the newlyweds some time alone. "Oh, I will. Of course." He cast June a look of stern reproach as soon as he thought Cary was no longer looking. Cary hid a smile. She was certain that Jason hadn't been aware of anything.

"I don't know..." Jason began with a frown, looking to Cary.

"The kids will be fine. And I'm sure they'd love to go," she said demurely.

Within minutes, it seemed, she had the kids dressed and ready to go. June and Jeremy were waiting at the door.

June and Jeremy. Hmm, Cary thought. Why not?

Jeremy paused to give Cary a kiss goodbye on the cheek, and she fluttered her fingers over his head.

"What was that?" he asked her.

"Christmas dust."

"What?"

"Never mind. Just go on and have a good time. And thank you."

"Sure. We'll see you later."

"Christmas dinner is here," Jason advised over Cary's shoulder. "I'm doing the stuffing."

"I'm doing the stuffing!" Cary protested.

"No, you're the turkey and the vegetables and the mashed potatoes and the pies. I'm the stuffing."

Cary laughed as his arms came around her. She shrugged. "Whatever. Christmas dinner is here. Just be back by then, okay?"

"Got ya," Jeremy agreed. June was telling him to get a move on. He rolled his eyes. "Is she coming for dinner, too?"

"Yes."

"Great."

"Christmas dust," Cary repeated.

Jeremy frowned with confusion, then the foursome left.

Oh, well, there was always next Christmas, Cary thought.

She turned in her husband's arms. His lips found hers, and when he kissed her deeply, she felt the familiar thrill sweeping through her.

Jason looked at the door again. "Are you sure they're going to be all right?"

"Yes, I'm sure!" She caught his hand and, smiling, pulled him over to the couch. "June and Jeremy only look flighty, honest. I couldn't trust the kids more with anyone else. And besides, I have another gift for you."

He grinned, cocking a dark eyebrow.

"Oh, yeah?"

She nodded.

"Where's the box?"

"There isn't exactly a box," she said. Her fingers still entwined with his, she started for the bedroom.

His brow arched higher. "Is it a foot massage?"

Cary laughed. "Maybe..." She stood on tiptoe, quickly kissed his lips, then began to whisper. He could still make her feel so shy at times.

"Remember when I told you there was nothing that I could give you that you didn't have? And you said that yes, there was—me. Well, you've got me."

"A gift I will cherish all of my life," he promised her tenderly.

She flushed. "Thank you. But you also said you'd like four kids—if I was willing, of course—and that I could give you the two that were missing."

"Yes?"

"Well, I thought that we could get started. We're alone, we're awake, we're aware..."

"And we're just as eager and as willing as can be!" Jason said, laughing.

He lifted her off her feet and into his arms. And then he was kissing her, deeply, richly, warmly. She felt herself coming alive, trembling, quivering inside.

The kiss seemed to last forever, but when he broke away, Jason paused, holding her tightly, tenderly.

And she realized that he was looking out the window. The North Star was still visible, a faint little flicker against the day that had dawned beautifully blue.

Cary felt a new trembling seize her. Thank you, thank you! she thought in silence. Thank you so much.

Jason's eyes met hers. She smiled. "I was just thinking..." he began.

"So was I."

"I'm so very thankful that I have you."

She nodded. "And I'm so thankful for you. And for Christmas miracles. And Christmas dust."

His grin broadened wickedly. "Christmas dust? That's one you'll have to explain."

"Oh, well, you see—"

"Later," Jason said firmly.

He carried her into the bedroom and laid her down. Then his lips touched hers, and she was in his arms, and very soon the day was exploding into a new splendor of excitement and wonder and enchantment. After the soaring and the magic and the ecstasy, the peace and the contentment remained, and his arms were locked around her.

"We have to get to the turkey," he mumbled lazily.

"Yes, we have to get to the turkey," Cary agreed.

But he didn't move, and neither did she. He might not know about the Christmas dust, but he did know a lot about Christmas miracles.

Indeed he did. He arose at last, pausing to kiss her on the nose.

"Miracles!" he whispered softly. "Thank God for them, and for you—my Christmas miracle!"

He kissed her again, then pulled her from her cocoon of covers.

"Someone really does have to see to that turkey! Unless you want to test our luck and see if any elves will appear to cook it for us?"

Cary grinned. No elves were coming. They already had their Christmas miracles. "I'm doing the stuffing," she told him. "You can be potatoes."

"You be the potatoes!" he charged.

She laughed, found her robe and hurried down the hall, then she opened the kitchen door very carefully.

After all, it was just a matter of belief.

There might be elves in her kitchen after all!

* * * * *

Author's Note

Christmas in the Sun—and Cold!

Christmas is definitely one of my favorite times of year, but sometimes getting there is hectic. There is still so much to do on a daily basis, and with five children, there are not only a trillion family gifts to deal with, but a vast assortment of teachers and friends.

Then . . . there's the house.

We have Christmas Day here—it has become a tradition—and with family and friends, there are usually forty to fifty people in and out. It's a wonderful time. The house is all decorated. Sometimes I think that the large deer head in the living room must be humiliated to no end, for ornaments dangle from his antlers.

It's lots of fun, even if getting there isn't all that easy. Because Christmas means cleaning, and I think we've decided that maybe we have Christmas every year just so that we *will* clean, really clean, and dig through the piles and piles of papers and things that have covered every flat surface in the house.

Now, I know that there are people who don't believe that you can have a real Christmas in a place like South Florida. No snow. No sleigh rides. But I grew up down here, and I've discovered that Christmas, like home, is where the heart is.

Every year, in the midst of all the frantic cleaning—all the staring at objects that were saved for some reason or another, though no one can remember what those reasons actually were—we also sit here and hope that the temperature will dip below eighty, because it is nice to have a little chill in the air.

Well . . .

Christmas just a few years ago came with a big, big dip in the temperature. Frost lay all over the land and the readings plunged into the low thirties. It was not a day for air-conditioning; it was a day for heat!

But in the midst of all the wild preparations—the turkey and the lasagna, so both sides of the family will be represented—we discovered that the heating system, so seldom used, was jammed with fur from the feline residents of the house. The furnace wouldn't tick out even a speck of heat.

The kitchen, at least, was warm.

And then they began to arrive, our family and friends. They showed up in their coats and jackets, walked in the door, took off their coats and jackets—and immediately asked for them back.

Pretty soon, they were all there in the kitchen with me, plying me with offers to help, jockeying around for the closest positions to the oven.

"Don't you all have heat?" I heard time and time again.

Yes, of course, we have heat, but we also have a Persian cat named Cougar and a Himalayan named Shenandoah, and though we sweep and vacuum, etc., etc., we just didn't think of the heating vents.

Luckily, we have a fireplace. And that's where our guests flocked once we had run out of space in front of the stove. Two deep, they stood before the blaze, only leaving it to run to and from the kitchen.

Then we began to run out of firewood. But that was really all right, too. Another cousin arrived and asked me where Dennis was. "Out back, chopping up the deck for the fire," I told him cheerfully.

I knew we had been keeping that faulty decking around for something. And that Christmas, it did come in handy.

They remained by the fire, the lot of them. The aunts who hailed from the frigid north were the closest to the flames. No one suggested removing a coat again.

But it worked out, with a group of them playing whist on one side of the fire, another group into poker on the other. And in the end, the day passed, the turkey and the lasagna were gone, and so were the shivering guests.

We went to bed wearing several pairs of socks and robes and any number of blankets, and all huddled together. Despite everything, it had been a wonderful day, which proved to me, once again, that Christmas is where the heart is.

Except that I did make a mental note to myself, promising never to ask the powers that be for a crispy cold Christmas—ever again!

Heather Graham Pozzessere

Angels Everywhere!

Everything's turning up angels at Silhouette. In November, Ann Williams's ANGEL ON MY SHOULDER (IM #408, $3.29) features a heroine who's absolutely heavenly—and we mean that literally! Her name is Cassandra, and once she comes down to earth, her whole picture of life—and love—undergoes a pretty radical change.

Then, in December, it's time for ANGEL FOR HIRE (D #680, $2.79) from Justine Davis. This time it's hero Michael Justice who brings a touch of out-of-this-world magic to the story. Talk about a match made in heaven . . . !

Look for both these spectacular stories wherever you buy books. But look soon—because they're going to be flying off the shelves as if they had wings!

If you can't find these books where you shop, you can order them direct from Silhouette Books by sending your name, address, zip or postal code, along with a check or money order for $3.29 (ANGEL ON MY SHOULDER IM #408), and $2.79 (ANGEL FOR HIRE D #680), for each book ordered (please do not send cash), plus 75¢ postage and handling ($1.00 in Canada), payable to Silhouette Reader Service to:

In the U.S.

3010 Walden Ave.
P.O. Box 1396
Buffalo, NY 14269-1396

In Canada

P.O. Box 609
Fort Erie, Ontario
L2A 5X3

Please specify book title with your order.
Canadian residents add applicable federal and provincial taxes.

ANGEL

YOU'VE ASKED FOR IT, YOU'VE GOT IT!

MAN OF THE MONTH: 1992

ONLY FROM
⬤ SILHOUETTE® *Desire*™

You just couldn't get enough of them, those sexy men from Silhouette Desire—twelve sinfully sexy, delightfully devilish heroes. Some will make you sweat, some will make you sigh . . . but every long, lean one of them will have you swooning. So here they are, men we couldn't resist bringing to you for one more year. . . .

A KNIGHT IN TARNISHED ARMOR
by Ann Major in January

THE BLACK SHEEP
by Laura Leone in February

THE CASE OF THE MESMERIZING BOSS
by Diana Palmer in March

DREAM MENDER
by Sheryl Woods in April

WHERE THERE IS LOVE
by Annette Broadrick in May

BEST MAN FOR THE JOB
by Dixie Browning in June

Don't let these men get away! *Man of the Month,* only in Silhouette Desire.

MOM92JJ-1

WRITTEN IN THE STARS

HE'S OUT OF THIS WORLD

in

ARC OF THE ARROW

Could Sagittarian R. G. Travers have finally met his match? Find out in Rita Rainville's ARC OF THE ARROW, the WRITTEN IN THE STARS title for December 1991—only from Silhouette Romance!

Brandy Cochran didn't *really* believe that R.G. was an alien—no matter what her zany Aunt Tillie said. But she did admit that his kiss put her in orbit!

ARC OF THE ARROW by Rita Rainville . . . coming from Silhouette Romance this December. It's WRITTEN IN THE STARS!

Available in December at your favorite retail outlet, or order your copy now by sending your name, address, zip code or postal code, along with a check or money order for $2 59 (please do not send cash), plus 75¢ postage and handling ($1.00 in Canada), payable to Silhouette Reader Service to:

In the U.S.
3010 Walden Ave.
P.O. Box 1396
Buffalo, NY 14269-1396

In Canada
P.O. Box 609
Fort Erie, Ontario
L2A 5X3

Please specify book title with your order.
Canadian residents add applicable federal and provincial taxes.   DECSTAR

 Silhouette Romance®

her turn at driving first and since she wanted to interview Scott, asked Jennie to sit in the back and take notes.

"Tell us how it all started, Scott," Gram said, after they'd settled in for the long drive. "What would cause a high-school boy to become such an avid environmentalist?"

"Actually, I've been interested in marine life for as long as I can remember. When I was about seven I saw this television special by Jacques Cousteau and decided then and there I was going to be a marine biologist when I grew up."

"You've been protesting since you were seven?" Jennie asked.

Scott shifted in his seat so he could talk to both Gram and Jennie. "No, I didn't get really involved until I decided to do a paper on dolphins. When I discovered how intelligent dolphins are and how well they relate to people, I decided I wanted to do something to help. I feel even stronger about it now that I've actually been in the water with them. There's something . . . it's hard to explain. It's like they know things."

"You mean like intuition?" Gram asked. "I've read some articles about how they've rescued people at sea."

"Yeah." Scott grew more animated as he talked. "But it's more than that. It's like they understand us. Anyway you'll see what I mean when you get in the water with them."

"Scott," Gram said, "I can understand why you'd protest and lobby against senseless killing of the dolphins by fishermen, but why protest places like Dolphin Playland?"

"That place is the worst. Dolphins shouldn't be captured so they can entertain people at fancy resorts or per-

"Most people don't realize it," Scott said, "but it can take years for some of these corals to grow one inch. Even touching the coral polyps can damage them."

After giving thorough instructions, Scott helped Jennie and Gram into their float coats and issued them masks and snorkels. Fully equipped, they descended the boat ladder and dropped into the water. At the reef they were greeted by some of the most colorful fish Jennie had ever seen. Their neon stripes flashed as they darted playfully in and out of the sea grass and coral. Scott pointed out a sea turtle and a queen conch, which he'd explained earlier was an endangered species. Jennie could understand why. Any shell collector would find it hard to pass up the beautiful seven-inch shell.

After what seemed like only a few minutes, Scott signaled them back to the boat. They'd been in the water for over an hour. During the sail back to Key West, they talked about the different species they'd seen, and identified them on a plastic chart Gram had purchased on the wharf.

As they approached the dock area, Jennie took Gram aside. "I've been thinking about your suggestion to ask Scott to come with us to Dolphin Island. We should ask him," Jennie said. "We must be good for him . . . at least you are. He's so different from when we first met him."

Gram nodded. "I could be wrong, but I think perhaps it's because we're offering him something he hasn't had in a long time."

Jennie frowned. "What?"

"Respect, friendship, a chance to prove himself. And maybe a feeling that someone cares about him. Last night when I asked him where he lived, he said his mom has a house in Orlando and his dad in Miami and that he lives somewhere in between."

"Oh, Gram. That is so sad."

"Yes. Yes, it is. What's worse is that he thinks neither of them wants him."

"So when are you going to ask him?"

"How about now?"

The surprise and excitement on Scott's face as Gram asked him about accompanying them up north and possibly working at the research center on Dolphin Island was all the thanks either of them needed to know they'd made the right decision.

When they got back to the house, Gram called the Coles to let them know Scott would be there. Scott called Melissa and told her he wouldn't be picketing Dolphin Playland for a while. During the rest of the afternoon and evening, Jennie sensed a change in Scott. After the phone call he seemed more subdued and maybe even a little nervous. Jennie began to wonder if he was having second thoughts.

After Gram had gone to bed, Jennie lingered in the living room, hoping he'd tell her what was bothering him. When he didn't, she asked. "You look upset about something. Have you changed your mind about coming? You don't have to, you know."

"You'd like that, wouldn't you?" he snapped. His bristling attitude reminded her of their first meeting.

"Hey, I don't care if you come or not. But if you do, at least try to act civilized. You've been sulking ever since that phone call you made to Melissa. Is she your girlfriend or something? Is she upset about you going?"

"No. She's real excited about my going up there. Thought it was a great opportunity."

Jennie leaned forward. "So what's the problem?"

Scott gave her a long, hard look. "You don't want to know." He stood and headed out the door. "Don't wait up."

7

Jennie felt a sudden sense of loss and guilt. Had she hurt his feelings by saying she didn't care whether or not he came? Or was it something else? Something to do with Melissa?

Jennie climbed the steps and paused at Gram's bedroom. Should she tell her Scott had gone? No. Scott hadn't taken his stuff, and that was a good sign. Maybe he just had to get away and think. There was no sense worrying her if that was the case.

But what if it isn't, McGrady? What if he doesn't come back? Jennie slipped under her covers and closed her eyes and did the only thing she could do. "God," she whispered, "keep Scott safe. And if you want him to come with us, then bring him back."

———

As it turned out, Jennie needn't have worried. Scott was up and packed at six A.M. Jennie flashed him a smile to let him know she was glad to see him. He greeted them both with a half-embarrassed, half-guilty grin and took their bags. They'd cleaned the house and set it in order the night before, and after Gram made a final check, they piled into the convertible and headed north. Gram took form circus acts. They need to be free."

"Really? When Jennie and I toured the facilities, we found it clean, and the animals looked happy and well cared for."

"Dolphins always look like they're smiling . . . that's what makes them appealing to people. But when they're in captivity they tend to get depressed and are prone to illnesses. Places like the Playland claim to be educational and say they're doing important research, but they're really exploiting the animals. The owners are making big bucks, and I think it's wrong."

"But what about the children that have been helped by dolphin therapy?" Gram asked.

"Yeah, well. That's the tough part, and I'm still struggling with that. Melissa makes it all seem so clear. I guess that's why I accepted your offer, Mrs. McGrady. I'd like a chance to get a feel for what the research center on Dolphin Island is really like."

They talked about ecology and the environment until Gram stopped in Key Largo for breakfast. From there, Jennie drove through Alligator Alley in the Everglades while Gram worked on her computer and Scott slept in the backseat.

When they reached Naples, Gram insisted they take a beach break. Jennie pulled into a beach-access park and the trio waded, ran, and collected shells for nearly an hour. After a quick stop at McDonald's for lunch, they were off again, this time with Gram at the wheel. As the distance to their destination shortened on the map, Jennie's excitement grew. If Lisa's information had been right, she'd soon be meeting Maggie and Sarah. She'd also be talking to Ryan. She frowned and guiltily turned to look at Scott, who was stretched out in the backseat, sleeping. She did like Scott, she decided—but she liked Ryan too.

The weary travelers reached the toll booth at Sanibel Island at exactly one-thirty. Twenty minutes later they crossed the bridge to Dolphin Island. They drove for about a quarter of a mile along a road bordered by tall palm trees and thick green vegetation. Just past a sign that read "Dolphin Island State Park" they came to an enormous gate bordered on either side by a high fence. A small white sign at the entrance read, "Private Property." Another sign, a blue one with official-looking white lettering, told travelers that this was the Dolphin Island Marine Research Center.

"Wow, this place looks more heavily guarded than Fort Knox," Scott offered.

"Debbie told me they've had some vandalism lately," Gram replied, pulling the car up to the guard posted at the gate.

"Afternoon," he said. "Can I help you?"

Gram told him who they were, and he looked each of the three passengers over carefully, then checked his clipboard. Even though they'd done nothing wrong, Jennie was beginning to feel like an intruder.

"Okay," he said, punching a button inside the guard house, triggering the gate. "You're clear. Just follow the main road until you get to the office. They'll give directions from there."

The road wound through more shrubs and trees for another quarter of a mile, then opened up to a spectacular view of the Gulf of Mexico. A white sandy beach bordered a lush green lawn, then ended at a cluster of buildings and docks fingering toward the water. The road curved to the right and ended in a parking lot near a simple rectangular structure. Gram parked and the three made their way along the short graveled path. Before they reached the door, a tall, willowy woman with straight shoulder-length blond hair emerged, swept down on them, and threw her arms around Gram as if they were long-lost friends.

"Helen, I can't believe it. You're finally here. It's so good to see you again." The woman backed away and turned to face Jennie and Scott. "And this must be Jennie." Without giving her a chance to respond, she added, "I'm Debbie Cole. Oh, you do look like Kate and Jason. I mean, your hair and eyes."

Who was this woman? Jennie stepped back and bumped into Scott. His hands grasped her shoulder to steady her. "You know my aunt Kate . . . and my dad?"

"Didn't Helen tell you?" She cast Gram a teasing shame-on-you look. "Kate and Jason are old school chums of mine. Kate and I roomed together at the University of Oregon. I went there for two years before I transferred to UCLA."

Jennie glanced at Gram, who looked surprised that Jennie wasn't aware of the relation. "Oh dear, I was certain I'd mentioned it." She shook her head in disbelief. "I must be getting old. Memory isn't what it used to be, I'm afraid."

Jennie laughed. "It isn't old age, Gram, and you know it." To Debbie she said, "She gets so involved with her writing, the whole world could fall apart, and as long as it didn't affect her computer, she wouldn't know what happened until she came up for air."

"Now, why doesn't that surprise me?" Debbie slung an arm around Gram. "Must be a McGrady trait. Jason was the same way. Half the time he'd be late for our dates, and the other half I'd be lucky if he showed up at all."

"Dates? You dated my father?"

"For almost a year." Debbie shifted her glance from Jennie to Scott. "But we can talk about all that later." She extended a hand. "You must be Scott. Welcome."

"Thanks." He dropped his hand from Jennie's shoulder and shook Debbie's hand.

"I don't know if Helen told you or not," Debbie said, "but you are a lifesaver. David, one of our trainers, came down with strep throat and pneumonia a couple of days ago. He won't be able to come back to us for at least two weeks. We were shorthanded to begin with, so how about stepping in?"

"Sure," Scott replied, surprise showing on his face at the quick job offer.

Debbie introduced them to her husband, Ken, who, in his white T-shirt and khaki shorts, looked so much like his wife they could have been twins. They were both tall, thin, and tanned, and Ken wore glasses with round wire frames. His sun-bleached hair was longer than hers, and he wore it pulled back into a ponytail at the base of his neck. He had an easy smile and hazel eyes that twinkled, making Jennie feel like an old friend.

Ken escorted Scott into the office to fill out employment papers. Debbie registered Jennie and Gram and gave them keys to their cabin. "We have five guest cabins on the compound," Debbie explained as she led Jennie and Gram along one of the many paths that led from the office. "The two on this end are being renovated." Debbie pointed to two rustic cabins that looked as though they'd been battered by a hurricane.

As they continued on the path, they passed two more cabins, a small A-frame and a cottage, both built on stilts, which Debbie explained was to keep them above flood levels in a storm. As they walked by, Debbie lowered her voice. "These are both reserved by a family from Portland."

Sarah and Maggie. It has to be them. Jennie glanced in the direction of the cottage, hoping to get a glimpse of the pair.

"You'll get a chance to meet them at dinner tonight. Oh, that reminds me. We serve rather simple meals here, family-style in the main lodge. Ken and I are vegetarians, but three times a week we try to provide our carnivorous guests and employees with chicken, fish, or meat dishes. You're welcome to join us, or, if you prefer, there are a number of excellent restaurants on Captiva and Sanibel."

"Carnivorous?" Jennie couldn't help but be amused at the term. It made them sound like monsters.

"Meat-eaters," Gram said. "I think she's hoping to convert us."

Debbie didn't deny it; she just smiled. The trail ended at the last cabin, and through a scattering of palms, Jennie could see another expanse of beach. Debbie turned toward Gram like an excited child showing off a new toy. "I saved this one for you and Jennie. It's a little more isolated, so you can hole away and write. It has a clear view of the water, and since it faces west, you can experience our spectacular sunsets every night."

"It's wonderful, but are you sure?" Gram said. "I didn't expect anything so glamorous."

"Well, it isn't exactly the Ritz," Debbie said. "It's really pretty basic." She unlocked the door and ushered them in. Light peeked in through the wooden shutters. When Debbie opened them, the afternoon sun poured itself all over the room. Jennie wasn't sure what she had expected, and it took her a few seconds to adjust. Basic. Debbie had that right. In the living room, directly in front of the door, a beige-pink sofa sat parallel to the window to capture the view. On one side of it stood a brown vinyl recliner and on the other a wooden rocking chair with a floral-print pad. The furniture came equipped with two end tables holding matching ginger-jar lamps, and a coffee table. A throw rug decorated the dark-stained wood floor. To their right was a kitchenette with a small refrigerator, stove, and sink.

"You can use the kitchen for snacks and tea, but it's really not set up for cooking meals. The fridge works and I've stocked it with plenty of pop and juice. Got tea for you, Helen . . ." She paused to open a cupboard containing a variety of teas and a few cups.

"You didn't have to do that," Gram said. "I can't believe you've gone to so much trouble."

"It's no trouble. Besides, it's not every day a famous writer comes to stay—not to mention the mother of two of my favorite people." Debbie glanced at her watch. "Oops, I've got an appointment in five minutes. Bedrooms are up there." She pointed to the stairs opposite the kitchen. "And you'll find the bathroom behind the stairs. Once you're settled, feel free to wander around the compound. Here's a map, and I think that's everything . . . oh, did I mention there's a road behind the cabins and a place to park your car?"

Debbie descended the front-porch stairs and turned back to wave. "Have fun settling in. See you at dinner?"

"We'll be there," Gram called, then closed the door and leaned against it. "Whew! I'd forgotten what a live wire that girl can be."

Jennie stretched and yawned, then offered to retrieve

the car and bring in their suitcases. By the time Jennie had hauled the last bag to their bedrooms, Gram had prepared two tall glasses of lemonade and had them waiting on the patio. Jennie plopped onto the chaise lounge and closed her eyes. She was almost asleep when she heard footsteps on the gravel walk leading from the driveway to their cabin.

"Hi," a voice said. "Debbie just told me we had new guests, and I thought I'd slip over and meet you. I'm Maggie Layton."

8

Jennie opened her eyes slowly, trying not to appear too eager. Questions crowded her mind, begging to be asked. *Back off, McGrady,* Jennie reminded herself, *take it slow and easy. This woman doesn't even know you exist.*

Gram rose and greeted their visitor, then offered her a chair. "I'm Helen McGrady and this is my granddaughter Jennie." Maggie nodded at Jennie and smiled.

Gram offered Maggie a drink and went inside to get another lemonade.

After a moment of uncomfortable silence, Maggie said, "I know this is going to sound strange, but you two look familiar . . . have we met before?"

This was the opportunity Jennie needed. *Yes, at the airport in Portland, I overheard you talking about a murder . . . no, not yet. Not so fast. You don't want to scare her away.* "Well . . ." she stammered, "I guess that's because we were waiting for the same plane at the Portland airport. I remember seeing you with a girl in a wheelchair."

Maggie clasped her hands. "Of course. You were with that adorable little boy."

"Attached to, is more like it. He's my brother, Nick." Jennie went on to tell her about Nick's scheme to accompany them to Florida.

"Oh . . . ," Maggie leaned back in her chair and accepted the drink Gram handed her. "That is so cute. I remember when Sarah was that age." Tears sprang into Maggie's eyes and she paused to fumble in the pocket of her white sundress for a tissue to wipe them away. "I'm sorry. I'm afraid I get teary whenever I think about how Sarah used to be before . . ."

Before the murder? Jennie wondered, wishing she could ask the question out loud.

Maggie blew her nose and stuffed the tissue back in her pocket. "Listen to me. Here you've just arrived and are probably exhausted from your trip, and I start babbling about my problems." She stood. "You must think I'm terrible."

Oh, no, she's going to leave. Stop her, McGrady, say something. "No, not at all," she and Gram answered together.

"There, you see," Gram added, "it's unanimous. Now, why don't you sit down and tell us about Sarah. What happened to her?"

Bless you, Gram. Jennie leaned back and listened.

"Sarah has been in a sort of semi-catatonic state for two years. She won't talk or respond to anyone. The doctors think it's a type of Post Traumatic Stress Disorder. She just sits there and stares as though she's lost in some obscure place inside her head. It happened when her father . . . my husband John died. She was with him. It's like something inside of Sarah died too." Maggie shuddered and retrieved her tissue, then dabbed the inside corners of her eyes again.

"So she really did witness the murder?" Jennie asked. *Oops. Nice going, McGrady. So much for taking it slow.*

"How did you know John was murdered?" Maggie

63

demanded, then just as quickly backed off. "I don't know why I bother keeping it a secret. It was on television and in all the local papers. You probably saw it."

"Um . . . no. I . . . I didn't mean to be nosy, Mrs. Layton . . ." she began. "But when we were waiting at the airport, my cousin and I overheard you talking to a guy named Tim."

Maggie shook her head. "That was my brother. He's so paranoid about Sarah. Tim thinks the person who killed John is still out there. Since Sarah is the only witness, he's afraid the murderer will come after her."

"I can understand his concern," Gram said. "I do remember reading about the case. As I recall, the police felt certain they'd solved it. Have any attempts been made on Sarah's life?"

"No. Nothing." Maggie stared at the ice in her glass. "Tim insists that as long as Sarah doesn't speak, she isn't a threat. He's convinced that the article in the paper about our bringing Sarah here for therapy triggered the bomb threat."

"How do you feel?" Gram asked.

"I don't know." Maggie set her lemonade on the glass-topped patio table and rubbed her temples as if she had a headache. "I think Isaiah Ramsey was guilty. He was one of John's clients, and the police found him the next day. He'd committed suicide and left a note. No one has ever tried to hurt Sarah. I just wish Tim could forget this nonsense. We all need to put the pain behind us and concentrate on bringing Sarah back."

"It must be difficult for you," Gram consoled. "In a sense, you've not only lost a husband but a daughter as well."

Maggie nodded. "We, my husband Carl and I, are

hoping that dolphin therapy coupled with counseling will help Sarah. So far, traditional treatment hasn't helped much. Sometimes I think she's drifting farther and farther away. I'm desperate to find an answer. That's why we came here."

"That would be Dr. Carl Layton?" Jennie asked, trying to remember what Lisa had said about him.

"Yes. Carl is a godsend. If it hadn't been for him, I'd never have made it through this. He and John shared a practice . . . they're both psychiatrists. In fact, Carl tried to stop the murderer and ended up getting shot. I just thank God every day that he didn't die too."

"Excuse me, Mrs. Layton," Jennie said, "but if Carl was shot, couldn't he have identified the killer? And wouldn't he be in danger too?"

"Call me Maggie. Mrs. Layton always seems so formal. And to answer your question, not really. Carl said the killer was wearing a black ski mask. After the police found Ramsey, Carl couldn't make a positive identification, but he had given the police a description of a jacket the man who shot him was wearing and it matched Ramsey's. I'm not sure how to answer your second question. I'm satisfied that the police have the killer, so I don't think either of them is in danger."

Maggie reached back to lift her brown shoulder-length hair off her neck. "As to why Tim is so concerned for Sarah, he adores her. She's his only niece. I suppose part of his concern is that we really don't know what Sarah saw. Only that it was more than what she could handle."

Jennie leaned back in her chair and took a sip of the bittersweet lemonade. Something didn't feel right. *So who are you, McGrady, Sherlock Holmes? Forget it. The police have solved the murder. Besides, solving one case does not make you a detective*. That was true enough, but she wasn't about to forget it, not yet. Jennie had phased out of the conversation and when she tuned back in, Gram was asking Maggie about her new husband, Carl Layton.

"I feel like I should know that name," Gram was saying. "Of course, wasn't there an article about him recently in the newspaper?"

Maggie nodded, pride evident in her smile. "Yes, he does a lot of work with people who were abused as children. His treatment program is one of the best in the country."

"Hmmm," Gram mused, "but he couldn't help Sarah?"

"He did up to a point. When it first happened, Sarah couldn't do anything. She'd just lie there all curled up. Over the months, she began to respond. Now she can walk, eat, take care of her personal needs, and even though Carl tells me it's wishful thinking, I'm sure Sarah can read. She's a bright, intelligent girl and in some respects seems almost normal. But she's like a robot. She functions, but emotionally she's just not there."

The lights are on, but nobody's home. Sarah had looked pretty spaced-out in the airport. Her eyes had a vacant look, but there was something there. Jennie was sure she'd read fear in those eyes. Or maybe a cry for help? Or was it just a feeling—the McGrady imagination working overtime again? Well, there was one way to find out for sure. "Where is Sarah?" she asked.

"In a session with Debbie, which reminds me, I'd better head back to the dock. I wish I could say Sarah would love to meet you. But I don't know that." Maggie stretched her long manicured fingers across her white cotton skirt as if trying to smooth out the wrinkles. She thanked them for the drink, stood, and started to leave, then turned back. "Oh, when you meet Sarah, try to act natural around her. I mean, talk to her as if she understands everything you're saying. Carl says we need to treat her as if she does." Maggie turned again and hurried down the path and disappeared into her cabin.

"What do you think, Gram?" Jennie gathered the three glasses and headed inside.

Gram followed. "I think that family is in a great deal of pain."

"No, I mean about the murder. Do you think Ramsey did it?"

"I have no reason to suspect otherwise. Do you?"

Jennie shrugged and set the glasses in the sink. "I guess I'm just wondering why her brother thought the bomb threat was meant for Sarah and why he's so sure it wasn't Ramsey. And why is he worried about Sarah being in danger and not Carl?"

"Perhaps he feels the crime was solved too quickly. Or that a murder/suicide is too easy a solution. Since there was no trial he may feel that the issue is still unresolved. There are a number of suppositions I could make, but the only way we can know for certain is to ask him." Gram raised her arms and stretched from one side to the other. "I'm not sure whether to go for a walk or take a nap, but I do know I need to get some of these kinks out of my muscles."

"Why don't we take a walk and you can help me work on this mystery."

"I'm not sure there is a mystery," Gram said, grunting as she dropped into a crouch and stretched one leg out behind her.

Jennie propped herself against the wall and folded her

arms. "Well, what if Tim is right? What if the bomb threat was meant for Sarah? What if the murderer is afraid the dolphins will help Sarah get better? What if the killer followed them out here? Sarah could be in real danger."

Gram switched legs and kept stretching. "Jennie, I know you're concerned about Sarah. And you're right. If Ramsey is not the murderer, and if Sarah was indeed a witness and gets well and is able to remember what happened, then yes, she could be in a great deal of danger. And from what we've heard, so could her stepfather. But there's nothing to indicate that that's the case. You heard Maggie . . ." Gram straightened and started running in place, ". . . there's been no attempt on Sarah's life—or Carl's."

Logically, Gram was right and Jennie told her so. "I know I should just forget about it and have a good time, but I just have this feeling . . ."

Gram stopped running and ran her arm across her forehead to push back her hair. "Whew," she panted. "It's too hot for this sort of thing. I think I'll have to go to plan B and take a nap."

"Gram . . ."

"I know, Jennie, I'm not ignoring you. I'm just not certain what to tell you. If there is a problem here, and the real murderer is still at large, I don't want you involved. I also know that you aren't about to forget it. You've got too much McGrady in you." She sighed. "Okay, we'll look into it. I'll see if I can get copies of the police reports and talk to whoever was in charge of the investigation. Just promise me you won't do anything that could put you in danger, and if you learn anything, you'll keep me posted."

Jennie pushed off from the wall and went to give Gram

a hug. "I promise. Thanks."

While Gram rested, Jennie took a shower, then settled down to read in a shaded hammock that stretched between two palm trees. After a couple of pages, the book dropped to her side and she fell asleep.

Jennie drifted in and out of consciousness, aware of the sweet musty scent of wet grass, of waves lapping on the nearby beach, and of the gentle breeze as it rocked the hammock. Something brushed her arm. A fly. Jennie brushed at it. "Go away," she mumbled. She felt it again. This time it brushed her cheek. Irritated, she lifted her hand to flick it away and came in contact not with a bug but a human hand.

9

Jennie screamed and bolted upright, almost falling out of the hammock.

"Hey, take it easy." Scott grabbed her arm and the hammock to steady her.

"What do you think you're doing? You nearly gave me a heart attack." Jennie swung her legs over the hammock's edge and hopped out.

Scott chuckled and spread his hands open innocently. "You sure are jumpy. I was just trying to wake you up gently."

"I wasn't sleeping." Jennie brushed by him and headed for the house.

"Yeah right. You were snoring."

Jennie stopped short and spun around, nearly bumping into him. "I do not snore."

"Okay, so you don't snore. Do you want to know what else you don't do when you're sleeping?"

Jennie gave him her best drop-dead look.

"Hey, take it easy. You were lying there so peaceful-like, I couldn't resist teasing you a little."

Scott's grin was infectious and Jennie relented. "Okay, I forgive you, but I'd watch my back if I were you." She raised her eyebrows and looked him in the eye. "I'll have my revenge."

Scott laughed and his green eyes sparkled like sunlight on the water. The butterflies in Jennie's tummy took wing and she looked away. "What are you doing out here anyway? I thought you were working."

"I am. My first official duty is to escort you and your grandmother to dinner."

Scott and Jennie went to collect Gram, who'd fallen asleep on the couch. After freshening up, they left the cabin by the front door and headed toward the main lodge.

Jennie hadn't realized how hungry she was until they approached the dining area and the wonderful scent of spices filled the air. The oversized multipurpose hall looked as though it served as a classroom, dining room, and recreation room. Four large round tables occupied one corner. In another corner stood a pool table, a bookshelf, and a cupboard bulging with puzzles and games. A stack of folding chairs hugged a back wall next to an overhead projector, a screen, and a podium. On the west wall three floor-to-ceiling windows overlooked the Gulf.

Good smells wafted out of a large kitchen off to one side. The atmosphere reminded Jennie of church camp. Except that at camp, loud hungry campers crammed the dining room and the noise level was high enough to shatter glass. So far, except for a couple of cooks preparing food in the kitchen, they were the only people there.

She was about to comment on that fact to Gram and Scott when Debbie and Ken joined them and motioned toward a table nearest the kitchen. "There'll only be eleven of us for dinner tonight, because you, Maggie, and Sarah are our only guests. We eat buffet-style . . ."

Debbie handed them menus and explained about ordering meals a day ahead, so the chef would know how much food to prepare. Jennie shifted her gaze to the door, anxious to meet Sarah. A group of four bustled in and took a second table. Debbie introduced them as their secretary Pam, trainers Heidi and Jack, and Dick, the head maintenance man.

It wasn't until the food had been placed on a reach-through counter adjoining the kitchen and dining room and everyone had gone through the line, that Maggie and Sarah made their entrance.

The first thing Jennie noticed was the absence of a wheelchair. The second was that Sarah was almost the same height as her mother—about 5′4″, Jennie guessed. Her cheeks were flushed and her skin had the healthy glow of a new tan. Sarah walked slightly behind Maggie and looked like a normal fourteen-year-old girl. Her light brown hair, still shiny and wet from swimming, had recently been cut in a short boyish style that didn't quite suit her face. Olive Oyle arms and legs protruded from her pale blue, shell-print T-shirt and white shorts. She was pretty, or would be if she weighed another ten pounds.

Maggie pulled out a chair and guided Sarah into it. "Jennie, Helen," she said, "I'd like you to meet my daughter, Sarah Stanford. Sarah, Jennie and Mrs. McGrady are from Portland. Maybe you remember seeing them at the airport."

Jennie wasn't sure what she expected, some sign of recognition maybe, but Sarah stared straight ahead into a place somewhere between her and Gram. Disappointment flooded her. She had hoped for a sign that the look Sarah had given her at the airport had meant something.

Now Jennie wasn't even sure of that. Maybe it had only been a trick of the lights, or Jennie's imagination.

She spent the rest of dinner trying not to stare at Sarah, listening to the others talk, and eating egg-flower soup, veggie-wontons, tofu-vegetable stir-fry, and white rice. Everything, even the tofu, tasted great. *Maybe being a vegetarian for a week and a half might not be all that bad— as long as Gram and I can sneak out at least once for a pizza or hamburgers.*

After dinner, Scott challenged Jennie to a game of pool. She almost declined when Gram announced that she, Maggie, and Sarah were going back to the cabins. *Give it up, McGrady. There's no mystery. Besides, what would you rather do, sit around trying to get a response out of Sarah or hang out with Scott?* Jennie glanced from Sarah to Scott. The girl's eyes were like two black holes—cold, dark, and almost inhuman. Scott's were warm and inviting. No contest. "You go ahead, Gram. I'm going to stay here and show Scott how to play pool."

"Show me how to play?" Scott countered. "Listen, frog face, I've been playing pool since I could walk."

"Frog face?" Jennie pointed a finger at his chest and poked him. "Well listen, toad head, my mother played pool when she was pregnant, so I learned how to play while I was still in the womb."

"Choose your weapon." Scott retrieved two cue sticks and held them up for Jennie's inspection. "Hey, Mrs. McGrady. You sure you don't want to stay and referee this match?"

Gram chuckled. "Not a chance. Don't worry, Scott," she teased. "The McGradys have always treated their opponents fairly. I'm sure she'll let you win at least one game."

Scott feigned a wounded look. "I'm hurt." Then, with an eyebrow raised, he turned to Jennie, "But I'm tough. You're dead meat, McGrady." Scott gathered the balls and racked them. "Just to show you what a good sport I am, I'll let you break."

"Break?"

"Ha! This is going to be so easy. Just take your best shot."

They stopped razzing each other to say good-night to Maggie, Sarah, and Gram. Gram started to leave, then turned back. "Try to be in by ten, dear. I'd like us to chat and have a cup of tea before we turn in."

"Okay," Jennie called over her shoulder as she chalked her cue.

"Don't worry, Mrs. McGrady," Scott said as Gram headed out the door. "I'll have her home in plenty of time."

Jennie elbowed him in the ribs. "I can get myself home. This is not a date, you know." When Scott didn't answer, Jennie added, "You okay? I didn't mean to hurt your feelings or anything."

"Sure. I'm okay. What's a broken heart? It'll mend." He heaved a deep melodramatic sigh, then said, "Actually, I was just thinking about what we can do to make this more challenging." Scott chalked his cue and blew off the residue. He cocked his head to one side and gave her a smile that reminded Jennie of the Cheshire cat in *Alice in Wonderland*. "How about this? We play three games. The loser has to take the winner on a date to Disney World."

"That's a pretty spendy date. Couldn't we just play for a couple of bucks?"

"Oh, I get it." Scott leaned his hip against the table.

"You don't even know how to play, do you? You're all mouth and no action."

You gonna let him get away with that, McGrady? Just because you've only played pool three or four times in your entire life is no reason to back down. "Okay," Jennie heard herself say, "you're on."

When the games ended, she'd had so much fun it hadn't mattered that he'd trounced her. Or that she now owed him a date to Disney World *and* Epcot Center. After the first game, he'd suggested they up the ante. Unable to resist the challenge, Jennie had agreed.

"Hey, how about we head down to the beach and view the sunset?" Scott asked, taking her hand. They strolled down the short walk and along the beach. When they'd gone to where they could no longer see the lights from the research center, they dropped to the ground. Jennie removed her sandals and pressed her feet into the still-warm sand.

A breeze lifted the loose stands of her hair. The sun, a blazing orange ball, hovered on the horizon, gifting the earth with its splendor. Jennie raised her face to it and closed her eyes. "It's so beautiful here," she whispered, afraid that speaking aloud would break the spell.

Scott picked up a handful of sand and let it sift through his fingers. "Yeah. It's a great spot. Makes you wish it could last forever."

Jennie glanced over at him and back at the sunset. "Do you think you'll like working here?"

He shrugged. "I guess. I'll be doing odd jobs while they train me to work with the dolphins. Ken put me in charge of feeding them."

"You don't seem very enthusiastic."

"I love the dolphins. I just don't like seeing them

used. There's a place in Australia where dolphins used to come in really close to shore. People fed them and they started coming in all the time. Some guys decided they could make a few bucks off the dolphins and research them at the same time. Anyway, they developed this elaborate park where people could interact with the dolphins. It seemed like a good plan at first, then the dolphins started getting sick. Several died. An environmental group tested the water and found high levels of E-coli bacteria." Scott picked up a seashell and stared at it.

"What happened? What would cause something like that?"

"The park toilets leaked raw sewage into the water." He tossed the shell into the water.

"But it was an accident."

"Right. So are all the oil spills."

Jennie didn't respond. What could she say? She wasn't about to defend people's destructive habits, but it didn't help to get depressed about it. In a way, she admired Scott, with his intense desire to save the earth. On the other hand, she felt concerned for him, but wasn't sure why.

As they watched the sun sink into the water and the sky turn to shades of purple and orange, Scott draped an arm around her shoulders. "Hey, look." He pointed to a bright star directly above them. "First star. Want to make a wish?"

Jennie closed her eyes and wished that Sarah would get well. When she opened them, Scott was watching her.

"I wished that you'd let me kiss you," he said softly.

Scott was so close. All she had to do was lean forward and their lips would meet. She liked Scott. She liked his sense of humor and his serious side—especially that side because he cared so much. *Go ahead, McGrady. Kiss him,* one voice in her head insisted. *Lisa would. But you're not Lisa,* another said. Still another asked, *What about Ryan?*

"I don't think that would be a good idea," Jennie said, turning to face the water. Then, thinking she should explain, added, "I have a boyfriend—sort of. I mean, we're not going steady or anything, but . . . I don't know, it just wouldn't be right."

Scott stood up and brushed the sand from his clothes, then reached down to give her a hand up. In the dark she couldn't see his expression. Why didn't he say something? "Are you mad at me?" she asked.

"Nope."

"Then why are you in such a hurry to leave?"

He chuckled and held up his watch. "It's ten o'clock."

Jennie tried to land a punch to his midsection. He ducked and ran ahead of her. She chased him as far as the lawn, then stopped to slip on her sandals. Scott waited for her, helped her to her feet, and walked her back to the cabin.

"Do you want to come in and have tea with Gram and me?" Jennie asked as they reached her cabin.

"I don't think I'd better. I have to meet Ken at five-thirty in the morning. And unlike you, I didn't get a nap this afternoon. See you tomorrow night?" Before Jennie could answer, he added, "I'll let you beat me at pool."

"I have a better idea." Jennie lifted her hand to brush some stray hairs out of her eyes and realized he was still holding it.

"Let me guess," he said. "You want to have a contest to see who can take the longest nap?" His sea-green eyes sparkled under the soft light of a nearby utility lamp.

"You nut."

"No, I know. You want to have a contest to see which of us is the best kisser."

"Be serious."

"I am."

"Scott . . ." Jennie pushed past him. "You're being a pest."

"Okay, I'm sorry. What's your idea?"

Jennie relented and turned back to face him. "How good of a swimmer are you?"

"Want to race me?" Scott loved a challenge as much as Jennie.

"Yeah," she said. "As long as you're not an Olympic contender."

Scott laughed softly. "You're on. Meet you at the pool at three, tomorrow afternoon." He leaned forward and kissed her cheek. Nothing dramatic, just the kind a person might give a brother or sister. Jennie touched her cheek. Then why did it feel like so much more?

Jennie watched him jog away. Even after the darkness had swallowed him up, she stood there. They had a lot in common, she and Scott. Maybe that's what attracted her to him. They both liked to joke around, but they had a serious side too, and a passion. His was saving the environment. Hers was finding Dad.

The phone rang, disrupting Jennie's thoughts. As she walked in the door, Gram held the receiver toward her. "I thought I heard you out there. This is for you." She lowered her voice to a whisper. "It's Ryan."

10

"Ryan?" Jennie pressed the receiver to her ear. Her heart was pounding so hard she could barely hear him. The static on the line didn't help either.

"Hey, Jennie!" Ryan responded. "You wouldn't believe this place. I'm taking tons of pictures. Maybe when I get home you could come down to the beach and I could show them to you—or I could come to Portland."

"I'd like that." Jennie imagined the two of them sitting on Gram's porch swing looking at pictures—and at each other.

"How's Florida?"

"Wonderful. And warm. The sunsets are fantastic. You'd love them. I'll get some pictures, but it won't be the same as being here in person." They went on talking about nothing in particular for about five minutes, both grasping for things to say.

"We're about ready to take off again," Ryan said. "I'll try to call you next time we're in port. Oh, say hi to Gram for me. Tell her I'll bring her back some salmon. You too."

"That would be great."

"Jennie?" Ryan hesitated. "I miss you."

Tears sprang to her eyes. "I miss you too," she said.

Oh, McGrady, her ever-present inner voice said, *you've got it bad. Three weeks ago you weren't even dating, now look at you. You've got not one but two boys interested in you.* She could hear Lisa now, "Oh, this is so much fun." Well, for Jennie it was about as much fun as getting her teeth drilled. Well, maybe not quite. But she was beginning to wonder if having boyfriends was worth the effort.

After hanging up, Jennie dried her eyes, blew her nose, fixed herself a cup of tea, and went in search of her grandmother. She found Gram in the bedroom. "You didn't have to leave," Jennie said, settling herself into the cushioned high-backed rattan chair.

"Nonsense. I thought you'd like some privacy."

Jennie shrugged. "He didn't have a lot to say except hi. He wants to show me pictures, he's going to bring us some salmon, and he misses me."

"I'd say that was quite a lot."

"I guess." Jennie hooked her leg over the arm of the chair and took a sip of the warm peppermint brew, letting the aroma soothe her senses. Gram asked about her evening with Scott, and Jennie told her about the bet she'd lost and how tired she was of liking two guys at once.

"What should I do, Gram? I keep going over and over things about Ryan and Scott, Maggie and Sarah, Mom and Michael, Nick, and of course, Dad. Now I'm starting to worry about dolphins. My brain feels so stuffed, if I add one more thing it's going to explode."

"I'm not sure what will work for you, but I can tell you what helps me. First I pray about it and try to put every worry, anxiety, and concern out of my mind."

"How can you do that? I used to be able to stuff things away and think only about what really mattered, but now it seems like there's too much."

Gram retrieved her Bible from the bedside stand and after flipping through it, bookmarked a page and handed it to Jennie. "You might also want to read this section in Matthew where Jesus reminds us that it doesn't really do much good to worry. Things have a way of taking care of themselves."

It seemed like good advice, and when they'd finished their tea, Jennie gathered up their cups, took them downstairs, and got ready for bed. The room was warm and stuffy, so Jennie opened the window and stretched out on top of her blankets. She prayed that God would give her the right attitude about guys and help her not to worry so much. It seemed as though lately she'd been doing nothing but worrying. It had gotten to the point where the most important thing in her life was fading into the background—finding Dad.

Jennie picked up the Bible Gram had given her and opened it to the marked page. *"Therefore I tell you, do not be anxious about your life . . ."* When she'd finished reading the entire passage, Jennie took a deep breath and mentally set aside the concerns she'd been having. One by one she stacked them in a neat corner at the back of her mind. As she'd done many times before, Jennie pulled the memories of her father into the foreground. In her mind's eye, she could see his dark hair and eyes, so like Nick's and her own. A few minutes later, she fell asleep.

The next morning Jennie felt more relaxed than she had in days. She and Gram greeted the morning by walking and jogging along the beach, which wasn't easy when they stopped every few feet to gather shells. After about an hour they made their way back to the cabin, set their treasures on the patio to dry, and got ready for breakfast. It was still only seven o'clock, but except for Debbie,

Sarah, and Maggie, the dining room was empty. Debbie had eaten and was getting ready to leave. She had explained the night before that they served breakfast from six to eight and most of the staffers ate early. A twinge of disappointment at not seeing Scott surfaced, but Jennie quickly sidestepped it. *Not today, McGrady. Today is for swimming with the dolphins.*

Jennie was in an adventurous mood and at Debbie's suggestion tried the granola topped with raspberry yogurt. She also helped herself to a banana muffin and a glass of milk. Her crunchy, tangy concoction tasted surprisingly good.

While Maggie and Gram chatted, Jennie studied Sarah. Nothing had changed as far as Jennie could tell, except that she felt more comfortable with the girl than she had the night before. *Just act like she understands,* Maggie had said.

"I'm swimming with Delilah today," Jennie told her. "Your mom says that's the dolphin who works with you and Debbie during your therapy sessions. Debbie and your mom told us it would be okay if we sat in on your session today. I hope you don't mind." After making several more mundane remarks, Jennie fell into an uncomfortable silence. *Now what? Come on, McGrady, you ought to be good at this, you talk to yourself all the time. Yeah, right, I could always say, "Hey, Sarah, snap out of it."*

Jennie contemplated her banana muffin, then took a bite. Talking to Sarah was like trying to communicate with a photograph. No matter what you said or did, the expression didn't change. It was like she'd been frozen in time. Jennie remembered how she felt when Dad had disappeared. She'd been numb and lost. Sometimes she felt as if her world had stopped and she had been locked inside herself.

Maybe later she'd tell Sarah about Dad, and that she knew, at least in part, what Sarah must be going through. Maybe, but not until they were alone.

When they'd finished eating, Jennie and Gram went back to the cabin to retrieve Gram's camera and note pad, then headed for the docks. Ken met them there and gave them a tour of the facilities. They first stopped at a pond, which housed a loggerhead turtle named Mr. Lucky.

"This really was a lucky turtle," Ken said. "A couple of marine biologists near Palm Beach found him washed up on the beach. He was still alive—though just barely—so they called me. We'd found another turtle like that a couple of months before, only he was already dead. I had done an autopsy and found some plastic bags and over a hundred cigarette butts in his stomach, so I played on a hunch and performed surgery on Lucky. Sure enough, his stomach was full of cigarette butts and plastic too. We removed the garbage and got him started eating again. Now he's almost ready to join his friends in the wild."

"Yuk," Jennie scrunched up her nose. "Why in the world would a turtle want to eat cigarettes?"

"Unfortunately, most people don't stop to ask that question. Smokers toss millions of butts on the ground, in the sand, off boats, and never give a second thought to the damage they can cause. The filters don't readily break down in the environment. Instead, they attract bacteria. Before long they're covered with algae. The turtles eat them, thinking they've just captured a nice juicy morsel. Since the filters don't break down, they don't pass through the digestive system. The more the turtles eat, the fuller their stomachs get."

"I see," Gram said. "So eventually, he feels full all the time, doesn't eat, and starves to death."

"Exactly."

Jennie was beginning to understand how Scott could get so worked up about environmental issues. While she didn't think she wanted to carry protest signs, she might be able to do something. "Do you have anything written about this?" she asked. "I was just thinking, maybe I could do a report for one of my classes."

"While you're at it," Gram said, "why not write an article for one of the teen magazines? I'll be happy to let you use my notes."

Jennie bypassed Gram's suggestion. She liked writing but wasn't ready for that kind of commitment. Besides, one writer in the family was enough.

Ken walked them through the rest of the facility, stopping briefly to talk to them about the various sea animals in their "hospital." Gram, of course, took pictures of each one, jotting down the details she wanted to remember. The menagerie included Pierre, a dolphin with ulcers who'd been sent to them from a zoo in Europe, and a sea lion named Max, whom they'd found wrapped in fishing line. The hook had been imbedded in his stomach, and they'd had to surgically remove it.

Ken then introduced them to several of the bottle-nose dolphins who'd chosen to live at Dolphin Island. Cleo and her baby, Squirt, approached the dock, eyed the humans, and dashed away. Squirt's was one of the few dolphin births they'd been able to observe at close range. Ken pointed to a dock across the lagoon where Scott and Debbie were feeding Splash and Corky.

From the opposite side of the dock, two dolphins headed toward them at breakneck speed, and Jennie was certain they'd crash into the dock. At the last second they both turned, spraying water onto the dock and barely missing their human targets. "This is our most friendly pair. Folks, meet Samson and Delilah." Ken gave them a series of signals, and they delighted their small audience by spiraling through the water then jumping high into the air in perfect unison.

"Since you'll be swimming with Delilah later, Jennie, why don't you come get acquainted with her?" Ken signaled her to approach the dock. Delilah lay in the water watching Jennie for a moment, then came in close so Jennie could pet her. The dolphin's skin was sleek and rubbery. "Giggle for her, Delilah." Ken signaled her again, and she lifted herself halfway out of the water and swayed back and forth, making a sound that really did sound like laughter. The dolphin then swam away, only to return a moment later, swishing her tail and sending a wall of water onto her audience.

"Delilah! Is that any way to treat our guests?" Ken scolded, removing his glasses and wiping the water from his face. "She loves to tease," he explained. After more discussion on dolphins and rules like, "Don't touch their blow hole," Ken announced that it was time for Jennie's swim with Delilah.

After changing into her swimsuit, Jennie donned a life jacket and entered the water. A wave of panic coursed through her. She wished her mother had never let her watch *Jaws*. Being in the water with a 400-pound animal was far different from watching them perform. Ken had told her that swimming with Delilah would be safe. Jennie gulped.

Gram's warning to be careful hadn't helped. Neither had Ken's informative remark that a flick of a dolphin's tail could break a man's arm. *Okay, McGrady, pull yourself together. You can do this. You've withstood a kidnaping, been held at gunpoint, and even been shot at. So what's the big deal?*

Jennie took a deep breath and moved away from the dock. Delilah circled her, swam away, then came back and gave her a nudge that sent Jennie farther into the lagoon. *"Help,"* she wanted to scream, *"she's going to push me out to sea. I don't think I want to do this."*

Jennie pushed her fears back and focused her attention on Delilah. "Okay, Delilah, what's the plan?"

Delilah swam close to Jennie as though she were sizing her up. Then the oddest thing happened. Suddenly all fear left Jennie, and she gently stroked the animal's side.

Ken tossed a ball into the water and Delilah caught it on her nose, tossing it to Jennie. Jennie laughed and threw it back. About half a dozen throws later, Delilah chuckled, dove deep into the water, then came back to circle Jennie again. Jennie wasn't sure, but there seemed to be a mischievous gleam in her eye.

Delilah ducked between Jennie's legs, sending her toppling. "You stinker," Jennie sputtered. "You could have warned me." Gram and Ken stood on the dock laughing.

The next time Delilah approached, she stayed at Jennie's side. "Take hold of her dorsal fin, Jennie. She wants to give you a ride."

She did, squealing with delight as Delilah circled the pool with Jennie in tow. On the second pass by the dock, Delilah dove deep and sped away.

"Sorry, kid," Ken said. "I'm afraid you're being dumped. It's time for Sarah's therapy session."

Jennie climbed out of the water and hung her life jacket on a post to dry. While she'd been swimming, Maggie, Sarah, and Debbie had arrived on the dock. Ken helped Sarah into a dry life jacket and lowered her into the water with Debbie. Jennie frowned. "Isn't it dangerous to let Sarah swim with Delilah? She was pretty rough with me."

Ken adjusted his glasses and smiled. "That's one of the things we find so fascinating about dolphins. They seem to have an inner sense of how tough or fragile humans are and what they need. Watch and you'll see what I mean."

Delilah swam close to Sarah, gently bumping her as she had Jennie. A few minutes later, Debbie took Sarah's hand and placed it on Delilah's dorsal fin, and Delilah took Sarah for a ride.

"I can't believe the difference," Gram said as she scribbled something on her note pad. "If I didn't know better, I'd swear you switched dolphins."

Jennie focused her attention on Sarah. Something had happened out there, but what? *Think, McGrady. What did you see? It might be important.* But the moment had slipped into a black hole in her brain. She replayed the scene over and over in her mind as Sarah finished her session, and she, Gram, Maggie, and Sarah walked back to the cabins.

It wasn't until Jennie and Scott were swimming laps in the pool that it came to her. She stopped dead in the water and Scott plowed into her. He came up sputtering. "What's going on? Why'd you stop? You had a good ten feet on me."

"She smiled!" Jennie grabbed his arms. "Sarah smiled!"

11

"You're nuts," Scott said, treading water.

Out of breath from the swim, Jennie gulped air and tipped her head back. "No . . ." she panted, ". . . it's true. She was out . . . with Delilah . . . had her back to us. Delilah turned and I saw it. I wasn't sure at first . . ."

"Probably a mirage. Or a nervous twitch." He leaned back and floated on the water's surface. "I just saw Sarah this afternoon. She still has that creepy stare."

Miffed, Jennie pushed his head under water and swam toward the sun deck at the deep end of the pool. Scott issued a challenge and raced after her. Jennie reached the deck ahead of him and was toweling off her hair when she heard him step out of the water. "I know what I saw . . ."

His arms went around her, and Jennie's feet left the ground. "Scott Chambers, put me down this instant."

"Okay." He let her go and she landed in the water.

Jennie came up sputtering but ready for revenge.

"You asked for it." Scott was still laughing as he reached a hand down to help her out.

Jennie took his hand and with a hard yank pulled him in with her. They splashed at each other until Jennie called for a truce. Since their towels were soaked, they sat beside the pool and dangled their feet in the water while

the sun dried their suits. "I did see her smile, Scott."
Jennie closed her eyes and leaned back on her arms.

"If you expect me to disagree with you again, you can
forget it. I think I'm beginning to understand what they
mean by 'a woman scorned.' "

Jennie jabbed his arm.

"You are one cruel woman, McGrady." Scott winced
and massaged his muscles, then lay back against the wood
decking. He lifted his arm to block the sun. "Anyway,
what's the big deal? I mean, so what if she did smile? It
doesn't seem to have made much difference."

"It could mean she's getting better." *Or, it could mean
she's faking*. This second thought popped into her mind
like a camera flash—too new and startling to reveal until
it could be developed. It was definitely time to talk to
Sarah Stanford.

———

Just before dinner Scott invited Jennie to go into Fort
Myers for pizza with him and a couple of the other staffers. Even though pizza sounded great, she decided to look
for Sarah instead.

When she arrived back at the cabin after her swim,
Jennie learned that Maggie had gone into Fort Myers to
pick up her brother at the airport and had asked Gram to
look after Sarah while she was gone.

After a dinner of lasagna florentine (which Jennie discovered meant a dish created to foist spinach on unsus-
pecting kids), Jennie asked Gram if she could take Sarah
for a walk on the beach. "It might be fun for her, even if
she doesn't . . ." Jennie paused, unsure of what to say.

"I think that's a wonderful idea," Gram replied. "I

need to finish going over my notes and get them into the computer."

"Great, but how do I . . . I mean, how can I get her to come with me?"

"Just take her hand. She'll go along."

Like an obedient puppy, Jennie thought sadly. Sarah followed Jennie down the path behind the cabin to the beach. Wanting to assure their privacy, she led Sarah away from the compound and, after about five minutes of walking, dropped to the sand. Sarah had stopped a few feet away and stood staring into the sea. A light breeze ruffled the skirt of her pink sundress, reminding Jennie of a pastel painting.

"You can sit down if you want," Jennie said. When the girl didn't move, Jennie shrugged her shoulders. "Whatever." She glanced at Sarah, then fixed her gaze on a sailboat in the distance. Jennie wasn't sure where to start and took a few minutes to gather her thoughts.

"Your mom told us about your dad's murder," she blurted out finally. "And that you were there when it happened. It must have been awful for you." Jennie picked up a pebble and tossed it in the water.

"My dad's gone too. He disappeared five years ago. He worked for the FBI, and they told us his plane had gone down and that he was dead. Afterwards I felt numb, like an empty shell. My body was there, but I wasn't—you know what I mean?" Jennie drew circles in the sand with her fingers. *What are you waiting for, McGrady? She's not going to answer you.* She looked up at Sarah and went on. "I don't know why I'm telling you this, except . . . well, I guess I'd like to help. And I wanted you to know I understand . . . I mean . . . I couldn't even begin to understand what it would be like to see somebody murdered—especially if it was your father . . ." *Oh shut up, McGrady, you're making a mess of things.*

Sarah turned and walked toward her, then sat on the sand at her left. The vacant look had disappeared. A tear trickled down her cheek and dropped onto her sundress, turning the spot it touched into a deep rose.

At that moment, Jennie heard a whisper so quiet it was barely audible above the lapping waves.

"You know, don't you?"

Jennie's heart caught in her throat. She closed her eyes, expecting that when she opened them the voice would have been a bizarre flash from the Twilight Zone. When her eyes opened and she saw that Sarah was waiting for a response, Jennie's mouth gaped open and she nodded. "I wasn't sure. At the airport, I thought I saw something in your eyes. Then, when you were swimming with Delilah this afternoon, I saw you smile."

"You won't tell anyone." It wasn't a question but a statement.

"Who'd believe me? You really put on a good act. What I don't understand is why."

A man's shout interrupted them. "How could you leave her with strangers?" The voice came from the cabins. "Especially without adult supervision! This whole thing was a crazy idea. Sarah doesn't need dolphin therapy. It's expensive and risky."

Jennie looked in the direction of the angry voice. Maggie and the man she'd seen at the airport were running toward them. "Tim, be reasonable."

Jennie looked back at Sarah, who'd turned to stone. *You won't tell anyone.* Sarah's haunting words lingered in her mind. *She's afraid.* And if Jennie's suspicions were right, she had good reason to be. If the wrong person learned Sarah could talk, and could identify the person who really killed John Stanford, Sarah could be in serious danger. "Don't worry," Jennie murmured. "I won't tell."

When Maggie and Tim approached, Jennie got to her feet. Tim squatted to the ground and picked Sarah up in his arms. "I don't know what you're up to, young lady," he barked in Jennie's direction, "but don't you ever take Sarah out here again." He gave Maggie an I'll-talk-to-you-later look and strode back toward the cabins.

"I'm sorry, Maggie," Jennie offered, still stunned by Tim's reaction. "I didn't know bringing Sarah out here would be a problem."

"No, I'm sorry. Tim's so afraid something will happen to her he gets a little crazy . . . but he means well." Maggie raked her fingers through her hair, pulling it away from her face. "I'm sure Sarah enjoyed her visit with you. And don't worry about Tim. He'll settle down." Maggie shook her head and smiled. "Tim's like an M&M, all crusty on the outside but soft and sweet in the center."

Obviously you've never heard of peanut M&Ms, Jennie felt like saying. Jennie did, however, intend to talk to Gram.

She found Gram curled up on one end of the sofa reading. When Jennie stormed in, Gram set aside her book and reading glasses. "I take it you've had a pleasant chat with Sarah's uncle." Gram patted the empty space beside her.

"Very funny. That guy is some piece of work. Did he talk to you?" Jennie kicked off her sandals, plopped down next to Gram, and stretched her legs over the coffee table.

"Yelled," Gram corrected. "His exact words were, 'A woman your age should know better than to entrust a child like Sarah to a . . .' what did he call you . . . oh yes, an 'unpredictable teenager.' How about you?"

Jennie recounted the beach scene, being careful not to reveal Sarah's secret. It was too soon for that. Besides, Sarah had confided in her, and there was so much more Jennie wanted to know.

"What do you make of it, Gram? I mean, doesn't it seem strange to you that an uncle would be that upset?"

"He did overreact a bit, didn't he?"

"A bit? That's like saying the nuclear bomb was a bit explosive."

Gram chuckled. "I wouldn't go quite that far."

Jennie tucked her legs up under her, turning so she directly faced her grandmother. "Either the guy's a certified nut case or . . ." Another possibility occurred to her. It was a frightening thought but one worth exploring.

"Or. . . ?" Gram prompted.

Jennie got to her feet and began pacing from the couch to the kitchenette. "I know this sounds really wild, Gram, but suppose Tim wasn't overreacting, but *over-acting*?"

"I'm not sure I follow you."

"Okay." Jennie stopped in front of Gram and dropped to the floor. "We know Tim is worried that the real murderer is still at large. We also know he doesn't want Sarah out here working with the dolphins. He claims it's dangerous. What if all that is an act to cover his real motive? What if he wants everyone to believe he's concerned about Sarah, when he's really concerned about himself?"

"Are you suggesting Tim had something to do with the murder?"

"It makes sense, doesn't it? Why would Tim be so suspicious if he didn't know something more than what the police turned up? Maybe he doesn't want Sarah here because he's afraid she'll remember who really killed her dad."

"Hmmm. An interesting point." Gram rose, reached for her empty teacup, and headed toward the kitchen. "Want some?" she asked.

Jennie shook her head.

Gram filled her cup and popped it into the microwave. "If Tim *were* the murderer, it might explain Sarah's emotional and mental reaction. If she really loved her uncle, it would be difficult, maybe even impossible, for her to believe he could have done it. I've heard of cases where people have been so shocked by their experience, they've completely repressed it and go on as though it never happened. Sort of an hysterical amnesia. With Sarah, the reality may have been so terrible, she shut the door to the outside world."

"So you think Tim is the murderer?"

"It's possible, but not likely. For one thing, what motive would Tim have? From what Maggie has told me, Tim and John Stanford were close friends, and Tim took his death quite hard." The microwave beeped, and Gram stopped to pull out the cup and drop in a tea bag.

"They could have had an argument."

"True, but according to Maggie, Carl saw the killer. If it had been Tim, Carl would have recognized him, mask or no. His description of the killer didn't fit Tim at all. Besides, if Tim killed John and was afraid Sarah would reveal his identity, wouldn't he have killed her too?"

Jennie's bubble of pride at solving the case began to deflate as Gram poked holes in her theory. "So you don't think he did it?"

"I didn't say that. Everyone connected could be a suspect—Tim, certainly, and even Maggie." Gram brought her tea into the living room and eased herself onto the couch. "Don't look so disappointed. You brought up a valid argument. And I agree, this overre-acting, or over-*acting* uncle of Sarah's bears watching."

————

The next morning Jennie and Gram joined Scott, Debbie, and Ken on the docks to help feed the dolphins. Debbie gave each of them a different colored bucket filled with fish, on which a dolphin's name was painted.

"Watch this." Scott held up Delilah's red pail and banged it a couple of times with a spoon. "They can tell which pail is theirs by the color." Before he'd finished his sentence, Delilah appeared at the dock, raised herself halfway out of the water, and made some clicking sounds. "You hungry this morning, baby?" Scott asked. He tossed her a fish, which she caught in her mouth, swallowed whole, and nodded for more.

Jennie and Gram followed his example with Samson and Splash, while Debbie and Ken fed the others. After feeding the dolphins what seemed like a hundred pounds of fish, they rinsed the buckets and headed for the large warehouse, which housed a laboratory and giant walk-in refrigerator filled with frozen fish. There, as Ken had explained the day before, they received new fish shipments every couple of days and prepared fish for each dolphin by adding vitamins and minerals and medications they might need.

When the buckets had been properly cleaned and stored away, Gram and Jennie returned to the dock to observe another of Sarah's sessions with Debbie and Delilah. While they waited for Sarah and Maggie to arrive, Debbie showed them several new hand signals to which Samson responded beautifully. Delilah, however, ignored them. "Looks like she doesn't feel like showing off for you today," Debbie said, signaling the dolphin to approach the dock. She reached out to pet Delilah and cooed. "You having an off day? Well, let's make it easy for you. Why don't you wave to them?" Debbie signaled her, and Delilah backed up, lifted her tail out of the water, and waved it back and forth.

"Isn't it amazing what they seem to understand?" Gram said.

Maggie, Tim, and Sarah had come up behind them. They all agreed, except for Tim, who leaned against the post and scowled. "I don't know what you're so excited about. You can get the same response from a dog."

Maggie patted his arm. "Ease up, Tim. You promised you'd come and watch with an open mind."

After lowering Sarah into the water, Debbie signaled Delilah, who raced toward them, then abruptly turned. Jennie heard Maggie's scream as the dolphin's tail came within about an inch of Sarah's face. "What's she doing?" Jennie gasped.

Tim pushed past them and leaned out over the dock. "That's it. I've seen enough. Get Sarah out of there this instant."

"Of course," Debbie said, guiding Sarah toward the ladder. "Delilah's never done anything like this before. I don't understand . . ."

Delilah came at them again, dove under Sarah, and carried her out to the far end of the lagoon. Jennie watched, horrified, as Delilah leapt over the low fence and headed for the open sea with Sarah clutching desperately to her fin.

12

Everything seemed to be moving in slow motion, yet it wasn't. Debbie had already swum halfway across the lagoon. Tim discarded his shoes and suit jacket and dove in. Jennie started to dive in after him, but Gram stopped her. "Wait. There's no point in your going out there too."

Jennie held back. Gram was right; Debbie would call for backup if she needed it. Scott and Ken had apparently heard their shouts and screams and hurried toward them, firing off questions no one could answer. "What's going on?"

"What happened?"

"Where's Sarah?"

Jennie started to explain when Maggie screamed again. "Where is she?"

Delilah had disappeared. Just outside the fence, Sarah's empty orange life jacket bobbed in the water like a fishing float. Debbie held it up, tossed it aside, and signaled the others.

"I was afraid of that," Ken said. "Sarah's so thin, the life jacket must have slipped off her. C'mon, Scott, we've got to find her. She may be hung up on the fence."

It took a moment or two for the realization to sink in.

Sarah may have drowned. "I'm coming too." Jennie raced after them.

Gram shouted. "Look! They're coming back."

Jennie turned her gaze in the direction Gram was pointing. She could barely make out the dorsal fin and the hand that clutched it.

"Hang on, Sarah," Maggie yelled. She dropped to her knees and gripped the edge of the dock. "Oh, baby, please hold on."

Moments later, the dolphin brought Sarah within reach of the ladder. Scott jumped into the water and handed her up to Ken. While Ken guided Sarah and Maggie to a bench, Jennie grabbed a couple of towels, which she wrapped snugly around Sarah's shoulders and legs. Sarah's face had gone completely white with fear, and she was shivering so hard the entire dock seemed to shake.

"Is she all right?" Debbie asked, having just arrived back at the dock. "I thought we'd lost her."

Ken hunkered down in front of Maggie. "I'm so sorry, Mrs. Layton. We've never had anything like this happen before. I don't know what to say."

"It's not your fault. I'm just glad Sarah's safe . . ."

"Don't say another word, Maggie." Tim bent to retrieve his shoes and jacket and approached them. "We're taking Sarah to the hospital and then I'm going to talk to a lawyer. I tried to tell you how dangerous this dolphin therapy business was, but you had to try it." He turned from Maggie and addressed the others. "I hope you people are satisfied. Sarah could have been killed out there. What is it going to take to get you to realize that these animals can't be trusted? I intend to close you down, Cole. Bet on it."

Sarah pulled the towel over her head like a turtle escaping into its shell. Tim hustled Sarah and Maggie off to the cabins, and within half an hour they'd changed and were heading into town. As they drove away, Jennie couldn't help wondering why Tim would react so violently over an accident. *If it was an accident.* Could Tim be over-acting again? Could he have been responsible for what happened to Delilah? What better way to stop therapy and keep Sarah silent than to make the dolphin therapy seem unsafe? *You're stretching things, McGrady,* she told herself. *Forget it.*

Ken told them he needed to talk to each of them so he could write up a report and suggested they all get into dry clothes and have lunch. Over soup, sandwiches, and fruit, they continued their discussion about Delilah's strange behavior. "From what you told me, it's like Delilah had a complete personality change," Ken said.

"What would cause something like that to happen?" Gram asked. "If I were dealing with a human, I'd suspect drugs. Is that possible?"

Jennie perked up at the suggestion. Maybe her idea about Tim wasn't so farfetched after all. She tucked the possibilities away, fully intending to pull them out when she had more information.

"Yes, but Delilah's not on medication. Still, it's worth checking out. I think I'll try to get her into the stretcher and examine her this afternoon."

"Delilah's gone," Debbie said. She took a deep breath and let it out slowly. "Samson was the one who brought Sarah back. Now he's gone too. I think he went out to find Delilah." To Ken she said, "I should have told you earlier, sweetheart, but I was so worried about Sarah."

Debbie crumpled her napkin and tossed it onto the table. "This is all my fault. I should have been paying more attention to Delilah this morning. She tried to tell me something was wrong. I didn't pay enough attention."

"Nonsense." Ken took his wife's hand. "Delilah started acting strange after she was fed, right?"

Debbie nodded.

"Then, I'll run some lab tests on the feeding pails and the prep tables and see if I can find anything. We might have some bad fish . . ."

"Oh, man . . ." Scott scraped his chair back and ran out looking like he was about to lose his lunch.

When they'd finished eating, Gram announced she was going to do some writing, and Jennie decided to check on Scott. When he wasn't in his room, she wandered through the compound, but no one had seen him. Worried, Jennie headed for the office to check with Debbie.

As she approached the building, she heard Scott's voice. At first she thought it was coming from inside, then realized he was using the pay phone around the back of the building. Jennie was about to step around the corner when Scott's angry words stopped her.

"Hey, I didn't bargain for this. What if they find out?"

After a few moments, Scott spoke again, this time his voice calmer. "Yeah, well make sure it doesn't." Scott hung up, and Jennie slipped around to the opposite side of the building.

It's probably nothing, McGrady, she tried to assure herself. But no matter how hard she tried not to connect them, she had the terrible feeling Scott's phone call had something to do with Delilah.

Jennie waited until Scott had moved away from the building, then ran after him. She wouldn't mention the phone call—at least not yet. Maybe he'd tell her on his own. As she raced past the office door, Jennie collided with a man coming out.

100

The impact threw her off balance, but the man pulled her up just before she hit the ground. Once she was back on her feet, Jennie nearly fell over again when she recognized him. Carl Layton. Sarah's stepfather.

"Are you okay, miss?" he asked.

"Yes. I'm fine," Jennie said, feeling off balance in more ways than one. "Oh, Mr. Layton, I'm so sorry. I didn't see you. I was . . ."

"Going after your boyfriend?" Carl nodded in Scott's direction, smiled, and winked.

Jennie could feel the warmth creeping into her cheeks. "No . . . I mean he's not . . ."

"You might want to let him cool off a bit. He looked pretty upset when he passed me a moment ago."

Jennie decided to let his comment pass. It would have been too hard to explain anyway. "Thanks," she said, finally. "I'll do that."

"By the way," Carl said, scrutinizing her. With his tanned muscular arms folded against his chest, he reminded Jennie of Mr. Clean with hair. "How did you know my name? Have we met before?"

Jennie introduced herself and explained how she'd seen him at the airport with Maggie and Sarah.

He nodded and flashed her a warm smile. "Then, you've met my girls. Do you know where I can find them? There doesn't seem to be anyone in the office."

"They . . . ah . . . went into town with Tim," Jennie offered, not certain whether to tell him the whole story.

"Well, then, maybe you could show me to their living quarters." He shook his head. "I don't understand why they'd leave. I phoned Maggie this morning to let her know I was coming in early." He stroked his chin and frowned. "Say, nothing's happened, has it? Is Sarah okay?"

"Sarah's okay," she said, unsure of how much to tell him. He was family and deserved to know what happened. *Better keep your mouth shut,* an inner voice cautioned. *With your luck, you'll just make things worse for Debbie and Ken.*

"Come on," she said, opting not to tell him. "I'll show you where they're staying."

Jennie left him at the Layton cabin and hurried on to her own. Gram was sitting at the patio table working on her computer. Jennie told her about Carl's arrival, but she didn't seem too interested.

"That's nice, dear," Gram murmured, her attention still on the screen. "By the way, your mother called. She sounded worried."

"She always sounds worried." Knowing Gram wasn't ready to talk to her about Carl yet, Jennie called home. "Hi, Mom," she said when her mother answered. "What's up?"

"Nothing really. I miss you. Are you doing all right? Eating okay?"

"I'm fine, Mom. The people who run this place are vegetarians." Jennie wrinkled her nose. "I'm getting plenty of greens."

"Oh, dear. Are you getting enough meat? I just read an article about teenage girls who diet and don't get enough protein."

"Mom, I'm not stupid. You don't have to worry."

"I'm sorry. Of course you're not." She hesitated. "I didn't mean to nag. Let's talk about something else."

After telling Jennie how great Nick was doing, Mom spent the next five minutes talking about Michael. Jennie felt depressed after hanging up. Her mother had shared lots of news—most of it bad—at least as far as Jennie was concerned. Michael was taking them out for dinner. Michael had brought her a dozen roses. Probably the worst news was that Michael and Mom had started seeing the pastor for pre-marital counseling classes. Ugh. She hoped the pastor would tell Michael and Mom they'd made a mistake and that they were incompatible.

It was all too depressing to think about, so Jennie grabbed a book and headed for the pool. She'd only read two chapters when Scott tossed his towel down on the lounge chair next to her, walked to the side of the pool, and dove into the water as if demons were chasing him. Maybe they were. The memory of the phone call she'd overheard came flooding back.

After swimming a couple of laps, he hoisted himself out of the pool and approached her.

"I came to say goodbye," he announced.

"What? But why?" Jennie stared up at him.

"Isn't it obvious?" Scott sat on the lounge chair next to her. "You heard Ken. He thinks maybe Delilah got some bad fish."

"So?"

"So that's what happened to the dolphin at Playland. And they blamed me. It's happening all over again. And once they get a look at my arrest record, I'm finished."

"Well, did you do it?"

"What do you think?" He looked hurt that she'd even asked.

"I . . ." Jennie thought about the phone call. "I don't know what to think. I overheard you on the phone earlier."

Scott frowned. "And you just assumed I was guilty?"

"No. I tried to keep an open mind. I still am."

Scott leaned forward and toweled his hair. "I was talk-

103

ing to Melissa. Before we came up here, Melissa asked me to collect data that they might be able to use against the research center. I thought maybe one of them had done it."

"Had they?"

Scott shook his head. "Melissa doesn't think anyone with the DPA would go that far." His shoulders slumped in frustration. "Look, Jennie, I wouldn't do anything to hurt dolphins, or any marine life for that matter. I know it doesn't look good, but you have to believe me."

"I do believe you," Jennie said. And she did. Scott would never have hurt the dolphin deliberately.

He smiled, but his eyes still looked a stormy-gray. "Thanks," he said. "That means a lot. But I still think I better split."

"If you're innocent, you don't have anything to worry about. But if you run, you'll look guilty. Besides, you can't leave. We have a date, remember?"

"Oh, I wasn't planning on letting you get out of that." He swung his legs onto the chair and leaned back. "You really want me to stay?"

"Yes."

Scott didn't respond. He lay on the lounge for several more minutes, then got up, said goodbye, and left. Jennie hoped he'd take her advice and stay at the research center. On the other hand, she could understand his wanting to get as far away as possible. *Don't worry about it, McGrady. Scott's bright. He'll make the right decision. He'll stay.*

Jennie tried to read, but concern for Scott kept getting in the way. After about twenty minutes, she gave up and headed back to the cabin. Gram had finished working on the computer and was straightening up the living room. Jennie grabbed a dustrag and furniture polish and pitched in to help as she told Gram about her conversation with Scott and about the phone call she'd overheard earlier.

"This doesn't look good," Gram said. "I can't imagine Scott doing anything that might harm Delilah, but I'm not sure I have the same kind of faith in the DPA."

Jennie frowned. "Remember our last night in Key West? Scott called Melissa to tell her he was coming up north with us and wouldn't be picketing Dolphin Playland. After the phone call, he acted like he was upset about something. I never told you about it, but when you went to bed, he got angry and left."

"Hmmm. That would make sense. From the articles and materials I've read about the DPA, they'd like nothing better than to close down places like this. Melissa may have been using Scott to achieve that end. It's hard to imagine that they would harm a dolphin, but . . ." Gram tossed the newspapers in a recycling bin and straightened. "I think maybe we'd better have another talk with Scott."

They spent the next hour looking for him, but no one had seen him since he'd gotten off work at two-thirty. When he didn't show up for dinner that night, Jennie's belief in Scott's innocence began to melt. *Face it, McGrady. You were wrong. The guy's guilty, and you're just too proud to admit it.*

13

Jennie tried not to think about Scott, concentrating instead on her food, which turned out to be a bad idea. The "hamburger" she thought they were eating turned out to be a concoction of soybeans and vegetables. It didn't taste too bad, as long as she used plenty of lettuce, tomatoes, onions, mayo, and ketchup—and if she kept her mind off what she was eating.

Fortunately, the Laytons and Sarah arrived, and Jennie was able to push Scott and the phony meat out of her mind. Maggie and Carl settled Sarah between them. When Jennie and Gram asked about Sarah, Carl reassured them. "She got a little cut on her arm, probably from the fence, but other than that she's fine."

"Speaking of cuts," Debbie said, "that's a nasty one on your arm. What happened?"

Carl seemed surprised, then rotated his arm so he could see the cut and frowned. A four-inch long, blood-caked gash ran from his elbow to about the middle of his forearm. "Must have scratched it while I was unpacking the rental car. Doesn't look too serious," he added. "A little soap and water ought to take care of it." He shook his head and grinned. "Talk about the absentminded professor. I didn't even realize it was there."

"You'd better come over to the office after dinner," Ken said. "We have a first-aid station there. I'd like to take a look at it—clean it up and make sure it doesn't need a stitch or two."

Carl nodded, then asked Debbie how she got started with dolphin therapy. From then on, with all their psychological jargon, they might as well have been speaking Swahili. Jennie switched her attention to Gram and Maggie, who were discussing writing, Gram's favorite topic.

She waited for a break in the conversation and asked a question that had been on her mind since the Laytons had arrived. "Where is Tim?"

Maggie flushed and shifted in her chair. "He's staying in town. He dropped us off here and left, probably too ashamed to face everyone after all the awful things he said."

"Do you think he'll really try to close down the center?"

It was Carl, not Maggie, who answered Jennie's question. "Not if we have anything to say about it." He wrapped an arm around Sarah's shoulders. "And we'll even continue Sarah's therapy. Naturally I'm concerned about what happened today, but after hearing about the success this program has had, we'd like to give Debbie more time."

When they'd finished dinner, Carl surprised Jennie by asking her if she'd like to take Sarah for a walk.

"But . . ." Jennie began.

"It's all right." Carl lightly touched her shoulder, his kind blue eyes meeting hers. "Maggie told me about Tim's rampage. I've assured both him and Maggie that interacting with others, especially young people, is exactly what Sarah needs. Go ahead."

Jennie took Sarah's hand and led her out of the dining hall, taking the same path she and Scott had taken the night before. "It's safe to talk now," Jennie said as she dropped to the ground. "No one can hear."

Sarah didn't answer, and Jennie wondered if the incident with Delilah had set her back. Jennie pulled off her sandals and wiggled her feet in the fine white grains.

"Thanks for not telling," Sarah said.

"I told you I wouldn't."

"I know . . ." Sarah glanced behind them.

"Why are you pretending? Don't you think you should at least tell your mom?"

"I can't. I can't tell anyone."

"Why not?"

"I know who killed my father."

"Then you need to tell the police."

"It's not that easy." Sarah pointed to her head. "It's all in here, but I can't find it. I get these nightmares and flashbacks. I remember being there when Dad was killed. I didn't see who did it, but . . . maybe I'd better start over." Sarah folded her arms and rubbed them as though she were cold. "A few months ago I woke up in the middle of the night, and I'd come back."

"Come back?"

"I know that sounds strange, but after Dad got killed, I felt like I was floating through a long tunnel."

"Your mom said you were sick for a long time."

Sarah nodded. "It was like being alive and dead all at the same time. Anyway, one night I woke up and I was alive—at least part of me was."

"I don't think I understand."

"I'm not sure I do either. Sometimes it's like I'm two different people. There's me, Sarah, a fourteen-year-old, who's working like crazy to make everyone believe I'm still sick, and trying to remember who shot my father before . . ." Sarah shuddered, ". . . before the killer figures out I'm faking it and kills me too. Then, there's the girl in my flashbacks."

"Wait a minute. What's all this flashback stuff? You sound like a psychiatrist."

Sarah shrugged. "You don't spend fourteen years around psychiatrists and not learn something. Besides, when I came back, I started reading Dad's books. Mom and Carl think it's an object-relations thing—that I need to have something of Dad's close to me—but I've been trying to figure out how to unlock little Sarah so she can tell me what happened."

"Little Sarah?" *You are dealing with a certified nut case, McGrady.* Jennie leaned back to study the girl.

"That's what I call the girl in my memory." Sarah glanced at Jennie and flinched. "Don't look at me that way. I'm not crazy. I know she's me. It's just easier to handle the flashbacks if I give her a name and keep her separate—at least for now.

"I first saw her that night, when I came back. I started to call to my mother and Carl, but something inside me panicked. A picture flashed through my mind. It was real, but it wasn't—kind of like a movie. Anyway, I closed my eyes, but the picture wouldn't go away. The girl was sitting in Daddy's chair writing a note. The pencil fell, and she crawled under the desk to get it. Then she heard an explosion, and everything turned red, then black. I could still see little Sarah, hiding under my father's desk, crying. She kept saying, 'No. Don't tell. You must never tell.' Little Sarah knows everything. She knows who killed my father."

Jennie had absolutely no experience in dealing with mental cases and had no intention of starting now. "I think we should talk to my grandmother."

"No." Sarah grabbed Jennie's arm. "Please. You said you wanted to help me. I need to remember who killed my dad."

"What about this Ramsey guy?"

"Ramsey didn't kill my father."

"How can you be sure?"

"I was there. I just know. It was someone else . . ."

Jennie heard a rustling noise in the shrubs behind them. "Shh . . . listen." The sound, whatever it was, had stopped. "Probably just an animal," Jennie whispered.

The noise had frightened Sarah back into her silent world. Having Sarah switch back and forth like that was spooky. Jennie had seen a couple of movies about people with multiple personality disorders. Could that be what had happened to Sarah? If so, could she believe anything the girl said?

"I'm going to take you back now," Jennie said as she stood and offered Sarah a hand up. "I know I promised I wouldn't tell, but you need more help than I can give you. I'm going to tell Gram. You can trust her. It will be all right, Sarah. It really will."

Jennie took Sarah back to the compound and handed her over to Carl, who was just coming to find them. "I appreciate your willingness to sit with Sarah," he said. "Not many young people would. It's difficult to carry on a one-sided conversation."

"It's no trouble," Jennie said. "Maybe someday she'll start talking back."

"That's what we're hoping." Carl took Sarah's hand and started up the path. "Oh, by the way, your grandmother said to tell you she'd be back in about an hour. She and Maggie went over to Sanibel to pick up a few things."

It took all the strength Jennie had not to run after Carl. *Sarah is talking,* she wanted to shout. *Only she's saying the strangest things and I'm scared and I think you ought to take her to a shrink.* That part was strange too, Jennie realized. Sarah was seeing a shrink—three of them, in fact. Between Debbie, Carl, and Sarah's regular therapist, they should have been able to see what was going on. Shouldn't they?

The one thing Jennie knew for certain was that she had to tell Gram about Sarah. Gram would know what to do. While she waited for Gram to return, Jennie wandered into the dining hall, shot a little pool, then wound around the paths and went back out on the beach behind the cabins. *Just killing time,* she told herself. *Liar,* her pesky conscience argued. *You're looking for Scott.* Jennie picked up a rock and flung it as hard as she could. *Great shot, McGrady.* It thumped into the sand about five feet away. She gave the rock a disgusted look, picked the thing up, and threw it again. This time it sailed an acceptable distance and disappeared into the water.

Nearly an hour had passed since she'd talked to Carl, so Jennie made her way back to the cabin to wait for Gram. She'd just opened the patio door when the phone rang. Jennie hurried over to answer it.

"Oh, hi, Gram. What's going on?"

"We're running a little late and I didn't want you to worry."

Jennie could hardly hear her over the music playing in the background. "Where are you?"

Gram laughed. "Would you believe there's an art fair

111

in town? Turns out that Maggie loves these as much as I do."

"That's great." Jennie had to work at trying to sound as though it didn't matter. She must not have succeeded because in the next breath Gram said, "You sound upset. Is everything okay there?"

"Yes, I just wanted to talk to you about Sarah. It'll keep until morning. Have a good time."

Jennie hung up, fixed a cup of peppermint tea, and plodded upstairs. Disappointment settled around her like a black cloud. It had been a bizarre day, and she wanted Gram to help her sort through it all. "Debriefing," Gram called it. She could call Lisa, but that would mean going back downstairs, and Jennie didn't have the energy for that. Instead she climbed into bed, pulled out her diary and wrote a letter to her father.

Thirty minutes later she turned out the light and snuggled under the sheet and lightweight blanket. "God," she murmured. "Help me to know what to do for Sarah. Please let her remember . . ." and at the risk of sounding just as crazy as Sarah had, she added, "and help little Sarah not to be afraid. Keep them both safe."

Jennie fell asleep thinking not of Sarah, but of little Jennie, who held so tightly to the belief that Dad was still alive.

14

The next day Jennie fully intended to tell Gram about Sarah, but at six that morning, Samson brought Delilah back home. Everyone in the compound gathered on the docks to watch Ken, Debbie, and two of the other trainers slip Delilah into a specially-made stretcher for dolphins. They maneuvered her through the water into an enclosed tank where they could more easily care for her.

"Is she going to make it?" Jennie asked. Her question hung in the silence. It was a question, Jennie realized, that no one could answer.

Over the next couple of hours so many people invaded the small island, Jennie wondered if it might sink. Reporters, along with other researchers, marine biologists, environmentalists, friends, and enemies came to get what they hoped would be a big story, to help or to criticize. Melissa, Scott's friend from the DPA, swooped in with a small band of demonstrators, reminding Jennie of a flock of vultures. They'd already prepared protest signs and flyers, and Jennie couldn't help but wonder how they'd been able to put them together so quickly. She tried not to come to the obvious conclusion—that Scott had somehow been involved or may even have been the cause.

At ten A.M., Ken emerged from the tank and briefed

them. "She's dead. She was badly air burned and dehydrated. We did everything we could."

"Any idea what caused this, Mr. Cole?" a reporter asked, pushing a microphone at Ken.

"I'm afraid I do. The autopsy will show for certain, but I found traces of methamphetamine hydrochloride in Delilah's feeding pail."

"That's speed, isn't it?" Melissa asked. "Are you telling us this dolphin was drugged?"

For the next few seconds the dock was so quiet you could hear the boards breathe. Then the crowd erupted, spewing questions and hurling insults. Jennie looked around for Gram and saw her up front with Debbie and Ken, probably trying to create order out of chaos. Feeling about as useless as a third shoe, Jennie pressed through the wall of bodies and headed toward the dining hall. At first she thought it was empty, then saw Sarah sitting in a chair, staring out the window.

Jennie hurried toward her. "What are you doing here alone?" She'd spoken softly, but in the large room it still seemed too loud.

"They figured I'd be safe enough here," Sarah whispered. "They're down on the dock with the others."

"Did you hear about Delilah?"

Sarah looked up at Jennie briefly, then continued to stare straight ahead. "It's my fault," she said softly, her lips barely moving. "If I'd told them I was better, Delilah would be alive."

"Don't be silly. This had nothing to do with you."

"You're wrong, Jennie. The person who did this to Delilah either wanted to stop the therapy, or wanted to use Delilah to kill me. Why else would anyone hurt a dolphin?"

Voices filled the room as dozens of people poured into it. Carl and Maggie came back to collect Sarah, and Jennie escaped to the cabin. Gram was in her element—interviewing, collecting information, and researching. She probably wouldn't surface until the last bit of information had been squeezed out of everyone there. Over a fruit and cheese snack, Jennie tried to decide what she should do while she waited for Gram to come back. *You could lie around feeling depressed. Or you could keep racking your brain to figure out what's going on.*

On impulse Jennie suited up, stuffed a book, a towel, some sunscreen, a candy bar, and chips—which Gram had smuggled in the night before—into a bag and headed for the beach. At the door she paused, went back inside, and left Gram a note.

After spreading out her towel, Jennie mentally pulled up all of her unanswered questions and worries and tossed them one by one into the ocean. Then, after applying sunscreen, she stretched out on the towel and immersed herself in another kind of mystery—one that would be solved by the end of the book.

It was always the least likely person. Jennie shifted her focus from the novel to real life—who killed Delilah? Was it Tim Stanford? Tim was obviously against having Sarah in the program. But that in itself wouldn't be motive enough to kill a dolphin. And Jennie didn't think he'd harm Sarah, unless . . . unless he was trying to keep her from remembering who killed her father. Or was it Scott and his team of environmental extremists? *No, think "least likely," McGrady . . . how about Debbie and Ken . . . or Maggie or Carl . . .* "Oh, no you don't," Jennie muttered. "The next thing you know, you'll be suspecting Gram. Now read."

Sometime later, Jennie set the book aside. The girl in the story reminded Jennie a lot of herself. She looked at the cover depicting the eyes of a murderer peering through some bushes, and shuddered. Winnie, the heroine in the book, had decided to solve her friend's murder. The murderer turned out to be the guy who'd been working on the case with her. Scary stuff.

A lot of mysteries were like that. The killer was often someone close, a family member or friend. And they always have a motive. *Why else would anyone want to kill a dolphin?* Sarah had asked. That's what Jennie intended to find out. Resolutely, she gathered up her things and wandered back to the cabin.

"There you are." Gram had a worried look, and Jennie didn't think it was for her. "I was about to come looking for you."

"Did something happen? Is everything okay?"

"I'm not sure," she said, handing Jennie a note. "I found this stuck in the door when I came in."

Jennie,
I've got something to tell you about Delilah. Meet me at
the lighthouse on Sanibel at eight-thirty tonight. Scott.

Jennie looked up from the note. "What should I do?"

"I suggest we meet him." She glanced at her watch. "In the meantime you'd best get dressed. Ken has called in the police to investigate. I've already given my statement, and you'll have just enough time before dinner to talk to them."

The "them" turned out to be Detective Angel Delaney, who Jennie decided had no resemblance whatever to any angel she'd ever imagined. Angel's dark hair had been casually swept up and clasped in a wide leather barrette.

116

She wore a don't-mess-with-me expression, and for a moment Jennie thought Angel and Tim Stanford would have made a perfect couple. From her stance and the questions she asked, Jennie had the distinct impression Angel had better things to do with her time than go after a dolphin killer.

"All right, Miss McGrady," Angel said, her pen poised above a small notebook. "Tell me what happened . . . and try to keep it short."

With Gram at her side, Jennie related the incident as best as she could, being careful not to mention Scott or the fact that Sarah could talk. She did, however, suggest that Delilah's death might be connected to John Stanford's murder. Angel raised her eyebrows. "What do we have here, a budding detective?" She looked at Gram and for the first time since Jennie had met her, smiled. "Teaching her the tricks of the trade, Ms. McGrady?"

Gram winked at Jennie and smiled. "She learns quickly. As I mentioned before, the fact that Sarah was in the water with the dolphin may be more than coincidence."

"Right. Well, if it will make you feel better, I'll check it out. But I wouldn't hold my breath. My bet's on the kid who disappeared yesterday." She flipped back a few pages in her notes and added, "Yeah, here it is, Scott Chambers. Which reminds me," she added, scrutinizing Jennie. "You didn't mention him. Any particular reason why?"

Jennie looked at Gram, who nodded. Reluctantly, she told Angel about the phone call and other things she remembered Scott saying. She finished with, "Scott wouldn't kill a dolphin. I just can't believe that of him."

After Angel left, Gram suggested they have dinner in

town before meeting Scott. On the drive into town it occurred to both of them that they'd neglected to tell Angel about the note Scott had left. "It's probably just as well," Gram said. "This will give us a chance to hear his side . . . and if he *is* involved, encourage him to go to the police."

Jennie took advantage of their time alone to tell Gram about Sarah. "She scares me," Jennie said when she'd finished. "She really believes whoever killed her father is after her too." Jennie sighed. "Sarah asked me not to tell, but I had to. I don't know what to do for her."

"You did the right thing coming to me. Obviously she's convinced herself that she's in terrible danger. It seems to me we have basically two possibilities. Either she's built up this fear in her mind, or it's real. Either Ramsey killed John Stanford or he didn't. And if he didn't, the real killer would want to be sure Sarah couldn't make a positive identification. What I don't understand is, why the killer, if it wasn't Ramsey, would wait so long."

Jennie leaned her head back against the seat and sighed. "Maybe since she was so sick, the killer didn't feel threatened. Or maybe he didn't want to kill her, but now that she's better . . ."

"I thought you and I were the only people who knew she was better."

"I'm not so sure about that. It doesn't seem like she'd be able to pull off an act like that without somebody figuring it out. I had a feeling something wasn't right the first time I saw her. She's got to have made some mistakes. Sarah told me she reads her father's books a lot. Wouldn't that make you suspicious?"

"You're right. It would be hard to live with a person

and not be aware of changes, no matter how subtle."

"Then, it makes sense," Jennie interrupted. "The person who killed John Stanford could be after Sarah and could have killed Delilah."

"Like Angel says, it's doubtful, but worth checking into. By the way, I got the information J.B. sent on the Stanford murder in the mail today. What with all the excitement, I didn't get a chance to study it. We'll take a look when we get back from our meeting with Scott."

Gram maneuvered the car into a small parking lot on Captiva at a restaurant called the Mucky Duck. "The Mucky Duck?" Jennie grimaced.

Gram chuckled. "Maggie recommended it . . . says the food's great."

"Whatever, as long as they have french fries and real meat in their hamburgers, I'll be happy." Not only did they have the real thing, Jennie learned, they served large portions of it.

Gram insisted they talk about more pleasant topics over dinner than murder, and Jennie reluctantly acquiesced. A little later, she was glad for the change. Jennie enjoyed dealing with safe subjects like school, friends, and plans for the future. For the first time ever, Jennie voiced her thoughts about studying law. Maybe become a police detective, a lawyer, or a federal agent.

"Aren't you going to try and talk me out of it?" Jennie asked. "Mom would."

"Yes, I suppose she would. I tried to dissuade your father, but it didn't work. He wanted to follow in his father's footsteps as well." Gram stopped to clear her throat. When she looked up there were tears in her eyes. She blotted them away. "I just hope you base your decision on what you want, not what you think your father would have wanted."

119

After dinner they drove to Sanibel. The lighthouse, a historical landmark, stood at the east end of the island and it took them almost half an hour to get there. By the time they reached the lighthouse area and parked, it was eight-thirty-five. The sky had turned a dusky rose. In another twenty minutes it would be completely dark.

They walked to the lighthouse and wandered around the surrounding area. No Scott. After waiting fifteen minutes, Jennie said, "I don't think he's coming."

"Perhaps he's been delayed. We'll wait until nine, then we'd better head back to the research center."

At Jennie's insistence, they waited until quarter after nine. On their drive back to Dolphin Island, Jennie wasn't sure whether to be angry or worried. Why had he asked them to meet him and not shown up? Had something happened to him? She rested her head against the seat and closed her eyes. Questions and concerns about Scott swirled through her mind. She gave up trying to sift through them, choosing instead to pray for him.

"We're almost there, Jennie," Gram told her when they reached the bridge to Dolphin Island. "Were you sleeping?"

"No." She yawned. "Just resting." Jennie lifted her arm to shield her eyes from the glaring lights of the vehicle coming up behind them.

"Hold on!" Gram yelled the warning only a split-second before the impact. Jennie's head snapped forward, then back against the seat. Their convertible swerved and bounced against the concrete guardrail.

"What's going on?" She braced her hands against the dash.

The headlights dropped back, then raced toward them again. Gram gripped the wheel and pressed her foot to the floorboard. "I'm going to try to outrun him."

"He's gaining on us." The words had barely escaped her lips when the vehicle bore down on them again. This time the phantom driver connected with such force, the LeBaron careened out of control, slammed into the side of the bridge, and flipped. Their car hung on the railing for an instant, then plunged toward the deep, dark water below.

15

Jennie heard herself scream. They were going to die.

The car slammed into the icy water with a force that knocked the breath out of her body. Jennie's scream died away, and she slowly opened her eyes. The car had landed upright and was bobbing in the water like a bathtub toy.

"Are you all right?" Gram asked as she rubbed her left shoulder.

Jennie nodded. "I think so."

"Okay, listen carefully. We have only a few seconds before this thing goes down." Gram unfastened her seat belt and asked Jennie to do the same. With the top down on the convertible, this will be much easier than trying to escape through the windows. Now all we need to do is ease out and swim away before it sinks and sucks us down with it."

She glanced over her shoulder toward the bridge. "We'll use the lights on the bridge to guide us. Looks like we're closer to Captiva, so head back that way." She sucked in a deep breath and took hold of Jennie's hand. "It'll be a long swim and the currents between the islands are strong. Now, get out and swim like crazy. I'll be right behind you."

"But . . ."

"We'll make it," Gram said, grasping Jennie's hand. "We have to. Now go."

Jennie climbed over the door and eased herself into the water. She pushed off and began to swim. When she felt she'd gone a safe distance, Jennie turned to check on Gram. There was no sight of her or the car. "Gram! Where are you?" Her cry echoed on the still night air. No one answered. Jennie looked back toward the lights. Even stopping so short a time, the current had pulled her away from them. Panic coursed through her, turning her arms and legs to lead. *Stop it, McGrady. Gram's going to be fine. She's in such good shape, she's probably on the beach waiting for you.* Jennie righted herself and forced herself to swim. *Arm up into the water, kick legs. Arm up . . . over. Fingers tight. You can do this, McGrady. You can do it. God, give me strength . . . and Gram. Please help Gram.*

She didn't stop again until she felt the sand beneath her feet. She relaxed and let a wave carry her in and deposit her on the beach. Gritty sand and shell fragments pressed into her face, hands, and legs. It smelled moist and earthy. "Thank you, God," she panted. Jennie dragged her hands up beside her chest and tried to push herself up. She rose about an inch, then collapsed. No use. Every muscle in her body felt like rubber.

She lay there until her breathing slowed, then tried again. This time, she rolled onto her side and sat up. She felt dizzy. Shock . . . she was going into shock. *Put your head down, McGrady. You know how it's done.* When the waves of nausea passed, Jennie took several deep breaths and slowly got to her feet.

She heard the sound of a car crossing the bridge. Jennie froze. The horror of the accident slammed back into her mind. Only it hadn't been an accident. The driver of that truck had meant to kill them. The car stopped. A door slammed. Footsteps. Had he come back to finish the job? Jennie scrambled up the embankment and huddled behind a concrete pillar under the bridge. A flashlight beam darted over the water and came to rest on the sand where she'd been lying only moments before. Fear wound itself around her so tight, Jennie could hardly breathe.

Above the sound of her own heartbeat pounding in her head, Jennie heard another car approaching. Red, white, and blue lights flickered over the water like a strobe light. A police car. Another car door slammed. "What's going on out here?" a woman's voice penetrated the stillness. *Delaney.* "Mr. Layton, isn't it?"

Layton? Had he been the one who'd hit them? For one horrifying moment, Jennie imagined him whipping out a gun and shooting Angel. *Cool it, McGrady. It couldn't have been him. The guy that hit you and Gram was driving a truck. Layton has a fancy Lincoln.*

"I was just trying to figure out what is going on," Carl said. "I was coming back from a meeting in Fort Myers when I saw the broken railing and glass on the road, so I came back to check. I was afraid someone had driven off the bridge. Can't see anything, though."

Another beam flashed through the darkness. It waved over the water and came to rest on a stumbling figure walking toward them on the beach. *Gram!*

"Ms. McGrady? Is that you?" The light jiggled and footsteps clamored overhead. Jennie raced toward Gram, reaching her only seconds before the others.

"Oh, Gram. I'm so glad to see you. I thought . . ."

"I'm fine. A little winded, and a bit shaky, but alive. Thank God." Gram pulled Jennie into a hug.

Jennie and Gram explained what had happened while

Carl and Angel helped the bedraggled and exhausted swimmers up the embankment and into Dr. Layton's car. Angel wanted them to ride with her, but Dr. Layton insisted they'd be more comfortable in his car. "They've been traumatized enough," he'd said. "No sense making things worse by subjecting them to a ride in the back of a squad car."

Carl drove them to the local hospital, where the doctor on call examined them. Except for a few bruises, they had both escaped without serious injury. They'd been extremely fortunate, he told them. Had they not been wearing seat belts, they might have been killed. While Dr. Layton drank coffee and read old copies of *People*, *Golf Digest*, and *Newsweek*, Angel escorted Jennie and Gram into an unused office just off the emergency room.

Once seated, Angel whipped out a notebook and pen. "Okay. You say some guy in a truck ran you off the road. Can you think of anyone who might want to hurt you?"

"No," they both answered in unison.

"Ms. McGrady. I did some checking on you. Seems as though you've been involved in some . . ." Angel glanced at Jennie, then back at Gram. "Ah, does she know?"

"That I do an occasional job for the FBI?" Gram nodded.

"Right. You've made a few enemies. Any chance one of them could be responsible?"

"I suppose anything is possible," Gram said, "but I don't think a hit-and-run with a fully loaded pickup truck would be their style."

"Maybe you're right. So talk to me. What's your theory about all this?"

Gram shrugged. "I can't think of anyone here who

would want me or Jennie out of the way. As far as I know, we haven't made any enemies."

"Looks like we've made at least one," Jennie voiced her thought out loud. She told Angel as much as she could remember about the incident, hoping they wouldn't have to tell her that they'd gone to Sanibel to meet Scott. Unfortunately, she asked, and Jennie had to tell her about Scott's note. "But Scott couldn't have been driving that truck. He had to hitch a ride up with us."

"He could have stolen it."

"He wouldn't do that." Why was she defending him? She'd only known him for a few days. "Scott's just not the type."

"That's what people said about Ted Bundy."

Jennie shrank back into her chair and listened as Gram related details of the crash to Angel. Jennie was surprised at how much Gram could recall. All Jennie could remember was the glare of lights and the sickening thud, the feeling of panic, and the car hurling itself over the railing and into the water. Gram, however, remembered specifics, such as how the vehicle was one of those sports pickups with running lights. Five across the top—the second light near the driver's side was burned out. Gram also said she didn't think the driver meant to run them off the road on the first hit. "It was too close to shore," she figured. "My guess is that he wanted us far enough out so we wouldn't survive."

When Angel had finished her interrogation, she left Jennie and Gram with Carl, who offered to take them back to Dolphin Island. Jennie wanted nothing more than to take a warm shower and crawl into bed. Every part of her body was beginning to ache. Gram climbed into the front seat and asked Dr. Layton what he thought about dolphin therapy. *Don't you ever quit?* Jennie wanted to ask. It was getting downright embarrassing. Gram had no business being so full of energy, when Jennie felt like she'd spent the last few hours competing in the Olympic decathlon. A smile crept to her lips. *Like the Energizer Bunny . . . Gram just keeps going and going and going . . .*

Jennie took advantage of the roomy backseat and curled up on her side. Lulled by the purring motor and the strains of gentle music flowing through the rear speakers, she began to drift off.

"Maggie told me you were shot trying to stop the murderer." Had Gram's voice gotten louder? Maybe it was just Jennie's radar letting her know the conversation had taken an interesting turn. She opened her eyes and tuned in.

"I thought we were talking about dolphins." Carl glanced at Gram, then focused on the road.

"Sorry about the switch. I'm an ex-police officer and can't help being curious. I was hoping you'd indulge an old woman's curiosity and give me your version."

"Old? You?" He chuckled, then his tone grew serious. "I don't mind telling you about it. Terrible tragedy. John was one of the brightest therapists in the country. He was more than a partner, Mrs. McGrady. He was a dear friend."

Gram nodded. "It must have been doubly hard for you, losing both a business partner and a friend. Did you actually see the shooting?"

"No. I was in my office when I heard the gunshot. I ran out to investigate and a guy was standing in John's doorway, holding a gun. I looked past him and saw John slumped in his chair. Blood everywhere." Carl paused. "Even after two years it's hard to talk about it."

"I can imagine. You don't have to go on, you know."

"It's all right." Carl took a deep breath and continued. "After I saw John's body, I looked back at the guy. He had his gun aimed right at me. I tackled him and knocked him down, but he got off a shot. Hit me in the shoulder. He pushed me away, then took off."

"And you phoned the police?"

"No, Maggie did that. She'd had a lunch date with John and came in, oh, couldn't have been more than a minute or two after Ramsey left. Fortunately, the guy took the stairs." Carl frowned. "I hate to think what might have happened if he'd decided to wait for that elevator."

"Or if he'd seen Sarah."

Carl sighed. "Poor kid. I didn't even know Sarah was there. The police found her under the desk in a fetal position. Her body was locked up so tight it took us two days to relax her muscles enough to straighten her out. I worked with her every day for months. Used a combination of drugs and hypnotherapy to bring her out and help her remember. We managed to bring her partway out, but who and what she saw is still locked inside her somewhere."

"Why did you stop working with her when you and Maggie married?" Gram asked.

"Ethics. I'm too close to be objective. I'm still involved, of course, but I called a colleague in, and a few months ago she suggested we try the dolphin program."

"Do you think Sarah saw who murdered her father?"

"We don't know what Sarah saw . . . only that she was severely traumatized."

"Her uncle, Tim, seems unimpressed with police findings. He thinks the murderer is still at large."

128

"That's a puzzle. I've never been able to understand why he is so adamant about Ramsey's innocence. My guess is that he's never been able to resolve his own guilt. The last words they said to one another were said in anger. Not a very satisfactory way for a relationship to end."

"Did the police question whether Tim could have killed John? They did have an argument."

Carl shook his head. "Tim is the right size and build, but he's not a killer. Besides, all the evidence points to Ramsey."

"So you think Ramsey is guilty?"

"It's the logical solution. I was able to identify the man's jacket, and he did have an appointment to see John that day. I've never had a reason to doubt his guilt. I'm satisfied that Isaiah Ramsey murdered John, then went home and killed himself. The police even found the murder weapon in his car."

"Sounds like an open-and-shut case," Gram agreed. "But suppose Ramsey was set up. What if the real killer wanted to make it look like a murder/suicide?"

"Look, Mrs. McGrady. I think I know where you're going with this, but it won't work. Tim may be outspoken at times, and even paranoid, but he's no killer. Besides, the police found smudges of blood on Ramsey's jacket that matched mine. There's only one way that blood could have gotten on his clothes and that was when he shot me."

When they got to the compound, Carl parked behind the cabins and walked them to the door. The ride had stiffened Jennie's joints and she could barely walk. She collapsed on the couch and fell asleep while waiting for Gram to finish showering. When Jennie awoke it was still dark. Gram had removed her shoes and covered her with a blanket. She shifted positions to turn on a light and wished she hadn't. Pain coursed through her neck and shoulders. Scenes of the accident replayed in her mind.

Jennie massaged the taut muscles, then made her way into the bathroom for a hot shower. When she emerged fifteen minutes later, she found Gram in the kitchen putting water on for tea. "What are you doing up so early?" Jennie asked.

"The same thing you are, I suspect. I ache in places where I didn't even know I had muscles." Gram stretched her arms out in front of her and winced. "Since I couldn't sleep, and I heard the shower going, I thought maybe I'd look through the papers J.B. sent on the Stanford case."

For the next hour they drank tea and read reports. They didn't find much more than what Maggie and Carl had already told them. "The only thing that strikes me as unusual," Gram said, "is that the secretary didn't remember Ramsey being a client. Don't you find that curious?"

Jennie shrugged. "Not especially."

"Most secretaries know more than their bosses. I asked J.B. to interview her. He's also going to see if he can talk to Ramsey's family for me. Maybe we'll learn more then."

"When did you talk to J.B.?"

"Last night after you went to sleep. I had to report in and tell him about the accident."

"Did you figure out who might have done it?"

"No, but I have a feeling it's someone who wants us out of the way. And since the only things we're really involved in right now are the Stanford case and the incident with Delilah, it must be someone connected with one or the other."

"Or both," Jennie added. She yawned and stretched.

"I think I'll go up and get dressed."

She'd just started for the stairs when the phone rang. Gram answered it. After listening for a moment, Gram said, "Are you sure?" She paused. "All right. We'll be there."

"What's wrong?"

"That was Angel. The police are certain they've located the pickup truck that hit us. It's registered to the Dolphin Research Lab. They found it in the park, not far from the gate." She took a deep breath.

"Do they know who was driving it?"

Gram nodded. "Scott Chambers."

16

"He's unconscious. They've taken him to the hospital," Gram continued, heading for the door. "I'm going to see if I can borrow a car from Debbie."

The idea seemed so unthinkable, it took a moment for the words to sink in. Scott was hurt. Scott had been driving the truck that had almost killed them. "I don't understand." Jennie's voice broke. "How could that be? He . . . he's our friend."

Gram shook her head. "Maybe we'll learn more when we talk to Angel."

"He seemed like such a nice boy," Debbie said as she took the keys to her Jeep Cherokee from one of the hooks behind the office door.

"Debbie, do you keep all of your keys here?" Gram asked.

She nodded. "It's easier. That way all of our employees have access to the vehicles."

"Did Scott know about the keys?" Jennie asked, hoping that he hadn't.

"I'm afraid he did. Funny thing though, you'd have thought that if he was going to take the truck, he'd have done it the day he disappeared."

"What do you mean?"

"The truck was here until sometime after dinner last night. I distinctly remember because I did a count. It's sort of an automatic thing. I take inventory of just about everything here—people, dolphins, vehicles . . . that sort of thing. I suppose he could have come back last night and taken it."

Or someone else could have taken it. Jennie's defense was immediately shattered by her own opposing view. *Give it up, McGrady. The guy's guilty. He suckered both of you. Remember the phone call? What more proof do you need?*

Jennie and Gram drove to Sanibel in silence. Gram seemed deep in thought, and Jennie didn't feel much like talking. *I don't understand all this, God. Why would Scott want to kill us?* When they reached the hospital, a nurse wearing surgical greens updated them on Scott's condition. "He's coming around. Dr. Stone is stitching up a gash on his head. You should be able to see him in about thirty to forty-five minutes." The nurse disappeared behind the automatic emergency-room doors.

A few minutes later the doors swished open again, and Angel came out. "Good, you're here. I'm starved and my feet are killing me. Let's go down to the cafeteria." She pushed the elevator button, then tipped her head back and massaged her neck and shoulders. "Guess I shouldn't complain. Most hit-and-runs aren't this easy."

"So you really think Scott did it?" Gram said as the elevator bell dinged and the doors opened. They stepped inside, and Angel pushed "B" for what Jennie imagined was the basement.

"Think? Oh, believe me, there is no doubt. Not only did we find him in the vehicle that hit you, we also found some uppers in his shirt pocket. The same drug that killed that dolphin . . . ah . . ."

"You mean Delilah?" Jennie furnished.

"Yeah, that's it. We figure he arranged to meet you. Then, when you left the lighthouse, he followed you . . ." She shrugged. "You know the rest. His last hit sent you over the bridge. I suspect that's when he whacked his head on the steering wheel. He managed to drive into the park before passing out."

Disbelief, confusion, and anger all battled against a shredding thread of belief in Scott's innocence. *It's a nightmare, McGrady. Pretty soon you'll wake up and things will all be back to normal. You'll be in your bed at the research center. You'll go to breakfast, swim with Delilah, and after dinner Scott will challenge you to another game of pool, and you'll go for a stroll on the beach.*

"Jennie?" Gram's voice broke through her confusion. "Dear, are you all right? You look pale."

"What? No . . . I'm fine. Did you say something?"

"I asked if you wanted anything to eat."

Jennie didn't feel hungry, but at Gram's insistence took some cereal and a glass of milk.

"I just can't believe this," she heard herself saying. "It doesn't make sense. Why would Scott want to kill us?"

"I'm not sure he wanted to kill you, probably just scare you," Angel said as they made their way to a table and sat down.

"But why?"

"It's very simple. He and that environmental group he's involved with would like to see the research center closed down. How do you do that? Bad press. First he drugs the dolphin. She goes wild and nearly kills one of their clients. This puts a big question mark on the dolphin therapy programs. Are they safe? What parent is going to put their kid, or themselves for that matter, in the water with a dangerous animal?"

"But what would running us down do to hurt the center?" Jennie asked.

"More bad publicity. A truck driven by an employee from the research center runs down a couple of guests. Not good for business." Angel stuffed a forkful of scrambled eggs into her mouth and took a drink of coffee to wash it down.

"I know the evidence against him seems strong," Gram mused, "but suppose someone framed Scott."

"Look . . ." Angel said, setting down her cup. "I understand how the two of you must feel. It's always tough to swallow the fact that you've been taken in by a con artist—especially when he's a nice-looking kid like Chambers. But, hey. You were a cop, Ms. McGrady. You of all people should know things aren't always like they seem."

"That's exactly right, and I'm afraid what seems to be evidence pointing to Scott's guilt could be meant to steer us away from the real issue," Gram said. "I don't suppose I could talk you into holding off on the arrest. I'd like to check into another possibility."

"If you're talking about the Stanford case, you can forget it. I talked to the police commissioner in Portland. No offense, Ms. M, but I think you're ruffling your feathers over nothing."

The determined set to Gram's chin told Jennie that her grandmother was not convinced. Somehow the knowledge cheered her. When they'd finished breakfast, they went back up to the emergency room, and the doctor agreed to let them see Scott.

Jennie gasped as the nurse opened the curtain to usher them in.

In that instant, all the anger and doubts vanished. Scott peeked out at her through a bruised and swollen face. A dressing covered what Jennie imagined was the gash on his left temple that Angel and the nurse had mentioned. An IV pumped fluids into his left arm. He opened his mouth and lifted his head, then winced and collapsed back on the pillow. "Jennie."

Jennie stepped up to the gurney and took hold of his hand. "Hey, Scott . . ." Jennie reached an arm up to brush the moisture from her eyes. "You look like you've been in a fight with a cement mixer." *Dumb thing to say, McGrady. Real dumb.*

"Yeah." He grimaced and squeezed her hand. "But you should see the other guy."

"Scott . . ." There were so many questions she wanted to ask. So much she needed to know.

"I think we'd better let him rest," a deep voice behind her whispered. "You can see him tomorrow." She let herself be guided back through the curtains.

"I'll be keeping him overnight for observation." Doctor Stone raised an eyebrow and sent a disparaging glance in Angel's direction and shook his head. "No questions yet. He's just regained consciousness from a severe head injury."

Angel sighed. "Okay, I'll post a guard outside his room. Call me when his condition improves. As soon as he's alert, I want to be here to read him his rights."

He nodded and excused himself, then disappeared behind the curtains.

"He didn't do it," Jennie said adamantly as they slid onto the Jeep's vinyl seats. "If he'd wanted to hurt us, he would have acted . . . I don't know . . . different, surprised or scared or something. He seemed glad to see us. Does that sound like somebody who tried to run us off the road?"

"I don't believe for a minute that Scott is guilty. It's too pat. The entire thing smacks of a frame. Question is, who would do such a thing and why?"

Jennie pulled her braid from between the seat and her back and twisted the silky brown strands at the tip around her finger. "What about Melissa? Maybe she's using Scott."

Gram chewed on her bottom lip and maneuvered the car out of the hospital parking lot onto the main road. "If the motive really is to discredit the research lab, I'd say that's a possibility, but I'm not so sure. Melissa's group may be radical, but . . ." She paused to make a lane change, then continued. "Somehow, I don't think they'd stoop to drugging dolphins or forcing us off the road. Besides, whoever hit us did it hard enough to send us over that guardrail. I sincerely doubt that we were meant to come out of it alive. But why get rid of us? What do we know that could make us a threat to anyone?"

"We know Sarah can talk and that she doesn't believe Ramsey killed her dad," Jennie offered. "If Sarah is right about Delilah's murder being connected to her dad's death, maybe the real killer is afraid we'll dig up something."

"We have been asking a lot of questions, and it's no secret that I was once a police officer." Gram slowed as they approached the bridge to Dolphin Island and glanced in her rearview mirror, then at Jennie. "Just making sure no one is following."

Jennie felt uneasy as well. She hugged herself as they

approached, then passed, the crash site. Scenes from the night before reeled through her mind. She was missing something important but couldn't think what. Gram patted her arm. "Are you all right?"

Jennie nodded. "I just wish we could figure out what this is all about."

"When we get back to the cabin, I'll call J.B. Maybe he can shed some light on the case. In the meantime we'll need to be careful. It might be best if we act as though we agree with Angel's suspicions about Scott for now. And we'll need to be careful. If Scott didn't run us off the road, whoever did is still out there."

"But . . ." Jennie frowned. "I need to talk to Sarah, find out if she's remembered anything else."

"I agree. And I want to be there when you do. I'd like Debbie there as well."

"Why? Sarah won't talk to anybody else. I think she'll be okay with you, but if you bring Debbie in she might never talk to anyone again."

"I have a feeling she will."

Jennie slumped in her seat. *While we're at it, why don't we invite the whole group? We could pin up a banner in the dining hall that reads "Sarah's Coming Out Party."* She'd expected Gram of all people to understand. "Sarah trusted me."

"And I hope you can trust me. Dealing with psychological trauma like this is not something we should be taking lightly. There's a possibility Sarah could regress . . . have a mental breakdown. Debbie would best be able to handle that. Don't you agree?"

"I guess," Jennie acquiesced. "But at least let me talk to Sarah alone before you tell Debbie."

They arrived at the research center just in time for

lunch. Tim was back, looking more sullen than ever, and Jennie couldn't help wondering again if his reactions were simply an uncle's concern for his niece, or concern for himself. Gram brought them up-to-date on the investigation into Delilah's death and the hit-and-run. "At this point," she said, "Angel is certain that Scott is guilty of both."

When they returned to the cabin, Gram phoned J.B. After a number of "aha"s and "interesting"s, and a suspicious-sounding "That sounds wonderful. I'll be looking forward to it," Gram hung up.

"Are you and J.B. dating?" Jennie asked. Strange. Only a couple of weeks ago, Jennie would have been horrified at the idea of Gram's dating. Now she found the prospect exciting.

Gram looked up from her notes in surprise. "J.B. and I are good friends. He's taking me to dinner when we get back. Says he wants to talk to me about a job. Now," she said, clearing her throat, "are we going to talk about J.B. all afternoon, or would you like to know what he's learned about the Stanford case?"

Jennie grinned. "Okay. What have we got?"

17

J.B. had discovered some interesting details. He'd confirmed that the receptionist, who'd been fired shortly after the murder, had never heard of Isaiah Ramsey. Which was strange because when the police investigated they found his name penciled into the appointment book.

"She swears it wasn't her writing," Gram said. "Unfortunately, no analysis was ever done on the handwriting, so J.B. is checking it out."

"Do you think Dr. Stanford's killer put Ramsey's name in the book to throw everyone off?"

"It's a possibility. Remember, though, Dr. Stanford could have written in the name as well."

"Yeah." Jennie looked back at Gram's notes. "So what else did J.B. come up with?"

"Their receptionist confirmed what Carl said about Tim and John Stanford having had a heated argument. She didn't know what it was about, only that Tim stormed out of John's office. Says he left about five minutes before she went to lunch."

"I guess that lets Tim off the hook," Jennie said.

"Not necessarily. He could have come back. Since Tim was the firm's financial manager and handled the books, she suspected the argument had something to do with money. It's possible John found a discrepancy in the books and blamed Tim."

"So you think he did it?"

"It's a possibility. Somehow, though, I don't see Tim as the kind of person who'd resolve a problem with a gun. He's quite verbal," Gram smiled and adjusted her reading glasses. "A fact to which we can both attest."

"You're confusing me. How come you keep going back and forth?"

"It's a way of exhausting the possibilities. A detective has to look at a crime from all angles—you suspect everyone remotely connected and a few who seem to have no connection at all. You dig up as much evidence as you can, probe until you come up with the most reasonable answer, and use your intuition."

"Well, I think Tim did it."

"You may be right, but before you make up your mind, let's look at another motive—money. According to J.B., Carl Layton had been having money problems around the time of the murder. The death of his partner and subsequent marriage to Maggie made him a millionaire. Not only that, he now has full control of their lucrative practice. Financially, Carl gained a great deal from his partner's death. That certainly doesn't make him a murderer, but it's worth considering."

"But he was shot trying to catch the killer."

"True, but the gun was fired at close range. It's farfetched, but he could have shot himself."

"Gram!" Jennie leaned back and looked at Gram in surprise. "That's awful. A person would have to be desperate to do something like that."

"Murder is a desperate act, Jennie."

"So you think Carl did it?"

Gram shook her head. "I'm just looking at possibilities. Carl had both the motive and the opportunity."

"Right, but he couldn't have killed Delilah. He didn't come in until after she was drugged."

"True . . ." Gram chewed on the tip of her pen and frowned. "And from what I've seen of Dr. Layton, he seems like a wonderful man. He's kind and generous and cares a great deal about Sarah and Maggie. And speaking of Maggie, we need to look at her part in all this as well."

"You don't suspect her, do you?"

"Let's look at the facts. The receptionist told J.B. that when she went to lunch, she ran into Maggie in the lobby. Carl says Maggie came up after the murder. What if she had come up before? Maggie gained from John's death as well. She received $500,000 from a life-insurance payment and half the business."

"So you're saying Maggie could have killed John because she needed money for something?"

"It's possible. There's also the fact that she later married Carl. The two of them could have been working together."

"But Carl said she came in after the killer left."

"Carl could be protecting Maggie."

"But why? Gram, you're confusing. None of this makes any sense. We'll probably decide that Ramsey did it."

"You're right. I feel like we're trying to swim upstream." Gram set her note pad aside. "I'm going down to the beach to clear my head. Want to come?"

"Sure, but I need to get my suit on." Jennie stood and stretched. "You go ahead, I'll catch up in a few minutes."

Gram left and Jennie slipped into her suit, grabbed a book and towel, and headed out. On impulse, she stopped at the Laytons' cabin to see if she could take Sarah along.

It might give her the chance she needed to talk Sarah into confiding in Gram and Debbie.

Carl answered the door and readily agreed to let Jennie take Sarah to the beach. He asked Maggie to help Sarah get ready, then joined Jennie on the porch. "You and your grandmother went through quite an ordeal last night. How are you doing?"

"We're okay. A little sore still—actually a lot sore in some places, especially my shoulder. I'm just glad you and Angel came by when you did."

He nodded. "Glad I could be of help. If there's anything else I can do . . . if you need a car or anything, just let me know."

"Thanks."

Maggie brought Sarah out onto the porch. It unnerved Jennie to see how Sarah could so totally space out. As though she had a split personality or something. Gram was right. They did need to be careful.

Once they were away from the house, Sarah tipped her head back and took a deep breath. "I have to talk to you," she whispered. "Not at the beach . . . alone."

Sarah glanced behind them and grabbed Jennie's hand. "Quick." She pulled Jennie off the walk, toward one of the cabins damaged by the hurricane. "We can talk in here." She climbed the stairs, opened a door, and scrambled over the boards nailed across the entry to keep people out.

"Sarah, wait." Jennie hesitated. "I don't think this is a good idea."

"It's okay. I've been in this one before . . ." She glanced over Jennie's head. "Hurry, someone's coming."

Jennie took the stairs in one long stride and ducked inside and closed the door behind her. The footsteps paused outside the cabin. Jennie peaked through a shuttered window. "It's your uncle," she whispered.

"Did he see you?" Sarah pressed herself against a wall.

"I don't think so." Tim looked toward the cabin where they were hiding, frowned, and walked on toward the A-frame in which he was staying.

Jennie let out the breath she'd been holding and leaned back against the wall next to Sarah. The cabin, she noticed at closer inspection, had collapsed at one end, destroying what had once been a bedroom. The corner in which she and Sarah stood seemed sturdy, but Jennie had no intention of testing it. "Let's go," she said. "This place looks like it could fall down at any minute."

"No, please. I need to talk to you. I remembered something else." Sarah dropped to the floor.

Against her better judgment, Jennie sat beside her. "Okay, but just for a minute."

Sarah pulled her knees up and leaned her elbows on them. "Thanks for coming by to get me," she said in muted tones. "It's getting harder and harder to keep this up, especially with Carl around so much. After Delilah dumped me, he put me back on those awful tranquilizers. I don't take them, but I have to pretend like I am. I'm so afraid they'll find out."

"Sarah, I don't get it. Why don't you at least tell your mom and Carl what's going on?"

"I told you. Ramsey didn't kill my dad."

"I know but . . ."

"It was one of them." Sarah bit her lower lip.

"One of who?"

"My mom, Uncle Tim, or Carl. One of them killed my father."

"Are you sure?" Jennie asked. "You suspect your own

mother?" Even though she and Gram had discussed the possibility, it seemed impossible to Jennie. Maggie was a *mother*, for Pete's sake.

"I don't want to, but in my flashbacks I keep hearing her voice."

"Sarah, she came to the office after the murder."

"I know that . . . I mean . . . oh, Jennie, it's all a blur in my head. Maybe it would be better for everybody if I didn't try anymore. What if I remember what happened and it turns out to be my mom? I don't think I could stand that. Maybe I should just forget about it. It's not so bad not talking to anyone. At least I'd be safe."

"You know you can't do that. Anyway, how can you be sure they don't already know? Seems to me it would be better to know the truth, no matter what it is, than to keep going like you have been. Sarah . . ." Jennie paused, deciding to take her own advice about the truth. "I told my gram. She wants you to talk to Debbie." When Sarah didn't answer, Jennie continued. "I had to. We can trust Gram. She thinks Debbie could help you remember."

"Debbie knows?" Sarah grabbed Jennie's arm. "She'll tell Carl . . ."

"No. Gram said she'd talk to you about it first."

"Please, Jennie. I don't need Debbie. Just let me talk to you." Sarah leaned forward and rested her head on her arms.

"I don't . . ." Jennie started, but Sarah had already begun.

"When I crawled under the desk to get my pencil I heard Uncle Tim's voice. I started to come out to say hello. But he was yelling something at Dad about stealing some money from the business. He sounded so angry, I was afraid to move. A door slammed. I thought he'd gone, and I started to get up. My father was standing at his desk, and the door opened again. Dad said, 'I think you and I better have a talk.'

"I heard a loud bang and Daddy . . ." Sarah covered her ears and sobbed.

Jennie scooted closer and placed a comforting hand on Sarah's shoulder. "Sarah, don't . . . let me get Gram."

Sarah threw her arms around Jennie's neck. "No . . . don't leave me. I have to do this. I have to remember."

Jennie leaned against the wall for support and patted Sarah's head. *Oh, God, help me . . . I don't know what to do.*

Sarah's muffled sobs subsided, but she continued to hold Jennie tight. "Daddy fell into the chair. Blood was everywhere. It was on me. I tried to scream but nothing came out. I couldn't move. I had to stay . . . he'd find me. He came to the desk. I remember." Sarah panted, her breaths coming in short puffs. She tightened her grip on Jennie's neck. "No . . . don't let him hurt me . . . don't talk . . . don't move . . . he'll kill you."

Steady, McGrady. Don't panic. Jennie took a deep breath and continued to stroke the back of Sarah's head and back. It was like holding Nick after he'd had a nightmare. Maybe that was the answer. "Shhh," Jennie whispered, rocking Sarah and holding her close. "It's going to be okay. I'm here."

As Jennie continued soothing her, Sarah quieted. Her breathing evened out, and she loosened her grip on Jennie's neck. Sarah pulled away and held her hands over her eyes. "I'm sorry."

"It's okay," Jennie reassured her.

"I saw him this time . . ."

"Who?"

"The man who killed my father . . . not his face. I saw his pants—gray pants like the kind you wear with a suit . . . and shiny black shoes." Sarah swallowed and closed her eyes. "He took some papers from Dad's desk, then left.

"I heard another shot and . . . and then the elevator bell. My mother screamed . . ." Sarah turned to Jennie. A faint smile flashed across her wet face. "She didn't do it. Mom came in after."

"Of course she didn't do it. I told you . . ." Jennie stopped as she heard a rustle in the bushes outside.

"What was that?" Sarah scrambled to her feet.

Jennie rose and peeked through the wooden window slats. "I don't see anything." An odd smell penetrated the room and seemed to rise through the floorboards. *Kerosene. Someone is getting ready to torch the place.*

Correction, McGrady, they already have. Smoke seeped into the cabin from the collapsed bedroom and through the front door.

"Come on! We've got to find a way out of here!" Jennie turned to grab Sarah's hand. Sarah stood frozen, staring at the flames licking the wall.

"Oh no, you don't. You're not going to turn zombie on me now. Let's go." Jennie glanced around. Other than the door, the only way out was through a window covered by wooden shutters. Jennie pulled at the knobs. They wouldn't budge. The shutters had been nailed shut, probably to keep trespassers out. Now they would be keeping them in.

Going out in a blaze of glory. For some reason, the words to the old hymn popped into her head. The fire stretched across one wall, obliterating the wood panels. They were going out all right, but there was nothing glorious about it.

18

"Help! Somebody help!" Jennie screamed, pulling Sarah to the floor. "Stay down. There's more oxygen down here." Hot smoke rolled over them, seeping into their lungs.

Jennie coughed and yelled for help again. This time Sarah joined her. "Here, put this over your head," Jennie said, reaching for her beach towel. They spread it over their heads and shoulders. Minutes passed like hours as the girls continued screaming for help, their cries muffled by their makeshift mask.

An alarm sounded. Voices shouted orders.

"Someone's in there!" came a man's voice from outside the cabin.

"Uncle Tim. . . !" Sarah yelled, then started coughing. Smoke filled the room. Jennie's lungs ached from the heat.

"Stay back!" someone shouted. The door crashed open. Tim appeared with wet blankets. He threw one to Jennie and wrapped the other around Sarah. With one arm around each of them he half-dragged, half-carried them outside and away from the burning cabin.

After depositing them on a patch of grass, Tim lit into Jennie. "What were you thinking of, taking Sarah into a broken-down shack like that? Are you out of your mind?"

Jennie couldn't have responded even if she'd wanted to. Her chest, throat, and lungs felt as if they were on fire. Every time she tried to breathe she'd go into a coughing fit.

"No!" Sarah cried, her voice raspy. "It wasn't Jennie's fault." Sarah gasped for air between coughs. Jennie took her hand and squeezed it, well aware of what the admission had cost her.

The paramedics loaded the girls onto stretchers and stuffed them into a waiting ambulance. They checked pulses and blood pressures, slipped oxygen masks over their noses, and hooked them up to IV's.

For the next hour the emergency room buzzed with excitement—not about the fire, but about the girls trapped in the cabin. About one girl in particular who, after two years of silence, had regained her voice. Jennie hadn't been able to speak to Sarah since the fire. Aside from the doctors and nurses, Maggie, Tim, and Carl floated around her as if she were a rare and delicate porcelain doll. Not that getting close to Sarah would have done much good. Neither of them had been able to talk without breaking into bronchial spasms.

The girls were transferred out of emergency into separate rooms on the third floor. Jennie had hoped they'd put them in the same room, but Sarah's family, the nurse told her, had insisted on a private one. Once they were separated, Jennie realized how much danger Sarah was in. And it wasn't the smoke inhalation that worried her. If Sarah's memory was right, one of the men with Sarah had murdered John Stanford and was now after them.

A deep breath triggered the bronchial spasms again. *Got to quit thinking, McGrady. It's distracting. Concentrate.*

Short even breaths. Even the pain medication she'd been given didn't help when the spasms started. All it did was make her sleepy.

After the nurses had settled her into bed, then checked the IV and the oxygen tubing, they let Gram in. She pulled a chair up next to the bed and sank into it. Gram looked tired. Her beautiful salt-and-pepper hair had a limp, wash-me-now look. Jennie started to reassure her, then sank back into the pillow. If she tried to talk, the coughing would start again.

"Shhh," Gram whispered. "You just rest. Whatever you have to say will keep until tomorrow."

Would it? Jennie wasn't so sure. She needed to tell Gram about the gray suit and something else . . . She closed her eyes for a moment and must have drifted off.

"Helen?" Maggie's soft voice floated on the air and into Jennie's consciousness. "Would you like a ride back to the island? The doctor has assured us that the girls are going to be fine. Sarah's sleeping, and we thought we'd go back, get a good night's rest, then come back in the morning."

"That sounds good, but . . ." Gram frowned and glanced at Jennie. "Will you be all right?"

Jennie nodded and squeezed Gram's hand. It would be best. Gram needed rest much more than Jennie needed company.

Maggie and Carl approached her bed. "Sarah's doing fine. She said to tell you thanks," Maggie said.

Carl leaned against the side rail and took hold of Jennie's hand. "Jennie," he said, his light blue eyes gazing directly into hers, reminding her of pale aquamarine gemstones. "I want you to know that Maggie and I don't blame you at all for what happened. In fact, we're grateful to you. The doctor told us that your quick thinking may have saved both of you."

Jennie frowned. What quick thinking?

She didn't say it, but Carl must have understood. "Staying low and using that towel to cover your heads was a smart thing to do." He smiled and straightened, then patted her hand. "Thanks to you, neither of you was seriously injured."

"It was no big deal," Jennie whispered. "I'm just glad she's okay."

Gram leaned over the railing and kissed Jennie's cheek. She lifted her hand from the bed rail and stroked Jennie's hair. For some reason, it reminded her of something Mom would do. The thought released a tear that escaped her eye and slid down the side of her face, onto the pillow. *Get a life, McGrady. You're too old to get all mushy.*

"You're sure?" Gram asked. Jennie gave her the best I'll-be-fine smile she could manage and nodded again. Gram started to leave, then paused at the door. "I'll be back in the morning. Call me if you need me sooner."

Jennie took a sip of the water from the cup at her bedside and glanced at the clock over the door. Seven-thirty. Strange. It felt like an eternity since she and Sarah had entered the cabin, since she'd smelled the kerosene.

Suddenly Jennie felt as though her veins had been infused with ice water. In all the excitement, she'd almost forgotten. The fire had been intentionally set. Who had meant to kill them?

At least she knew one thing for sure. Angel Delaney wouldn't be able to blame Scott for this one. She was more convinced than ever that the person who killed De-lilah, sent her and Gram over the bridge, and set the fire was the same person who had killed John Stanford. And if Sarah was right, the killer was either her stepfather or her uncle.

Jennie tried to reconstruct the scene in her mind. Carl had been the last person to see them. But they were out of his sight when they left the path. Tim had stopped beside the cabin. Had he seen them? Had he sneaked up on them and overheard Sarah? Had he been the man in the gray suit?

Jennie shivered. Maggie and Carl had gone home, but they hadn't mentioned Tim. Had he gone too? Or was he still with Sarah? With no one around, he could put a pillow over Sarah's head, suffocate her, and do the same to Jennie. Everyone would think they had died of smoke inhalation.

Stop it, McGrady. Tim pulled you out of the fire. He saved your life. Besides, you're in a hospital. No one's going to hurt either of you. Not with all the nurses running around.

As the door to her room opened, Jennie brushed the thought aside before it could expand into an unreasonable fear.

Fear? Had she said fear? The man who entered her room sent an explosion of terror ripping through her. *The call button, McGrady. Hit the button!* She reached over the edge of the bed until her hand connected with the cord. Slowly following it down, she felt for the small button at the end and pushed.

Tim shifted from one foot to the other and glanced from Jennie's face to the floor. "Hi." He looked more like a teenager getting ready to ask for a date than a murderer.

"Hi," she croaked and leaned back in the bed. *It could be a trick, McGrady.*

"Look, I don't blame you for being afraid of me. I

. . . ah . . . haven't been very nice to you."

Not nice? That's the understatement of the year.

"Anyway," he said, stepping closer. "I just wanted to apologize. I know you were just trying to help Sarah. I overreacted and I'm sorry."

"It's okay. Ahh . . . it's a good thing you came along. Thanks for pulling us out of the fire."

"Don't thank me. Your grandmother engineered the rescue. I just followed orders. If I'd done it my way, all three of us probably would have been killed. She made me take in the wet blankets and wait till the doorway was cleared."

Right. Or maybe, if Gram hadn't come along you would have stood there and let us fry. Jennie remembered her first impression of Tim Hudson. He seemed sincere now, but Jennie still didn't trust him. *Ask him about the suit.* The command echoed through her head. *Are you crazy?* she argued.

"It's just that I'm nuts about that kid," Tim was saying. "Sarah's the only niece I have and . . . well, she's like my own daughter. It's pretty great about her being able to talk." Tim reached up and brushed his fingers over his mustache, then shoved his hands into his pockets. "Has Sarah told you anything . . . I mean, about her father's murder?"

Jennie shook her head. Why had he asked that? *Is he afraid she knows too much?*

"I'm sorry," he continued. "You can't talk very well right now either. It's just that . . ."

The eyes, McGrady, look in his eyes. Gram had often told her she could tell a lot about a person from their eyes. When she looked directly into Tim's chocolate-brown ones, she saw sadness and warmth. Still, he could be acting. *Ask him about the suit. Yeah, right. And just how am I supposed to do that?* "Yo, Mr. Hudson, what color suit were you wearing the day Dr. Stanford was killed?" *That could get me killed.* No, she had to be more subtle.

"Do you ever wear gray?" she croaked out. *Good going, McGrady. That was about as subtle as a two-ton truck.*

He looked at her like she'd just escaped from the mental ward. "Gray? No. Makes me look like a candidate for the morgue. Why?" He took a step toward her and frowned. "This has something to do with Sarah, doesn't it? What did she tell you?" Flashes of anger replaced the warmth in his eyes. Jennie's heart leaped into her throat. He lifted his hands from his pockets and reached for her.

"Hi!" Anna, the evening-shift nurse popped in. "Oh, hello," she bubbled, turning to Tim. "I didn't mean to interrupt, but I'll have to ask you to step out for a moment while I check her vitals."

Tim lowered his arms and stepped back, sending Jennie a we'll-finish-this-later look. Jennie gulped. Not if she had anything to say about it.

"Did you need something?" Anna asked, turning off the call light.

"Ah . . . the bathroom," Jennie whispered, "I need to use the bathroom."

After a shaky trip, she climbed back into bed. Anna checked her vitals, which, Jennie discovered, was short for checking a patient's pulse, blood pressure, temperature, and respirations. The nurse jotted the information on the chart and asked, "How are you feeling?"

"Better," Jennie answered carefully, so as not to upset her throat again. Surprisingly, she did feel better. Her chest was less constricted, and she could breathe almost normally.

"Would you like some Jell-O? Might soothe your throat. We need to get more fluids into you."

"Sounds good." Not wanting to be left alone again she asked, "Is Mr. Hudson still waiting?"

Anna disappeared for a moment then stepped back into the room. "Nope, sorry. I guess we took too long. I thought he might be in with Sarah, but he's not. Must have gone home with the others." She left again, and a few minutes later returned with two cups of green Jell-O. "Hope you like lime." She crinkled her nose. "Prefer raspberry myself, but it's all gone. If you don't like this, I'll see if I can get a different flavor from the kitchen."

Jennie shook her head, ripped the lid off, and downed the contents of one cup, then started on the other.

"Keep that up and we'll be able to get rid of your IV." After Anna left, Jennie leaned back against the pillows, but she kept her hand on the call button just in case. Not that it did much good. Tim could have easily killed her if he'd wanted to. *But he didn't. And he doesn't wear gray.* He could have lied. But there was no reason to. She thought about his olive skin and brown eyes. He probably would look terrible in gray. Come to think of it, Carl Layton probably wouldn't look too good in gray either. It would be great with his eyes, but his skin was too dark . . .

The niggling thought that had bothered her so much when she was around Carl edged into the periphery of her mind. He'd had a tan the first day he arrived at the research center, but not when she'd first seen him, at the airport. She closed her eyes and tried to remember. His skin had been as washed out as hers. She hadn't paid much attention, but then nearly everyone in Oregon, unless they made regular trips to the tropics or tanning booths, was pale by the end of winter. Had he been wearing a gray suit? She closed her eyes, trying to remember. No, he'd had on a light blue shirt and dark slacks. Which proved a big fat nothing. Tanning quickly wasn't reason enough to suspect someone of murder, especially someone as nice as Dr. Layton. Still . . .

The puzzle pieces flitting through her mind blurred and faded. Something important still hung on the edge of her consciousness. Something to do with the bridge. Jennie closed her eyes, but her mind refused to clear. She finally gave into the exhaustion and slept.

"Miss McGrady?" Angel Delaney's voice broke through the barrier of sleep. Jennie opened her eyes. "I just came by to see how you were doing." She paused and gave Jennie a worried look. "And to tell you we think we know who started the fire."

"It was Tim Hudson, wasn't it?" Jennie whispered, still not trusting her throat to behave itself.

"No. We think it was Scott Chambers."

The words slammed against Jennie's heart like a sledgehammer. "But that's impossible," she rasped. "He's here, in the hospital."

"Not anymore. He escaped this afternoon, about thirty minutes before the fire started. If it makes you feel any better, he probably didn't know you were inside. Most likely he wanted to give the research center more bad press."

Angel folded her arms and leaned over the railing. "Look, I know this is tough for you, but you're going to have to face facts. The kid's a loser." Angel straightened and stepped away. "I have a hunch he'll try to contact you, especially when he finds out you were inside. If he does, call me."

Jennie frowned and looked toward the wall. Angel was wrong.

"I mean it. Harboring a criminal is a crime. What I'm trying to say here, McGrady, is that I don't care what your grandmother does for a living. If either of you are protecting Chambers, I'll take you in."

"I haven't seen him." Jennie's voice cracked.

Angel's stern look softened a little. "Hey. I know this is rough for you, him being your boyfriend and all, but it happens."

"He is *not* my boyfriend," Jennie argued. "He's a friend, that's all." The realization surprised her, but it was true. Somewhere along the line, Jennie had resolved her struggle. She felt as strongly about Ryan as she had two weeks ago when he'd kissed her for the first time. Scott *was* just a friend. But that didn't mean she wasn't concerned.

After Angel left, Jennie dropped back against the bed. Her throat and lungs still hurt, but not nearly as much as her heart. Scott couldn't have done all those things.

But suppose you're wrong, McGrady? You've been wrong before. What if Sarah is wrong too? Her dad's murder might not have anything to do with what's been happening here. After all, what evidence did they really have to tie them together? A paranoid uncle. A stepfather who tans easily. A neurotic child who's been a silent witness for two years. Sarah was convincing, but she was also confused.

Jennie sighed and took a deep breath, sending her into another round of coughing. She was just recovering when Anna came in to "disconnect" her. The nurse took out the IV, removed the oxygen, and helped Jennie into the bathroom again.

Once the initial dizziness wore off, Jennie was able to

stand without wobbling like an unbalanced top. Except for her sore lungs and throat, she felt almost normal.

Anna took her for a short walk down the hall where she learned that Sarah's room, 319, was just across the hall from hers.

Ten minutes later, Anna steered Jennie back to her room and helped her back to bed. The exercise left her weak and shaken. Her lungs burned, and she felt more like she'd run a hundred-meter dash than having taken a leisurely stroll down a hospital corridor. Next time, she'd go farther. If there was a next time. *Why are you doing this to yourself, McGrady? You're fine. Nothing can happen to you here.*

While she waited for her breathing to return to normal, Jennie loosened her hair from what had once been a neat braid and now looked like a bird's nest. Her hair still smelled like smoke. She brushed it and used the rubber band to tie it in a ponytail.

Jennie felt restless, unsettled—as if she had to do something but couldn't think what. Finally, she called Gram. No answer. Worry forced its way into her restlessness. Why wasn't she home yet? *It's only eight-thirty, McGrady. They probably stopped to have dinner.* On impulse she called Debbie, who told her Gram hadn't come back. Jennie left a message to have Gram call and hoped she would get it before it was too late.

Too late for what? Jennie asked herself. She wasn't sure. It was only a feeling—her intuition sending out a warning. Jennie shook the feeling off and eased out of bed. Since she couldn't talk to Gram, Jennie decided to check on Sarah. She slipped into the pink sock-slippers and the pink-and-white-striped hospital robe that Anna had brought for her earlier walk. The hallway was empty, except for a nurse at the desk who seemed engrossed in reading a patient's chart. Jennie stepped out of the room and pulled the door closed behind her, then crept across the hall and into Sarah's room.

The room was dim, lighted only by a night-light near the floor. Strange. There should have been a light on by her bed. "Sarah?" Jennie whispered, willing her eyes to adjust to the darkened room. When there was no answer, Jennie tiptoed closer. Sarah was gone.

19

Don't panic, McGrady. She has to be here somewhere.
Jennie checked the bathroom, then hurried to the sliding
glass door at the opposite end of the room that led to the
visitors' hallway. No one. Her heart hammered inside her
chest. *Where is she?*

Jennie held on to the bed to steady herself. *Think,
McGrady, think.*

Jennie slipped back into the inner hall and padded
toward the nurses' station. Anna chose that moment to
step out of a room, and the two nearly collided. Jennie
told her what had happened.

"I'm sure it's nothing to worry about. Her doctor
could have ordered a chest X ray." Anna took Jennie's
arm and walked her back across the hall. "You get back
in bed. I'll check it out. And don't worry—I'll come back
and let you know."

Jennie reluctantly climbed into bed. She was beginning to feel like a tennis ball being hit from one side of
the net to the other. First, she was in Sarah's court, seeing
everything that had happened to them as being connected
to Dr. Stanford's murder. In the other court her perspective changed. Delilah's murder, the car crash, and the
cabin fire could be unrelated to Sarah.

If she viewed the situation honestly and objectively, she had to admit that Scott could be guilty. Everything had been fine until they met up with him and his DPA buddies. Coincidence? On the other hand . . .

Jennie bumped back into Sarah's court. Sarah had witnessed a murder. If Ramsey hadn't killed her father, Sarah would be in danger, especially if the murderer knew she could remember specifics like gray suits and voices.

Jennie remembered the murderous look Tim had given her when she'd asked about the gray suit. Carl, Maggie, and Gram had gone, but Tim had stayed behind. He could have taken Sarah.

Anna poked her head in the doorway. "Don't panic. We haven't been able to find her yet. She may have gone for a walk. We have a security guard out looking for her now."

When Anna left, Jennie placed another call to Gram. If Jennie's suspicions were correct, they wouldn't find Sarah. This time her grandmother answered.

"Oh, Gram, I'm so glad you're back." Jennie squeezed the words past the lump forming in her throat. "He's got Sarah."

"What? Who's got Sarah?"

"Tim. I went into her room to talk to her and she's gone. I think Tim took her. He was here after you left and . . ."

"Wait a minute. Slow down. Tim couldn't have taken Sarah anywhere. He brought Maggie and me back to the island. We stopped to eat dinner and arrived here about five minutes ago."

"Wh . . . how? Tim came by my room after you left."

"I know. We waited for him in the lobby. He said he owed you an apology."

161

"I thought . . . I thought Carl took you home," she stammered.

"He had some business to attend to in town."

Jennie frowned and rubbed her forehead. This wasn't making any sense. She told Gram about the gray suit that Sarah remembered seeing from beneath her father's desk after he'd been shot. "Tim acted really upset when I asked him if he wore gray. But if Tim was with you, then Carl must be the murderer."

"Let's not jump to conclusions, Jennie. For one thing, we can't be certain that Sarah's memory is accurate. I'll talk to Maggie and Tim, then call you right back. Oh, and Jennie, be careful. I want you to close the curtain and lock the door to the outer hallway just in case."

Jennie agreed. After hanging up, she tossed aside the sheet and swung her legs off the bed. A shadowy figure appeared in the dimly lit visitors' hallway and reached for the handle on the sliding glass door.

The bedside curtain obstructed her view. She couldn't see his head, only the outline of his body. *Which means he can't see me.* An empty bed stood between her and the inner door to the nurses' work station. If she could crawl under it and to the door, she might be able to get away. Not fast enough. She had to figure out a way to delay him. The door hissed open.

Jennie put a hand to her throat. She couldn't scream. If only the nurse would come in. *That's it, McGrady. You're brilliant.* Jennie reached up and switched on the bright light above her bed and at the same time yanked the curtain shut. Hoping she had deterred the intruder, Jennie slid out of bed. Staying as close to the wall as possible, she dropped to her knees and crawled under the empty bed, toward the inner door.

She reached up to grab the handle. A hand clamped down on hers and forced the door shut. Her captor covered her mouth with his hand and pulled her up tight against him.

"I'm not going to hurt you, just promise me you won't scream."

Jennie nodded. He let go of her and she whirled around to face him. "Scott Chambers, you scared me half to death. What are you doing here? Angel said you ran away. She thinks you set fire to the cabin."

Scott shook his head. "I'd never hurt you, Jennie. You've got to believe that."

Her throat ached, and she was beginning to feel light-headed. "Then how did you know I was here?" Jennie said, leaning against him for support.

"I went to the research center to look for you." He put a hand under her arm and guided her to a chair. "You don't look so good." He lowered her into the chair and plopped into the one next to it. "The place was burning when I got there. They'd already pulled you and Sarah out. I hid in the bushes and watched the whole thing. You believe me, don't you?"

"I'm trying to. Why did you leave the hospital?"

"What choice did I have? They were going to arrest me for killing Delilah and forcing you off the bridge." He shoved a hand through his wavy brown hair. "I didn't do it. Any of it. You've got to believe me."

"Why? Give me one good reason why?"

Scott pulled a rumpled T-shirt from his pack. The back of it was splotched with dried blood. "From the looks of this shirt, you'd think my back would be all scratched up, but it isn't." He turned and lifted his shirt to show her. "See, not a mark. I don't think this blood is mine."

"I don't understand."

"I didn't either at first. I can't remember anything from the time I left you at the pool that day until I woke up in the hospital. I think somebody must have hit me over the head, then kept me drugged. I've got a lump the size of an ostrich egg on the back of my head, and the doctor said he found needle marks on my arm. I don't do drugs, Jennie, so how do you explain that? Somebody set me up. Whoever it was must have cut himself or something. I'll bet anything this is his blood."

Jennie pressed the palm of her hand against her forehead. "Of course. The cut. Carl Layton."

"Who's Layton?"

"Sarah's stepfather. He came to the research center the day you disappeared. I overheard your phone call and was going after you when I ran into him. He was coming out of the office. At dinner that night we noticed a long cut on his forearm. The cut could have been a coincidence, but if you add the tan . . ."

"You're not making sense."

"Scott, do you remember seeing anyone around the research center the day Delilah was drugged—who shouldn't have been there?"

"Just the health inspector. When I went to pick up the food for the dolphins, he was in the lab. Said he was just finishing up." Scott shrugged. "Seemed like a nice guy. Said his name was Hans Larson."

"What did he look like?"

"Big, blond, pale blue eyes."

"Sounds like Layton. He must have been in Florida all along. He killed Delilah. And he must have been the one who ran us off the road . . ."

Jennie leaned forward and gripped the arms of the

chair. "Dr. Layton told Delaney he was coming back from town when he saw the broken glass and damaged concrete. He crossed the bridge, then turned around and came back." She grabbed Scott's arm. "But he couldn't have. The whole time I was in the water until I reached shore, I only remember hearing one car on the bridge." Jennie closed her eyes to bring the memory into focus. "I was lying on the beach and heard a car . . . only it wasn't coming from town. It was coming from Dolphin Island. I was afraid the truck driver had come back to make sure we were dead."

"Maybe he did." Scott put an arm around her shoulder. "This Layton guy could have stashed the truck with me in it, then driven back in his own car to make sure he'd finished the job."

Jennie leaned back in the chair and closed her eyes. "It still doesn't make sense. Dr. Layton was so kind and understanding that night. He gave us a ride and stayed at the hospital. If he'd wanted to kill us, why didn't he just stop the car on the way back home, murder us, and toss us off the bridge?"

"He wouldn't have had an alibi. Besides, Delaney knew you were with him."

"True . . . still, he was always so nice about my spending time with Sarah . . ." Jennie shook her head. "Of course! The noises I heard each time Sarah and I were together. I'll bet he was listening. That would explain why he'd want me out of the way. I'm the only other person who knew."

The phone rang. She rose from her chair to answer it. Scott stopped her. "Don't tell them I'm here."

"I'm not making any promises, Scott," she said. "Let go of my arm. You're hurting me."

"I'm sorry." Scott withdrew his hand and looked down at his shoes. "I just don't want to end up in jail for something I didn't do."

"You won't." Jennie picked up the phone.

"I talked to Maggie and Tim," Gram said after Jennie's hello. "Carl was wearing a gray suit that day."

Jennie told Gram about the blood on Scott's shirt and filled her in on the details she'd remembered.

Scott wandered out the sliding glass door and stood in the hallway, gazing out the window, down at the parking lot. He whipped around to face her. "It's Larson, or Layton, or whatever his name is. I'm going down to see if I can catch him."

"No . . ." Jennie placed a hand over the mouthpiece. "Scott, wait."

"Jennie," Gram called, "are you still there?"

"Yes, but . . ."

"Listen carefully. If Carl has Sarah, he may come after you next. I've called Angel. She's on her way. We'll be there in about ten minutes."

"Okay, hurry. I think Layton's here, and Scott's gone after him." Jennie hung up and hurried to the sliding glass door. The hallway was empty. She ran to the door marked EXIT and hesitated. One direction led to the elevators, the other to the stairwell. Deciding Scott would have taken the stairs, Jennie pulled open the door, entered the stairwell, and started down.

She stopped on the second-floor landing to catch her breath. A door opened somewhere beneath her. "Scott," she whispered as loudly as she dared. "Is that you?" Her voice bounced against the concrete and came back sounding like someone else.

Jennie glanced down. A man's hand gripped the rail-

SILENT WITNESS

ing one floor beneath her. He raised his hand, and she saw the dressing on his arm. At that moment Jennie realized what a foolish move she'd made. Why had she run out here? She should have stayed in her room.

Slow, deliberate footsteps hit, then scraped on the steps, like a brush beating and sliding against the head of a drum. One-shhh. Two-shhh. Three-shhh. Jennie bolted for the second-floor door and grabbed the handle. It was locked. The white writing on the glass read SURGICAL SUITE NO ADMITTANCE.

Four-shhh. Five-shhh. Six-shhh. There was only one way to get out—back to the third floor. *Oh, God . . . please let it be unlocked.*

She grabbed the railing and pulled herself up two steps at a time. Her lungs felt ready to explode. *Don't think about the pain. Just run.*

She reached the third-floor landing and stopped. The footsteps kept coming. Seven-shhh. Eight-shhh. Nine-shhh. Jennie grabbed for the doorknob. The footsteps stopped. A sinister chuckle shattered the silence. "It's only me, Jennie. You don't need to run away."

Jennie turned and looked back. Carl stood poised on the landing below, staring at her across the stairs that separated them. His pale blue eyes were now hard as ice; the smile on his face no longer kind, but evil. How could she have misjudged him? How could she have been so blind?

"Sarah wants to see you," Carl said, ascending another step toward her. "She's waiting in the car." He extended his hand up the stairway. "Come on. I've decided to take you both home."

"N . . . no," Jennie gasped. "You killed Dr. Stanford. You shot yourself in the arm to make it look like you were

167

a victim. You killed Delilah and . . ."

He raised his eyebrow and advanced another step. "Of course not. Did Sarah tell you that? She's been hallucinating, you know. That's why I'm taking her home. So I can care for her properly."

Still facing Carl, Jennie gripped the doorknob behind her and twisted. It wouldn't open. The knob slipped through her sweaty hand as though someone had greased it. She froze. *You're dead, McGrady. You can't get by him.* Carl stopped four steps short of the third-floor landing. "You don't have to be afraid of me, Jennie," he said smoothly, his arm still extended toward her. "I won't hurt you."

"I don't believe you. You were wearing a gray suit that day. Sarah saw you."

His eyes flickered in anger. "Sarah is very ill. No one will believe her. I hoped you would cooperate, Jennie. Now you leave me no choice." Carl reached into his shirt pocket and pulled out a syringe. He took another step toward her.

"No!" Jennie gasped. She flattened against the door.

Another door opened beneath them. The stairwell erupted with voices and laughter. Carl glanced toward the sound. Taking advantage of the disruption, Jennie slammed into him. He staggered back, teetered on the top step, and fell backwards. His head slammed into the cement with a sickening thud.

Jennie leaned against the wall and sank to the floor. Carl's limp body made a slow-motion slide down the stairs to the landing below. A pool of blood trickled from his head onto the gray concrete. His ice-blue eyes stared unseeing into hers. The syringe lay beside him, still loaded with whatever he'd planned to use on her.

Voices echoed in the stairwell again. Jennie tried to call for help, but managed nothing more than a scratchy whimper. She felt sweaty and chilled all at the same time. And dizzy. Everything around her drifted into colors of yellow, pink, red, blue, purple, then black.

20

"Is she going to be all right?" The question swam into Jennie's murky consciousness, then out again.

"I hope so." Gram's familiar voice edged in, crowding out the darkness. "The doctor is certain she didn't get any of the digitalis in the syringe. She just fainted, but they've kept her mildly sedated."

Jennie opened her eyes. Scott stood beside her bed, holding a vase containing a fern and two pink roses.

"Hi," Jennie croaked out.

"Hi, yourself." Scott smiled and set the flowers on the nightstand. "I brought you these. Kind of as a peace offering."

"Don't keep blaming yourself, Scott," Gram said. From the other side of the bed, Gram placed a straw to Jennie's lips. After drinking a few sips, Jennie looked from one to the other and frowned. "What are you talking about?"

"It was my fault Layton cornered you. I shouldn't have gone after him. Ran into Delaney in the lobby and she busted me. I tried to tell her about Layton, but she wouldn't listen."

"Layton . . ." Jennie shuddered as the picture of Dr.

Layton lying at the bottom of the stairs leaked back into her memory. "I killed him."

Gram shook her head. "He's alive and in custody. After we found the two of you in the stairwell, I suggested Angel have her people look for his car. They found Sarah in the trunk."

Jennie raised up on her elbows. "Is she okay?"

"She's fine. Maggie and Tim took her back to the research center this morning."

Morning. "How long have I been out?" Jennie said, glancing at the clock.

"About eight hours. The doctor said we had to let you sleep off the trauma."

"They found something else in the trunk too," Scott added. "My fingerprints and traces of my hair and blood. Layton must have knocked me out and stashed me in his trunk. When I showed Delaney the blood on my shirt, she had the lab run a test. It matched Layton's."

Jennie glanced back at Scott and smiled. "So you're in the clear. I'm glad." She looked back at Gram. "Did he kill Delilah?"

"It looks that way," Gram said. "Angel is still trying to fit all the pieces together. I think with the evidence she's found and with Sarah's testimony she'll be able to come up with a good case against him on all counts."

"You got that right, Ms. McGrady." Angel Delaney stepped into the room. "Just got off the phone with your friend in the bureau."

"J.B.?"

"Right. He's been rattling a few cages up in Portland. Looks like Layton left enough loose threads to trip himself up. Once we started pulling them, his alibi unraveled like an old piece of burlap." Angel sauntered over to a chair and dropped into it. "A handwriting expert compared the Ramsey entry in the appointment book with Layton's handwriting, and it matched. Not only that, we can tie him to the car Ramsey was in when he died. Back when they were investigating what they thought was a murder/suicide, the forensics team found a couple strands of blond hair on the passenger seat of Ramsey's car. Lucky for us they kept them."

"Carl's?" Gram asked.

"Bingo. They were able to match those hairs with some they found on Layton's suit. I owe you two an apology for not taking you more seriously in the beginning. Layton's good."

"But not as good as Jennie and Gram," Scott said, his sea-green eyes filled with admiration.

"I don't understand it," Jennie asked. "How could someone like Dr. Layton do such terrible things? Doctors are supposed to help people, not kill them."

"I doubt Carl planned to hurt anyone, initially," Gram said. "From what Tim has said, he liked having money. Got greedy, started gambling and borrowing large sums of money. Then, to pay off his debts, he embezzled money from the counseling center he and Dr. Stanford ran together. Tim found a discrepancy and confronted Stanford. Carl must have overheard them and figured the only way out of the situation was to kill his partner. To avoid suspicion he shot himself, then framed Ramsey and killed him too."

"How did Ramsey fit into it?" Jennie asked.

"J.B. thinks Carl may have owed him money."

Jennie grimaced. "It seems so cold-blooded. I'm surprised he didn't kill Sarah as soon as he found out she was there."

"He didn't have the opportunity. Remember, Maggie came to the office right after he'd shot himself. Besides, as long as Sarah remained silent, he was safe. He used hypnosis and drugs to make certain she wouldn't recover or remember who killed her father."

"The guy's a real gem." Angel cleared her throat. "You ready, Chambers?" She took hold of Scott's arm and started to lead him away.

"Where are you going? I thought you'd been cleared."

"Almost," Angel answered for him. "We still have the little matter of fleeing an officer to deal with."

"Never run from a cop, McGrady," Scott said as he stepped into the hall. He turned to Delaney. "Couldn't we talk about this. . . ?" Their voices faded as they walked away.

"Is he really going to jail?" Jennie asked. "It seems so unfair. After all he went through."

"He broke the law. He shouldn't have left the hospital." Gram smiled and patted Jennie's arm. "Don't worry, dear. I'm sure they'll take all that into consideration."

They did. By the time Jennie and Sarah got to Dolphin Island the next day, Scott had been released and was back to work. Ken and Debbie were acting more like parents than employers. They not only gave him back his job, they offered him an internship at the center while he worked on his degree in marine biology.

After lunch, Jennie pulled on her swimsuit and made her way to the docks. As she approached, Sarah's laughter danced over the water of the lagoon. "Come on, Samson, toss me the ball."

Samson lifted the multicolored beach ball with his nose and instead sent it flying in Jennie's direction. She caught it and tossed it back. "That was a pretty poor aim,

Samson," Jennie chuckled. "Better try again."

"He did that on purpose, Jennie," Sarah said. "He wants you to play too. Don't you, Sam?"

Samson lifted his sleek body out of the water and nodded, making a clicking noise that sounded to Jennie like an enthusiastic invitation to join them.

Jennie shrugged into a life jacket and climbed into the water beside Sarah and Samson. The dolphin sliced between them and offered a fin. They held on as he gave them a wild ride to the far side of the lagoon, then abandoned them.

"Come back here, Sam," Sarah called. She turned to Jennie and gave her a knowing grin. "He knows I'm well, so he's being a tease."

"Are you really okay?" Jennie asked as Samson approached them again to offer a ride back.

Sarah petted Samson's side and nodded. "Thanks to you." Tears sprang to her eyes and she lifted a wet hand to wipe them away. They both giggled at the soggy result.

Later that afternoon, while Scott worked and practically everyone she knew was taking a nap, Jennie stretched out on a lounge chair by the pool. She'd promised Gram to get some rest, but after all that had happened, she was almost afraid to close her eyes. *It's over, McGrady. Done.* So why did she still feel restless?

She knew what it was. She just didn't want to think about the possibility. Even so, the thought snaked in and coiled itself around her heart. Sarah's father was dead. Even though they'd solved the mystery and Sarah's silence had been broken forever, they couldn't bring Sarah's father back. Would the same be true for her? Would she and Gram solve the mystery of her dad's disappearance only to discover that he too had died?

Oh, no you don't, McGrady. It's not the same. Dad's alive. He has to be. And with Gram's help, you'll find him. In the last month, you've solved two mysteries. You can solve this one too. Count on it.

Jennie pillowed her head in her arms and closed her eyes. Tonight, dinner on Sanibel, and later, a game of pool with Scott. Tomorrow, Disney World—the next, Epcot Center. Then home. Soon she'd be seeing Mom and Nick and Lisa and . . . Ryan. The thought brought a fluttering to her heart and a smile to her lips.